D1260908

Julia Stone

Julia Stone

Charlotte Hardy

PIATKUS

First published in Great Britain in 1995 by
Judy Piatkus (Publishers) Ltd of
5 Windmill Street, London W1

**The moral right of the author
has been asserted**

*A catalogue record for this book is available
from the British Library*

ISBN 0–7499–0283–3

Set in 11/12 pt Times by
Datix International Limited, Bungay, Suffolk
Printed and bound in Great Britain by
Butler & Tanner Ltd, Frome and London

Prologue

(He) does not admire women with minds . . . He would
have us all mild unoffending creatures . . . writing a
small delicate hand, and expressing little thoughts in
the most strictly proper and polite terms. Why am I
not like this? Why am I born with reason and with
power to comprehend readily and to argue?

Nina Lehmann

William Stone did well at Oxford. He took a double first, received holy orders and was elected to a fellowship of All Souls, and all before his twenty-third birthday. During the next six years he worked on his Commentary on Leviticus, which was well received when it was published, and thereafter settled down to a study of the historical background to the Book of Revelations, which was intended to demolish all previous efforts and to make his name.

At the age of thirty-three he was presented to the living of Stallbridge in Wiltshire, through the influence of the Bishop's wife, a second cousin through his mother's family. He seized this opportunity. Stallbridge was a prosperous village, the tithes were good, he would have a comfortable house, a large income and lots of time to work on Revelations. He would also be able to marry. As a celibate fellow in Oxford he lived a reclusive life, refused invitations to tea-parties, avoided boating expeditions, and never went into taverns.

But he felt it was the appropriate thing at his time of life, and his mother found him a suitable candidate, a girl of seventeen, another distant relative, one of five unmarried daughters, and whom her mother was gratified to bestow on a 'rising man', as she put it in a letter to his mother. Agnes had been educated at home, if that is not too strong a term; actually, she knew less than nothing, but had a pretty singing voice, and a passionate love of dancing and flirtation, picnics and parties. William Stone's mother was satisfied her son would be able to mould such an unspoiled and simple girl to his wishes, and chose her accordingly.

So, in the year 1840, on a blazing June day, after three brief meetings, and a long talk from her mother, she was married and came to Stallbridge to take up residence in the rectory with her husband. The bride had no idea what to expect, but vaguely believed she had made a good match, and would preside over a respectable

3

establishment. Her sisters had certainly been staggered by her good fortune so young.

Her husband seemed to her a man of powerful physique and convictions, immensely learned, who would care for and protect her, and she came prepared to give him her loyalty and duty.

He for his part thought he would be able to 'form her mind', but he found her unreceptive to his teaching, frivolous and immature, and as his disappointment grew, became harsh and demanding, asserting his authority with an increasingly sharp tone of voice.

On their wedding night he had almost raped her, seizing and taking her with such force – a girl who had only the vaguest idea what to expect – and afterwards as she lay dazed and bleeding, fell on his knees in the darkness by the bedside and prayed for divine guidance.

She could never hope to understand him, but she hoped at first to reach him by devotion and obedience. He would not allow her near him however and for twelve years never approached her again. From this solitary union, their daughter Julia was born.

After the birth the Reverend Doctor Stone retired to his study to work on his book, and his wife centred her life on her little girl. When Julia was twelve, William Stone took it into his head to approach his wife again. She became pregnant, but both mother and child died in childbirth. The clergyman was left alone with his daughter. Dr Stone tried to make up for the loss of her mother, and now took it upon himself to educate his daughter. Julia was intelligent and learned fast.

A housekeeper was engaged after her mother's death, but when she left three years later, Julia took over all the duties her mother had undertaken. She was now mistress of the house, and thenceforth ran it alone. This suited Dr Stone perfectly. He was free to devote himself entirely to his studies, and in the big silent house Julia grew up into a thoughtful, educated young lady, fluent in French and Latin. She was well-known in the village, dressed as became a rector's daughter, modest, quietly spoken, genteel in her manners, of medium height and well-rounded figure, with dark hair and eyes, and a clear ivory complexion. A young lady who spoke little but always to the point, saw clearly, was not fooled, and controlled the household in every department. She had become indispensable to her father in his studies: his secretary and assistant, translating, copying, abstracting learned articles.

In their position in the parish and the county, the Reverend Dr Stone and his daughter had a circle of acquaintance, though Dr Stone discouraged visits and seldom went out. He also tried to

4

discourage Julia; it was easy to find a letter or a sermon to copy, or some other task connected with the house. Dr Stone dreaded the loss of his daughter. He was now at work on a Commentary on St John's Gospel, intended to be the definitive version, but as yet nowhere near finished. New writing bearing on his subject was constantly coming into print, not only in England but elsewhere, especially in Germany; it all took time, and he was oppressed by a sense of rising urgency, of time slipping away and so much left to do.

To this end he asked Julia to learn German; things would get along quicker if she could translate some of the important works coming out in Germany. Like all scholars he lived in fear that someone else would beat him into print – that someone else would produce a Commentary on St John's Gospel before he did, and the labour of so many years would have been wasted.

Julia took up German but had little success. Her spare moments were devoted to it; she found the language uncongenial, and worked away from a sense of duty, but it was slow going.

Their near neighbours Mr and Mrs Cunningham were the principal landowners in the village and from her childhood Julia had known their children, Peter and Elizabeth. Lizzie was her closest friend, and as far back as she could remember Julia had been in love with Peter. She thought of this as an 'astronomical' phenomenon; being in love with him was like observing some distant planet. He knew nothing of it and treated her with the same childhood familiarity he always had. Lately, since he had gone to Oxford, they had seen very little of each other, until unexpectedly one March morning, when she was twenty-two, he came back into her life.

PART ONE
March–May 1862

Chapter One

Peter was looking down at her, smiling into her eyes. They were in a secret place of their own, though she did not know where, a mysterious magical place, alone together unseen by anyone, all the pretences and restraints of normal life gone. She was lying back on a rug, the hot sun beating down, and she could feel the heat in her body, suffusing her, flowing through her limbs as she reached up to pull him down to her; her clothes were loosened, all flowing round her, and she was opening, opening to him, desiring him with an intensity, an unbearable sweetness, and the most divine tingling heat flowing through her as she opened herself to him, desiring him so badly she couldn't bear it, a fathomless yearning, an aching sweetness, and they were melting and flowing together . . .

'Miss Stone! Miss Stone!'

She was being shaken; something, a horrible intrusion, a rude sacrilege, was breaking in on her, a searing cold feeling in her body, pulling, dragging her up, up into the light. She opened her eyes.

'Miss Stone, I've brought your tea. And your father's asking for you.'

Annie was bending over her.

Julia raised herself on one elbow.

'What time is it?'

'Half-past eight, miss.'

'Oh Lord.' She fell back on the pillow and closed her eyes again. The dream was still half present to her, a fugitive memory, Peter's face already dispersing like an image in smoke. With an effort, she dragged herself into wakefulness.

'Half-past eight – why didn't you wake me sooner?'

'Sorry, miss. There's been a bit of a muddle in the kitchen this morning.'

'Bring me some hot water, Annie, please.'

'I've brought it, miss.'

Julia pulled herself up and threw back the bedclothes. She sat for a moment, her face in her hands, then stood up.

'Get out my grey dress. What muddle?'

She padded across the cold floor and threw back the curtain. A bright glare of March sunlight flooded the room.

Annie had poured out the hot water. Julia threw off her nightdress and, naked and shivering, quickly washed herself.

'Soon as you're dressed, miss, could you come and talk to Mrs Oldham?'

'What's happened?' She was towelling herself down.

'Mrs Oldham's gone mad, miss. She just threw the breakfast all over the floor.'

'What? Why?'

'She had a letter this morning –'

Julia pulled the long shift down over her head. She had overslept and was dressing hurriedly. She pulled up her long loose cotton drawers and tied them with their drawstring, smoothed down her shift and clipped her stays round her waist. Annie was bringing her grey day-dress from the wardrobe. Julia fitted the crinoline round her waist, Annie tied up the drawstrings at the back, then helped to ease the dress over her head, and smooth it down over the crinoline cage.

'She's been crying and shrieking, miss, she smashed the tea pot –'

'Oh Lord! For heaven's sake, Annie, put up my hair as quick as you can, there's a dear.'

She sat at her mirror, and while Annie ran a brush through her hair and pinned it up, Julia pulled on her stockings, and slipped her feet into her shoes. This alarm, whatever it was, had driven the dream out of her mind, and yet for a moment, looking into her own eyes as she checked her collar was straight, she felt a hint of it in her body still, remembered for a moment that ineffable, divine feeling.

She remembered again the intense warmth, a warmth she had never felt in real life, that had coursed through her body, deliciously alive, tingling in her veins, and the wonderful sense of Peter above her, hovering there about to kiss her. What could such a powerful dream signify, and where had such feelings come from, feelings a thousand times stronger than anything she ever experienced in her waking life?

She ran down into the dining room.

'Julia, do you know what time it is?'

'Yes, Father, I'm sorry I overslept.'

10

'And where is breakfast? There seems to be bedlam in the house this morning. I hear shrieks from the kitchen.'

'I will look into it. Breakfast will be served as soon as possible, Father.'

She went quickly into the kitchen, which was on the ground floor of the house, behind the dining room, and looked out on the yard. Mrs Oldham was sitting at the table, her head in her hands, sobbing uncontrollably. Annie and Becky were on their knees, apparently cleaning the floor.

'Mrs Oldham, what is going on? Why has breakfast not been served?'

Mrs Oldham did not look up but Annie turned to her with a warning look in her eyes.

'Mrs Oldham, what is the matter?'

The cook raised her face in an agony of grief. 'What's the matter? What's the matter? Everything, that's what!' She was staring about her blindly, her face streaming with tears. She turned sharply. 'What does his breakfast matter? What do any of you matter?' With a sweep of her arm, several plates clattered loudly off the table on to the tiled floor. Becky turned quickly and started picking up the pieces.

'He's lucky if he's got nothing worse than his breakfast to worry about!' It was a long loud wail, to the whole world. Again Mrs Oldham buried her head in her arms on the table in a storm of sobbing.

Julia looked to the other girls.

'Mrs Oldham – Annie – for heaven's sake –'

Annie came over and, leading her a step away, whispered: ''Tis her son, miss.'

'Jacob?'

'He's gone for a soldier.'

Jacob was the despair of his mother, a foolish boy, a ne'er-do-well in the village, who had disappeared several days before.

'Mrs Oldham, when did you hear of this?'

'She had a letter this morning, miss, from him in Aldershot.'

Without looking up, Mrs Oldham half stretched out her hand which held a crumpled tear-stained sheet. Julia took it and read the few scrawled lines. Mrs Oldham sobbed afresh.

Becky had gone back to clearing up the mess of bacon and eggs, the broken plates, the remains of the tea pot. Julia rested her hand on Mrs Oldham's shoulder.

'I see.' She drew up a chair close to her. 'I am so sorry for you, Mrs Oldham. It has been a terrible shock.' She ran a hand over the

11

cook's shoulders and spoke softly to her. 'Come to my room after breakfast and I will give you something to send him. Annie, make Mrs Oldham a cup of tea.' She looked about. 'Are there any bacon and eggs left? Dr Stone must have his breakfast.'

She gave Mrs Oldham a little squeeze on her shoulder, then crossed to the range, opened the lid and poked up the fire inside. 'I can cook it myself. Becky, finish cleaning the floor.'

But seeing Julia reaching down a frying pan, Mrs Oldham started up.

'Oh, Miss Stone, I can't have you doing that. Give it here.'

'Mrs Oldham,' Julia said cheerfully, 'sit and drink your tea. I am not so helpless that I cannot fry an egg, you know. And we will send something to Jacob. I am sure everything will turn out all right. This could be the best thing for him. I believe he will make an excellent soldier; I cannot wait to see him in his red coat.'

Mrs Oldham smiled a wan smile.

Ten minutes later Annie carried Dr Stone's breakfast in to him.

After breakfast Julia went back to her room. Becky had already made her bed. The room was barely furnished. A bed, a wash-stand, a wardrobe, and a large table by the window covered with papers and books. She took her seat at the table and began to order the papers on it. Her first task was to finish copying out in her neat handwriting her father's Sunday sermon, passed on to her in a mass of illegible scrawl, crossing out, and transposition. Many years' experience had taught her his methods and ways of thought. She sharpened her pen, opened her ink-bottle, and set to work.

However she was not halfway down the page when she heard the distant jangle of the front door bell, and a few moments later Annie's head appeared round the door.

'It's Miss Cunningham to see you, Miss Stone.'

The Cunninghams' home, the Old Manor House, was less than half a mile away.

As Julia came down into the drawing room Lizzie darted forward and seized her hands.

'Julia, I have such news!'

She quickly pushed the door shut behind Julia, then dragged her to the covered window seat.

'Now, my dear.' They sat facing each other. Lizzie took Julia by the hands again.

'I have a few minutes while Mama and Peter go into the village. Julia, can you imagine – only imagine, my dear – the dearest, sweetest man . . .'

'Adolphus?' Julia smiled.

'Has proposed!'

This news had been hourly awaited for some weeks. Julia and Lizzie threw their arms round each other.

'Were you in doubt?'

'Julia, I had to know! How could I plan anything until the silly man actually spoke the words? Of course I knew he was coming round eventually –'

Lizzie undid the ribbon of her bonnet and shook out her blonde curls. She was a petite girl of eighteen and that March morning was wrapped in a thick cloak over her olive green dress. Her cheeks were pink from the cold air, and Julia thought she had never looked prettier.

'I wish you every happiness.'

Lizzie looked down for a moment and spread her skirt out neatly over its crinoline hoops.

'I have thought it all out, everything, the wedding, the house – Dolly and I are going to look at houses straightaway. Do you know he suggested moving in with his people? He said they had oodles of room and how cosy it would be, having all the furniture laid on. You can imagine what I said to that! I mean, Julia, with all due respect, the Emersons are the most charming people in the world – but I put my foot down. I must have a place of my own. A married woman has the right!'

'Will Adolphus be able to afford it?'

'Lord, yes! Well, anyway, Mama and Mr Emerson have got to talk about all that. But I shall have a place of my own if I have to live in a shoe box!'

She burst into a peal of musical laughter.

'Of course we shall have to go and live in Devizes to be near the brewery. Dolly says you get used to the smell of the malt in the end – I only hope he's right. He also says,' Lizzie lowered her voice, 'Julia, if his Papa plays his cards right – that one of these days there might a baronetcy for the family.'

'Goodness.'

'I waited and waited. Dolly hummed and hawed until I thought I'd never get any sense out of him. Of course I knew he doted on me, but you know how men are – very happy to call and chat; very happy to come to a dance or flirt at a croquet party. But bringing them up to the mark – sometimes I was in despair. In fact it was only yesterday, by chance a friend of Peter's at Oxford was down and we were all sitting round –'

'Is Peter down from Oxford?'

13

'Yes – well, anyway – you would have known if you had come.'

'Lizzie, I wanted to come. I was going to come but Father and I were very busy yesterday. He's been asked to do a series of articles for the *Church Times*, and what with the Commentary.' She brightened. 'Never mind. Do go on.'

'Julia, I'm sorry to say this, but your father really is the outside of enough! When do you ever get out? And it would have been such fun.' Lizzie's pretty features were screwed up in vexation for a moment; but then her own thoughts swept her on.

'Well, you know it was pouring with rain, so we couldn't go out, and there was nothing to do, so I thought I'd teach Dolly a lesson, and I invited this young man, Frederick, or Cedric, or Edgar – I forget his name – to look through an album with me. And that did it! I knew Dolly was watching, and I really played up to him, this Frederick, telling him about my childhood, making him laugh, smiling at him, and our heads almost touching over the album. Of course all the time Dolly was going demented watching us. Served him right! So that evening as they were going he got me to one side out of the light and demanded to know what I was doing. So I asked him who he thought he was talking to – he didn't own me, did he? And he said he thought we had an understanding, and I said what understanding was that? And that did it, Julia! He said he thought we were engaged! And I said it was the first I'd heard of it, and if he thought we were engaged, it was jolly well up to him to ask me – so he did!'

Julia smiled with amusement as Lizzie rattled on. 'And do you think you'll be happy with Adolphus, Lizzie? He won't be too dull for you?'

She looked up shrewdly. 'So long as I have my way, I shall be happy. I know exactly how everything is to be ordered. I have worked it all out, I assure you. Dolly's a dear sweet boy and I know he'll behave himself. The main thing is I shall have a home of my own.'

She leant forward and took Julia's hands.

'And I want babies! Lots and lots of babies!'

She looked up.

'There's Mama and Peter, I must go. Dearest Julia, don't tell anyone for the moment. Of course it will be announced by Mama, and we're to have a ball. Then all the world will know.'

Julia had looked quickly out of the window at a black carriage which had drawn up in the lane, just visible beyond the laurels.

'And you must tell your papa to let you come to my ball. I shall insist!'

'Lizzie, you know I'd love to come. I'll do my best. Perhaps on this special occasion it will be possible.'

'Mama will send you an invitation anyway. He can't stop you. At least –'

'I'll do my best.' Julia couldn't bear to dampen Lizzie's exuberance.

Lizzie leapt up. 'Goodbye for now, dearest. Come and see me as soon as you can. Now Peter is down from Oxford he'd like to see you again, I know. Oh dear –'

'What is it?'

There was a jangling at the door.

'Well,' she glanced out of the window, 'oh, that's him.' She began pulling on her gloves, and tying the ribbons of her bonnet. She leant closer and spoke fast. 'Perhaps I shouldn't tell you. You see, Peter's down from Oxford –'

'Yes, you said, the vacation –'

'No, Julia, not the vacation.' She looked into Julia's eyes conspiratorially. 'For good. Rustication. No, not even that. He's out, Julia.'

'But why?' she whispered.

'He wouldn't say. Mama wasn't too pleased, of course, but she never criticizes him – her favourite – Peter could rob the Bank of England and she wouldn't care. But that's mothers for you!'

'Lizzie –'

The door opened, and Annie was ushering in a young man, light-hearted, grinning, his hands in his pockets, and a lock of fair hair falling over his pale face.

He looked down at the girls. His dark eyes had thick eye lashes which gave him an almost feminine beauty, but his manner was boyish and hearty.

'Come on, Lizzie, visiting time's up! The carriage awaits! Hullo, Julia.'

If the god Apollo had come down to earth, dressed in a battered old blazer, his neck-tie knotted negligently, one hand in his pocket and the other run casually through his hair, a being not of the same common clay other men were fashioned out of, someone who did not notice the usual obstructions and difficulties that confused and impeded ordinary mortals, a being for whom everything was effortless, as if the whole world had been constructed round him for his especial convenience; he might have looked to Julia the way Peter Cunningham looked that March morning in her cold drawing room.

Julia stood to one side as Lizzie went out into the hall again, and responded almost inaudibly to his greeting.

15

Lizzie turned to Julia and they touched cheeks. 'Come and see me soon, darling! When you can get away.'

Annie held open the door as Lizzie gathered up her skirts and dashed down the drive where the carriage was waiting. Peter lingered for a moment.

'Thank you, Annie,' Julia said, and the girl went back to the kitchen.

'Beats me what you girls have to say to each other.' He smiled down at her, a mocking grin.

'I expect you'll be told when it's good for you,' she said with an effort to be arch. Why had he left Oxford? she wondered.

'Good for me? I don't like the sound of that. I never liked anything that was good for me.'

'Peter!' There was a call from the carriage.

'Your mother is calling.'

'Let her wait. I say, Julia, it's about that ass Adolphus Emerson, isn't it?'

'What on earth gives you that idea?'

'What? Well, it could be the way he's been mooning about the place for months after her. The way he's been in and out of the house night and day, getting under everybody's feet; carrying her shawls, running her errands, handing her her paint brushes, turning the pages of her music and breathing down her neck while she plays the piano; it could be the fatuous remarks he makes, the way he never answers a question when I ask one, the expression of complacent idiocy as he hands her a cup of tea; that *may* be what made me suspicious.'

Julia couldn't help laughing.

'It'll be a relief for all concerned when they make up their minds,' he went on. 'Anyway, more to the point, how are you?'

'Well, sir, as you see, I breathe, I occupy space.'

'You're still breathing? Well, that's something. Nothing like breathing, I'm told. Oh, yes, I remember, you used to win prizes for it.'

'And you? Have you won any prizes lately?'

'Let me see. Prizes? Well, I won a bet with Morley once to see who could stay in bed the longest. Would that count?'

She laughed.

'Staying in bed? That doesn't sound like you. Far too strenuous.'

'I made a special effort. Just on that occasion.'

'And who won?'

'I did, of course. Morley's scout turfed him out.'

'Ah. He lacked the moral stamina.'

16

'You can say that again. It was a real effort. Nothing worse than staying in bed, Julia, believe me. Utter Purgatory.'

'Oh, I know.'

'I mean it. Probably all right for you. You like thinking. You can lie there staring at the wall and think all sorts of uplifting thoughts. But spare a thought for me. There's nothing I hate worse than thinking. Really.'

There was another distant shout from the lane.

'Your mother is calling.'

'Put me in a bed, Julia, I'm at my wit's end. I whistle, I do my sums, anything, but it doesn't help. The thoughts keep coming.'

'Poor soul. Your guilty past.'

'You may laugh. You lead a blameless existence. Very right and proper. But think of me – a mere human mortal. It's very hard. By the way, what happened to you yesterday? I thought you were coming over.'

'Oh.' She was sobered. 'No. I was unable to come. I was very busy yesterday. We are very busy just at the moment.'

'That's what you always say. You should have come. You could have helped me cope with Emerson.'

'I thought that was Lizzie's job.'

'Ah. So he has proposed!'

'You will be told all in good time.'

'And no doubt Lizzie will want her ball. A girl's hour of triumph must be celebrated in style. The ogre will have to let you come to that.'

The smile left her face.

'Are you referring to my father?'

'You know I am.'

'You should not speak disrespectfully of him to his daughter, Peter.'

'Somebody should. It's criminal the way he treats you.'

She had become severe, tense.

'Peter, really, you must not speak that way. I cannot listen.'

'Come off it, Julia, you know what I mean. You are entitled to a life of your own, I mean to say.'

'Peter, thank you for your consideration – look, your mother is calling.'

'Don't change the subject. We expected you over yesterday.'

'I explained to Lizzie. I was busy. I sent your mother a note.'

'Busy be hanged. Your father invented some excuse to stop you, didn't he?'

'You seem to forget sir,' she tried to regain a light-hearted note,

17

'that I am in charge of my father's house. I have many duties which a thoughtless young man would not dream of.'

'Bosh.'

'Peter!' Another call from the lane.

'There, you see, you are keeping your mother waiting.'

'Well, I won't give up. If he won't let you out more often, I shall come round myself.'

'Hush! I will call over in a day or two, I promise.'

'Julia!'

A stern voice from the hall behind her. 'Are you going to keep that door open all the morning?'

'No, Father. Goodbye, Mr Cunningham.'

Her face was a mask. Peter made a wry expression and turned away. She closed the door, and crossed the spacious hall towards the stairs.

'Julia!'

'Yes, Father.' She was on her way upstairs. 'I haven't forgotten the sermon. I'll finish it now.'

'Come into my study.'

As she followed him in, he said, 'That was Peter Cunningham, I suppose?'

'Yes, Father.'

The study was a large room on the ground floor at the back of the house, overlooking the garden. The wall opposite the door was lined with books, there were books along the window sill and along the mantelpiece, and in the centre of the room Dr Stone had his big desk, covered with papers and opened books. He bent over the desk, pulling papers about and turning over books and periodicals.

'I wonder he has nothing better to do with his time.'

'Better than what, Father?'

'Disturbing us with his idle chatter, girl.'

'I hope you weren't disturbed.'

'This house has no more privacy than Piccadilly Circus.'

'Actually it was Lizzie who came to see me. Mr Cunningham was simply calling to collect her.'

'Oh, he was *simply* calling to collect her, was he?' Dr Stone's voice was heavy with sarcasm. 'And no doubt you were *simply* passing the time of day, and no doubt *simply* lost all sense of time as he *simply* bewitched you with his flattery?'

'Was I to shut the door in his face?'

'Were you to waste the whole morning prattling like a housemaid?'

Julia drew a deep breath.

18

'The Cunninghams are our neighbours, Father. And our friends. How should I behave?'

'Ah, here we are.' He took up a heavy black book. 'This has been sent me by a colleague who assures me it is important. It is in German.'

Dr Stone handed it to her. She took the book and looked into it. It was page after page of close-printed black-letter Gothic script.

'It is a study of the composition of the Gospels. I saw a mention of it somewhere else. I have a feeling it may be crucial to our work.'

'It was reviewed in *Miscellanea*.'

'Oh. Yes, I remember. Of course.'

She turned the book over in her hands. It was heavy; the print was small. '*Miscellanea* thought very highly of it.'

'Exactly.' Stone took the book from her. He held it in one hand, pressing on it with the other. 'This may be the key. Think, Julia – the key to our work! In these pages may be the answer to some of our most pressing problems. It is of the highest importance. We must begin at once.'

He thrust it into her hands.

'Start this morning!'

'Yes, Father, of course.' She looked down hesitantly at the black book. 'You know, I still have a lot to learn . . .'

'Well, do what you can. It is most important.'

Julia looked through the book again.

'I will try.'

There was a pause.

'Well, get on with it then.'

'Yes, Father. Dinner will be at six.'

Dr Stone's study door closed behind her and Julia stood alone, silent for a moment, holding the heavy book, before she continued up to her room.

As she sat at her table again, she looked down into the garden. It was the end of winter, and Goodrich the gardener had been working all week preparing the beds for planting. She could not concentrate.

She could think only of Peter. How strange life was; Peter, whom she had known all her life. With whom she had passed so much of her childhood in the village. She remembered afternoons with Peter and Lizzie, on expeditions across the downs behind the village, tree-climbing expeditions, berry-gathering trips.

Peter had been the captain, Lizzie and Julia his trusty lieutenants. They had built a dam in the stream. They had climbed trees. They had stolen the juicy young peas from villagers' gardens, stolen apples from orchards. And one day Peter had kissed her. It was an experiment; to see what it was like. Peter quite liked it, but forgot it soon after when other novelties came along.

But Julia never forgot it. That afternoon when he had kissed her by the stream while Lizzie had gone off paddling further up; that hot afternoon, she remembered the heat of the sun on her neck, the smell of the brackish water of the stream, Peter, his shirt neck open, the smell of him, the specialness of him. That evening she had written in her diary: 'Peter kissed me three times. I love him'. It changed her life.

It wasn't her fault. It wasn't anybody's fault. It was just her bad luck that she had been in love with him ever since. The little moments when they could talk were for her magical spaces in the continuum of time, moments set apart from reality. She accepted that. She knew he could never fall in love with her, that he never even noticed her, except as a friend; that he could take his pick from any one of a dozen girls – two dozen, three, a hundred, any of them.

And just now how easy it had been between them; the silly banter probably meant nothing to him yet it had been a rare treat for her. Could he have any idea what it meant for her in the bleak round of her days here, the duties, the steady hours at her desk; understand what it meant, those few minutes of light-hearted chat? How could he?

She finished the sermon, stacked the sheets neatly to one side, and opened the black book. She read the title with difficulty. *Forschungen zu den Urquellen der Heiligen Schriften*: 'Researches into the Original Sources of the Holy Gospels'. She pulled across her big *Langenscheidt's Lexikon*. It was going to be a long job.

Mrs Oldham had by now recovered. Julia had given her ten shillings to send to Jacob, and the kitchen had been cleaned. All deferred to Mrs Oldham, partly on account of her age, partly on account of her erratic temperament. In any case it paid to be in with her; however sharp Miss Stone's eye, there were often little perks for Mrs Oldham's friends – a pot of dripping, odd half-used candles, produce from the garden, coal. It was a good house to be in, the best in the village, and there was usually a way round Miss Stone's soft heart.

With the cook that morning were Annie and Becky Loveday, sisters. Annie was senior – she was parlourmaid, nineteen years old, and carried the tea-tray into the drawing room and opened the front door to visitors, when there were any; Becky, fifteen, was general housemaid and cleaner. There was another woman, of middle years and unmarried, called Gertie who was scullerymaid and did all Mrs

Oldham's dirty work. Present too were Goodrich the gardener and his assistant William, a gangling youth of twenty.

'Have you got the back room ready for the new curate, Becky?' Annie said suddenly.

'What new curate?'

'The new curate that's arriving by the five o'clock train, dear, and is expected to dinner at six.'

Becky leapt up.

'Why didn't anyone tell me?'

'Miss Stone told you last Tuesday.'

'She didn't say he was coming today, did he? Oh Lord!' She began quickly tying her apron.

'Let's hope he's an improvement on the last one,' said Mrs Oldham drily, 'I never could stand that namby-pamby Mr Tresham. He didn't last long. Bit too high for Dr Stone – I reckon if he'd been any higher, he'd have been floating up the aisle. The way he used to come mincing in in his lace and frills – more like a bride than a vicar!'

'Dr Stone said he went over to Rome.'

'Good riddance.'

'You'd better light a fire in there, Becky, to give it a good air. Make sure the bed's well aired too.'

'All right, all right, miss. I suppose I know what's needed.' Becky dashed out.

Julia had given up the uneven struggle with her German, had put on her bonnet and cloak and was now in the churchyard, looking down at her mother's grave. She often came here to be alone.

Here
In Patient Expectation of the Coming of Our Lord Jesus Christ
Rests what was Mortal of
Agnes Stone
Beloved Wife of William Stone Rector of this Parish
And Daughter of Mr and Mrs Anthony Maxwell
of Streete in the County of Kent
Who was called to Rest on February 19 1852
Aged Thirty Years
Quam Maxime Dilexit Primam sibi Deligit

She knew the words by heart. The Latin epitaph had been composed by her father: 'She in whom He delighted most He took first unto Himself'.

21

All her earliest memories – before even she knew Peter and Lizzie – were of the afternoons playing with her pretty mother, dancing together in the drawing room as Agnes sang, telling each other riddles, reading together, or working at their needlework. Her mother loved music and would sit at the piano and sing to Julia. In the summer they would be together in the garden beneath the broad cedar tree.

Sometimes Dr Stone would come upon them, and would watch them together, awkwardly approving and nodding his head as if his attention had been briefly distracted, but there was no sympathy between them, and a shadow would fall over mother and daughter. Silent, morose, Dr Stone would return to his studies, and the sun would shine again.

When Agnes died Julia would not speak, would not eat, and was so reduced that for months it was feared she might even die herself. She did make a slow recovery however. Dr Stone tried to make up for the loss of her mother, and now took it upon himself to educate his daughter. Julia submitted to her lessons, but privately she blamed him for the death of her mother, and relations between them had a formal quality, cool and restrained. In her imagination the memory of her mother glowed with a never fading warmth.

Outwardly she was her father's child: intelligent, learned and precise. Inwardly she was her mother's, and longed for pleasure and dancing sometimes so intensely she thought her mind must be turning.

The consequence was headaches, and those dreams, more disturbing than her headaches, dreams difficult to acknowledge even to herself, when she would awake sweating, her body suffused with the intensity of her feelings, and lie awake in the darkness wondering at herself and what meaning such a strange vision could have.

Chapter Two

The new curate did arrive by the five o'clock train, but he was not present to dinner at six. Dr Stone naturally assumed that he would come up from the station, a distance of five miles, by the station fly – a broken-down one-horse carriage – and should have been at the rectory within forty-five minutes.

The new curate however saw no need for a ride over such a trifling distance. He set out to walk. Besides, he was not so rich that he could easily afford it. Mrs Oldham need have no fears of the Reverend Arthur Grahame going over to Rome, or of 'mincing up the aisle in lace and frills'. Mr Grahame was built like the son of a farm labourer, which is what he was.

On that cold bright March evening as he walked with his long easy stride through the village in his frock coat and top hat, it amused him to think that he was now a person of consequence in a community like this. To his right a labourer in shabby moleskins who was turning over the soil in his garden ready for the spring planting looked up and touched his forehead; Arthur responded easily with a 'Good evening'. In a garden opposite, a little girl in boots that were too big for her was feeding chickens.

Seeing these country folk Arthur was looking not across some gulf of incomprehension, as the village gentry did, the Cunninghams or the Emersons; he was looking at himself. He had grown up in a cottage just like the one that little girl had run out of.

He knew that cottage, its earth floor, the open hearth with the kettle hanging over it. Arthur was one of six brothers and sisters; he remembered them as children, four in a bed, his eldest sister tucking them in every evening. He remembered the sound of his father coming home from the Fox and Hounds at night, singing, and cursing as he stumbled in the garden path. He remembered his mother hanging out washing like the woman in the garden here on

23

his right; remembered her calling him and his brothers in to supper, like her over there. And looking at that woman's weather-beaten, care-worn face, remembered his mother's, too.

Looking at the cottages as he walked through the village that evening, everything came back to him.

But unlike his brothers and friends, Arthur had been befriended by the schoolmaster, and then by the squire; he had been bright, apt, and ambitious. And to the amazement of the whole village Arthur had gone to Oxford. The church was one of the few ways in which a poor man could rise in the world, his schoolmaster told him; Arthur had never wavered.

When the Bishop unexpectedly offered him this place, curate to Dr Stone, it seemed another important step forward. Dr Stone was a legend in Oxford – who did not know *Stone on Leviticus*? Arthur had come a long way. And yet as he walked through the village on this cold bright March evening it was as if he had come home.

He was passing an imposing gateway. The squire's residence, no doubt. He looked up at it.

He had come home, and yet there was a difference. He had fought his way to Oxford, endured the buffets of snobbery and prejudice, laboured and studied hard; and in so doing had leapt the invisible fence which surrounded the gentry. As a curate he was now acceptable in polite drawing rooms on terms of equality.

He smiled wrily to himself: what a victory. Years of study, of concentration, of endurance, of idealism, to qualify him to take tea with the squire's lady, to commiserate with her on the ailments of her pets, or to offer an opinion on her daughters' ball-gowns. This was not what he had gone to Oxford for. It had been a mistake to accept this post.

Up to his right he now began to see the square flint tower of the church. Tall beech trees shaded the churchyard round it. And now here to his left was the gravelled drive which must lead in to the rectory. He passed clumps of laurel, and there came into view a broad stately house of the eighteenth century, set among elms and a beautiful cedar. He remembered coming up to a house like this with his father to pay his tithes, remembered his father paying money down over a deal table at an outhouse door nodding and bowing to the vicar.

This evening however he was walking up the drive, not as a labourer's son, but as a clergyman in his own right, a gentleman, not to go round to an outhouse but to walk up to the front door and knock boldly and be admitted by a servant. It might take some getting used to.

24

He pulled at a brass bell-pull.

'Yes?' Annie was mystified for a moment. 'Oh – you must be the new curate! Lord, sir, we thought you was lost! You was expected an hour ago!'

Arthur walked into a spacious hall with a black and white chequered marble floor.

'Please to wait in here, sir.' Annie led him into a room to the right – the room in which Lizzie had confided in Julia that morning. He waited, uncertain, looking about him. A spacious room, with a wide curved window. The low evening sun threw a golden light through the room, across large portraits on the walls; across a marble fireplace, unlit, and old comfortable leather chairs. But the room had a chill unwelcoming feel, as if it were not much in use.

The house seemed quite silent, but after a few minutes he heard voices, the door opened and a young woman of his own age stood before him, calm, upright, in a grey dress.

'Mr Grahame.'

She crossed to him and shook his hand. 'Welcome to Stallbridge, sir.' Arthur looked down into her dark eyes, her neat hair.

'I find I am late. I had no idea.'

'We naturally assumed you would come by the station fly, and when you didn't I am afraid we thought you had missed the train. My name is Julia Stone. My father will be here in a moment.'

'The station fly. I see.'

The station fly was for gentry. Arthur had walked. And now he was late, and here was this serious young lady, with her level gaze and her firm hand-shake . . .

'Do you have your things with you?'

'The carter is bringing my box in the morning.'

He was a broad-shouldered man, with a countryman's healthy complexion. He was standing easily, looking down at her with a little smile on his lips. His manner was modest yet relaxed. He had too a slight country burr in his voice which she thought curiously attractive. He was already a great improvement on the prissy, self-important manners of the late Mr Tresham.

Behind her appeared a stocky strong-built man, probably in his fifties, his hair grizzled, with serious grey eyes looking up from beneath strong brows and a beaklike nose which gave the impression of some bird of prey. He stood hunched forward, his hands behind his back.

'We expected you an hour ago, Grahame. You should have wired. We have dined without you.' He turned to his daughter, 'Julia can

25

something be done for Mr Grahame?' He turned again. 'Where are your things?'

'Mr Grahame walked from the station, Father,' the young woman said calmly, attempting to alleviate the harsh and awkward tone of her father. 'His box will come in the morning.'

'How do you do, sir?' Arthur reached forward his large hand.

'Hmm,' Dr Stone grunted, and almost absent-mindedly shook it. 'How do you do?' He looked round for a moment, as if in search of something to say. 'Well, my daughter will take care of you. We will talk in the morning. Now if you will excuse me, I have business . . .'

He gave Arthur another penetrating glance, and went out. Arthur was left facing the young lady.

'Let me show you your room, sir,' Julia said quietly. She led him up a broad staircase and along a short corridor at the back of the house and into a small bedroom.

'A maid will bring you some hot water in a moment. I expect this will be cold by now.' She crossed to touch the jug on the wash stand.

'You need not trouble your maid. That will do me well enough.'

'Dinner is ready whenever you wish.'

He undid his neck cloth, opened his shirt and washed his face and hands. As he was towelling himself, he looked down from his window into the yard below. To one side were stables, and on the other some outhouses, a laundry, and a brewhouse. The gardener and his young assistant were just finishing for the day and as they carried their tools into a barn at the farther end a girl came up the path carrying a basket of bulbs. She must have been working because her face was flushed, and her dress was open at the neck, and her full figure was accentuated by two buttons left undone. There was a ripe, luxuriant feel about her which made it difficult for him to drag his eyes away from her.

Now the young man came out of the barn again and they were talking, and though he could hear nothing, Arthur was aware of the coquetting of the girl; she had rich chestnut hair and as they talked she reached up to arrange it, turning and twisting the heavy tresses through her fingers, and setting her little cotton cap on it, and all the time the young man watching her mesmerised. The girl had a cheery off-hand manner, not seeming to pay him much attention as she fiddled with her cap and her hair, but Arthur could easily see her absolute hold over him. The old man came out, and after locking up the door, the three of them set off round the building and were lost to sight.

26

As he retied his neck-cloth Arthur could not help smiling to himself at the little rustic comedy played out there below him; it was as familiar to him as his own childhood.

He opened the window, and taking off his boots, opened a large clasp knife and scraped off some of the mud they had accumulated on his walk.

When he went downstairs again he found the dining room opposite the drawing room. The young lady was waiting for him.

'Father is busy, I am afraid, and he has asked me to entertain you. I hope your walk has given you an appetite?'

'I've not eaten since this morning, and that's a fact.'

He sat at the dining-room table. Much of the recent dinner remained.

'There's some cold mutton and the remains of a fowl. Would you like some soup? I have told Cook to warm it up for you.'

Annie set the soup before him, and he ate quickly. Julia sat at the table and watched him. He took some bread and tore it to pieces in his hands.

'Would you care for a glass of claret?'

'Thank you, I never take wine.'

There was silence for a moment.

'You hold strong views on temperance, Mr Grahame?'

'Only for myself,' he said, looking at her mildly. 'After all, Our Lord turned water into wine; He was no teetotaller. But I prefer to be fully in command of my actions.' He still had that unassuming but relaxed manner, and yet there was in him a certain definite quality – as if deep in him, there might be a hard core. Anyone less like Mr Tresham she could not have imagined.

Arthur Grahame had finished the soup and was demolishing what was left of the chicken as well as the vegetables. He had a man's appetite, that was certain.

'Father says you were at Jesus College, Mr Grahame.'

'I'll make no bones about it, Miss Stone, I was a servitor in college. A poor scholar. I had no money, so it was my privilege to wait on the fellows, to run their errands, clean their boots, brew their brandy punch, and on occasion defend their honour.'

'I beg your pardon?'

'The college is situated near the town market. You can imagine that there might on occasion be some difference of opinion between their lordships of the college and the market boys. I would be on hand to see that the dignity of the college was upheld. In between times I got on with my studies. I also enjoyed a small college exhibition which provided me with books.'

27

'Mr Grahame –' She was astonished.

'Yes?'

'About the market boys – were you joking? I mean, surely you did not actually fight them?'

There was a humorous light in his eyes as he looked up at her. 'It nearly came to it once or twice.'

She couldn't help smiling. Yet there was something about him, a certain masculine presence, that suggested it wasn't entirely a joke. She felt that she would not like to be a market boy facing this man. She warmed to him, relaxing.

'Did you graduate quite recently?'

'I was ordained a priest by the Bishop of Oxford last summer. Since then I have been working with a group of friends in a mission in the East End of London.'

'How interesting.' Then a thought struck her. 'I wonder, did you by any chance come across a Mr Cunningham at Oxford – Peter Cunningham? I believe he was at Christ Church.'

Arthur frowned.

'The name doesn't mean anything to me. But Jesus men had very little to do with the House.'

There was another silence. Arthur started work on the mutton. 'I wonder if I might request some more bread, Miss Stone? And would a cup of tea be too much to ask?'

Julia had already risen to ring for Annie.

'I beg your pardon, of course you shall have more bread. We usually serve tea at nine o'clock, if that would be agreeable?'

Agreeable. Yes, he would have to learn to be agreeable. He was in a genteel home now where tea was handed round with ceremonious courtesy at nine.

'Tell me something about yourself, Miss Stone.'

Julia raised the bunch of keys which hung from her waist.

'I am the housekeeper, sir, at your service. Should you have any problem, any difficulties or enquiries, I beg you will refer them to me.'

'Your father's housekeeper? But your mother, surely –'

'Dead, sir.'

In the silence the two candles on the table flickered. Julia crossed and laid a shovel of coal on the fire.

'I am sorry. Has your mother been dead long?'

'Ten years last month.' Julia was looking into the fire. Arthur studied her back as she rested one arm on the mantelpiece, and looked down into the renewed flames.

'And you have no brothers or sisters?'

28

'None. My mother died in bringing forth a sister. She never survived.'

'So you and your father live here alone?'

'In a manner of speaking. We are well attended, I assure you. The girl who brought you your soup was Annie. And you will soon meet Becky our parlourmaid. They are sisters and are quarrelling and twittering all day long like two sparrows. Then there is Mrs Oldham our cook. You may judge for yourself of her cookery.'

'You have not yet told me anything of yourself.'

'Have I not? Well, sir,' and she turned at the fireplace, 'look your fill. Housekeeper, secretary, my father's assistant in his parochial duties, translator –'

'Translator?'

'I translate various articles from French and Latin for my father. He has also asked me to learn German in order to translate some important theological treatises. But I am afraid –'

Julia looked at him frankly.

'I have only recently begun, and so far my progress has been dismal. I try, Mr Grahame; the spirit is willing.'

'I will help you,' he said, looking up from his plate. 'I am no great scholar myself, but I understand German well enough. Your father is right: German scholarship has had a great influence at Oxford.'

'Really? It is not simply some whim of my father's?'

'By no means. In the last fifteen years the Germans have transformed our views of the Bible. It was a great shock when Holy Scripture was analysed like any other historical document. When inconsistencies were pointed out, you may imagine the effect: much fluttering in the dove-cote, Miss Stone.' He smiled a sly smile at her. 'It has been proved scientifically that if Noah's Ark were built according to the dimensions in the Bible, it could not float.' He paused. 'Think of it, Miss Stone, poor Noah launching his ark, with all the animals on board, and watching it sink.'

She could not help smiling.

'Are you serious?'

'Quite serious.' He pushed away his plate and sat back in his chair. 'And in the meantime, the poor will not cease to want, the homeless to seek shelter or the orphan a kindly hand.' He paused. 'But I will gladly help you with your German.'

'Thank you.'

That night as Arthur undressed in his cold bedroom and the candle flickered in the silence he picked with cold fingers at his studs and thought of Miss Julia Stone. He had not been prepared for her; of

29

course there was no reason why Dr Stone, the famous theologian and scholar, should not have a daughter to keep house for him. Yet she behaved more like a house-keeper than a daughter. There was something joyless about her. She desperately wanted cheering up. He could not explain it; as if she had given up her hope of happiness in this world.

Julia too, not far away, was preparing for bed. Arthur Grahame had understood her immediately. She saw her life stretching before her, a maiden lady, running the household with an increasingly sharp tongue, and in her old age, when her father should have passed on, perhaps in charge of the village school like Miss Pearson. Staring into the candle flame as she buttoned her night-dress she thought of Miss Pearson, who conducted a sort of bedlam in the village under the name of a school, in which Miss Pearson, a large mob cap on her head, spectacles on the end of her nose, and a birch in her hand, failed entirely to instil obedience into the twenty five children who ran screaming in and out of her house.

A disappointed woman, growing older, withered, shrewish, all hopes and possibilities dried into a sterile nullity. A wasted life. Julia got into bed and blew out her candle.

Chapter Three

The following morning, as every morning, before breakfast, Dr Stone conducted morning prayers. The servants filed into the dining room, and all knelt in prayer as Dr Stone went through a short service.

Afterwards in the kitchen all were agreed that the new curate was a great improvement on Mr Tresham.

'He's no gentleman though,' said Mrs Oldham. 'He's a farmer's son – I could tell the moment I set eyes on him. I'm surprised at Dr Stone.'

'I don't care,' said Becky, 'I think he's nice.'

'A bit sober though.'

'He's got a very nice smile.'

Annie laughed. 'He smile at you, then?'

'Well, what if he did?' Becky turned away quickly.

'You mark my words,' Mrs Oldham went on, 'Dr Stone won't be pleased. You expect a curate to be a gentleman. Otherwise how will he gain respect?'

'Come with me, Grahame. I'll show you the parish. We'll beat the bounds together.'

Breakfast was over and it was another bright cold day.

'Julia, tell Annie to fetch Mr Grahame's coat and mine.'

'Yes, Father.'

She went out, and Arthur was aware of her shadowlike existence in her father's presence.

'There are some letters on my desk to be copied. Have you made a start on that article for the *Church Times*?'

'Yes, Father.'

Presently the men were tramping down the gravelled drive.

'It's a compact parish, Grahame. I have a trap, but I seldom use it. No need. The principal landowners in the village are the Cunning-hams, and we'll look in this morning to pay our respects. The other important families are the Laidlaws and the Emersons – not really a county family, made his money in brewing but we should call on them too. Then there are three good-sized farms, all Cunningham land, good tenants, give no trouble. Trefusis is the most important – that's his farm.' Stone gestured away to the right. 'You'll find him good for a fat goose at Christmas. And three stalwart sons to be proud of.'

They were striding at a brisk rate down the lane towards the centre of the village. To their left, set back from the lane, was a row of low thatched cottages. A woman was cutting a cabbage.

'Morning, Reverend.' She bobbed a curtsy.

Stone grunted and ignored her.

At the bottom of a shallow slope they crossed the ford, passed a smithy to their left, and climbed again towards the centre of the village.

They came into the main village street. Here the cottages to their right were up a small grassy slope. Several of them were shops, and more were public houses.

'The devil is busy in Stallbridge, Grahame. You can take your choice: the Fox and Hounds, the Grapes, the Royal Oak, the King's Head, the Nag's Head, and the Bush. They each have their particular clientele. The Bush – down there at the end of the village – is the rowdiest. Cider, sir. Potent stuff.'

He swung round.

'The house over there is our village school. Miss Pearson does her best – a foolish woman. I shall expect you to assist on Sundays.'

At that moment a girl came out of one of the cottages opposite, and walked up towards them carrying a basket. Arthur recognised her from the previous evening. It was difficult to avoid looking at her. It was not merely that she was strikingly beautiful with an abundance of rich chestnut hair, and large brown eyes in a regular oval face. Those were as nothing compared to her body, her whole self, which she carried in such a public fashion, as if knowing that all eyes must be on her; an instinctive knowledge that she was being watched, so that her hips swayed as she walked and her dress was open a button or two more than was necessary at the bosom, especially on this March morning, as if she did not care for the cold. Worst of all there was a cheery innocence about her as she passed them and gave them a morning salutation. Arthur could not help returning her smile, but was conscious of the rector turning away and grunting. The girl walked on quite unabashed.

When she was out of earshot, Dr Stone said, 'That's Amelia Goodrich. My gardener's daughter, and a shameless baggage. I've spoken to him about her. I pray he gets her settled soon. There are more fights over her in the village than anything else.'

Later that morning they came to the gates that Arthur had passed the previous evening and, walking up a gravelled drive, came out before a long low Jacobean mansion of lichen-covered limestone, with mullioned windows: the Old Manor House, home of the Cunninghams.

A butler told them however that Mrs Cunningham, Mr Peter Cunningham and his sister were out.

'We'll pay our respects to Mr Cunningham, Parker.'

As they were led through the house by the butler, Arthur noticed that the interior, unlike the outside, was furnished and decorated with a glossy newness, as if the decorators had barely packed up and left the day before. Everywhere the wallpaper was light and colourful, and the paintwork gleamed. The furniture all seemed quite new.

They were led through to a conservatory where they found an elderly man in a wheel chair, strangely aged, his hair white and his skin of a thin papery quality. His manner was nervous and timid, his hands clutching and unclutching at the plaid wrapped round his legs, his attention wandering. He offered an emaciated hand to Arthur. Among the exotic plants in this hot and humid atmosphere, he felt a revulsion as if in the presence of death.

'I am glad to see you looking better, sir,' Stone said loudly.

'Only wish I were,' the invalid whispered, 'my physician is not hopeful.'

'Come, come, sir, while there's life –'

'No doubt, no doubt,' he whispered.

Dr Stone introduced Arthur, and after one or two pleasantries, seeing the invalid's mind beginning to wander again, judged it time to be off. 'We'll look in again, sir.' But Mr Cunningham had not heard.

'Is the nature of Mr Cunningham's illness known, sir?' Arthur asked as they were walking down the drive.

'No.' Dr Stone gave Arthur a significant look from beneath his lowered brows, but would say no more.

The following day was Sunday. In the morning Julia sat in church as her father intoned a sermon over her head, chafing her fingers to keep them warm, and thinking about Lizzie's ball, and whether there was any chance of her going. Supposing her father by some miracle gave his permission, what would she wear? The undignified fact was

33

that she had nothing to wear, no ball gown. It was a dismal prospect and Julia's thoughts that morning were gloomy, her mind half on her father's sermon; on the one hand his relentless tone, the severe, rasping note in his voice, the threatening, implacable voice of one certain of what he said; on the other the convoluted and intricate arguments, the winding processes of a mind too turned in on itself, a mind that spent too much time alone, devising theories ever more complex and subtle. No one understood a word he said.

Lizzie and her mother and father were in the Cunningham pew; and opposite, the Emerson family in theirs. Peter was not present. 'Still in bed,' said Lizzie.

In the afternoon Julia also attended to hear Arthur's maiden sermon. He surprised her. The congregation was smaller even than the morning, which had not been great. After their conversation together, she was not surprised to find Arthur had a simple and unaffected manner in the pulpit which made for a more direct communication with his congregation. He lacked the kind of stage-fright which had made other curates stumble over their texts, mumbling downwards or staring up into the rafters.

With him the shepherd and the flock were one, and his country burr seemed stronger than ever so that the few labouring women, their husbands and children, had a sense of kinship with him which was quite different from their view of Dr Stone. Standing up in the pulpit, there was in him a certain tight, contained strength. The hands which grasped the sides of the lectern looked like those of a man who might crush a pewter tankard with ease, or bang together the heads of two drunks from the Bush if need arose.

As the congregation filed out afterwards it was clear that Mrs Oldham had been quite wrong in her prediction. There were many who thrust forward to shake his hand and welcome him to the parish. Furthermore the takings in the plate exceeded those of the morning.

Julia waited for him until he had disrobed, and reappeared in his day clothes.

'I believe you have made a hit, Mr Grahame,' she said as they walked back to the rectory.

'Time will tell,' was all he would say.

The following morning saw her fears realised. As she brought the morning post in to her father, she recognised one large envelope with a local postmark, and inscribed in Lizzie's handwriting. She knocked at her father's door and, laying the letters on his desk, waited to see his response.

'Have you nothing to do, Julia?'

'I noticed a letter there addressed to us both. I wondered what it might be.'

He opened it, and drew out a stiff printed card. He looked at it briefly, looked at her, and then quickly tore it in half.

'Father!'

'What is it?'

'May I – what was that? The card you have torn up?'

'Nothing of importance, Julia. Nothing that need concern us.'

'May I see?'

She leant across his desk and took up the pieces of the card. It was, she knew, the invitation.

There was a crisis here, which she must not avoid. Fortunately Mr Grahame was out.

'Father –' she hesitated '– would it not be very ungracious of us to refuse Mrs Cunningham's kind invitation?'

'I have much to do.' He looked up, as if surprised to see her still there. 'You know very well I never attend such functions.'

'With respect, as rector of the parish is it not part of your duties to participate in its joys as well as its tribulations?'

She wanted the argument focussed on him as long as possible.

'Julia, I have much to do. I sometimes wonder whether you comprehend the importance of my work.'

'How can I not? Every day I am working upstairs, copying, making notes, abstracting, drafting letters – how can you say that? But still, there must be time for rejoicing too! It is wrong of you to shut yourself away here in the rectory.'

He looked up at her from beneath his brows.

'Wrong? What is this? My foot my tutor? No, Julia, I understand very well – it is you who wish to go to Elizabeth Cunningham's ball.' Resting his elbow on the desk, he pointed up at her with his pen. 'You, miss, who would gad after pleasure; you who are so easily lead astray by folly and giddiness.'

Julia had known this was coming; she strove with every nerve to keep the argument cool and reasonable.

'Father, you may regard it as folly, but there are many no less God-fearing than you who do not.'

'You set yourself in judgement on your father? You presume to know better than I?'

'Father, that is nonsense –'

'Nonsense? Are you my child? Do you live in my house?'

Julia clenched her teeth.

'Yes, Father.'

'Very well. As long as you live under my roof, I will be obeyed.'

35

He changed tack, in a way she was familiar with. 'And, Julia, I must say, I am very disappointed in you. What has happened between us? Years ago you enjoyed helping me. We worked together; you were very happy to make my fair copies for me. You were my little handmaiden.'

'Father, I know I did. And I still do, and willingly. Do I complain?'

'Now I find you fractious and obstinate.'

'Obstinate? That is unjust. When do I ever cross you?'

'You have behaved in a manner disrespectful to your mother's memory.'

This was another dizzying change of tack.

'How can it be disrespectful to go Lizzie's ball? I don't understand.'

'You do not understand.' He became sharp again. 'That is the point. Your understanding is immature, deficient. It is my responsibility to judge for you.'

'Father, I am twenty-two! If I cannot understand now, when will I ever be able to? It is unfair to treat me like a child.'

'Twenty-two? Pooh, that's nothing!'

'Nothing? Many women are married and mothers at my age.'

'The more fools they! Bringing children into the world they cannot afford to maintain. This is all beside the point. So long as you live in this house I will be obeyed. If you choose to leave the door stands open to you.'

Even so, Dr Stone sensed in some inner core of his understanding that he had lost the argument. He picked up his pen, and shuffled papers on his desk. The interview was over. Julia went quickly out into the hall and up to her room. She could feel the blood in her cheeks, feel her heart beating painfully.

She found she still had the pieces of the card in her hand, and standing alone in her room stared stupidly down at them. Sitting at her desk, she took the glue pot and a piece of pasteboard and glued the pieces together on to it.

When she had finished she sat a long time staring at the fine copper-plate engraving: 'Mr and Mrs Cunningham request the pleasure of the company of the Reverend and Miss Stone at a ball to celebrate the engagement of their daughter Elizabeth to Mr Adolphus Emerson'.

To celebrate the engagement; what could be more natural or right? Why did her father hate such things? Why did he shy away from them? Why did he refuse to let her go?

As she set out her paper, opened her ink bottle and sharpened her pen, the card lay on the table before her, and as she worked through the morning, her eye would stray back to that card and she would read those words again, 'Mr and Mrs Cunningham request the pleasure . . .'

As Julia Stone prepared for her morning's work, Arthur was in the village. He knew that hardship existed here no less than in the worst city slums, and sometimes, he reflected, it might be worse for being among such picturesque surroundings. He needed no reminder. His own youth was full of memories of poverty, which degraded a man and stripped him of his dignity. He had made a plan to visit every home in the parish in time, to learn to know every family, to seek out want and need and use his small store of influence where he might.

Dr Stone was a great scholar; Arthur thought he himself could best use his time going about the parish and supplying the rector's place as he laboured over his books.

He turned down from the road by the smithy, along the stream through a strange narrow valley called the Kennel. Beside the stream stood a row of low squalid cabins, the entrance to each across a bare plank of timber. The place had a dank, cold and gloomy atmosphere. It was the poorest part of the village.

Here he found himself facing an elegantly dressed lady in a black habit trimmed with dark red, which exactly suited her complexion, pale, but with clear dark eyes. She had a sharp profile, and a thin-lipped smile which spoke of power. He thought she might be in her forties but it was difficult to tell. She was what they called 'well-preserved'; her lips were a little too red, and had he but known it, Mrs Cunningham was not above the aid of certain French products which could be had in Bond Street. A gleaming black boot was just visible at the hem of her wide skirt.

To his surprise she spoke to him, and her manner was easy and natural.

'I believe you must be our new curate.'

'That is correct, madam. Arthur Grahame at your service.'

'Mr Grahame, we are about like errands.'

'I beg your pardon?'

She smiled at him, with a flash of gleaming teeth.

'You are on some errand of charity, are you not? And so am I.'

'To tell you the truth, madam, I am so lately arrived here that I am even now only beginning to seek out where I may be of some service to the poor.'

'Bravo! Well spoken, Mr Grahame. Come with me – I am on my

way now to visit old Wentworth. He is a Peninsular veteran, you know.'

'I beg your pardon, madam, but may I know –'

She turned, looking into his eyes with an amused smile.

'But of course. My name is Alicia Cunningham. How do you do?'

They shook hands. She was an elegant woman, and he had had time to see now, expensively dressed. She gave him a smile of complicity, and led the way.

Together they were admitted into one of the dark cabins where on this cold March day a wizened shrivelled old man, unshaven, his hair disorderly, but with a bright eye, was huddled over a small fire.

'Wentworth, I have brought our new curate to see you. He's very anxious to hear your stories. And I have brought you half a pie for your supper.'

The old fellow was quick to take possession of his pie, wrapped in newspaper. He unwrapped it, and sniffed it, before putting it on a plate up on a shelf above his head.

'Don't want Grip to get hold of that,' he chuckled.

A dog, as old as his master, had stirred in the hearth at this.

'Still, boy!'

Later, during his rambling talk, he brought out an old rusty sabre in a shabby, broken sheath to show it with pride; and a medal, bestowed personally by the Duke of Cambridge, he claimed, now tarnished.

'I wears it on the Queen's birthday and drinks her health. The old squire would set a hogshead of beer in the village for any man to drink the Queen's health – but times are changed. Now, 'tis all temperance . . .'

Afterwards they made their way up into the village. Mrs Cunningham picked her way carefully, and taking his arm as she crossed the narrow plank across the stream, lifted her skirt to reveal a glimpse of lace petticoat.

'Mr Grahame, you and I must co-ordinate our efforts. My carriage is waiting by the King's Head. Come with me now, and we can go through my list of deserving cases.'

A glossy black carriage, square and upright, with new leather harness and gleaming brass, and a coachman, stood waiting. Once they were inside she turned to him.

'A man of your energy, Mr Grahame . . . I feel there is much we could accomplish together,' giving him a long straight look in the half light of the carriage.

Arthur felt strangely and unexpectedly excited to have this vivacious and elegant woman so close; flattered too that a woman so

38

obviously wealthy, the wife of the squire no less, should value the assistance of a raw curate.

When they arrived at the house Arthur went first to pay his respects to her husband in the conservatory, wrapped in plaids despite the hot and humid atmosphere, huddled in his wheel-chair, his hands never still, clutching and unclutching, his eyes moving here or there, unable to concentrate.

'I am sorry to see your husband so sadly reduced, Mrs Cunningham. Is there any hope of a recovery?'

She was silent for a moment, then shrugged.

'In a case like his, the cure may be worse than the illness.'

She clearly wanted to say no more and they went into a spacious office where she took a seat at a wide table and invited him to draw up a chair. She drew out a sheaf of papers.

'Dr Stone takes no interest in his parishioners, but there is much to be done nevertheless. You and I together might achieve much. It is a question of identifying those truly in need. As you know there is always an indigent rump who would rather beg than work. It takes skill to separate the two. And then there is the question of raising funds.'

Sitting erect at her desk, she radiated energy and determination. Looking at her, Arthur could see she was a woman who got what she wanted.

Later, as he was about to leave, she rested her hand on his arm for a moment.

'I look forward to seeing you at my daughter's ball.'

'I beg your pardon?'

'Mr Grahame, surely Julia has told you of my daughter's engagement? We are giving a ball to celebrate and I sent Dr Stone and Julia an invitation yesterday. Whether or not Dr Stone will come, I have no idea. To tell the truth he is not a sociable man, although of course very pious and learned. Let us hope that Julia will be able to come at any rate. Poor girl, she does not have much pleasure in life. It will be your pleasant duty to escort her, Mr Grahame.'

'You will not find me much of a dancer, Mrs Cunningham.'

'Nonsense. You are young. It is the time for dancing. I shall personally expect the pleasure of your company in a quadrille.'

Afterwards Arthur felt pleased with himself that he had encountered an ally so soon in the village; together he and Mrs Cunningham might be able to accomplish much – then he realised with a faint chagrin he was repeating her own words back to himself. He would have to be more careful, he thought with a smile: she was a powerful woman.

39

Chapter Four

As Julia and Arthur sat down that afternoon to their German lesson, he mentioned his meeting with Mrs Cunningham and asked her about the invitation.

Julia's eyes turned to the glued-together card lying on the table between them. Arthur picked it up and turned it over, studying it for a moment.

'Why has this been torn? Was it an accident?'

Julia took it from his hands and put it away beneath some papers.

'It was accidentally torn,' she said.

'And you glued it together?'

'Obviously. Shall we get on with the German?'

'I have no great experience of such things, Miss Stone,' Arthur said cheerfully, setting the large dictionary on the table, 'but it will be an honour to escort you.'

'I am not going.'

There was a long silence. Julia was looking down at her papers, shuffling and arranging them, and then self-conscious, folded her hands on the table, unable to look up. Outside the window, beneath them the gardener and his assistant were at work in the kitchen garden.

'I do not understand.'

'It is perfectly simple.' She looked up quickly into his face. 'I wish you a pleasant evening, Mr Grahame.'

'It's nothing to me, I assure you – and I certainly shan't go if you don't – but I assumed –'

'Never make assumptions.' She looked away, out of the window. Goodrich and William were bending over the rows of fresh-dug earth, working methodically along. There was another silence. Arthur spoke softly to her.

'And yet you have glued the card back together.' He was silent for a moment. 'You would like to have gone but your father has forbidden it?'

'As I said, never make assumptions, it won't help,' she said in a colourless voice, still looking out of the window.

Arthur reached over and picked out the card again. He turned it over in his hands. How serious was this exactly? He had never been to any ball himself in his life.

'Do you want to go, Miss Stone? Surely Dr Stone cannot prevent your going?'

She spoke so softly that he barely heard her.

'There is almost nothing I can do without his permission.'

She was still staring out of the window. Arthur tried to sound cheerful.

'So you won't be going to the ball, eh? And young ladies must have their balls, I dare say.'

'Mr Grahame, I beg you, do not mock me! It is so easy for a man! You are free! You can walk out of that door at any time! You can go anywhere! You may choose to emigrate, you may travel to China or Africa; any profession is open to you. You may walk the streets unmolested day or night. You may enter an hotel, a restaurant, a public house alone, and no one will question you, notice you, laugh at you or make improper suggestions. Do you have *any* idea what it means to be a woman? Do you understand that I do not own a penny in the world? Everything in this house, every knife, fork and spoon, every piece of coal on that fire, is my father's property. If he chose to evict me I should walk out of that door possessing nothing but the clothes I wore. And what would my prospects be in such circumstances? I leave it to your imagination. Do you realise, Mr Grahame, I do not even own a ball-gown? Even if by some miracle my father changed his mind about Lizzie Cunningham's ball, what should I wear?'

Julia had become so agitated that tears were starting into her eyes. Arthur did not like to look at her for a moment, as she turned again to the window. He waited, looking down at the dictionary on the table.

'I beg your pardon – I had no idea,' he said quietly. 'Does he make you no allowance?'

Julia regained control of herself.

'There is sometimes a little latitude in the household accounts out of which I may afford a pair of shoes or trimming for a gown. Father prefers to keep me on a short rein, Mr Grahame.' She drew herself together. 'It is disloyal of me to say what I have said, but it is a relief to speak to someone.'

41

She pulled the black book across the table and, opening it, tried to focus on the first page. Arthur was watching her carefully.

'Loyalty has its reciprocations too, Miss Stone. What of your father's obligations to you?'

'Has he any? Does the Bible enjoin us to "Honour our Children"? In any case, I am wasting your time. Let us try our hand at German.'

She pulled a tiny handkerchief from her pocket and blew her nose, straightened a stray hair round her ear, took a deep breath, and appeared to dismiss the subject.

They spent the afternoon working through two pages of the heavy book Dr Stone had consigned to her. Julia found it difficult to pick her way through the words, but they came easily to Arthur, and he helped her.

Later he was in his own room in the silent house, looking down at the yard below, turning over in his mind what he had seen. It had seemed at first a trivial matter – a ball, what was that? Yet there had been something deeply touching about the way that invitation card had been glued together again. It was very important to her. It was difficult to understand. The famous Dr Stone – he remembered still the man's reputation in Oxford, the great scholar, the author of such important books – what was he to his daughter? A bully and a tyrant.

But more than that, there was something about the woman, something in the passionate look in her eyes, in her unhappiness, that unsettled him, that kept returning, intruding in his thoughts.

Yet he could not see what he could do to help her. He was so newly come, he had barely met them; how could he intervene in such a personal matter?

He could not stand by either. There was something in Arthur that would not wait for things to right themselves. When she had looked at him in that extraordinary speech, with that extraordinary light in her eyes, he knew he must act. And there was in him a force that would act. Dr Stone's tyranny was intolerable, and newly arrived or not, he knew he must speak.

But if he did speak what would he say? This was the crucial factor. What could he say that might weigh with Dr Stone: a man so powerful, of such fixed opinions, a man who knew his mind in all things? How was he to be turned?

'Come in.'

It was getting towards dusk, and the room was in semi-darkness.

'Ah, Grahame, come in. What have you been doing?'

42

'Shall I have the candles lit, sir?'

'In a moment, Grahame. I have been sitting thinking over one or two problems. And you – I trust you have been profitably occupied?'

'I have taken the liberty of reading a little German with Miss Stone, sir.'

Arthur was holding the heavy black book. Dr Stone leant forward over his desk.

'Have you? My dear fellow, I am eternally grateful. Julia has been most dilatory in her studies, most remiss. And I need it more than anything. It is most vexatious to me that I do not read German myself – but the time, my dear sir, the time. You see –' He waved his hand across the desk before him, crammed with papers and books. 'I have years of work ahead of me, Grahame, and with the best will in the world –'

He slumped back in his chair, raising his hand over the papers, and letting it fall again.

'Julia is not as zealous as I could wish. It is very frustrating when there is so much to be done. It will be my life's work.'

'You have already achieved as much as many men might pray for. Your commentary on Leviticus –'

'Yes, yes; very well in its way, though I cannot bear to open it now. A juvenile work. But this –' He tapped the papers on the desk in front of him with a sharp finger nail. 'This, this, will make me. If the Lord spares me to the work, Grahame, this will be the standard work on St John's Gospel – perhaps for ever.'

There was a sharp gleam in his eye.

'You may understand my frustration sometimes when Julia –'

'Yes, sir.' Arthur planted himself squarely before the rector in the gloom of the fading light. 'It is of Miss Stone I should like to speak. Without in any way wishing to give offence –'

Arthur sensed that the rector had stiffened, and was watching him carefully.

'Well, Julia – what of her?'

'I met Mrs Cunningham in the village today, and she invited me to a ball in honour of her daughter's engagement.'

There was silence. Stone was watching him, waiting. Arthur continued.

'She told me that you and Miss Stone had also been invited.'

The rector looked up at him from beneath his brows. 'What has Julia been saying to you?'

'It was I who raised the matter. Dr Stone, it does seem –'

'Mr Grahame,' Dr Stone began quietly, 'you are but recently arrived in this house. You do not yet properly understand the

43

position – a position, which I may say, in no way concerns you. It would be wisest if the matter were not to be raised between us.'

'With gravest respect, sir, I cannot keep silent. Mrs Cunningham has specifically asked me to escort Miss Stone to the ball, and I feel –'

'You feel?' Stone intruded with the withering sarcasm Julia knew so well.

Arthur sensed he was on the wrong tack. He decided to begin again. He held up the black book. 'As I said, I have been reading some German with Miss Stone. She has a long way to go, Dr Stone, before she will be able to read this. Years probably.' He paused, looking directly down into Dr Stone's eyes. 'It must be very frustrating for you. I can see how important it is to your work. Crucial. The *Forschungen* is the single most important book in German on the composition of the Gospels. So I have been thinking,' he spoke carefully, 'I *could* do it myself. At least the parts you need.'

Stone leant forward.

'What are you suggesting?'

'I *could* – I would be quite happy to. And then, perhaps –' He paused again.

Stone sat back in his chair, looking away.

'I see.' There was silence. Arthur waited. Stone was staring out of the window. At last he turned again, and spoke coldly.

'You leave me little option, it seems.'

'Dr Stone, you will not regret your generosity. I will begin tonight.'

My Dearest Lizzie,

You will never believe this. I can hardly believe it myself. Last evening we were sitting at dinner, the three of us; Father was his usual self, hardly speaking, as if his day's work was still revolving in his mind. As you know, he is so involved in his studies, that it requires a severe effort on his part sometimes to realise that there are others present at all. I have sat through dinner with him many times in complete silence. Mr Grahame, our new curate, was attempting to make conversation; though, with Father, as you can imagine, it was uphill work. Then, apropos of nothing at all, Father said – and I think these were his exact words – 'Julia, I have been thinking. I was perhaps a trifle hasty in deciding against Mrs Cunningham's ball. I do not myself wish to go, of course, but if you should wish it, you have my leave to go.'

You may conceive of my feelings. Was I dreaming? How was this possible? For a moment, I could not recognise my own father.

Lizzie, what can possibly have happened to make him change his mind? I have racked my brains for some excuse, but can find none. It is a mystery to me.

Of course I was profuse in my thanks, but he would say no more. Then Mr Grahame said he had met your mother in the village, and she had invited him too, and he would be very happy to escort me, though he said he wasn't much of a dancer! I am not much of a dancer either, if the truth were told.

Dearest Lizzie, may I beg a great favour of you? You are such an expert on clothes and fashions and all that sort of thing, and I confess I am a complete dunce. Will you come and inspect my meagre wardrobe, and advise me on what I should wear? I have looked through my dresses and nothing seems appropriate to such a very important event, my darling. Will you come, and assist your very dear friend,

Julia Stone

The following morning as Arthur sat down in his little room at the back to translate the *Forschungen*, Lizzie arrived at the front door clasping a large paper parcel and they went up to Julia's room. Julia's own clothes were laid out on the bed and examined. There was no ball gown among them, as Julia had told Arthur. Her best dress was a simple black gown, severe and high-necked, with very little flounce – nothing like the great bell-like skirts that were in fashion. It was an attractive enough dress in its way, sober, dignified, a clergyman's daughter's dress, but it was hardly a ball gown. The two sat staring at the clothes scattered on the bed and on the floor.

'It won't do, Julia,' Lizzie said with finality. 'Let's try this.'

She opened her paper parcel: it was a ball gown in pink and apple green, off the shoulder, and with layers of flounces. It was a few years old, though, and a little out of fashion, Julia could see. Somebody's cast-off.

'I don't know if it'll fit; it belongs to my cousin.'

Julia undid the back of her own dress and let it crumple to the floor, and Lizzie helped her into the gown. It was an unaccustomed feeling to bare her shoulders; a strange feeling of nakedness at once frightening and exciting. The gown did not fit however; Julia was a buxom young woman, bigger in the bust than Lizzie's cousin. Lizzie turned her round, pushing and pulling at the gown.

'I'm sure we could work on it . . .'

Suddenly Julia wanted the gown to fit very much. She wanted to wear a ball gown, wanted to bare her shoulders, wanted to go to a ball and dance.

45

'Take it off again.'

Together they were leaning over it, examining the inside stitching.

'We can let it out down the back. Trouble is, the material's faded. It's going to show.'

They sat staring at the dress.

'I don't care if it shows, Lizzie, I'll carry a shawl or something. I want to wear it.'

'Do you? You don't mind it being a bit old? We'll work on it together.'

'And I don't care what Father says either.'

'A limb of Satan,' Lizzie giggled.

'Tell me about your own gown.'

'It's a surprise. But seeing as it's you, Julia, I shall be all in white with a simply enormous skirt over a crinoline – and the most daring decolleté. I don't care what Mama says, I shall jolly well show myself off. What are balls for? If I don't annihilate every girl in the room, I mean to say – except you, my darling, of course.'

Julia smiled, the soft smile in her eyes which were her chief attraction. 'I shan't offer any competition, my dear.'

'Julia, you are a dear, and my dearest dearest friend. Now I promised Mama . . . oh Lord, is that the time?'

After Lizzie had gone Julia took her work scissors and began carefully unpicking the back of the pink and green ball gown. It had astonished her that the very moment she had put on this gown such a powerful feeling should have come over her – something quite unexpected: to dance! But then, as she sat picking out the stitches, the thought arose – she hadn't danced in years – could she remember all the different dances? Life was unjust: Lizzie Cunningham undoubtedly knew every dance under the sun; and if she didn't her mother would have engaged a dancing master for her.

It was extremely vexing: Julia knew about dances, she vaguely remembered them – the Lancers, quadrilles, polkas, waltzes. It was an important matter. When was she likely to get another invitation? And she so longed for gaiety, for lightness, for pleasantness and fun. She wanted to dance so badly that it ached within her. It would be heartbreaking to go to Lizzie's ball, and be compelled to sit them out for fear of making a spectacle of herself. To sit by and watch every dance simply because she couldn't remember the steps. What a pair she and Mr Grahame would make – side by side, neither able to dance.

And then there was Peter. He would be there. Of course he would dance, no doubt every girl in the room would be ready to kill for the chance of dancing with him. That would be an agreeable sight: to watch him dance with every belle in the county, and to speculate on which took his fancy. She bent over her work with the scissors, and tried not to think of Peter Cunningham.

After three days at work Arthur began to ask himself if his gesture on behalf of Miss Stone had been so wise. There was months of work on the table in front of him. If anyone had told while he was still at Oxford that he would be assisting William Stone on his Commentary, he would have regarded it as an honour that would make him the envy of every man in college. Now that he knew what sort of man the Reverend Stone was, he was not so sure. Shut up in this rectory, poring over a book all day until his eyes and his back ached, cooped up over this table; this was not what he had fought his way to Oxford for. For him, Christ was the healer of the sick, the feeder of the hungry, the raiser of the lame. Arthur felt again, as he had done the first evening he had arrived in the village, that he allowed himself to be diverted from his course.

Another thing was that he had made an enemy of Dr Stone; he would never forgive Arthur for forcing him to change his mind.

Annoyed with himself, he let himself out into the rectory garden. A few minutes of air, just to walk a little, to breathe and refresh himself, might put him in a better frame of mind before renewing his labours. As he walked he thought of Miss Stone again. She was an enigma; usually so quiet, so reserved, there had appeared to him, that once, another passionate side. Was that more nearly her true self?

'Annie.'

Julia was looking into the kitchen.

'Yes, miss?'

'Come into the drawing room for a moment.'

Annie wiped her fingers, on a teacloth, and followed Julia. When they were in the drawing room, Julia closed the door behind them and turned to the girl. Annie was nineteen, three years younger than Julia, yet Julia felt that Annie knew the world in ways that she did not.

'Annie,' she threaded her fingers together, looking down, a little flustered, 'you know about all the various dances there are, I dare say?'

'What, miss?'

Julia made an embarrassed gesture. 'I mean, the waltz, the polka, the galop, the schottische and so on.'

'Well, miss, only what most folks know.'

47

'Annie, the fact is, I have got out of practice at – dancing and so forth.'

'And you're going to Miss Cunningham's ball, miss?'

'Yes.'

Julia could not look at her, biting her under lip.

'And you want to get in a bit of practice?'

Julia nodded.

'I'll help you, miss,' Annie said gaily.

'Will you?'

''Course, miss. What do you want to know?'

'Well, as I said – perhaps the waltz first?'

'Come on, then, miss, I'll be the man. It's ever so easy. You just count one-two-three.'

Annie took her in the embrace for a waltz. Julia felt extremely awkward, but there was a desperation in her to learn. She rested her hand on Annie's arm, and took her hand.

'Off we go then,' Annie said. 'Ready? I'm leading off with my right foot, so you go back on your left. Just count in threes. Ready?' Annie began to sing *Over the Waves* under her breath, to give them a rhythm. Julia was looking down, concentrating on her feet, awkward to be dancing with a maidservant. Annie had a good natural rhythm, and an easy lilting movement, and swung her round the room, round the old leather arm-chairs, lightly singing the sentimental tune, and Julia began to relax a little and let the rhythm of the dance carry her along.

'That's it, miss, you got the idea.' Annie swung her along, floating round among the chairs, and then Julia began to feel it, to feel the wonderful infectious pleasure of the dance, and a spontaneous smile broke on her face.

'You got it, miss.'

The door opened, and Becky burst in.

'What's going on?'

'Come in, and shut the door, Becky. We don't want Dr Stone to hear.'

Julia had broken away abruptly.

'Beg pardon, miss, didn't know you was here.'

Julia put her hand to her hair to tidy it. 'It's quite all right, Becky, it's nothing.'

'Now, miss. You got that all right.' Annie grinned wickedly. 'Want to try the polka?'

Julia glanced awkwardly at Becky.

'Very well.'

'Now, miss, first off,' Annie took her arm, and stood side by side with her, 'just watch my feet; see, one step forward – and then bring the other up to it, and hop – that's all there is to it really. Becky, you give us a nice polka rhythm.' Annie took Julia in her arms. 'Come on, miss, we'll take it slow first.'

She launched them off together, gently, as Julia looked down, watching her feet.

'Don't watch your feet, miss. Watch me!'

As they circled round the room, and Annie sensed that Julia was getting the idea, she gradually increased the speed, and at last she could resist no longer.

'Now really let yourself go!'

She dashed into full speed, and sent them galloping round the room. Becky clapped her hands to the rhythm. But before Julia had time to be frightened or cautious, it had come back to her; oh, it was divine, yes, it came back to her now, all those years ago when her mother used to swing her round this room, this wonderful, divine floating, as if she were on some great steed, flying about the room, all light on her tip-toes, and Annie so surely in charge, holding her lightly, but not letting her go.

'Now, miss, dip down this way, and then that – that's it – you got it! Now point the toe – see, and let go at the knee a bit, to give it more style, like, that's it –'

'"Oh, I love to dance the polka,"' Becky sang, clapping in time to the rhythm.

They swung round, the infectious rhythm carrying them whirling about the room. Julia could not help the smile on her face, just swept along by the sheer pleasure of the dance.

They came to an end and both stopped, resting their hands on their ribs for a moment to get their breath.

'She's got it, ain't she, Becky?'

'Oh yes, miss, you needn't worry. You dance very well.'

Julia pushed the hair back from her face. She was quite warm.

'Want to try it again? Make sure?'

They launched off, and Julia felt much surer now and could really let herself be carried by the rhythm, ducking and curving through the motions, to give it grace and elegance. It was wonderful – she could dance for ever, and never want to stop.

The door opened and Mr Grahame was there.

'I beg your pardon.'

The girls stopped. It was a cold breath through the room.

'What do you want?'

'Eh? Nothing – I just wondered –'

'Can't you see I am occupied, Mr Grahame?'

He raised his eyebrows.

'I beg your pardon,' he said again, and went out.

Wasn't that just like him, to walk in – Mr Grahame, the very person she would least have wished to see her dancing. No doubt he would take a very high moral line, look down his nose, just like her father, and no doubt he must consider her a very frivolous young lady by now – as if she went to balls every week, as if every moment of her day were taken up with the cut and set of her gown, and how she was to do her hair, and which young officer she was planning to flirt with. Why were churchmen always such prigs?

This might be the only the ball she ever went to, and no Mr Grahame was going to face her out of her right to it.

'Now, Annie – what about the schottische?'

Chapter Five

The gown was not a perfect fit, there was no helping it. Lizzie and Julia had worked on it, had done what they could, but still it did not sit on the shoulders evenly, and there was the strip down the back where the let-out material looked newer. It had also been a little too short, but Julia and Lizzie had sewn a fringe round the hem; it was the best that could be done. Julia had a clear idea of how it would compare with the dresses of the other girls. Every one of them would have had a new dress made for this occasion; they would be criticising and comparing each other's, and she knew exactly the sort of glances she would receive as she entered the room. She had a paisley shawl, which she planned to drape round her shoulders to hide the back as well as she could.

She and Arthur were walking up the drive to the Old Manor House. She had her dancing slippers in a bag. Arthur was dressed in his clerical black, with a white neckcloth tied in a neat bow. He was surprisingly neat for a man whom she thought would have despised such things. She was conscious of a sense in him of following his duty, rather than his inclination; while for her – there was a deep hunger in her that evening for lights, dancing and fun.

'You know, Mr Grahame, I shall never understand why father changed his mind about tonight, but whatever the reason I shall be eternally grateful.'

Julia's thoughts were not on Arthur. Her main concern was how Peter would receive her. Would he ask her to dance? Lizzie had given her a dance card, and Julia had looked down the list: quadrilles, Lancers, waltzes ... and against each a blank space. There was something daunting about those blank spaces; she had her pencil, but would she be called upon to use it?

As they approached the house, it was ablaze with light. It was a cold April evening, but the front door stood open, and a carriage was there, people were getting out, and there were shouts and greetings. Old family friends, no doubt.

As Julia and Arthur arrived at the front door, Parker was there to greet them.

'There is a room upstairs where you may change your shoes, Miss Stone. Mr Grahame, if you would care to let the footman have your coat, and then perhaps you would like to go through to the drawing room. Miss Cunningham and Mr Emerson are waiting.'

Julia went up to a spare bedroom. A fire was burning, and there were three girls in it already, one adjusting her gown in a long pier glass, one bending over to pull up her stockings, while another was monopolising a looking glass on a chest of drawers. The bed was covered with coats and shawls. Julia knew only one of these girls, Miss Violet Trefusis. Miss Trefusis' father was Mr Cunningham's tenant-in-chief, and their farm lay next-door to the rectory. This was a very special moment for her, as special as it was for Julia.

'Oh, Julia.' Her eyes unconsciously took in Julia's dress, but she was just able to refrain from speaking. Julia was aware how, even in that split second, Violet had taken in the dress, appraised it, realised that it was someone else's cast off and didn't properly fit ... why was it girls had such needle eyes for these things, Julia thought? Was it going to be like that all evening?

'How marvellous you were able to come. Is your father here?'

'No, I have come with Mr Grahame.'

'Who?'

'Our new curate,' Julia said drily.

'Oh.' She could hear the disappointment. A curate; hardly husband material. Still, at least it was a man, if only just. Julia understood Violet very exactly.

She was able to get at a looking glass, and dressed her hair a little, pulled and pushed at the dress round her bust. How strange, how exciting to bare her shoulders, to experience that nakedness in public, with men looking at her. How odd. She didn't care what the other girls would say, she was glad she had come. Oh, if only someone would ask her to dance!

She looked at herself in the looking glass. Was she attractive to men? She had not the faintest idea. How could you tell? It was obvious in the case of Lizzie or Violet Trefusis, but with herself ... She took a final look, a final pull at her gown, a final adjustment to her shawl, and went downstairs.

Lizzie was waiting to greet her with a round-faced, vacuous young man, looking very pleased with himself. This was Mr Emerson. Lizzie was a dream in her wide crinoline gown, white with the palest of green trimming round the hem, and a green sash; and her hair put up, with a rose in it.

'Julia, you can't imagine how glad I am you were able to come.' She gave her dress a quick glance. 'The dress hasn't come up too bad. You look lovely. Look, Mama has the arrangements for dinner. We shall be sitting down at eight.' She was turning to a another arrival.

Mrs Cunningham was looking elated and brilliant in a gown of blood red and black, which set off her white shoulders and coal black eyes.

'Julia, my dear, I am so glad to see you here tonight. I have asked General Conyers to take you in to dinner.' And she led Julia to an elderly general, a merry old fellow of sixty, retired from the army, a man who had never known a day's illness in his life, and didn't understand what the word boredom meant.

Julia was relieved at what she thought of as Alicia's tact, that she had not exposed her directly to the critical gaze of some of the young girls, who were scattered about the drawing room. There were already twenty or so guests here, and soon they would go in to dine. Afterwards many more would arrive for the dancing.

Julia adjusted the shawl about her shoulders as she answered the General's questions; which was easy because he was a man with no malice in him, who simply enjoyed everything, as far as she could ascertain.

Alicia had also met Arthur and introduced him to an elderly lady.

'This is Mrs Sloper, Mr Grahame, she is one of my trusty lieutenants in our good work. Will you take her in to dinner?'

Arthur attempted to make small talk with Mrs Sloper but he had noticed Julia across the room talking to an elderly gentleman. He saw the way she adjusted the shawl about her shoulders, he could see she was ill at ease, unused to this sort of gathering – as he himself was. He still could not make her out. Unless he had been dreaming, when he had walked into the drawing room the other day, Julia had been dancing with the parlourmaid. Her embarrassment would account for the way she had snapped his head off. He didn't mind. It had made her singularly attractive. He watched her as she listened attentively to the old man. She had an interesting quality, Arthur decided; a strong centre of gravity, so that even when she was clearly in difficulties, in awkward or unusual circumstances, she had the presence of mind to remain calm.

Julia was thinking, Is Peter here? There were a number of other girls she knew vaguely, through Lizzie. There was Fanny Emerson, Dolly's sister: she was a very pretty, bird-like girl; though bird-brained would be perhaps closer to the mark, in Julia's opinion. And then there were the two Scots girls – the Laidlaw sisters. Beattie Laidlaw was a rather tall, angular young woman, with red hair and sharp intelligence; her sister was Sarah, a horsewoman, shorter than Beattie, and considered rather 'fast'.

Parker announced dinner. The General gave Julia his arm, and they went in. The dining room was decorated in opulent taste: thick swags of curtains, paintings in heavy gilded frames, ornate carved dining chairs. The long table had been set with big set pieces, great epergnes laden with fruit, floral displays culled from the hot house; decanters and glasses of crystal; there was a beautiful porcelain dinner service; gold-plated cutlery – everything was shiny and gleaming. As the old gentleman helped her into her chair, Julia saw in her place a little card with her name inscribed in an ornate copper-plate hand. She adjusted the shawl at her back.

At one end of the table Mr Cunningham had been wheeled into his place by a footman, and at the other Julia saw that Mrs Cunningham had placed Mr Grahame next to herself. Lizzie and Dolly were sitting in state in the middle of one side of the table. Next to Lizzie was the General, and next to the General came Julia. Opposite them sat Peter.

Mrs Cunningham asked Arthur to say grace.

While they were waiting for the first course Peter, who was in high spirits, began twitting Dolly.

'You realise she'll take a lot of keeping up, Emerson? She'll need a complete overhaul and fitting out every year.'

'Peter, shut up!' Lizzie called clearly.

'I think Emerson has a right to know,' he went on in a tone of sweet reasonableness, looking round the table. 'He has a right to know what he's letting himself in for. Well, doesn't he?' He looked round innocently. 'You see, Emerson, you should have come to me before committing yourself. That would have been the wise course, the prudent course. A man should not go blindly into these things. I could have advised you. No, Lizzie,' he saw she was trying to intervene, 'a man has the right to know. Emerson should have come to me and I could have given him a clear idea what was in store for him.'

Young Adolphus could think of nothing witty to say and sat in silence, meditating revenge. Fortunately he was rescued by the arrival of the soup.

At moments like this Peter dominated the table effortlessly. As Julia watched him she was dazzled by his easy assured manner, his good looks, the casual way he would turn to his companion at the

54

table and make some glancing remark which would raise a smile. With him everything seemed easy, everything flowed smoothly. Any woman with him would have the most elegant, good-looking and eligible man in the room. It was as simple as that.

To her gratification he had actually noticed her and given her a quick smile, which had caused her a momentary blush as their eyes met. Every girl would be out to get him tonight, that was certain. Julia would have to be content with the likes of General Conyers.

The general was telling her a funny story.

'I was in some theatre in London – Haymarket, I think it was, and the memsahib had gone off somewhere – this was after the play when everyone was coming out, and I was standing there, and all of a sudden this officious-looking, pompous fellow, surrounded by a gaggle of females – wife, daughters – appears. "Call me a cab!" he says – bless me if he didn't take me for the manager! "You're a growler," I said. "Whaa-a-a-at!" he says. "Well, I can't call you a hansom," I said! All the ladies giggled. Collapse of stout party! Pretty smart, eh, Miss Stone? For an old-timer? Eh?'

Julia had heard this one before, but she laughed with the general. Then she was distracted by Fanny Emerson, further along the table.

'Now listen everybody, here's a riddle!' Fanny called out. Heads turned along the table. 'Ready? Now, why is a man like a telescope?'

There were a lot of earnest guesses.

'No, Mr Cunningham, you are *not* to answer – I bet you know it already!'

'Should think I do, it's got whiskers on it,' Peter said in a world-weary tone.

Now as it happened Julia knew the answer to this riddle, and without thinking she spoke out,

'Because a woman can draw him out, see through him, and shut him up again whenever she likes!'

Everyone laughed and clapped her. This minor triumph, and the general good spirits helped Julia to relax and forget about her shawl.

Arthur realised he knew Peter Cunningham. He remembered him now from Oxford. It was something he had not foreseen – yet he should have remembered him when Julia Stone mentioned his name. He was studying Peter, when he became aware that Mrs Cunningham was speaking to him.

'I have not seen you lately in the village, Mr Grahame. You are grown remiss in your pastoral duties. I looked for you.'

'I have been occupied with some work that Dr Stone asked me to deal with. I hope to continue, however, in the not too distant future.'

'What could be more important than the care of your parish, Mr

Grahame? I need some of your man's energy. I am only one frail women, and there is so much to be done.'

In everything Mrs Cunningham said to him, there was an undercurrent of suggestion. She looked at him so straight, so deep in the eyes, he could not understand what she was thinking. At least there was one explanation, but it was so preposterous, that he would not consider it. He was conscious of the low neckline of her red gown, and the white skin of her bosom as she leant towards him. He found her powerful and disconcerting.

Mrs Cunningham produced her dance card.

'Now, Mr Grahame, you promised to dance with me, and I shall hold you to it. I do not get so many invitations that I can afford to refuse any. I think we said the quadrille, did we not? See, I am marking you down.'

She wrote his name on the card.

'Do not fail me.' She gave him a very straight look, and smiled.

As dinner came to an end the guests began making their way to the library where the dancing was to be held. A band from Devizes had been hired for the evening – three fiddles, a flute, a cornet and a bass fiddle – and they were hidden in a corner behind a barrier of hot-house plants. The room had been lavishly decorated with pot plants, and was already quite warm from the wide chandeliers, blazing with candles.

Other guests were arriving. It was after ten, and the room was crowded. Julia thought she had never seen so many pretty girls in lovely gowns, all with wide skirts and in strong, sometimes violent colours: cerise against purple, viridian against royal blue, pink with a magenta sash; it was very colourful, and Julia allowed herself the luxury of admiring the girls, the rustling of silk and satin, the flowers in their hair, the glimpses of tiny slippers, before reminding herself of her own modest creation.

Peter was among the girls, and had said something funny because they all suddenly burst into laughter. They twittered about him, every one of them a thousand times more attractive than herself, switching and clattering their fans, like a flock of exotic birds.

The first dance was announced, and Peter led a girl out of the crowd on to the floor, and couples formed up the centre of the room for a country dance – as Julia knew from her card. She had not been claimed for this one.

Dolly and Lizzie took their places at the head of the set, the band struck up and the couples moved in and out, back and forth, ducking and weaving through each other, up the line, down again, the music tripping along in its light-footed rhythm. Peter was easily the most accomplished dancer, the easiest and most graceful man on the floor. He looked so handsome, so elegant, making every other man in the room look foolish or old, clumsy or boorish.

Julia envied the girl opposite him. Then, as Peter was coming down outside the line, near her, he caught her eye and gestured to her. He was gone before she could make out what he meant. It was nice to be noticed, though; it would of course have been even nicer to have been in the dance. General Conyers was sitting beside her and she answered him with some random remark, her eyes never leaving the dancers.

The dance came to an end, and the couples dispersed, and the general was speaking, and after a while, as the band was striking up again, said, 'I say, I've stood by long enough. If none of these young bloods have got the sense to claim you, I'm damned if I won't! Come on, Miss Stone, could you bear to stand up with an old stager, eh?'

'General, you know I should be delighted!'

'You'll find I can still shake a leg,' he said with a gleam in his eye.

It was a polka and Julia wondered if the old fellow was up to it, but he was. He took her in his arms, and as the music started swept her away with splendid old fashioned gallantry, sweeping her around the room as the other couples galloped round about them.

'General, I won't insult you by congratulating you on your dancing,' Julia tried to say, as the old man whirled her about. 'But I have not enjoyed myself so much since – oh, I can't remember when.'

In the pleasure of the movement she could not help flashing a smile, and just then Peter went whirling past with Fanny Emerson, and saw her and returned her smile, and she wanted to blush – it was as if she had deliberately been smiling at him – as if – oh, she didn't know, her thoughts were muddled, but it was just such a pleasure to be swept round like this, and she said a prayer of thanks to Annie.

However, in the swirl of the dance and the bumping of couples against each other, the shawl became disarranged from her arms, and before she could stop it, had fallen, and been lost on the floor. The general swept her on, not noticing, but now Julia's pleasure was converted into panic. She had lost her protection; so long as she had had the shawl she had felt safe, but now, as the general continued to dash her about the room, she knew every girl would be noticing and remarking the tell-tale signs down the back of her dress; how the rector's daughter was in the shabbiest dress in the room, someone's cast-off, and the rector too mean to buy his daughter a proper dress for this important occasion, pitying her and despising her. The general was enjoying himself hugely, laughing and telling her things, and she was fighting to remain cheerful and follow his lead, but in her mind there was only desperation, and finally as the dance came to an end, and the general was escorting her to a chair, she was looking round her in an agony of nakedness. She sat, and the general was beside her, thanking her, and she could think of nothing but her shawl.

But now she saw Peter coming across the floor towards her, and then he was in front of her, and said, 'I say, come on, Julia, can't have you sitting out. You're not booked for this one, are you? Off we go!' and was already taking her hand, but she became terribly agitated, pulled it away and said, 'Thank you, Mr Cunningham, I should love to, but I really must decline.'

Chapter Six

At that moment, she felt something on her shoulders, and looking round saw Mr Grahame replacing the shawl. He looked into her eyes but was already turning away when Peter repeated, 'I say, come on – they're starting,' and before she could say anything, he had taken her hand again and was leading her out on the floor.

'Excuse us, General,' Peter called over his shoulder, and Julia looked round too but Mr Grahame had disappeared already, she was unable to thank him, and now here she was dancing with Peter.

'I say, Julia, I never knew you could dance so well. I saw you with old Conyers – you were floating like a butterfly, by Jove.'

But she didn't need to answer. To be here, in his arms, lilting round to the swaying rhythm of a waltz, was enough. If nothing else tonight she had been dancing in Peter's arms, and everything else was distant, out of focus. The room swept round them, and she could only be conscious of Peter here before her, so relaxed, so charming, making amusing remarks. What did he care? Nothing was difficult for him, all flowed so easily, all as easily as this dance as they moved round the room, among the flowing dancers, and everything was a blaze of lights, music and pleasure, and she could have gone on for ever, just floating in his arms.

She forgot everything, forgot the others in the room, forgot the knot of girls, whisking and clicking their fans as they watched her, forgot the general, forgot Mr Grahame whom she saw briefly standing talking to Mrs Cunningham, forgot everything, only the pleasure of the dance. Round and round, oh, it was infectious, the physical movement, intoxicating, she wanted nothing more in life, only this to be in Peter Cunningham's arms, sweeping round in the waltz.

But even then, even in that moment of which she had dreamt so often, she thought, I must not let him see how much I am enjoying this, I must stay in charge, it would never do if he were to see how I worship him. And at the end, as she readjusted her shawl, she turned to him in the middle of the floor, and said, 'Thank you, Mr Cunningham, I did enjoy that,' and walked away before he could answer.

As she stood for a moment by the fire, getting her breath back, she was joined by Alicia Cunningham who said, 'You should congratulate me, Julia. I have got your fierce Mr Grahame to dance the next dance. I have brow-beaten him into a quadrille! He swore solemnly he was not a dancing man, but I think I got the better of him! Now, let us see if he will honour his pledge.'

She flicked open her fan, and at that moment Peter came across. 'Did you see Julia, Ma. Danced liked a butterfly.'

'I did indeed. Julia, you are a sly-boots – you never told us you were such a an accomplished dancer. I assure you, I am quite envious.'

Arthur Grahame was beside her at that moment, and said, 'Mrs Cunningham, I believe I have the pleasure of this dance?'

He spoke in a very studied way to Alicia, but Julia swung round and said, 'Oh, Mr Grahame – I must thank you for retrieving my shawl. I wonder, may I introduce Mr Peter Cunningham?'

But to Julia's astonishment Arthur looked into her eyes with an expression of cold indifference, then turned back to Alicia as if he had not heard her, and said, 'This is our dance, I believe?' And offered her his arm.

Peter's attention had been distracted so he had missed the moment, but to Julia it had been like a slap in the face.

Arthur was gone with Alicia, and now Peter turned again to Julia and said, 'Come on, can't miss this one!' and led her back into the dance.

She could feel a heat in her face. Mr Grahame had ignored her as if she had never spoken. As if she were invisible.

They took their places in the set, but all the time she was glancing towards Mr Grahame, could not take his eyes from him, confused and angry. He moved through the interminable windings of the quadrille, politely, but with a seeming indifference, as if it gave him little pleasure.

Soon after the dance finished, Julia excused herself from Peter and went in search of Mr Grahame. She found him alone, on his way through the hall into the drawing room.

'Mr Grahame.'

He turned.

'I should like to know what you thought you were doing just now?'

'I beg your pardon?' he said with polite indifference.

'I think you know what I mean.'

He thought for a moment, and at last replied with difficulty, as if he would rather not have had to to answer, 'I had no wish to hurt your feelings, but I did not wish to be introduced to Peter Cunningham.'

'Oh, really?' She was astonished. 'Is there anyone else you do not deign to know? Perhaps I am not good enough for you either? I suppose the fact that you are the guest of his mother might not make you change your mind?'

'If I had known who he was, I would not have come.'

'I suppose –' Then she heard what he had said. 'Whatever do you mean?'

He looked her straight in the eye and said without inflection, 'I knew him and his cronies at Oxford.'

'You are a boor, sir. You have been invited here tonight as a guest; that does impose on you at least a duty to be civil. You boasted to me that you had been a servitor at Oxford. I wish while you had been there, you had learnt to be a gentleman.'

She thought this would finish him off, but he replied quickly and vehemently, 'There are more important things in life than being a gentleman!' and turned and walked quickly away from her, leaving Julia staring at his back.

She turned away, and made her back through the crowds; the man had disturbed her composure, had thrown everything into confusion and disorder, and what was intended to be an evening of pleasure and fun was turning into one of frustration and annoyance. It was obvious that Mr Grahame was not a gentleman and should never have been invited.

She made her way into the conservatory where she found General Conyers talking to Mr Cunningham in his wheelchair and the old general welcomed her and they sat and listened to their host's complaints, his stories of doctors and cures. The general, robust and hale, listened with polite incomprehension, and would interject bluff remarks on the efficacy of cold showers, sea bathing or a thorough purge. The mutual incomprehension of these old gentleman helped to settle her mind, until she was able to say to herself that after all Mr Grahame was not important, and the whole house was full of people enjoying themselves, and that was what mattered, and how well Alicia had arranged everything.

Dolly was by himself. He did not seem to be very happy.

'Adolphus, I wonder, would you be so kind as to give me an ice cream? I confess I have become quite warm.'

Dolly came to life.

'Oh, hullo, Miss Stone. Excuse me, I was miles away.'

Dolly offered his arm and they went together into the dining room, which had now been set out with a buffet serving cold drinks and ice creams. Dolly helped them to ice creams.

'Now then, Adolphus, what was making you so thoughtful?'

Dolly looked as thoughtful as he ever could, an expression of vacuous emptiness in his face.

'Oh, I don't know, Lizzie's gone off somewhere, and sort of left me becalmed.'

'Haven't you asked anyone else to dance?'

'Oh, yes – well, I was going to ask Lizzie, you see, in case she wanted –'

His voice trailed off.

'In case what, Adolphus?'

'Well, I don't like to engage a girl, then find Lizzie wanted to dance that one with me, in a manner of speaking.'

Julia ate her ice cream for a moment.

'I see. Well, Adolphus, you know I think we should take the bull by the horns. I think you should invite me to dance. I don't get so many invitations that I wouldn't be grateful for another.'

'Oh, I say, do forgive me, Miss Stone. Of course, unpardonable of me – of course, it would be a pleasure. Er. Was there any dance you had in mind?'

'I tell you what, Adolphus – why don't we just dance the very first dance after we've finished our ices and that way we'll just take pot luck!'

Dolly was amazed and delighted at this daring suggestion; Julia seemed positively transformed this evening, actually asking a fellow to dance and then saying they'd just take the first one that came along. It made him quite dizzy.

'Are you enjoying yourself Adolphus?'

'What? Oh, of course, Miss Stone – no end.'

'Are you quite sure?'

'Oh, yes.' He glanced over her shoulder, and his mood changed. 'I say, Miss Stone, do you think we could go and dance now?'

'If you wish.' She had nearly finished her ice cream, and put it hurriedly down on the buffet as Dolly suddenly took her arm. As they turned Peter had just come through the door.

'Ah, there you are! Come on, Julia, they're just starting up again, off we go! Hullo, Dolly.'

He had already seized her arm and was about to drag her away.

'You are too late, Mr Cunningham, I am engaged for this dance.'

'Engaged? To whom?'

'Why, to Mr Emerson here!'

'What, Dolly? He won't mind, will you, Dolly? You'll excuse us, won't you? You can have her for the next one.'

And again he was about to drag her away.

'No, I really must insist, Mr Emerson has secured me for this dance. If you would like to come to me after it, I will see if I have any vacancies left on my card.'

She smiled at Peter, an arch, amused smile, took Dolly's arm, and went off with him to the dance, leaving Peter to watch.

She could have kicked herself for her Quixotic streak: she felt sorry for Dolly, but how easy it would have been to have looked helplessly at him and gone off with Peter. She bit her lip. But she mustn't be easy on Peter. It would never do.

As they were dancing, Dolly said in a husky, unfocussed voice, 'I say, thanks awfully, Miss Stone.'

'Thanks for what?'

'Well, you know, I mean to say, it's a real pleasure to dance with you, you know.'

'Thank you, Adolphus. And it's a real pleasure to dance with you too.'

She saw at that moment over Dolly's shoulder Peter dancing with Fanny Emerson.

'No, what I meant was – well, I mean to say, thank you for dancing with me, and all that.'

'Adolphus, I don't understand. We had engaged the dance. Why shouldn't I dance with you?'

'Oh, I don't know . . . ' His voice trailed off, and he looked away over her shoulder.

But Julia did understand very well. Poor Dolly, he was a man of few words, and Peter was so terrifyingly fluent, it was not fair . . .

But Julia had to pay the price for her strength of mind. Peter did not come near her for the rest of the night. She had the mortification of sitting with General Conyers, then talking with Lizzie, then dancing again with General Conyers and Dolly, and all the time watching Peter among the gaggle of girls twittering about him, their fans clicking, fanning clouds of flattery around him, their laughter like the bubbling of champagne; and he intoxicated by it, revelling in it, taking it as his natural due, easy amusing, relaxed, and the girls aching to dance with him, as she was.

Chapter Seven

Arthur woke early. It was his habit to sleep with the window open in all weathers, and at the first hint of sound from the kitchen below he was awake. Although he felt tired, he threw on his clothes, went down into the kitchen to beg a crust of bread, and in a fitful restless state went out and walked down through the village, pulling at the hunk of bread in his hand.

Where was he going? He had no idea. There was only in him an urge to walk, to subdue his feelings and rearrange his thoughts, to settle his mind before returning to the Rectory.

The situation was more complicated than he had thought. Wouldn't it be wisest to move out into a cottage in the village? Or go back to London to his friends in the mission? That was where he should be. He walked quickly along as the thoughts passed through his mind.

It might be wisest. He still could not get over what he had seen the previous evening. It was the one thing he had not anticipated. Fall in love with Julia Stone? It was a thing he must not do. He remembered again the vision of her as she had danced with Peter Cunningham. Arthur could never have believed it. Julia Stone was beautiful. Why had he never seen it before? The sight of her being swept round the room in that man's arms, throwing back her head, her face lit up in an ecstasy of pleasure, and then – it was so touching – looking down suddenly to see if her feet were in the right place.

She was quite beautiful. Her whole body swaying to the music in light quick movements, turning her head suddenly, a flashing smile breaking from her in the sheer pleasure of the dance. A man might wait twenty years – all his life – and never see such a sight.

That was a woman – that was a woman to fight for, a woman to struggle for. But was he in a position to fight or struggle for her? As if he were to go to her father and ask for her hand – on seventy pounds a year!

He would have to keep a strong grasp on the situation. It was only by the utmost will power and determination that he had come this far. It would never do to fall in love with that incomparable woman, a woman of her fine intelligence, her sensitivity, her gentleness, her kindness – no, it would never do. Everything would be muddle and confusion, out of his control. Better to move out. Better to move, go away, go back to his real work.

He had walked almost through the village before he turned off along a path which ran beside a beech wood. The village lay in the lee of the downs, snuggling at the foot of the western slope of low chalk hills, with their sinuous feminine curves. Just beyond the village a valley ran up into the downs and beech woods clung against its slopes.

Across the valley to his right hung a faint mist, and the gentle downs swelling on the far side caught the early morning sun, the woods in their fresh greenery, in their first spring flush. Two cottages were partly visible among them, a tall thin wisp of smoke rising straight in the clear air. Somewhere in the distance up on the downs he could hear the faint sound of sheep bells. He stopped to take in the scene; it was one of those rare moments when there is a palpable sense of the wonder of existence, and as he surveyed the scene, Arthur offered up a silent prayer of thanks for God's goodness. The view soothed him, strengthened him, and he made a vow that let things turn out how they might, he would not be deflected from his work.

As he turned to continue his walk, he saw old Granny Leggatt coming towards him. She was bent beneath a bundle of sticks twice her own size. Arthur greeted her, and as she looked up with difficulty to see who it was, took the bundle from her shoulders and swung it with an easy movement on to his own.

'I'll take that, Granny.'

He turned and they continued back towards the village. Mrs Leggatt was one of the poorest inhabitants of the village; she occupied a tiny squalid cottage in the high street and scraped a precarious living making gingerbread.

'It'll soon be warm enough to do without a fire, Granny,' he said cheerfully.

'Not for me. My old bones feel the cold more than most, Reverend.'

They were abruptly stopped by a man who stepped suddenly out from among the trees. He was holding an old muzzle-loading shotgun, and had a large game satchel slung across his shoulders. He wore a battered bowler hat, gaiters on his legs, and was scowling at the old lady.

'Now then.'

Mrs Leggatt shrank closer to Arthur.

'Morning, friend.' Arthur did not know this man.

'I've told you before, you old rag-bag, you're trespassing. What did I say? Eh? I'm danged if I don't report you to squire, and you can look for other lodgings. He'll turn you out in a twinkling, you old witch.'

'Hold on, friend.'

''Beg pardon, Reverend, but you stay clear. I knows her of old.' He menaced her with his gun. 'Didn't I tell you before? Stealing squire's property, that's a felony, that is.'

'You were picking up dead wood, weren't you, Granny? No harm in that.'

Arthur stood above the two of them, large and relaxed. he held the great bundle of sticks on his shoulder still. 'And you needn't wave that gun about, friend. We aren't going to attack you.'

'No I shouldn't think you are. Now then, Reverend, you just put them sticks back in squire's wood and depart peaceful, or I'll report the both of you.'

'Put your gun away,' Arthur said. 'Mrs Leggatt is within her rights to pick up dead wood.'

'Not without squire's say so.'

'With it or without it, friend.'

'I say no, and I ain't no friend o' yourn.'

The man was still menacing the old lady with his shot-gun. Now Arthur swung the great bundle of sticks on to the ground, and as the man's attention was distracted by the motion, deftly took the gun from him and before he could do anything, discharged it into the air. The report made him jump. Arthur handed the gun back to him.

'Now stand aside, friend, and we'll go on our way in peace.'

Once more he swung the bundle on to his back and he and the old lady walked past the man who for a moment was too stupefied to say anything. Then he called after them, 'Squire shall hear of this!'

They came down into the village, and Arthur deposited the sticks in a little yard behind Granny Leggatt's cottage, dank and smelling of drains.

'You'll be all right now, Granny?'

She thanked him with tears in her eyes, clinging on to his big hand with both her own, emaciated and twisted with arthritis.

'And don't worry about the squire. He wouldn't throw you out of your house.'

''Tis only Mrs Cunningham I fear . . .'

'What?'

'If it comes to her ears, Reverend –'

'Mrs Cunningham would never harm you, Granny.'

'If you could only speak to her for me, Reverend.'

'Of course I'll speak to her. But you needn't worry.'

'Only promise me you'll speak to her, Reverend.'

She wouldn't let him go until he had given his promise again and he turned away up towards the rectory, puzzled by her frenzied insistence.

Arthur was walking up past the gates to the Old Manor House. He was beginning to need his breakfast. The sun was higher now and it was warmer. He was still puzzled by Mrs Leggatt's confused remarks about Mrs Cunningham. Obviously she ruled the village – that had been obvious since the morning he'd met her – but at least it seemed a benevolent rule. He would have to make some more discreet enquiries before he spoke to anyone, he thought.

He wasn't far from the rectory when he heard his name called out from down the lane behind him. Turning, he saw a hundred yards away Emmy Goodrich running towards him, a basket in her hand.

'Reverend Grahame!'

He waited as she caught up with him, and for a moment she stood before him, out of breath, her cheeks flushed with the effort, and her eyes bright. Her straw bonnet had fallen down behind her head. As usual she was clad in an open-necked dress, and she seemed oblivious of the early morning chill.

'Oh, Reverend, I can never thank you enough!'

Arthur waited for her to go on, as she still fought for breath.

'Gran just told me. She was so afeard, and you saved her from Randall this morning, and she'll never forget it so long as she lives, I declare, and neither will I.'

Emmy had never spoken to him before, though he had often seen her coming and going from the rectory. He knew some of the old prudes thought her a Jezebel who flaunted her all too obvious charms shamelessly through the village, but it seemed to him she was quite innocent, as if she wanted, in her abundant and generous way, to share her pleasure in life with everyone.

It was a pleasure just to look at her, but Arthur was embarrassed by her thanks.

He smiled.

'How did you hear of it?'

'She do live next-door, Reverend! And she came in this minute to

67

tell us, and I want you to know 'twas a kindness in you, Reverend, a right Christian act. That Randall is the very devil.'

'Your granny has a right to pick up dead wood, Emmy.'

'That's what we all do say, but 'tis Mrs Cunningham won't have it, and do threaten us if we touch so much as a twig of her wood, 'ceptin' it be by her leave.'

They turned and continued up towards the rectory together. Arthur was thinking.

'Mind, I knew you'd never let such a thing pass, such a man as you be, Reverend,' Emmy went on quickly. 'Ever since you preached your first sermon, we all did know you was a good man that would care for the likes of us, and we all do like you for it. We never had a curate before that cared a farthing for poor folks.'

'Why shouldn't I care, Emmy? I am a poor man myself.' He smiled.

'That's what I did say, Reverend! He be a man such as ourselves.'

'But I'm sure Mrs Cunningham cares too. I know she goes about on many errands of charity.'

Emmy who was walking close beside Arthur, turned sharply up to him, and spoke quietly in a conspiratorial whisper.

'Every crumb bought with humiliation! She do rule us, night and day. There's nothing happens in this village but she do know of it, and there's nothing that do pass but by her leave and say so.'

They were at the rectory gate.

'Are you coming to see your father?'

'Oh, yes, 'tis his dinner – him and William.' She indicated the basket on her arm.

'Well, now listen, Emmy. I make no promises. But I shall speak to Mrs Cunningham about your granny, and we'll see if she can't be persuaded to change her mind.'

'Reverend, you're an angel!'

Without thinking, Emmy reached up and kissed Arthur hard on the lips, and then went lightly running off round the corner of the rectory towards the kitchen garden.

He was abruptly aware that he was standing on the rectory lawn in full view of the house, and that anyone could have seen Emmy kissing him. He must be be more on his guard, he thought. Above all in the delicate position he now thought himself to be in the rectory he must beware for his reputation.

As it happened Becky, who had been in the dining room setting the breakfast, had been watching them.

Peter looked down at her, smiling into her eyes. They were on the bank of a river, though which river she did not know, and she was lying back on the grass. Somehow her clothes had all gone, as once before when they were children they had taken all their clothes off and paddled naked in the stream, only this was not the stream, and they were adults now. It was confused, but somehow they were there, and she was aware of the sun's heat on her naked body. It did not seem at all strange she should be naked like this, and he was leaning over her, nearer, his lovely face nearer and nearer, and was about to kiss her. She could feel the sun's heat right through her, a wonderful warmth, which flowed up through her arms as she reached up to take him into her embrace, her whole body suffused by an aching sweetness and yearning as she strained up to him. She was pulling him down over her, and she felt herself opening, opening, and yielding, receiving him into her, a piercing intense pleasure. . . .

'Julia! Julia!'

Everything was falling away, something was breaking in, she was being wrenched out of a deep, deep trough of sleep and now, her head dizzy and swimming, she opened her eyes.

It was her father, bending over her.

'Do you know what time it is?'

'Father – oh –' She tried to pull herself up on one elbow.

'Twelve o'clock, miss!'

'Oh Lord!'

She fell back on the pillow for a moment and closed her eyes.

Annie came into the room, crossed it and drew apart the curtains to let in a flood of light.

The dream was still half present to her, the delicious warmth and pleasurable tingling that had flowed through her, a fugitive memory evaporating from her limbs.

'Julia!' He seemed to bring a gust of cold air into the room. 'Have you finished the letters I gave you yesterday?'

She struggled up, pulling a robe round her, and tiptoed across the cold floor to her table, and shuffled through the papers on it.

'They are here somewhere. I finished them before I went out.'

'Also, miss,' said Annie, who had brought her a cup of tea, 'please could you speak to Cook about dinner tonight? She's asking. And Goodrich says can you tell him what about the strawberry beds? Also Becky dropped that vase off the side table in the drawing room. She must have knocked it off with her new crinoline.'

'What on earth was Becky doing in a crinoline?' Dr Stone turned to her abruptly. 'Neither of you is to wear a crinoline while you are on duty.'

'No, sir.'

'Bring me some hot water, Annie, and I'll get dressed.'

'Yes, miss.'

Her head still swam.

'It's all right, Father, your letters are here.' She had found them now, and held them out.

Stone took them, and couldn't resist giving her a long appraising look.

'Do you know what time it is?'

'Yes, Father, you told me.' She picked up the cup of tea. 'Don't worry, I'll get dressed straightaway.'

'Twelve o'clock.'

'Yes.'

'What time did you come in?'

'Oh – I really have no idea.'

'Through idleness and debauchery, your work is neglected, Julia.'

'I hardly think Mrs Cunningham's ball counts as debauchery, Father. Besides, I have finished your letters, as you see.'

'It was fortunate I reminded you, young lady.'

'Father, I wish to get dressed now. And Mrs Oldham has not been given her orders for dinner.'

'Has she not? The household seems to have been turned upside down, to satisfy you; your duties neglected, your work undone, turning night into day –'

'I am very sorry. I will speak to Mrs Oldham right away.'

Dr Stone had taken his letters and went out as Annie returned with a can of hot water. Julia finished her tea, and Annie helped her to dress.

'Hope you enjoyed the ball, miss.'

'Oh, yes. Have you woken Mr Grahame?'

'Lord, miss, Mr Grahame was up hours agone. He's down in the village.'

Julia pulled the nightgown over her head, while Annie poured out her hot water.

'It must be lovely to go a ball, and see all the finery, miss. Did your dress hold out all right?'

'Yes, thank you, Annie.' The girl's tactful juxtaposition of her own faded dress, which was still hanging over the chair where she had left it, and the wonderful creations worn by the other girls, brought back vivid memories of the ball.

She towelled herself down, shivering naked for a moment, and took the shift which Annie was holding out for her.

'Course us poor folks don't get such chances. Do tell us about it, miss.'

70

Julia fitted the stays round her waist and clipped them up. Annie's idea of the ball and her own memory were two different things.

'How did Miss Cunningham look? 'Tis said her gown was the finest ever seen in Stallbridge.'

'It was lovely,' Julia said faintly.

'And Miss Emerson's, I dare say.'

'Oh, yes.' But was it all so wonderful? After that first period when she had danced with Peter, it had gone strangely wrong for Julia. There had been the ugly moment with Mr Grahame – she remembered his arrogant expression. Then she had sat with General Conyers and he had asked her to dance, but Peter had remained at the other side of the room, and whenever she allowed herself a glimpse in his direction, he was laughing with the girls round him, their fans fluttering, and she would hear their tinkling laughter. And she would realise again what a distance separated them. She had had to drag out the rest of the night, and it must have been after four o'clock when at last she had walked home in silence with Mr Grahame.

Annie helped her to step into the crinoline cage, and was doing up the drawstring at the back.

'Did you dance with Mr Cunningham, miss?'

She could read her thoughts.

'Oh – yes, once or twice.'

'Such a handsome gentleman,' Annie sighed.

'I'm afraid he hasn't much time for me, Annie.'

'No, miss.' Tactful as ever. 'Mr Cunningham isn't for everyday use, miss, only for bringing out on Sundays.' She laughed.

'What do you mean, impertinence?'

'Oh, sorry, miss. Nothing really.'

Annie fetched Julia's grey day-dress from the wardrobe, and helped her pull it over her head and smooth it down over the crinoline cage.

'What do you mean?'

'Nothing, miss. Only,' she couldn't help going on, 'I mean to say, such a handsome gentleman, he's bound to have ever so many girls after him, isn't he? I mean, so to say, he can have his pick of 'em.'

His pick of them. Annie had said it all. Julia finished dressing, and when Annie had brushed her hair and pinned it up, she went down to the kitchen. After she had given her orders to Mrs Oldham, she went out to the garden where Goodrich and his assistant William were turning over what were to be the strawberry beds, and discussed that. She had a headache, and the bright light hurt her eyes, but the air revived her and presently she went back to her room and sat herself at her desk to arrange her papers.

There was always something to be done. When no letters needed copying; when no sermons had to be transcribed from Dr Stone's minute and incomprehensible handwriting; when there were no articles to be copied or abridged from journals, or translated from French and Latin; when nothing was left of all that, there were always her German studies, and once again she opened her grammar.

For some reason Mr Grahame had taken the book away and never returned it. She would have to ask him for it.

She could not focus on the page, and leant her head on her hand and closed her eyes, while unexpectedly her dream of the morning came back to her. What a strange fantasy had that been. She wondered if her mind wasn't turning. Where had such a powerful dream come from? In it she had felt everything, felt her hunger for Peter a thousandfold more vividly, more passionately than she had ever been aware of in her waking life. What sort of creature must she be, she thought, to harbour such brutal and unrestrained cravings?

She turned her gaze out of the window. What was Peter doing at this minute? She could not easily imagine him away from her. Had he slept late? What was his bedroom like? Manly it must be, neat, probably rather spartan, not at all like a girl's room. He must have a man, too, who would lay out his clothes each morning. She imagined, or tried to imagine, Peter washing – and he would have to shave. How strange that must be. Everything about him had been so elegant, so perfectly arranged; his clothes fitted so well, his hair so neatly combed – and none of those ridiculous dundreary whiskers some of the men affected.

Really, the more she thought about him, the more perfect he seemed to be. And the more remote from her. She drew in a long sigh. Why couldn't she have been more – well, more forthcoming with him? He had asked her to dance, twice; at first she had thought he had really been enjoying her company, and then somehow it had all gone off the rails, as they said. It must have been her own fault. When she thought about it harder, she knew perfectly well why he had gone off and left her. She had snubbed him. It was true. She'd snubbed him with Dolly Emerson. Why? Because she was frightened he would see how much she loved him.

That little daydream was over. For once her father had broken his rule. For once he had allowed her to go out to a ball. There would not be such another opportunity, not for a long time, not perhaps ever. And she had snubbed Peter. The ball had come and gone, and she was left once again in the house, but now in a worse plight than before. Of course it had been a lovely evening, of course she had enjoyed the lights and the hospitality, and oh how she had loved to dance. It had been like wine, and she had been drunk on the dancing, but the memory of it made her present condition worse than ever, more unendurable. No wonder she had strange dreams. It was a wonder she was sane at all.

Chapter Eight

Dr Stone had gone out for a walk, his usual custom of the early afternoon, and she was in his room, tidying his papers and setting some letters out for when he should return. As she set the letters on his desk, however, she noticed a sheaf of papers covered in neat writing in black ink, in a hand she did not recognise, a large neat hand, a man's hand.

Puzzled she picked up the sheets, and could not make out for a minute what they were, but then realised suddenly that they were translated from the *Forschungen*. There were pages and pages of it; she turned the sheets over, looking through it. The arguments were complex and abstruse, and she found difficulty in following the thread. She noticed sometimes that there would be gaps, and page references. It did not appear to be a complete translation, only selected passages. That was just as well, the whole book would have taken for ever.

But who could – not Mr Grahame? Holding the sheets in her hand, in that room in the silent house in the afternoon, it came to her – who else? He was doing the work. That was the why the book had disappeared from her room. Yet he had never mentioned a word to her.

She came out into the hall in a very thoughtful mood. She simply did not know what to make of him. He was so contained; even the things he had said to her on his first evening in the house had been in a spirit almost of defiance, as if to say: I come of a poor family, and you are free to make of it what you will, because I don't care what you think.

Yet this was unquestionably a great kindness to herself. She ought to mention it to him, and thank him. At the least. She decided she would swallow her pride, and speak to him when a suitable moment arose.

*

'My dear Julia!'

She came down the stairs to where Annie was holding the door open for Mrs Cunningham.

'How are you? Fully recovered from the rigours of our ball? Not too stiff?'

Mrs Cunningham smiled and gave her a peck on the cheek.

'You did us all proud, Mrs Cunningham. I don't believe Stallbridge ever saw such a ball. I hope you got my note?'

'Indeed, my dear.' She took Julia by the arm as they passed into the drawing room, and Julia crossed to the bell pull by the fire place. 'Everyone was saying how charming you looked in that gown. So becoming.'

Julia wondered whether she was being sarcastic. She was not on intimate terms with Mrs Cunningham who did not encourage intimacy; her natural posture was that of the ruler vis-à-vis the ruled, as Peter had once remarked to her.

'Have Lizzie and Adolphus decided on a date yet?'

'Well, my dear, you know how it is – so many relations to consult, arrangements to make. Lizzie is determined on a house of her own. And such things take time. Perhaps some time in September. She is such a headstrong girl, as you know.' She laughed, pulling off her gloves and undoing the ribbon of her bonnet. 'And Peter was saying how much he had enjoyed dancing with you. My dear, I had no idea you had such a talent for dancing. You were positively flying about the room. A pity you don't have more opportunities to show us your skills.'

'I believe I did not realise it myself,' Julia said faintly, amazed that Peter should have remembered her.

'He said it was a delight to dance with you – that you had winged feet.' Mrs Cunningham would not let her escape. 'You know, we really do not see enough of you. Lizzie is always talking of you, saying we should invite you over – as a matter of fact, that is the very errand that brings me. Lizzie and Peter have taken it into their heads to hold an archery contest. And you are positively invited.'

'I don't think I ever held a bow in my life,' Julia said. Mrs Cunningham laughed.

'None of us has. What matters it? It will be an agreeable afternoon party.'

Annie opened the door.

'Annie, bring tea into the drawing room, and tell Dr Stone that Mrs Cunningham is here.'

Her father hated visitors, and Mrs Cunningham above all.

*

75

'Archery is the rage now, Dr Stone,' she told him shortly after, as they sat in the drawing room. Arthur too had been invited to sit with them, though he took little part in the conversation.

'Archery? I thought it was croquet?'

'Archery *and* croquet. And you know archery is very good for the posture.' She tapped him on the knee. 'It stretches the back and opens the chest – especially good for those who spend too much time cramped over a book.'

Stone attempted a muffled laugh. He always seemed to Julia strangely subdued in Mrs Cunningham's presence.

'I really feel – a pity that my work precludes me from accepting your invitation, Mrs Cunningham, but Julia and I are at this minute most particularly occupied. Our labours seem to multiply – one problem solved serves merely to reveal another. A pity therefore that –'

'Dr Stone, of course we all know you are a busy man, and we all respect the importance of your studies – but one afternoon's relaxation. It will refresh you, and enable you to return to your desk with renewed vigour. Isn't that so, Mr Grahame?'

Arthur coughed slightly and muttered something.

'We shall expect you all three. I shall send you a note when we have fixed on a date. You too, Mr Grahame.'

'I fear not, Mrs Cunningham. I am very, very busy just now.'

Julia turned to him. She remembered his refusal to meet Peter Cunningham, and his arrogant condescension towards herself.

She sat between these two heavy serious men dressed in black, and felt for a moment like a criminal between two warders, harbouring a guilty and felonious desire for pleasure. How on earth could she accept Mrs Cunningham's invitation when both men had declined it? At this moment, however, Arthur coughed, and Stone looked up suddenly towards him, and seemed to receive some sort of hidden message, for he abruptly changed his tack.

'However, I am sure Julia would be happy to accept your very kind offer, Mrs Cunningham.'

Arthur realised that Stone's rapid conversion on Julia's behalf had been through his own agency. That accidental cough had served like an electric shock to remind Stone of the *Forschungen* still lying uncompleted on his desk.

She stopped, frozen, in the hall. Mr Grahame's name had been clearly spoken. In the dining room Annie and Becky were laying the table for dinner. Mrs Cunningham had departed and her father and Mr Grahame had both gone their own ways.

'I did! I saw him! Don't believe me if you don't want to, I don't care. I saw him kissing Emmy Goodrich, right outside that window in broad daylight, large as life! And I didn't notice her shrinking back!'

'Mr Grahame?'

'Who did I say? Anyway, I shouldn't mind – and nor would you, if you was honest!'

'What, being kissed by Mr Grahame?' Annie giggled.

'Yes, silly, be honest now, would you or would you not like to kiss Mr Grahame – if you had the chance?'

Julia was as petrified as the marble paving of the hall as she listened to this conversation. There was a pause in the conversation as the girls went on with laying out cutlery and plates. At last Annie spoke.

'Anyway, he's only a curate, ain't he? He ain't got two pennies to rub together – he only comes from a poor family, same as us. What's the difference? Why shouldn't he marry a poor girl as well as a rich one?'

'Would you marry him?'

Annie thought.

'I wouldn't say no. He's a real man, I'd say. He'd know how to do the business, you could bet on that!'

They giggled. Julia blushed and turned quickly to the stairs, ashamed of herself for having eavesdropped.

Mr Grahame kissing Emmy Goodrich? It was incredible. Incredible. She was more agitated than she could account for. And yet – she tried to puzzle it out – it was so difficult to tell. After all, if he himself came from a poor family, he had not been brought up a gentleman, and would not have the same standards as she was used to. He simply would not understand things that were obvious to a gentleman born.

Of course, Emmy was very attractive in her way, in that common, obvious sort of way – that rather obvious, flaunting way she had; Julia supposed it must appeal to a certain kind of man. She tried to be rational for a moment, tried to place herself above the whole thing, and see it as a stranger might.

She herself had no interest in Mr Grahame, far from it. Nor would she want to – certainly not – a man who went round kissing village girls? Hardly. Even if it was and this was the hard part – someone who was as obviously, blazingly, beautiful as Emmy Goodrich, someone who put herself – her Julia Stone – completely in the shade. That was the hard part.

She wasn't sure what to do. Should she do anything? Should she

77

mention it to her father? Should she speak to Mr Grahame? That might be best. This was after all something that must not be countenanced. If her servants were discussing it, it was only a question of time before it was all round the village.

Julia pondered. First of all, she had meant to thank Mr Grahame for the translation then she had changed her mind when he had so pompously refused Mrs Cunningham's invitation to the archery and now it appeared she was having to reprimand him for taking liberties with her gardener's daughter. She did not know what to do.

It was dark in the passageway, and Arthur had come out suddenly from his room and almost run into her.

'Oh – Mr Grahame.'

'Miss Stone.' He was subdued, rather grave, but she could not very well make him out in the gloom of the passage.

'There is something I should like to – that I –' She was flustered. 'I should like to thank you for the translation you are doing for my father. I know he is not an easy man to get on with, and may perhaps not have expressed his thanks in the way he would have wished to.'

'Thank me? Why?'

She was taken aback at his blunt, direct way.

'Why? Well, – you know very well why. I was going to have to do it myself. And it would have taken me years. I have hardly started at German.'

He looked down at her. In the half light, she looked up into his face and thought, This is the man who kissed Emmy Goodrich, and she didn't mind.

'It really is nothing, I assure you. Dr Stone pays me, and I like to earn my keep. How's that? Does that satisfy you? Besides, I can see that you have quite enough on your plate already, Miss Stone. Good afternoon.' He was going past her.

'Mr Grahame!'

He turned.

'Why – why did you refuse Mrs Cunningham's invitation?'

'I thought we had already discussed that,' he said quietly, and turned away from her.

He was gone and she was left in the passage. Reprimand him? What was she thinking of? How could she possibly have raised the subject of Emmy Goodrich?

'I should like to speak to Mrs Cunningham.'

Parker showed no trace of expression.

'If you would care to wait in the drawing room, Mr Grahame, I will inform Mrs Cunningham.'

Arthur remembered the house from the evening of the ball. He stood looking about him as he rehearsed in his mind what he was going to say.

Why was he allowing himself to be alone again with that woman? It was not a curate's duty, yet perhaps he was all that stood between her and the likes of Mrs Leggatt.

He looked round the room. By daylight he could examine it more clearly. It was newly papered and the furniture was new too. In the morning light which streamed from the old mullioned windows everything had a new shiny quality – the sort of thing one would expect from Mrs Cunningham.

His gaze was arrested by a large portrait of the woman on the wall; life size, bright and new. She was in a black evening dress, and the painter had worked hard to bring out the glossy sheen as the light caught the folds of the dress. A tiny, gleaming pointed slipper emerged from beneath the skirt.

But Arthur was not looking at it because far above it the dress had a low neckline, a great V stretching from shoulder to shoulder and plunging at the centre; to emphasise this the sitter leant forward towards the viewer as if to invite him to look down the front of it. There was something indecent about it, as she leant forward and then looked up, as if to say, 'Do you see anything you like, sir?' As in life her eyes fixed Arthur, black and glowing like coals, like a hawk's, and her red lips were slightly parted in a wicked, conspiratorial smile.

Arthur had been standing before this picture for some time when he became aware that he was not alone. He turned.

Mrs Cunningham was near him, leaning, half sitting, against the edge of a table, her arms folded, watching him.

She said nothing, just looked at him, with that slight smile on her lips. At last, as the silence was becoming embarrassing, and Arthur realised she was not going to open the conversation, he said, 'Was it recently done, Mrs Cunningham? I don't remember to have seen it when I was here before.'

'Oh, it was there – but you had more important things on your mind at the time.'

Arthur searched for the appropriate remark.

'It is a remarkable work.'

'And like?'

'Oh, very. That is – certainly very striking.'

79

'You don't think – just a little provocative? My family don't approve of it. They consider it indecent. Do you?'

'What?'

'Consider it indecent?'

Arthur did not wish to be drawn any further down this particular line of discussion.

'Mrs Cunningham, I called this morning in the hope of having a word with you about Mrs Leggatt.'

'You haven't answered my question.'

'I fear I know nothing about such matters. But it is certainly very striking.'

'And indecent?'

What did she mean by that? What did she want him to say?

'Do you find it, shall we say, attractive?'

He wanted to withdraw his gaze, to turn again to the portrait, but found he could not take his eyes off her face. It was not the picture she was talking about. She had fixed him with a stare.

'Mr Grahame, do you find me attractive?' Her voice was low, she spoke concentratedly, seriously, but with a speculative, querying tone. Arthur could not wrench his gaze from her.

'You are very attractive,' she went on hypnotically, 'since we first met I have thought so, very attractive. You have the qualities that a woman most values in a man, Mr Grahame, strength and a generous and frank disposition. There is nothing of the niggard about you, and yet you are discreet. I could tell as soon as we met that you were a man on whom I could rely.'

This was a direct challenge and Arthur saw there was no evading it.

'You can rely on me, Mrs Cunningham – in your charitable work.'

'You know that is not what I mean.'

'But it is what I mean.' He said it with finality.

She ignored that.

'You see, Mr Grahame,' she got up at last and moved across the room, 'we have a lot in common, you and I.'

'Indeed?'

'Oh, yes. You have come up from nowhere – I am right, am I not?'

'I am not sure my mother and father regard our home in that light, but I take your drift.'

'My drift, Mr Grahame, is this. That you come from a common labourer's family, and have by your own courage and resourcefulness fought your way into the place of a gentleman. You are here, this morning – accepted as my equal in my home.'

'Many thanks.' Arthur could not help bowing slightly.

'You see, Arthur – may I call you Arthur when we are alone? – it may or may not be apparent, but I myself have done much the same thing. When I was eighteen, I was a poor governess, and when I found that my employer – who was then more than twice my age – was in love with me,' she sighed, 'well, that is putting it perhaps too strongly. At any rate he was dying to get me into his bed. When I found that out, I had the wit to take advantage of the situation.'

She continued to look at Arthur.

'I married him. Like you, I was ambitious. And what I am saying to you, Arthur, now, this morning, is this. You are an ambitious man – oh, you are, however you may hide it beneath your humble curate's coat. You are ambitious, Arthur, and you are right to be so because you have ability, and you have strength and courage, and you are going to go a long way.'

'Mrs Cunningham, you are right, I am ambitious – but not in the way you think.'

She had come across to him, stood before him, and rested one hand on the front of his coat, looking into his eyes.

'You are ambitious, and in your position there is one thing that can help you more than anything else – the friendship of a wealthy and powerful woman.'

There was a long moment as she looked into his eyes, and her hand rested against the front of his coat. Arthur had not yet moved, but now he gently took her hand and moved it away. Then he spoke softly, in a collected way, concentrating his gaze on her.

'I have fought my way through Oxford, as you say. And all that time – and it took me quite a while, Mrs Cunningham, many years – I had a goal ahead of me. A task. Because ever since I could see and had the wit to understand what I was looking at, I saw all around me poverty, injustice, and misery. And I did not think I had any right to be on this earth, or any right to sit down and eat my dinner, unless I did everything within my power to ease that poverty and fight that injustice wherever I could. That is my ambition, Mrs Cunningham, and that is why I have come to talk to you about Mrs Leggatt.'

'Mrs Leggatt?' She laughed. 'Arthur, we have better things to talk about!'

'What better things?'

'Why can't you understand? There will always be Mrs Leggatts in this world! What does the Bible say – "The poor you have always with you." Unfortunately, Arthur, when you get to my age, you will understand the truth of that. The sick, the halt, the lame – they will

81

always be there – but an ambitious man, a man of ability, that is something else. That is someone to be encouraged, and assisted.'

'Mrs Cunningham,' Arthur took out his watch and glanced at it, 'I won't waste any more of your time. Whatever your gamekeeper may have told you, Mrs Leggatt was within her rights to pick up dead wood in your woods. I was present, I saw what happened, so I give you notice that if any threats are made, or any charges laid, I intend to defend her myself. You will find me a formidable opponent. Now please excuse me.'

He turned towards the door.

'Arthur! Not so fast! Goodness, how impetuous you are!' She crossed quickly in front of him, and smiled. 'Who said anything about prosecution?'

She shook her head, still smiling.

'But, my dear, if you knew how much timber is stripped from my land every winter, if it were your accounts that were made up, and the debit and credit set out for you, to see how much you were losing, you would perhaps take a different line.'

'Mrs Cunningham, I have only one line. Justice for Mrs Leggatt. Now excuse me.'

'Arthur, before you go.' She rested her hand on his arm. 'One last word. You are hot with idealism, and full of laudable sentiments about justice. But just let me give you a piece of advice. You have ability. But a man who does not seize his opportunities when they are offered – what is he? Hmm? You must take your chances. Do not forget.'

Chapter Nine

'Bullseye!'

As Dolly handed another arrow to Lizzie, he looked sheepishly into her eyes.

'Your arrows never fail to reach their mark,' he sighed.

'Oh Dolly, don't talk such piffle,' Peter said over his shoulder, fitting an arrow to his bow. 'You're engaged. You can leave off all that sort of rot now, you know!'

'Mr Cunningham, shame on you!' said Julia. 'You mustn't stand for that, Lizzie! If gentlemen are to leave off saying pretty things to ladies the moment they become engaged, it will be an end to all domestic harmony.'

'Hear hear, Miss Stone. I certainly shall never leave off paying compliments to my dearest Lizzie so long as there is breath in my body.'

'Oh, well,' Peter took aim and let fly, 'I must say, it would drive me to distraction.'

'You were not made for domesticity, I am afraid,' Julia said, tapping him on the chest with an arrow. 'You will live and die a crusty old bachelor.'

'Not crusty, I hope.'

'Oh yes. You will be the terror of little boys and courting couples in the park. And you will be very mean with tradesmen and servants' Christmas boxes, too.'

'I say, steady on, Julia! I'm not as bad as all that!'

'Well, you have been warned. And it all starts by being niggardly with compliments to young ladies. We all like to hear pretty things, Mr Cunningham. I'm surprised your mother never told you.'

'My mother never told me anything of use.'

'Well, there's Fanny Emerson. I think you should offer to fetch her arrows. You are the host, you know.'

'You think I should?'

'You wouldn't want to be thought crusty, would you?'

Julia turned away with a smile.

It was now mid-May, and the chestnuts were heavy with their first thick green. It was hot too, and the girls had ventured into summer frocks. Julia had nothing special in this department, but was wearing a simple cotton dress in a lavender stripe, and a straw hat. But some of the other girls were in more striking costumes – Fanny Emerson was in a puffy white lawn blouse hanging over a a billowing skirt of green shot silk; a thin knotted ribbon of coral red emphasised her slender waist.

The archery had by degrees become something of a competition between her and Lizzie. After the first novelty of the sport had worn off many of the other young men and women had tended to gather in chattering groups. Lizzie and Fanny however were battling it out, and it had already occurred to Julia that Fanny might have been wanting to make a show in front of Peter.

Julia watched now as he crossed to her. Fanny was quick enough with a flattering remark, and that was what Peter was used to.

Julia walked up towards the house where Mrs Cunningham was superintending the servants who were setting out tea things on two rustic tables. It was better than watching Peter flirting.

Mr Cunningham had been wheeled out in his invalid chair on to the terrace.

'It was most kind of Mrs Cunningham to invite us all this afternoon, sir. The party has been a great success. I never thought there were so many talented archers in Stallbridge.'

'Don't you find it rather chilly? Would you mind tucking in that rug round my feet? Thank you. Somehow I can never get warm. I don't know why Parker brought me out here. Tell him to take me inside.'

Julia was quite happy to wheel him in herself. It was easier to engage in these domestic duties than to take part in conversation with the other girls. Conversation with them always became competition, and she did not feel her lavender stripe equal to Fanny's shot silk this afternoon.

As she came out again on to the terrace, Mrs Cunningham was there. She was in a fine pink silk dress which rustled as she turned and bent over the table to set everything to her own satisfaction.

She was in high spirits, and particularly pleased that Julia had been able to come.

'It is a special triumph for me to have dragged you away from that house, my dear. Quite a victory.'

84

Julia smiled, but did not speak. At such moments she always felt obliged to defend her father.

'It was very kind of father to spare me,' she said at last.

'Fiddlesticks! What is the point of being young, if it is not to enjoy oneself? You will be old long enough, believe me.'

They turned and looked down over the sloping lawn to where the archery targets had been set up. Lizzie was drawing back a bow almost as tall as herself, and Dolly was beside her holding a large shawl, and a sheaf of arrows. Near them were Peter and two other young men together with a group of young girls.

'Is everything ready, Parker?' Mrs Cunningham turned briskly. 'Tea is served!'

As they sat round the table, however, Julia again found Peter by her side.

'May I help you to a slice of bread and butter, Miss Stone?' He leant in towards her unctuously. 'Or perhaps you would care to partake of this excellent plum cake? Or perhaps a custard tart? May I press you to a bloater paste sandwich?'

'Thank you, sir,' Julia could not help laughing. 'I think I am able to find my own way to the bloater sandwiches, but I am gratified that my lesson has been taken to heart.'

'Ah.' Peter heaved a great sigh. 'To heart. Indeed.'

'Peter!' Lizzie called from the other side of the table, as they crammed round, helping each other and themselves to tea. 'Do you intend to eat all those bloater sandwiches or are we allowed to have any? Honestly!'

'I hope you realise by now what you've let yourself in for, Emerson,' Peter called across the table as he passed the dish. 'This girl has the appetite of a horse. She could eat her own weight in bloaters, so watch out for those sandwiches, if you intend to have one yourself.'

'Oh,' he looked back at Julia, 'what am I saying?'

'Too late, I am afraid. You are well on the way to a crusty bachelorhood. I really don't know what we are to do with you. You are quite incorrigible. No woman is going to listen to you, until you mend your manners.'

'Thank you, Julia,' Lizzie called across. 'He has been spoilt since infancy, and you are the only girl I know who has the sense to put him in his place.'

'That's because I've known him since the days when he pulled my hair, and threw mud pies at me; it gives me the right to lecture him, don't you think?'

'So long as someone does,' said Lizzie, her mouth full.

Peter didn't mind the banter, so long as he was the centre of it.

'Now listen, everybody,' Fanny called, 'here is a riddle! No, listen, Mr Cunningham, and if you know the answer you are not to tell before the others have had a chance to think of it.'

'Why does she always pick on me?' Peter looked round the table in mock earnestness.

'Now listen! What is the connection between the Prince of Wales, an orphan, a gorilla, and a glue-pot?'

There was deep silence among the guests, with looks at one another, muttered suggestions, and finally complete bafflement. Fanny looked highly delighted with herself.

'Because one is an Heir Apparent, one has ne'er a parent, and one has an hairy parent!'

Roars of laughter, and then as the laughter subsided, 'But what about the glue-pot?' Dolly asked.

'Ah, that is where you get stuck!'

There was another burst of laughter.

''Fraid you fell for it, Dolly,' Peter said in his world-weary tone. Dolly blushed, and looked down.

'Now then, which of you Dianas took the palm?' Peter took charge of the conversation again, and looked round the table between Lizzie and Fanny.

'Fanny,' his sister said, while Fanny gave him a smile.

'She must have her prize,' Mrs Cunningham cut in. 'Peter, where is Miss Emerson's prize?'

'Prize?'

'Fanny has won and shall have her prize, you know.'

'A nosegay!' Peter, reaching across, took a bunch of flowers from the vase in the centre of the table and presented it to Fanny. 'Sweets to the sweet. To our fair huntress.' He leant across and gave her a peck on the cheek.

Fanny blushed.

'Peter, really! You can't give Fanny any old bunch of flowers! Shame on you!'

'Oh no, Mrs Cunningham, I assure you! They are admirable!'

'Peter! No wait – Anderson! There is a nosegay of flowers in the conservatory, I made up this morning. Fetch it, will you?'

The old housekeeper went indoors.

'Peter, really! What must Miss Emerson think? My dear, I beg you to wait a moment.'

Fanny Emerson was looking desperate.

'Mrs Cunningham, these are lovely, and I would not dream of accepting any other, I assure you! I beg you not to make a fuss!'

Mrs Anderson came out again holding a pretty nosegay, made up with a neat handle.

'Give it to Mr Cunningham. Now, Peter, do it properly.'

'Miss Emerson, I crown you Queen of the afternoon and beg you to accept this prize!'

'You are silly.' Fanny couldn't help laughing with pleasure. 'Now I shall have two nosegays.'

'Mother's on at me to marry – preferably money. "What's wrong with Fanny Emerson? Or one of those Scotch Laidlaw girls?" Can't stand Scotchmen, Julia – God, it's tiresome! "You can't remain a bachelor for ever, Peter." Why in Heaven's name not?'

He had become querulous. Dusk was falling when the archery party finally broke up and he offered to walk her home. She had seen the expression on Fanny's face, but there was nothing she could do about that, so she had graciously accepted. They were alone together in the lane. The air was warm, and overhead the trees were thick with new summer foliage. On either side the wild grasses and flowers grew thickly in their first summer flush – cowslips, foxgloves, harebells, and the tall rank cow parsley. There was a magical stillness in the air, warm, pregnant with the coming summer.

'Oh Lord, isn't life a bore.'

'Am I supposed to answer that?'

Peter said nothing, but swiped aimlessly at the cow parsley with his stick.

'Anyway, who cares? It'll soon be over.'

'What on earth do you mean?'

'The Cunninghams are a doomed lot.'

'Peter, what *are* you talking about?'

'You've seen my father, haven't you? Rotten. We all are. It's in the blood.'

Julia stopped and looked at him seriously.

'You must never say such things. It is impious and unchristian. You are not rotten, neither is your mother or sister. Your father is ill, that's all.'

Peter cut through the cow parsley with his stick and stared moodily away. Julia watched him anxiously.

'You don't know. It's all rotten. Oh, God, sometimes I wish I'd never been born.'

'You are in a strange mood.' She thought it best not to take him too seriously. 'Well, if you're unhappy here, why not go to London?'

'Wouldn't mind at that, instead of just idling about here. It's

87

damned unfair. Mother watching me like a hawk. It's no life for a man, believe me.'

'I can see that. You're too old to be still living at home. It must be irksome.'

He was a little soothed.

'If you were to go to London, I imagine you could rent bachelor apartments. I don't know anything about such things, but obviously they exist. You could have a man to look after you.'

'Yes.' He had cheered up as she spoke. 'Yes, take Franks, then one would be able to get out, go to the club, and that sort of thing, go about. Enjoy one's freedom.'

He gave the cow parsley another swipe, this time with more relish.

'Do you know something, Julia, you always manage to cheer a fellow up. Here am I talking a lot of balderdash and getting in the dumps, and in two minutes you put everything straight, and I can see what to do.'

Julia felt a stab even as she smiled at these spontaneous compliments; just a regular good fellow, that's what she was.

Peter stopped and looked down at her.

'You really are a first-rate girl.'

She could feel the blood in her face. Their eyes had locked, and it was if he were seeing her for the first time.

'I don't know what it is. When I'm with you, everything seems easy. No one's trying to pretend or show off, we can just be ourselves with each other. You're the only person I know who doesn't mind me just as I am.'

They had been looking into each other's eyes. On an impulse he leant over awkwardly, and seemed about to kiss her on the cheek. Again there was a pause; clearly he didn't know what to do next, while she stared into his eyes, and felt her heart beat painfully.

He broke away from her, and they walked on in silence, each trying to digest what had happened; conscious that a new aspect had entered their relationship.

However, they now heard an approaching horse, and in a few seconds there appeared a mounted figure at the bend in the lane ahead of them, a silhouette in the encroaching gloom.

It was her father. He reined in his horse.

'Who's this? Julia?'

'Good evening, sir.' Peter raised his hat.

Dr Stone nodded at him, and grunted.

'Julia, where have you been? You know we waited dinner for you? I expected you two hours ago.' His voice was without feeling, as inexorable as a biblical injunction.

Julia seemed confused.

'I had no idea – surely – I hope you and Mr Grahame were able to dine without me, Father?'

'You were expected to dinner.'

'The archery rather ran on, and then Mrs Cunningham kindly invited us all to tea, and I don't know somehow, it all ran on – anyway, I am on my way now. Mr Cunningham kindly offered to escort me.'

'I am indebted to you, sir. I shall be able to escort my daughter from here on. I wish you a good evening. Come, Julia.'

He turned his horse, large in the lane, as if physically to exclude Peter from their company. Julia, however, went to him.

'Thank your mother for me. It was a lovely day, and I am most grateful to her for inviting me.'

She still remembered the unexpected nearness of him, the imminence of a kiss. Peter again raised his hat, and made a funny face at Dr Stone's back, before turning and setting off whistling along the lane.

Dr Stone did not look back, but kicked his horse into motion. They proceeded in silence for several minutes, and Julia was beginning to think her father had nothing more to say.

'You surprise me, Julia.'

'In what way?' she said quietly.

'I am not accustomed to the idea of my daughter walking unescorted with a single man.'

'What were you afraid of?'

'Are you being impertinent, miss? You are my daughter. It is not proper that you should be alone with that frivolous young man.'

'Father, I assure you you need have no fears on my account.'

'Oh, but I do have fears. You are in my charge, and your reputation, of which you yourself take so light a care, is also my responsibilty.'

'I assure you I am old enough to watch my own reputation. You can trust me.'

'Frankly, I do not trust you. You are a young woman, giddy and thoughtless; like all young woman, your mind is full of vanity, confused with thoughts of pleasure.'

She drew a deep breath, staring straight ahead, and said in a low voice, 'If that is your opinion of me, then you little know me.'

'Do I not? Then perhaps I am not your father? Perhaps I have not had sole charge of you since your mother died? Perhaps we do not inhabit the same house? This is mere foolishness. Of course I know

89

you, and I know that like all young women your head is full of idle nonsense, and like all young women –'

'Father, this intolerable! I will not be addressed like this! You know you are entirely dependent on me, that without me, your house could not function. If I am old enough to manage your affairs, I am old enough to arrange my own, and will not be treated like a girl.'

He reined in his horse, and looked down at her in what was now almost total darkness.

'How dare you address your father in this fashion? Do you know what you are? You are my child. This boldness shows a pernicious and unwomanly independence of spirit, Julia, retrograde to all christian feeling. You have been corrupted with frivolous and loose company, mixing in –'

'Corrupted?' Julia was angry. 'Are you calling your daughter corrupted?'

Stone would not retract a word once spoken, though he slowed down.

'I perceive a corrupting influence in that young man, Julia.'

'Oh, I see. It is Peter Cunningham you object to,' she said ironically.

'Yes, miss, I do object to him, and I will not have him in my house, and I will not have him consorting with my daughter.'

Julia would not continue with this conversation any longer. Ignoring her father, she set forward at a fast pace.

Chapter Ten

Dear Mr Cunningham,

I really do not know how to put this – or indeed whether I should write to you in this fashion at all – my head is in such a whirl, I really cannot order my thoughts at the moment. Yet I must write to you.

Well, perhaps you can guess my message. Needless to say, my father was not very pleased to see us together unchaperoned this evening, and read me a lecture on the subject, which I confess I took with a very ill grace, as I feel I am old enough now not to need it. He of course was further incensed at my want of filial piety – as if I did not show my love and duty to him a dozen times every day – and in a fit of what I must call pique has forbidden you this house. I am writing this in order to spare you any embarrassment should you have had occasion to call in future.

What must you think? It is not merely discourteous, but shows a barbarous want of grace in him. I blush even now as I write on his behalf.

Please convey to your mother my thanks again for a most pleasant afternoon, and believe me to remain,

Yours sincerely,
Julia Stone

(On second thoughts, this must seem very forward in me, for what reason indeed should you have to call? To tell the truth, as I said, I am still rather in a whirl about the matter.)

The fact was this letter expressed the barest iceberg-tip of Julia's frustration. She could have screamed; she could have thrown herself against her father's horse, pulled him to the ground and pummelled him. How dare he order her in this manner? In her room she walked back and forth, back and forth, unable to settle, the letter on the table before her. Forbid Peter Cunningham the house? How dare he? Was she a prisoner? Had she committed some heinous crime? She was an adult woman, capable of ordering her life – and his – fully in control of her feelings, a rational, educated being. It violated the deepest sense of her integrity to be so humiliated.

In the silence of the night, alone in her room, she stretched, arching her back for a moment, and stared into the candle's flame standing on the mantelpiece. She was drying up. She was a flower that no one would water. She could feel her bloom fading, withering. For a moment Peter Cunningham had seemed to offer her a drop of moisture and her very soul had soaked it up. And in that very moment her father had appeared, abruptly breaking it off, dismissing Peter so rudely.

Yet she did feel guilty too. She remembered the nearness of Peter, his masculine presence, felt it still. It was not just that it had been so *pleasant* walking alone with him. Of course he was in a funny mood – he was a moody boy, if the truth were told – spoilt by his mother, used to having his own way. She didn't mind that; she could handle it easily. It didn't matter. It was just that he was so beautiful to look at, so light and airy, amusing and inconsequential. If he was in the dumps, that didn't matter, she could soon chaff him back into a good humour.

No, it was not that even – it was rather that in his nearness, she had sensed his maleness, and felt in herself the unmistakable sting of desire. She felt guilty because she desired Peter Cunningham, and in that desire there lurked an implacable disloyalty to her father.

But he was forbidden the house. Was this to be be her life henceforth? Trapped here, her father's secretary, his bond-maiden, his slave? Unable to speak to the only man who brought any charm or life into her monotonous round? Her whole body cried aloud at this injustice. Other girls got married. Lizzie had caught foolish Adolphus. Her father was marrying village girls all the time – and many of them barely in the nick of time, too. They mocked her with their reckless fecundity; rushing into marriage, rushing to produce children, when they had so little to live on.

During that dinner, when Julia had not appeared, Arthur had sat and watched Dr Stone growing more and more irritated, more and more moody. It was a puzzle – so far as Arthur knew, she had simply gone to the Old Manor House for an afternoon of archery, a frivolous but harmless pastime. It was not clear why Dr Stone sat opposite him gloomily chewing his food, staring down at his plate, until he had become positively black with rage.

At length Stone had stood up, pushed his chair back violently and gone out, and soon Arthur saw him ride past the window on his horse.

Later Arthur himself went out. He walked down into the village to call on Granny Leggatt. She was not alone. Emmy Goodrich and her mother were there too – three generations of the family.

In the little cottage with its earth floor they were sitting by the fire on low stools, and the flames supplied the only light there was in the room. Emmy for once had a shawl round her shoulders. They started up when he came in, and he joined them by the fire. He looked into the worn and lined face of the old woman, highlighted by the uncertain light.

'Well, Granny, I've done what I can. I told her I'd stand by you all the way. Not much more I can do, I'm afraid.'

Emmy impulsively reached across to Arthur's arm. Full of concern as she was, yet her clear smooth skin and the lovely soft light in her eyes contrasted with the faces of the two other women, lined and worn, frowning, used to worries and difficulties.

Afterwards Emmy followed him to the door, and in the darkness took his arm and said quietly, 'I *knew* you'd not forget us, Reverend.'

The evening of the day after the archery party, Julia was in her room. Dinner was over, and Mr Grahame had gone out. She meant to get down to work, but it was hard to start. Her father had not spoken to her all day; they had sat over dinner in silence. She was determined not to begin, and he was as obstinate himself. Mr Grahame had attempted to make conversation, asking about the archery contest, but her replies had been monosyllabic. It was impossible to expand or bring any warmth to the conversation with that unbending presence there, the heavy figure of her father solemnly chewing his dinner in silence.

She sat at her desk and stared out of the window. Beyond the kitchen garden, beyond the wall, away over the glebe fields, the woods looked enchanting in their new covering. It was a calm clear summer evening, everything spoke of renewal and growth, new shoots, new beginnings, and increased in her the sense of nullity, of hopes trodden carelessly into the ground.

The was a light tap at the door. It was Annie.

'Beg pardon, miss,' she whispered, and came in and shut the door behind her.

Julia was surprised by the conspiratorial manner.

'Message for you, miss.'

Julia took the envelope into her hands. The handwriting was immature, ungainly and scrawling. She did not recognise it. She ripped open the envelope and as she unfolded the sheet it contained, saw it was from Peter. She closed the paper quickly.

'When did this come?'

'This minute, miss.'

'Thank you. That will do, Annie.'

'Yes, miss.' Annie smiled knowingly and went out.

Hullo, Julia – I am in your orchard.
Why don't you come and see me?

She sat still, her hand on her heart. For a moment she could see nothing, could only feel her racing pulse, a tightness in her throat. In another second she had leapt up and was reaching for her shawl. She looked up and caught sight of herself in the looking glass. She hardly recognised herself – the heightened expression, the flushed cheeks, the eyes large and dark, glowing, her lips parted – was that her? Where was her composure? Her calm control? Was she running like this, thoughtlessly, like a young girl to her lover? Her lover? She was dizzy. And disobeying her father, too? Yes, she was. She was.

She didn't dare stop any longer to think, but swinging the shawl round her shoulders, ran lightly down the stairs and into the garden.

The fruit trees were heavy with blossom. Somewhere a blackbird sang as if it were the first blackbird that had ever sung on earth. The air was warm and charged with the scent of the blossom.

The orchard was deserted. Across the bottom the high old brick wall closed it off, and and beyond was the field. No one.

She stopped, and felt almost faint, breathless. He wasn't here. What had happened?

A mistake? Was he joking? Had he got tired of waiting? Anything was possible, knowing Peter.

'Hello, Julia.'

His face appeared at the top of the wall, and in a minute he had pulled himself over and dropped lightly down beside her.

'I read your letter. Looks like I got you into trouble with the ogre. Can't have that. Thought the least I could do would be to come and cheer you up.'

'Peter –'

She didn't know what to say.

'Anyway, how are you apart from that? All right, I hope?'

'Oh, Peter, I shouldn't have written.'

'Shouldn't you? I am jolly glad you did, though. What a beastly

94

old tyrant. Honestly, Julia, you've got to breathe. I mean to say, it's not fair. Stifling, I should say. Anyway, are you glad I came? You don't seem too sure.'

'Glad? Oh, yes, it's just that –'

'What?'

'It's so unusual, that's all. And I'm always afraid –'

'Of your father? Let him come. What can he do?'

'It would be awkward, and I should hate to have unpleasantness between you and him.'

'Don't worry about me! What can he do to me?' Peter laughed. 'In fact if you ask me, he ought to be jolly glad to see me. Why not?'

She looked into his face. Oh, he was wonderful – carefree, beautiful – she simply worshipped him. He caught her gaze, and their eyes locked.

'You know, Julia, after that walk of ours, I got to thinking. I don't know – well, there's just no one like you.'

Her heart beat rapidly, but she turned and looked up into the blossom thick on the apple branch.

'No, listen,' he caught her by the shoulder and turned her to him, 'and I thought and thought, couldn't stop thinking about you, you see, how good you were, and –'

Taking her more firmly, he pulled her to him, and kissed her.

Even then she wasn't sure whether she dare let herself go. Wouldn't the depth of her feelings simply swamp him?

'I think you're the grandest girl in the world.'

This time she could no longer help herself. She reached up, pulling him to her, reaching out and up to him, answering his kiss greedily. Peter was surprised at the strength of her feelings.

'God, Julia, you are wonderful.'

She could say nothing. They could not drag their eyes from each other. She felt faint and could scarcely breathe, her ribs constricted by her clothes, as if she struggled for air. Peter clasped her to him.

'After what you said about me going to London, and taking rooms, and having Franks to look after me – well, I thought, dash it, why not have Julia to look after me? Mother won't hear of me taking rooms on my own, anyway – and she keeps me on such confoundedly short commons here – but with you – well, if it was you and me – I mean, you're just the girl. Do you see?'

'Peter – how?'

'I don't know. Sort of go off and get married, I suppose.'

'Peter – you mean – you want – are you asking me to marry you?'

'Suppose I am.' He grinned at her; but she pulled away a little.

'Heavens, you must give me a moment.'

'Is it such a terrible shock?'

'No – gracious me – only it is very unexpected.'

'You look as if you had been shot.' He seemed a little put out.

'No, my dear – oh no.' She took his hand. 'You are the dearest creature to me in the world. It's –'

'Your father?'

'Peter, you will have to give a little time to think, that's all. Heavens, it was so unexpected. Oh my darling!'

On impulse, she put her arms around his neck and kissed him. He responded passionately and they stood locked together, her head against his chest: it was something she had imagined a thousand times in the past, as if in a painting, but now, on this warm evening, it was actually real.

'We could have a gay old time of it, couldn't we? Get some snug little place, you know. There's so much to do in London, all my chums are there. And get away from here – that's the main thing. The country's so stifling, don't you find?'

'Peter, have you spoken to my father?'

'No, not yet.'

'I think – Peter, it would be better to let me speak to him first.'

She couldn't even begin to imagine the scene between them.

He pulled away.

'You're a free person, Julia. This isn't a prison, you know.'

'You don't understand. Of course I am free, in a manner of speaking. But still, there will have to be arrangements. I shall need to – oh Lord. You must give me time to think. I don't know –'

Her mind went blank at the thought of what was involved. She turned and walked a step or two among the trees while he watched. Then she turned.

'I think – for the moment – we must not say a word to anyone. No, trust me, my darling, I will work it out. But just for now, let us keep it between ourselves.'

And then would he change his mind? It was possible. Perhaps this was the best way – it would be a small trial of his feelings for her.

After he had left, shinning back over the wall without effort, she was left alone in the evening gloom to think. Pulling the shawl round her shoulders, she wandered between the fruit trees back towards the house.

Chapter Eleven

Arthur spent the afternoon with old Wentworth hanging a new front door to his house. He had seen the door lying in a barn in Trefusis' farm, and persuaded him to let him fit it in Wentworth's house. The existing door was in a such a dilipidated condition that it was impossible to keep out the weather.

That evening as he left the old man's house it occurred to him to walk back to the rectory through the fields instead of the direct way up the road. It was a warm, tranquil evening, and he was in no hurry to get back.

So instead of turning up the road he followed the stream up the valley into the fold of the downs, hearing the chuckling of the water over the stones, the gentle sound of the breeze through the rushes, and sometimes the plop of a frog. He stopped at the part where it widened into a pond, and sat on the grass for a while looking up towards where the stream narrowed again, where the valley became steeper and the stream was choked with wild cress and overhung with trees. Looking up at the great sweep of the downs stretching beyond and away to the south and west, on that evening he thought of Julia.

What would she think of a proposal from a man who had seventy pounds a year? It had come to him as he awoke that morning: to ask Julia to marry him. It would come as a surprise to her for sure. He smiled ironically to himself. She was a lady, used to having servants about her, living in a spacious house; besides, he was not sure whether she even liked him. In fact he had the strong suspicion that she did not. How long was it going to take him to talk her round?

He got up again. Well, maybe it didn't matter how long it took. The business was worth it. As for the seventy pounds – that was for her to decide.

The path crossed the stream here by a number of large stepping-stones, and passed along the other side of the pond for a while before turning off through a patch of wild brambles, winding its way back across a hay meadow and down a lane before picking up the road above the church. The air was warm, and there was the wonderful deep stillness of a summer evening, a feeling of the ripeness and abundance of the season bringing forth its plenty with careless prodigality. The profusion of scents was intoxicating.

Arthur was tired, but the thought of Julia had infused him with a feeling of optimism. She might reject him, but she was worth the fight.

He crossed the stream, took the path up the other side, and then passing between the clumps of brambles, came upon Peter Cunningham sitting in the grass with Emmy Goodrich. Her clothing was disordered, her bodice open and off her shoulders, and her breasts exposed.

As they saw him, she gave a little scream and jumped up, pulling her bodice together, and fled away back along the path. Arthur watched her go and then looked down at Peter in silence. He looked up at Arthur.

'You haven't changed, I see.'

'Mind your own business.'

'I make it my business,' Arthur said, 'in matters like this.'

Peter snatched up his jacket and leapt lightly to his feet. He pointed his finger in Arthur's face.

'Listen to me. I don't want to hear a word from you. Now or ever. You're a curate. Nothing. Just remember that. Father's patron of this living. I can have you thrown out any time I like. So hold your tongue.'

He turned away, and would have walked off, with his jacket swung over his shoulder, but Arthur went after him quickly, and pulled him abruptly round.

'First of all, don't ever turn your back on me. And secondly, if we're threatening each other, I know exactly what happened in Oxford.'

Peter looked at him with an insolent stare. Arthur went on.

'I went round to that boy's home after he was released from hospital. He is never going to walk properly again. He'll never be able to work. He is afraid to go out of doors, he suffers from nightmares, and is permanently and horribly scarred. That means nothing to you, I suppose?'

'He was paid off.'

'Paid off? Well done! Of course it was only a student prank to you and your friends – very amusing, a bit of mild horse-play with a pot-boy in the Mitre. A pity he was nearly burnt to death. He was only saved because the landlord had his wits about him and got him to the hospital in time. If that boy had died you would have been in court on a charge of manslaughter, which is what you deserve. But never mind, because your mother was able to hush things up! She is a capable woman. You're lucky to have her. It cost you nothing but your degree, and I don't suppose you'll miss that much.'

'Not much.' Peter stared at him for a moment. 'Who do you think you are, lecturing me? You're a labourer's son, aren't you? The dirt still under your finger nails – and you have the impudence to tell me what to do? Get out of my way.'

Arthur took him by the shirt and pulled him roughly up to him. 'Listen hard. From now on I'll be watching you. Seducing village girls is about your level, I can see. But if any harm comes to that girl, I'll be after you. Mind now.'

He released Peter with a contemptuous shove. Peter was breathing hard.

'You'll pay for that.'

Arthur pointed his finger in Peter's face.

'Mind now.' He turned and walked away across the field.

There was one person in the world Julia could consult before she broke the news to her father. This was her great-aunt Frances, an unmarried aunt of her mother with whom Julia had always kept in close touch. She visited the old lady from time to time in her house in Kent, and they would talk about her mother. It was a link that was precious to Julia, and as they talked, sitting in the drawing room in Kent, keeping the memory of Agnes alive, Julia could believe that her spirit was still there with them.

Dear Aunt Frances,
I have a piece of news which will astonish you, as it has astonished me. It is at the moment a deep secret, so I beg you will keep it so, until I can announce it to the world.

I have received a proposal of marriage! I will not disguise the fact that the young man is one whom I have 'worshipped from afar' for years. I never expected he would reciprocate my feelings, but when he asked me to marry him tonight, I knew this was my chance of happiness and I must seize it with both hands.

I am approaching you first because you know my circumstances best and are my dearest counsellor and friend. Is it wrong of me? Father relies on me so completely, the very thought of deserting him is almost inconceivable. How can I? I am his prop and staff.

My head aches even to contemplate the upheaval it would cause in this household. You cannot imagine – well, you can, I know – how everything here runs through my hands. However, I am determined not to be cowed by the enormity of the task. 'If it can be done it will be' is my attitude, and it will not be for want of exertion on my part.

But it is my father I am thinking of; how he will take it. I am writing, first of all to acquaint you with this momentous event, and then to seek your advice. First and foremost, if I am to leave this house, I must find someone to come in and act as housekeeper. Will you give this some thought and let me have your opinion?

The other problem, that of a secretary, is more difficult. I cannot at the moment think of any satisfactory solution. Our curate might have been the man – he has already undertaken some work on my father's behalf – though he is not one of nature's secretaries, to be sure.

Do write and give the benefit of your advice to
Your affect. niece,

Julia Stone

The answer to this letter came by return of post.

Dearest Julia,
My dear, I am on my way! Tell Annie to air the bed well!

I embrace you by post in the meantime, and offer you my warmest felicitations! What a surprise you gave me. Oh, I don't mean that – not a surprise, for if ever a girl deserved a husband, you do, my darling. I wanted to hug and kiss you on the spot, but there was no one here but Tib, and he had to do instead!

When I see you, we can put our heads together and draw up our plans!
In haste,
Yr loving aunt,

Frances Maxwell

Julia's problems came to a head quicker than she had expected because her father opened this letter by mistake, and did not scruple to read it.

About the middle of the morning he opened her door without knocking and stood in the doorway holding out the letter.

'Can you explain this?'

Julia looked up from her table where she had been writing.

'What is it?'

100

'It is a letter from your great-aunt in which she appears to be felicitating you upon your forthcoming marriage.'

Julia stood up to face him, and said calmly, 'Let me see. When did this come? Father, did you open a letter addressed to me?'

'I opened it in error. It came this morning.'

'And read it?'

He grew rather huffy.

'I cannot imagine – or rather I should say, I *could* not have imagined – that you had any secrets from me, Julia. It now appears that you have.'

He was back in a position of moral superiority.

Julia had by this time read the short note. She took a breath.

'I have received a proposal of marriage.'

'May I know from whom?'

'Peter Cunningham,' she said after a pause.

'And you have accepted?'

'As you see.'

Silence.

'Well, Julia,' Dr Stone looked down for a moment, summoning his thoughts, 'I had thought it a matter of common courtesy that I should be consulted in such a matter. It is customary, I believe, that a gentleman should approach the father of his intended bride and seek his sanction, before opening his heart to the young lady. That, I believe, is the honourable course. One does not run, hole in corner fashion, behind the back of someone who is to say the least most nearly concerned in the business. I am more upset than I can say.'

Julia was struck dumb by this unexpected turn.

'Nothing has been arranged,' she stumbled. 'As a matter of fact, it was I who asked Peter – Mr Cunningham – not to speak to you.'

'Why?'

'In the circumstances, I thought it better to tell you myself.'

'Instead of which you have consulted your aunt.'

'There are so many things to consider. I wanted to talk to her, and endeavour to make arrangements before I broke the news to you.'

'Arrangements?'

'Of course. For one thing, when I have left you will need a housekeeper –'

'Julia,' Stone interrupted, 'I cannot approve of this match. I cannot approve of Peter Cunningham.' He glared sternly down at her, his hands behind his back. 'I consider him a most unsuitable husband for my daughter. I certainly have no intention of giving my consent.'

'Father –'

101

'You have acted in a shameful and dishonourable fashion! Have you forgotten that you have duties in this house, that you owe a duty to me and the others who depend on you? It is quite improper that you should seek to run away in this irresponsible manner. And with a young man who is quite unfit to be your husband, immature, and of very unsound character.'

Julia spoke quietly.

'Father, we have no intention of running away. I would wish to be married from this house.'

'Can you seriously ask that?'

'Why not?'

In spite of everything, Julia could feel tears in her eyes.

'I am your daughter. Will you not give me your blessing?'

He stared at her, silent and unblinking.

'Are you refusing to give me in marriage?'

Stone was implacable. Julia, however, would not give ground. They stood in her room, facing one another, even as the tears gathered in her eyes, even as she could hear her voice cracking.

'Father, it is my right! You cannot refuse! How can I be married if you will not give me away?'

'Right? You talk to me of rights? To the one who gave you birth? To the one who has nurtured you, sheltered you, educated you? You have no rights, miss! You have duties, however, which you are shamefully neglecting. You ask me to give you in marriage, when I have not even been consulted? When my wishes have been ignored? When my interests are to be completely abandoned! You ask me that?'

He turned and went out of the room.

Julia could no longer hold back. She stood silent as the tears began to trickle down her cheeks, slowly, one after the other. And she would not reach up a hand to wipe them off.

She could not think of touching lunch, and had been lying on her bed, trying to get her thoughts in order, when Annie appeared with another note, this one from Peter again.

Why don't you come over? It would be better to have you here when I break the news, I think.

P.

She pulled herself together and stared at the note. Her first feeling was of relief. For one nightmare moment she thought he might have discovered some reason, some caprice, for backing out.

She looked at it again. Come over when? Straight away presumably.

She poured out some cold water and splashed her face and eyes which were red from weeping. Then, drawing a deep breath, she threw a large shawl round her shoulders, tied on her bonnet, and set out for the Old Manor House.

Mrs Cunningham was all smiles. She was very pleased indeed, she said; it had been her secret wish, and she had watched with increasing hope and pleasure the growth of their friendship. Julia was surprised at this. She looked across at Peter. Any apprehension he had felt had been well concealed. Now he looked his usual jaunty self.

Later Mrs Cunningham took the opportunity for a little tête-à-tête with Julia when Peter had gone out of the room.

'My dear,' kissing her on the cheek, and taking her hands, 'I am more pleased than I can say. We both know Peter. He is still rather a boy; young, sometimes a little wild and undisciplined. You are the very best woman I could have hoped for as a wife for him. You will be able to – shall we say – lead him into quieter ways, help him, through your gentle and feminine influence, to learn moderation and control.'

'I cannot be a mother to him, Mrs Cunningham. He is a grown man.'

'All wives have to mother their husbands a little, I am afraid.'

She gave a weary smile.

Afterwards as she was about to leave, Julia spoke to Peter alone.

'My father found out this morning, before I had had a chance to prepare him for it. It doesn't matter how. Of course he was unhappy, I expected that. But I never thought he would refuse his blessing.'

'Blow me. So he won't give you away in church? Hmm. Lucky for us there are one or two other churches in the country, eh? I say, we could run away to London and get married by special licence. What a lark that would be.'

'I will be given away by my father. He has no right to refuse. This is my home and I have the right to be married here. He said this morning it was "hole in corner". It will not be "hole in corner".'

'What does it matter? Forget him.'

'How can I forget him? He is my father. I am not running away, and I will not be married until I have made proper arrangements for him. But I do insist that he should be at my wedding. It is my right. So I am just warning you, it may take a little time.'

'Oh – well, if that is what you want. I don't mind.'

The following afternoon Great-aunt Frances arrived. Dr Stone was

103

locked in his study and didn't emerge as the old lady bustled through the door in a flurry of shawls, boxes, baskets, reticules, and umbrellas.

'Annie, take these up to my room. Here, and be careful with it, is a capon pie of my own baking – we can have it for dinner, it only wants warming through. And I have brought you a couple of bottles of my own elderberry cordial – my dear, how pale you look! Come and give your old aunt a hug, that's better. Now, Annie, tea! In the drawing room. Come, my dear' – taking Julia by the hand 'I want to hear everything.'

Julia waited until they were in the drawing room together. She closed the door.

'I could have spared you the trouble, Aunt. Father knows everything. He opened your letter in error.'

'And what does he say?'

'He is opposed to my marrying.' Julia looked down at her hands. 'He refuses to give me in marriage.'

'Hmm.' Aunt Frances looked at her for a moment. 'My dear, I can see that it has been a strain for you. Have you been losing your sleep?'

Julia nodded without speaking.

'Tell me about your young man.'

After dinner, Aunt Frances headed Dr Stone off before he could retire to his study; she was not one to let the grass grow.

'William. We must have a talk.'

Arthur had gone to his room. Julia watched, pale-faced, as the old lady confronted her father.

'Now, Julia, has told me everything. I understand your position. Very difficult. You have come to rely on Julia – too much so possibly. She has been running your house for you so long, you have forgotten that she too has a life of her own. Still, it will be difficult for you when she leaves.'

'When she leaves?'

'When she leaves. And because she is a conscientious and dutiful girl she has asked me to help. And since she is the dearest girl in the world to me, I have come at once as you see.'

'Where is this tending?' Stone glared rigidly at her, not prepared to unbend an inch.

'Cannot you see, you obtuse man? *I* shall take over from Julia until some other permanent arrangement can be made.'

'*You?*'

'And why not? Do you doubt my capabilities?'

'Is this some joke? It is perfectly clear that Julia cannot be spared from this house. Her duty requires her to remain here.'

'*Your* duty requires you to accede to your daughter's future happiness. It is your duty to facilitate her future plans.'

Julia watched the two of them. Her father's patience had run out.

'Madam, I must tell you that you are meddling in matters which do not concern you.'

'Stuff and nonsense! Julia's happiness concerns me.'

'I repeat – which do not concern you. Julia knows her duty; if her head has been turned – temporarily – by a young man who should know better –'

Julia could not keep silent.

'I love him!'

'Pooh! Mere foolishness.'

'Father, you shall not continue! Peter has asked me to marry him, I have given my consent, and no power on earth can prevent us getting married. I am prepared to do everything in my power to arrange matters so that you do do not suffer by the change – but you have no right to prevent it!'

'Be silent!' He turned to the old lady. 'Frances, you fail to understand the seriousness of what you propose. I have been working now for many years on the Commentary. It is, as Julia very well knows, far from completion. Do you understand? I have devoted a large part of my life to this work. Do you imagine that I can simply let it go? It is absolutely essential that Julia remains in this house. I cannot and will not permit her to abandon the work on some frivolous whim.'

He again tried to make for the door, as if this had somehow concluded the argument. Julia put herself rapidly in front of him.

'Father, I am prepared to do anything – anything – to help you continue with your work.'

'I will not listen. Step away from the door.'

'Father, you have no right –'

'Do you still persist? Stand away, I say.'

'Father! You will hear me!'

'No! Be silent. Julia, I give you solemn warning – if you leave this house to go to that young man, you leave it for ever. Be under no illusion. Now, let me pass.'

He thrust himself past her at last, slammed the door, and in a moment the door of his study could be heard closing behind him.

Julia's face was white. Frances took her in her arms, and at last she collapsed into a burst of violent sobbing.

Chapter Twelve

Julia did not sleep that night. Her shock and perturbation had given way to a deep anger. She realised that she was locked in a struggle for survival with her father. All the years of self-delusion, of misunderstanding or ignoring the hints and remarks of her friends, were at an end and it was clear to her now that her father was cold-bloodedly prepared to sacrifice her happiness, her whole future life, to his book.

The following morning she rose early, restless and unable to lie still, and dressing herself without sending for Annie, sat and waited until she thought Peter might be awake. Then she left the house and walked quickly to the Old Manor House.

Parker let her in, and went up to announce her to Peter; she sat alone in the drawing room, pale and light-headed from lack of sleep, huddling in a cloak. Her mind however was ice-cold; everything was clear to her.

Peter finally appeared. Late as she thought she had left it, it was still too early for him, and he was in shirt-sleeves, doing up his cuff-links.

'Peter, listen to me.' She drew him down beside her on the sofa. 'You said the other day you would run away with me – to get married by special licence. Did you mean that?'

'What? Yes, I suppose so, why?' Peter stopped wrestling with his cuff-link.

'My dear, I will not weary you with my woes, but there is no dealing with my father. He is opposed to our marrying, on any terms. If you have any scruple about marrying me, if you simply want to forget the business, if you wish to back out, I will perfectly understand and make no complaint. But if you want the matter to go forward, then I am ready to go with you wherever and whenever you choose – tonight if you please.'

Her eyes were alight with determination.

'By Jove Julia, do you mean it? And let the old man go hang, eh?'

She searched his face.

'Kiss me, strengthen me.'

'By Jove, you're a girl in a million,' he said as he took her in his arms.

'Oh Peter, let us go as soon as possible. I cannot bear to be in that house a day longer.'

He could feel her shaking.

'I say, Julia, you're cold, and as white as a sheet. Haven't you had any breakfast?'

'Never mind that. Just tell me. Will you go with me?'

'I should say so. What a lark, eh?'

'Will you go tonight?'

'Eh? All right – why not? It's going to take Mother by surprise. Still that's what mothers are for, eh?'

'Peter, find out the times of the trains to London, and send me a note to say what time you'll collect me. I want to go. I cannot wait any longer, really, I can't.'

There were tears in her eyes.

'Here – I say, steady on, old girl. Yes, by all means, leave it to me. It's been a strain for you hasn't it?'

She clasped him in silence. Then she gave a long sigh, pulled herself away, and drew in a deep breath.

'That's better. So long as you love me, I can do anything. Now, I must go back and try to make arrangements. Send word what time you'll come.'

'Rather.'

She walked back in time to find the family at breakfast. The table was subdued, and no one remarked on her arrival. As soon as breakfast was over, she drew her aunt into the drawing room.

'Aunt, you may be shocked or not, I don't know, but I have made up my mind to go away. Tonight. Don't worry, it will be quite respectable. We shall be married in London by special licence. After that –'

She turned away towards the window and looked out at the great cedar overhanging the lawn, twisting her hands together, as the thoughts passed through her mind.

'Tonight? Dear, is that quite wise? There will be the most frightful scandal in the village. You will make things very difficult for your father.'

'He has made life quite difficult enough for me. Aunt, I rely on you to take charge here. We'll go and talk to Mrs Oldham in a

107

moment. You won't have any difficulty – only you must watch her carefully. But I know you, you will be more than a match for my servants; they are simple souls, and Annie and Becky are as good as gold most of the time.'

'Julia dearest, let me counsel you. I really think we should take a little more time. I am sure your father may be softened, and come to some agreement.'

'I don't want to hear any more. I will speak to him once more, just to say goodbye – if he will hear me. I am convinced now that he is not prepared to –'

She stopped. After a moment, Frances said, 'What is it, dear? You were saying?'

Julia was staring out of the window at the cedar.

'I was thinking of my mother.' She was silent again, then went on quietly, 'Remembering the times when we used to sit together under that tree. Perhaps that was the only time I was truly happy. And now I am going away, and may never see it again.'

Frances was subdued by Julia's tone.

'Your mother was a dear gentle soul – not right at all for your father, poor dear.'

'I often think of her. I don't believe he can have made her very happy. Now she is beyond the reach of care. I wonder if she is looking down on me?'

'I am sure she is, my dear.'

Julia roused herself and turned.

'Come, Aunt, I will take you to the kitchen and we can go through the housekeeping with Mrs Oldham.'

Later that morning Julia was in her room, turning over in her mind what she should say to her father. She was surprised that she should be free from any hint of remorse or guilt. It was as if she had sloughed off her old life like a dead skin, and only wanted to go forward to a bright new life. She had already had a note from Peter telling her to be ready at six that evening.

Then she thought of Mr Grahame. She must speak to him too. What must he make of the comings and goings in the rectory? It might be easier to get that interview over first; she went and knocked on Arthur's door.

He opened it, and was visibly surprised to see her.

'Mr Grahame, I should like to have a few words with you if I may? Would you come with me to the dining room?'

The room was likely to be empty at that time of day.

As they went in Becky was in fact dusting, but Julia sent her out and closed the door behind her.

'Mr Grahame,' she said, turning, with the door handle still in her hand, 'I am sure you must be aware that something has been going on in this house, and I owe you an explanation.'

She paused, but he waited in silence for her to continue.

'The fact is, I am going to leave, and I –'

She was struck by the extraordinarily concentrated expression in his eyes. 'Is anything the matter?'

'No. Go on.'

'As I say, I am about to leave this house.'

'When?'

'Tonight.'

'Tonight?' His voice was unexpectedly loud, and she was startled by it.

'Yes – I – that is, it is impossible for me to remain here any longer. I am going away.'

'Going away? Why?'

She was taken aback.

'Why?' She was confused, and then, realising again the purpose of this meeting, drew herself up, and spoke quietly and with dignity.

'If you want to know, I am to be married.'

'Married! To whom?'

And then even before Julia could answer Arthur understood.

'Miss Stone – are you going away with him?'

'Who?'

'Him. Peter Cunningham.'

She did not know what to say. He seemed inexplicably ahead of her in this discussion, as if he had taken it over. She looked into his face, which was alight with feeling in a way she had never seen before.

'You must not do it.'

'Mr Grahame –'

'Miss Stone, I tell you, you must not. I will not allow you.'

'I beg your pardon?'

'Let me only say he is not worthy of you, you cannot know what he is.'

Julia understood in a flash that he had been put up to this by her father. She stiffened.

'I will not hear you. I know what you are going to say. I understand, and I have heard it before. Thank you, Mr Grahame, you may spare yourself the effort.'

'What have you heard?'

'Oh –' in fact Julia had heard nothing about Peter '– the usual slanders which surround any young man.'

109

'Yes, but what have you heard?'

'Mr Grahame,' she was becoming tense, 'I will not listen to tittle-tattle and gossip. I know what I am doing.'

'You have not heard –'

'I say, I will not hear,' she tried to drown him out, 'I beg you to be silent!'

He came a step towards her, and was standing over her now.

'I will not let you go to that man until you have heard me!'

In her refusal to hear anything bad of Peter she had worked herself into a tense, nervous, state.

'Mr Grahame!' she said quickly, backing to the door. 'I do not think you are the man to lecture me on this matter! Your own conduct hardly bears deep scrutiny.'

Arthur was staggered.

'What do you mean?'

'You know very well what I mean.'

She had him on the defensive now.

'Mr Grahame, your own conduct, I say, will not qualify you to lecture me or Mr Cunningham on morals.'

'My conduct? I don't know what you are talking about.'

'No? It is hardly something you will wish to discuss with me, I am sure!'

'Unless you tell me what it is, I cannot say.'

'You have been seen consorting with village girls.'

'*Consorting?*'

He said this such with undisguised disgust that she was driven to shout in his face, 'If you want to know, you were seen kissing Amelia Goodrich! And if you were a gentleman –'

'Emmy Goodrich? That has nothing to do –'

'Excuse me, but I think it has everything to do with it. It shows the kind of man you are, and I think it relieves me of the necessity of any further conference with you. Good afternoon!'

She wrenched at the door handle and went quickly out before he could say any more.

Two o'clock. Time was passing. She went to her room to make last minute arrangements. Should she take Annie with her? The trouble was that Annie was the most capable girl in the house. Julia could not bear to think of her father ministered to only by Becky and Mrs Oldham. Annie must be left at home; she would take Becky with her. It was time the girl was given a little more to do, anyway. Now was a good time to start. She rang for her, to take her into her confidence, and assist Julia in packing some boxes. The business of

110

packing brought home again the reality of what she was doing, the enormity of it. A kind of coldness settled over her. There was to be no more hesitation.

Then she sat down to write a letter to her father. Another interview could achieve nothing, except to lacerate her feelings further. Later, when it was after five o'clock, she gave the letter to her aunt, and asked her to give it to her father as soon as she was out of the house.

At six there was a knock at the door, and when she opened it, already with her bonnet and shawl on, one of the Cunninghams' grooms was there. She silently indicated the three boxes she had prepared, they were carried out, she kissed her aunt, and went out to where the carriage was waiting.

PART TWO
May 1862 –
August 1864

Chapter Thirteen

As she awoke she was aware first of the scent of the early-summer morning, a heavenly freshness wafting from the nearby fields, and promising another glorious day. It lifted her heart with joy as she opened her eyes. Across the wall opposite were the bars of light, which had greeted her every morning since they had arrived, the early sunlight shining through the shutters. In the dim room she looked up at the thick beams above their heads, alive with decorative painting – flowers, heraldic devices, scrolls of leaves; she had lain there on previous mornings staring up at them as her mind came into focus after sleep.

She turned her head slightly. There beside her, Peter was asleep. She studied his face on the pillow, his eyes closed, hearing his steady breathing. His hair disordered about his beautiful face, the soft eyelashes. She wondered again at herself. Could it be real? Was this herself, Julia Stone, the staid rector's daughter, the translator, and copyist, here in bed with this beautiful man, her husband? A shaft of joy went through her, and with it energy, and she climbed carefully out of the high bed, so as not to disturb him, and crossed to the window, unhinged the shutter, and opened it just a little so as to be able to look out.

Somewhere a church bell was tolling. Quite unlike the church bell at Stallbridge, lighter, with a merry, early morning note. Below her in the square, no one was moving yet. No, there was a girl coming across the cobbled square towards her in her quaint costume, the long heavy skirt, the white lawn blouse, her hair under its pretty starched cap. The houses opposite seemed centuries old, tall, oh, four or five storeys, leaning out, timbered in pale brown and white, their shutters still closed. Looking to her left, she could just make out the tall church steeple, pale with yellow stucco. About her were the roof tops, higgledy-piggledy with their red tiles, and all crowded

115

in on one another, so picturesque, and with their tall twisting chimney stacks, and the cranes' nests on top of them. And then, beyond, rose the mountainside with its steep rows of vines, grey yet in the early morning. How did they manage to grow them up such steep slopes? It was early yet the sun was already warm, and later it would be hot.

She turned, and there in the bed Peter was still fast asleep. She watched him, as his chest rose and fell with his breath, a breathing living being; the wonder of it, she thought, looking down at him asleep, the wonder of his presence, and she felt an outpouring of love towards him, a flood of warm love and she sent up a silent prayer of gratitude for her happiness. What miracle had brought her here?

Now was a good time to write Aunt Frances a letter. Once Peter was awake he would demand all her attention. The habit of years did not lightly desert her, and she sat at the little table in the half light, near the window, opened her writing box, set out her paper and unscrewed the ink bottle.

Dearest Aunt Frances,
At last I have moment to write you a proper letter. I hope you got my notes from London and Rotterdam. Well, we are here, in the prettiest little town on the Rhine, and are in no hurry, but idling our way along, stopping here and there as the fancy takes us, and not aiming to get anywhere at all. It is quite delightful. The weather is perfectly charming, in fact during the middle of the day very hot, and every day glorious. So we feel thoroughly lazy, and are enjoying the scenery which is magical. I cannot describe it; the river, and the little old ruined castles on the mountain tops, every one with a tale to tell. I am thankful now that father forced me to learn German – even the little I have has come in *very* handy. I am become a perfect authority on mediaeval German history, I assure you!

Well, you will want to hear properly about our journey to London and our marriage. As you know, Peter and I left Stallbridge and took the train to London. Peter has Franks with him, and I of course have Becky. We went to the Charing Cross Hotel when we arrived, and the following morning Peter went to arrange about the special licence, while I with your very generous gift in my purse went in search of a bridal trousseau. I thought since I am only getting married once in my life, I had better be dressed for it! Becky and I traipsed up and down Regent Steet and in and out of the bazaars, but I was able to find some things, and with a

116

few alterations, I made a fairly presentable bride. Oh, Aunt Frances, I beg you don't criticise me – how I would have loved you to be there – but Father would have none of it so there was no helping it, and I had to take matters into my own hands, if I was ever to get out of the house. Basta!

Next day the four of us went to St Stephens, and Peter and I were married by the Revd Mr Hobson, MA, a worthy young curate, and Franks and Becky were witnesses. Peter had booked us on the steamer for Rotterdam the following day at noon, so we spent the day wandering about London, which, entre nous, is *not* my favourite spot on earth, but all the same we did see the Queen's palace, and St Paul's Cathedral.

Next morning I went early to pick up the things I had left to be altered, and fortunately the work had been done, so I now felt I was fit to be a bride on her honeymoon, and we went along to London Bridge to take the packet. My dear! I have never seen such confusion. The whole river was packed from side to side with boats and ships of every size and description. And every destination too, I might add. There were sea-going barques – one the *Santa Maria* from Valparaiso, can you imagine? I barely can – side by side with lighters and red-sailed wherries, coal barges, quite black, bumping in among them, and everywhere a shouting and bustling, with steam cranes constantly whirring and banging, as bales and packages swung through the air, with no regard for anyone as they dropped down to the quayside. What confusion! Well, we found our boat, and there sure enough was a tiny cabin for Peter and myself, though Becky and Franks were huddling somewhere at the forward end. Poor Becky, I did feel sorry for her. The boat seemed to become more and more crowded, and then a number of gentlemen's carriages were swung over, and seemed to take up all the forward deck, just where I had thought it would have been so charming to stand and look out to sea once we were underway.

This was all rather exhausting and I was very glad to sit in the saloon for a while with Becky and drink a cup of tea. She was very excited as you can imagine at the prospect of a trip on the continent, and wriggled on the seat like a little girl. To tell the truth, I felt like a little girl myself sometimes, about to set off on an adventure. Peter was very happy to wander about the deck, and smoke a cigar, and chat to the other passengers, many of them English like ourselves off for a jaunt to the continent; a lot of them behaving as if it was something they did every year. (Perhaps it is, I don't know!)

117

Well, the ship eventually got underway and we steamed down the river, which is extremely dreary, ugly and flat, and I do not recommend it at all. The funnel was billowing out black smoke, and I must say worse than the train. I had to be very careful not to allow any specks of soot on my new dress. In fact I soon went down to the cabin and changed into an old dress I had with me – and that with Becky and myself crammed in there, and coping with crinoline hoops. Such a piece of vanity, really I must leave off wearing them – it was quite comical.

However, once we reached the open sea, I am afraid it became rather less comical, for the ship began to heave with the sea, and all the jollity of the departure vanished. It became silent in the saloon, and then people preferred to go on deck, only all the time there was the smoke from the funnel blowing among us, as the gusts of the wind caught it, and with the ship heaving and lurching, and then suddenly dropping into a hollow of the waves, I just stared at the horizon, and took deep breaths and hoped every thing would be all right. Peter was no better. He had long since since thrown away his cigar, and was sitting on a bench with a tartan rug round him, very pale, poor boy. I felt more sorry for him than myself!

The following morning we were in Rotterdam, and came by train to Cologne, which is a delightful city, very peaceful, and full of charming picturesque streets, with old gabled houses leaning into each other, and the great Cathedral. We attended a Lutheran service – which, by the by, is much like a Presbyterian order of worship – and there, I must say, my German was most useful.

And so the following day our honeymoon really began for we took the steamer up the river, and it was the most enchanting journey imaginable, as the river curved and snaked between the high and rugged outline of the mountain on either side; at every turn of the river there was some fresh vista to marvel at. The sky was clear, the sun warm, and the river gave a pleasant coolness. And all along the river side the most charming little towns, with their red-tiled roofs and slender church spires, which apparently are all Roman Catholic – this was something I had not realised. Apparently there are many such in the more southern parts of Germany.

We have been here for two days, and it is so charming we are in no hurry to move on, so I am hoping you will find time to write, my dearest aunt, and give me all the news. Your letter will find me here care of the Gasthof *Zum Grünen Baum*. Do write and tell how me how father is taking my departure. It has been a bad

118

business for him; he depended on me so, but I knew if I did not take my chance of happiness I might miss it forever. What a terrible urge there is in us, to be happy! (I felt truly like a drowning man beneath the water who strives to swim up to the surface to the light and air. And now I have found my light – my life, here with my husband, and I cannot regret what I have done.)

I will come and see you soon after we get back, and then we can make plans for the future.

Yr affect neice,
Julia Cunningham

As Julia wrote these words, she ran a slightly different version through her mind.

The days in London had in truth been very fraught, and at one point she wondered whether it was going to work out at all. In the end after Peter had entirely failed to find out about the special licence, it had been herself who had gone to the Archbishop of Canterbury's office in Doctors' Commons for the special licence and made the arrangements with Mr Hobson at St Stephen's.

She had also sent Peter to arrange the tickets for the ferry, but he had made a mess of that too, and when they had arrived at London Bridge, would have been on their way to Stockholm instead of Rotterdam, if she had not looked carefully at the tickets. Peter had been delightfully light-hearted about it, however. 'What does it matter my dear? Stockholm, Rotterdam, Fiji! So long as we are together.'

The other thing she couldn't mention in her letter, of course, had been their wedding night. Now, unlike many of her friends, Julia did have a pretty accurate idea of what was supposed to happen. It was partly that being an accomplished classical scholar, and having access to her father's enormous library, she was familiar with the work of Aristophanes and Ovid; again, being in and out of book-shops in Oxford and on her few visits to London, she'd had a chance to open medical textbooks on a few occasions, so that she had a rough working knowledge.

But in particular there had been one afternoon when she and her father had gone up to Oxford to see a colleague of his. Dr Stone and his friend had shut themselves up in a room in the college and left Julia to twiddle her thumbs in the adjacent rooms, of a colleague then on vacation. Having nothing to do for the next couple of hours at least, she had idly pulled a large folio volume, leather bound, out of the bookshelf and found to her astonishment that it contained erotic engravings.

119

Alone in the little room on that summer afternoon, the window open and the college quadrangle below her, knowing she was not going to be disturbed for two hours at least, Julia decided to make use of the time, and sat down at the table to look through the book.

The book was useful to her in two ways. First of all, it it confirmed her knowledge of the actual physical process of sex, of which she'd thought she had had a rough idea, but now saw in page after page graphically, copiously illustrated. But secondly and more importantly she learned that as well as the athletic young man, the young lady also appeared to be a full and energetic participant. Far from being a passive recipient of her partner's attentions, she was actively engaged. Julia thought, as she turned the pages carefully that if she were ever to experience a tenth of this young woman's enjoyment, and frankly ecstasy, she would be well content. In the end, feeling a decided warmth in her cheeks, she shut the book and pushed it back in the shelf, went down into the quadrangle and walked about for sometime to let the buzzing in her head subside, and the heat in her limbs dissipate.

So, on their wedding night, after dinner, she went up first to their room with Becky and undressed herself. Becky brushed her hair, put her clothes away and then wished her good night. Left alone Julia pulled off her nightdress, turned back the bed, and lay down naked to wait for Peter. She was confident that after four years at Oxford he was no virgin, and would have a clear idea what to do.

When he came in eventually, though, he had been drinking, and she could smell the brandy on his breath as he came to her. He was enthusiastic as he saw her nakedness, and appreciating her readiness for him, threw off his clothes. But to her disappointment, in place of the transports of pleasure, the athletic display she had seen in the illustrations, the night of joy she had anticipated, he was no sooner on her, no sooner entered her, painfully for her of course, than he seemed to be done, it was over, he rolled off her and was asleep almost immediately.

Julia was left wide awake; she sat up, pulled her nightdress on, and taking a grip on her feelings, told herself it was bound to get better. In fact it had. Peter was still far too fast, and seemed to have no idea that she too was supposed to gain any pleasure from their love-making, but at least he was young and energetic, and they made love many times over the next few days, and she hoped he might at last begin to get an inkling of what was going on in her.

Because she knew as soon as she had seen the drawings in that room in Oxford that she was going to enjoy this, and that she had a right to, and everything else was a lot of man's talk about woman being the purer one, and having a "higher nature", above the base instincts of men etc which she was supposed to endure with fortitude and patient resignation. As soon as she had seen those pictures, Julia had understood the truth, that women were every bit as capable as men of enjoying conjugal pleasures, and it was sheer humbug to say otherwise.

Peter would need educating, though, which might take time.

She heard him turn in bed and interrupting her train of thought she turned towards him. He lay in bed, and his eyes had opened.

'Good morning, pretty lady.'

'Good morning, kind sir. Shall I ring for your hot water?'

'Hmm? No, there's no hurry.' He raised his arm, beckoning her, and she went across and sat on the edge of the high bed, on top of its multitude of mattresses. They looked at each other, and he ran his hand over her breast, through the thin nightdress. She felt a thrill of pleasure and couldn't help moving against his hand, and it was only a moment before she was beside him and in his arms. In the lazy, relaxed early morning her body flowed against his, arching itself in readiness for him, opening itself, needing him. Peter, however, rolled away and laughed.

'I say, give a fellow a chance. Bit too early for that, don't you think?'

She turned and knelt beside him, looking down at him and then bending over him, her loose hair falling about his face, nuzzling her cheek against his, kissing the side of his neck. Oh, he was so beautiful, she could have spent all morning, all day there, just dallying, playing, and exploring the wonder of each other.

Peter, though, seemed bored with it.

He giggled.

'Stop, you're tickling, Julia.'

He stared across at the window where the shutter was half open.

'Extraordinary, isn't it?'

'Hmm?'

'I mean, us, here. Better than Stallbridge, eh? Are you glad you came?'

She kissed him without answering.

'And you Julia – the rectors's daughter. I mean you're nothing but a shameless hussy!'

She sat up.

'What do you mean?'

He laughed.

'Oh, you and your maidenly blushes, you in that rectory, you and

121

your studious life, and beneath it all – all that writing and copying – by God, you'd do credit to a sultan's harem!'

'What?'

He giggled.

'You kept it very well hidden.'

'Peter, what's the matter? Don't you like it? I only want to please you.'

'Of course I like it, you little fool, what fellow wouldn't? You took me a bit by surprise, that's all.'

'Oh,' she grinned, 'is that all? And I took you for such a man of the world.'

'Well,' he bridled now, 'of course, I've knocked around a bit, naturally.'

'Naturally.'

'A fellow sees things, gets around a bit, you know.'

'Of course.'

'I must say, though, Julia, it was you – I mean, I didn't quite expect –'

'What didn't you quite expect?'

'Well, all this, you know.'

'All what?'

He looked away thinking, and then spoke, looking away from her towards the window. 'This may sound rude, possibly, but Julia, can I ask you something?'

She felt a stab of alarm.

'What?'

'Were you, I mean, when we married, were you a – well, a virgin?'

She sat bolt upright.

'How can you ask that?'

She turned from him, her cheeks tingling. Peter tried to laugh.

'Sorry, I didn't mean to offend – it's just that, well, I wasn't ready for it, I suppose.'

'Ready for what?'

'Well, finding you so forward.'

'Forward!'

She got out of bed, walked across to the window and sat at her desk, where her letter to Aunt Frances lay.

'Oh, don't get into a wax! I didn't mean to upset you! Come here.'

Julia was bewildered.

He got out of the bed and padded across to her in his bare feet, and slid his arms round her neck.

'Sorry.'

She was silent.

122

'Julia, I said I'm sorry. Shouldn't have mentioned it.'

Slowly she reached for his hand, and turned to him; he bent over her and they kissed.

'Glad you are though.'

'What?'

'A shameless hussy. It'll be our secret.'

Looking down into her face, he saw the trace of a tear on her cheek.

'Oh God, Julia, don't cry, for pity's sake. I can't bear it when girls cry.'

But she was smiling now, and threading her arms round his neck, pulled his head to her.

'I only wanted to please you. Peter, I would do anything –'

'I know, old girl. Come, no tears, I beg you. I really can't stand it.'

He freed himself and threw open the window. Immediately the room was flooded with light. Outside the little square below was busy, shops had taken down their shutters, and cafe proprietors were setting out chairs and tables for the day.

'What shall we do today?' he asked with a brilliant smile.

Chapter Fourteen

Franks brought Peter his shaving water, and Becky came to brush Julia's hair and help her dress. Julia was not normally particularly interested in clothes and had never given them much thought at home except on those special – and rare – occasions when it was necessary to put on a display. But here, on her honeymoon, she knew she must dress the part, if only to please her brand new husband, and had spent a good portion of the present Aunt Frances had given her.

So this morning she was able, knowing it was going to be hot during the day, to put on a fine white cotton dress with a print of pale anemones, trimmed with violet braid, and looped up to show *broderie Anglaise* petticoats. Round her neck on a ribbon hung a gold locket, a gift from Peter with a photograph of himself inside. She had felt slightly apprehensive when she first put on this finery – as it seemed to her – but it was the least she owed to Peter, to do him honour, and he was certainly very pleased with the result.

'I say, Julia, you look a regular stunner,' had been his comment, when he saw her first in her going away clothes.

Eventually they descended to the terrace of the hotel, and sat out beneath an awning while the *Herr Ober* brought them coffee, *brötchen* and apricot jam, and they were able to sit, in the pleasant early morning, sipping their coffee and breaking open the crusty rolls, freshly baked, and make lazy conversation and silly comments on the townspeople going about their morning business.

'What are we going to do today?' Peter asked.

Julia licked her fingers, wiped them, and picked up Murray's *Hand Book*. 'There's a castle on the top of the mountain. Let's climb up and have a picnic.'

'Very good.' Peter was happy to let her make the arrangements.

So, with Franks and Becky, they set off, out through the little town, along the river, and then across the old bridge (which according to Murray had been built in 1463, though it was destroyed by the army of Louis XIV during some war or other and afterwards rebuilt), and then taking a narrow winding path, they made their way up between the vineyards past pretty little farm buildings so old they looked as if they had grown out of the earth, Julia in a straw hat with streamers, and holding a walking stick, and Peter with his jacket slung over his shoulder and a cigar between his teeth, behind them Franks with the luncheon basket, and Becky carrying several travelling rugs.

They came out higher, and higher, as the path curved and wound round the side of the hillside, and up narrow little valleys, and at last they came to the ruins of the castle. "Demolished by the retreating armies of Napoleon in 1813" Julia read out of Murray, as they surveyed them.

'Whoever had the task of demolishing them made a very thorough job of it.'

Around and beneath them the wooded countryside spread away until it lost itself in the blue-grey haze of the horizon; nearer, below them, the river, broad and lazy, curved past, and the little town nestled cosily beside it in a cluster of red roofs and slender church spires. Distantly they could hear a bell chiming.

'This'll do,' Peter said.

Later as they sat lazily admiring the view, Julia whispered to Peter to tell Franks and Becky to take a stroll, and then she and Peter lay on the rugs with their arms round each other, and Julia wanted him so badly just then, all the misunderstanding of the morning forgotten, and would have made love on the spot. How romantic it would have been, the two of them there, on top of the world, with that wonderful view spread out beneath them, and behind them the picturesque old ruins. But the thought intruded, the morning did return. He would think her forward. Was she immodest? Unladylike? Was there something wrong with her? And it cast a slight cloud over her enjoyment.

In any case, she realised Peter would be too nervous of their servants returning unexpectedly, so there was a strained atmosphere. However they lay looking up at the empty blue sky between the ruined battlements of the old castle, and made lazy conversation, and giggled and kissed and made plans about where they should go next. None of it seemed important, time just flowed along, and the whole world seemed to belong to them, and Julia felt that fate, or the gods, or someone, had been very good to her, and had given her more than she had had any right to expect, and her heart overflowed with thankfulness, and she could not resist pulling Peter over on to her, kissing, and holding him, and then wanting him again, wishing they could throw their clothes off here and make love, only of course they couldn't – someone might come, he said. She didn't care, would have taken the risk – but she took care not to say so.

Two evenings later it was decided to go to the opera. Amazingly the little town had its own opera house, and they were presenting *Don Giovanni*. Julia was able to get them a box.

The opera visit entailed a lot of work by Becky on Julia's hair, brushing it and coiling it and pinning it up, and then setting a wreath of flowers in it, and she unpacked a dress she had not yet worn and had reserved for a special occasion, which this clearly was, a white dress, a low off the shoulder dress, and inside it a mass of whalebone, all hooks and eyes at the back, and setting off her splendid bosom over a wide hooped skirt. What her father would have said to see her like this, her, Julia, the belle of the ball, she thought, looking at herself in the looking glass, as Becky, on her knees beside her, set the skirt neatly over the hoops. Last of all she unwrapped from their tissue paper a pair of the tiniest satin slippers.

Round her neck on a black velvet ribbon hung her gold locket.

Peter too was splendid in evening dress and white neck tie, extravagantly tied.

'Got to uphold the honour of Britain tonight, my dear. They'll be saying, whisper, whisper, "Who's that ravishing young lady in the box? Never saw her before. Oh, didn't you hear? It's that young couple from England, don't you know!"'

The theatre was not large – though Julia did not know that, never having been in a theatre in her life – but it seemed perfectly enchanting to her; there were four tiers of boxes, and every one filled with an entire family it seemed: children hanging out and waving to each other; staid mothers of seven fanning themselves and talking animatedly to their friends, pulling their offspring back from the balustrade; blushing young girls looking down at their fans while young officers in colourful costumes, jackets apparently half hanging off their shoulders, leant over their chairs and, judging by the concentrated expression on the young girls' faces, made remarks not altogether unwelcome.

In the pit on long benches sat what appeared to be the shop-keeping element with their families, all very respectable and proper. Julia had her fan, because it was warm here, and sat in the most perfect contentment and excitement. Eventually they heard a fanfare of trumpets, and a family made their way into what must be the Royal Box, or whatever it was called here, because everyone in the theatre stood up and bowed towards them, and they in turn very graciously bowed back to the assembled house. Julia found it most amusing, and wondered how the show on the stage could possibly compare with this? He must be a duke at the very least – perhaps even an archduke – a plump little man in an extravagant toy-soldier military uniform, pillar box scarlet, with a broad sash, tight white trousers, and half the medals of Europe, she imagined. With him his spouse, a plump, self-satisfied matron in a low-cut gown, with a sash too, and even a medal, and around her five children, from teenage down to seven, and behind them three young gentlemen in military uniform and two dowdy middle-aged maids of honour. So the box was quite full.

But at last, after all this entertainment, she noticed the orchestra had been gradually assembling, and finally a conductor popped up and received a rousing ovation, which he took with gracious aplomb before rapping with his baton on his desk. All was hushed and the music began.

Julia had never been to an opera, knew very little of music; there was no theological or intellectual bar to it in the rectory, it was simply that her father was not musical, and it never crossed his mind that she might be.

Presumably this was not the world's greatest opera house either, but Julia found it very interesting. After a while Peter excused himself and said he was going out for a smoke, but Julia wanted to watch. She quickly realised that the singers were well known in the town – each received a hearty welcome the moment they appeared on stage. She soon noticed too that the various female singers appeared to have their rival bands of supporters, because after each of their arias they received a tumultuous burst of applause, and it was clear that some received more than others. Julia was quite intrigued by this.

The music was far too much to take in at one hearing. There was so much contained in it, so many thoughts, suggestions, so much feeling; it was all very interesting. The young singer who played the part of the peasant girl – Julia could not afterwards remember her name – sang her two songs very affectingly and with great sweetness of tone as well as being a marvellous actress, and wound her way into the audience's heart with insidious skill.

The opera came to a thrilling finale with a most impressive transformation scene. The wicked Don having been repeatedly exhorted to mend his ways and having refused point blank, the scenery of the room all seemed to come to pieces and was transformed before her eyes to the gaping jaws of hell. A troupe of devils, their hands outstretched, drew him downwards while beneath them the conductor whipped the orchestra into a positive frenzy of excitement. The curtain came whisking down to a thunderous ovation, and afterwards the female singers came before the curtain to receive bouquets and people were on their feet crying 'Bravo!'

During the interval Julia ate a sorbet, something else she had never tried, and afterwards they came out of the theatre hearing the excited buzz of the other people as they dispersed, watching the carriages of the nobility and hearing the loud calls of the doormen, calling out the names of the families as the carriages rolled up beneath the *porte cochère*. They walked through the cobbled streets, her arm in his, very contented, and at last getting back to their dear little room, undressed, and fell into bed together to make love.

Next morning Julia had a letter from her aunt.

My dearest Julia,
I was so pleased to get your letter, and to hear that all is well with you, my darling. I have never visited Germany, but I am sure it must be very beautiful. Very glad too that all your arrangements turned out successfully. Also that you were able to get some nice clothes in time. Of course I would have loved to be at your wedding. Don't you think I have dreamed about it for years? Still, so long as you are happy, that is what matters, and I am thankful for it.

I don't need to tell you, your father has not taken it kindly. I wish in a way I didn't have to inflict this on you on your honeymoon, my dear, but I know you are a sensible young woman and would rather hear the truth. I am afraid he has been quite unmanageable for days – ever since you went. He is either in a black rage, or a brooding melancholy, one or the other. Either way there is no handling him. He would not even eat at first – a day went by and he did not come out of his study except to go to bed at some unearthly hour, four in the morning I think it was. Of course no one is allowed into his study, but glancing in yesterday morning, it seemed in a state of perfect chaos. I timidly knocked, thinking to tempt him with a cup of coffee, and had my head bitten off for my pains. Doors slam, we hear a heavy tramp as he comes out occasionally, but never a word to any of us.

Eventually he consented to eat. But I don't know which was worse: having him at the table, or not having him there. He sat hunched over, staring at his plate, chewing his dinner with a relentless implacable chew till I thought of Jack the Giant Killer, and he was the Giant wishing it was your husband he was devouring.

I must say the young curate, Mr Grahame, has been *very* good about it. What a pillar of strength that man is! So helpful, in unobtrusive ways, I mean. He has taken upon himself a host of duties, has quietly dealt with some of the things I imagine you used to do, and is in and out of the house at all hours, running errands, helping to prepare your father's sermons, going about the village and consulting with Miss Pearson over the school. I am sure your father could not have wished for a better curate. There is something very comforting about Mr Grahame too – I cannot say exactly what it is. Well, you certainly know he is *there* if you know what I mean. I know some of the ladies in the village find him a little uncouth, a little earthy in his ways, and I know he has no family to speak of. I believe he comes from labouring stock and has worked his way up by his own efforts, but I say well done and certainly wish him well. He has his own way to make in the world, and has already come so far and I for one respect him for it, whatever some old biddies may mutter behind his back.

What are your plans for when you get back? I know your father still imagines in some way you are going to come back and carry on where you left off, which I am sure you are *not*. You are a married woman, and will have your own life to make, and your husband to care for, and no doubt soon enough other cares on your mind.

As I say, there is no talking to your father. Let us hope he will be in a condition to see sense before you get home, and we will be able to sit down and discuss the future rationally. He is so obsessed with his book – well, you know all about *that*. If he were only a little more reasonable, I am sure it would be perfectly possibly to come to some working arrangement.

Do write when you can and let me know your plans for the future – where you intend to settle, and what your husband plans to do.

In the meantime, my darling, my very best wishes to you both, and do have a lovely trip.

Yr affect aunt,
Frances Maxwell

This letter threw Julia into deep thought. It had come just after breakfast, as they had been about to go out, so she did not have a chance to read it till later, when the day had become unpleasantly hot and they had retired to their room to rest.

With the shutters closed, the room was in a pleasant half light, enough to read by, and they lay side by side on the bed as she read the letter twice through.

'What does the old girl say?' had been Peter's comment, and Julia had made a slight glancing reply, and his curiosity had gone no further.

Eventually Peter dozed off – he had drunk several glasses of the very drinkable Rhine wine over lunch – and Julia lay in the half light, and tried to puzzle out the future.

Of course it depended on Peter. They had not yet talked of their plans, but she knew he wanted to live in London. That was where his friends were, he could go to the club, there was so much more going on and so forth. And of course if that was what Peter wanted, that was what they must do. There was no question of contradicting him.

The next thing was, what was Peter to *do*? He had no profession. He had been trained to nothing. He had floated through Oxford, had left under mysterious circumstances, she had no idea what and probably never would. Of course the Cunninghams were wealthy, and his father was in very poor health, so it was probable that in the not too distant future Peter would come into the property, and they would come back to live in Stallbridge anyway.

Where did that leave her father? The fact was there was no place for him in her future life. From now on her place was at Peter's side, The best she could do was to assist him in finding a suitable young man to act as his secretary. She knew the Commentary was nowhere near finished, and could easily take years yet. The problem was that it was such a big project; that even during the time he had been working on it books had come into print, both in England and elsewhere, that necessitated changes in those parts he thought he had finished. It was most trying; he would have to reopen questions he thought had been settled. In fact sometimes it appeared as if it might *never* be finished, a mountainous labour that rumbled on like some great Juggernaut, devouring everything – and everyone – in its path.

Her father had confided in her in the past, that sometimes he had wished he had chosen a less ambitious project – something he might have been able to see through in three or four years – instead of this, which seemed to have no end in sight, even after more than ten years' labour.

There was another even darker fear in Stone's mind, deeper than the mere fear of being beaten into print, deeper than his anxiety for mere worldly reputation. He had said to her one afternoon, and she could see that it had frightened him, that there were things in St

John that he himself simply didn't understand. She had tried to reason with him – pointed out that human wisdom could not hope to peer into the divine mystery etc – but he had looked up her from his desk, with a haunted look in his eyes. 'How can it be, Julia? It is inconceivable that God should bequeath to man this abstract of his wisdom, this summation of his message to humanity, and that it should be actually incomprehensible. Why should he? Even after making all allowance for corruption in the text, there are passages which simply do not make sense.' It had worried him more than anything else and – she pitied him his perplexity.

Anyway there was nothing that she could do about that. And closely as she had been connected with the Great Work, she had no relish for devoting the rest of her life to it, and resented more than anything her father's driving ambition that had been prepared to sacrifice her to it.

Chapter Fifteen

The following day Peter suddenly felt restless and announced it was time to move on, so their boxes were packed, and space was booked on the Diligence – a kind of enormous stage-coach – and they set off for Bad Homburg, a spa town.

'Bit more life there, Julia. This place was beginning to bore me,' he said as he helped her inside. He himself had elected to ride on the roof so he could enjoy his cigar and chat to the other passengers. Peter was very fond of striking up acquaintances – and flirting with pretty girls, Julia had already had time to note – and everywhere they went, quickly made himself agreeable, so that people were often congratulating her on what a fine young man her husband was, and, she thought, adding the unspoken comment: And you're very lucky to have caught him! Well, she didn't mind that, she agreed with it, after all. So that day she sat inside with Becky, and the two men sat on the roof, and Peter struck up acquaintances, and made up conversations in a pidgin English which he believed must be comprehensible to poor benighted foreigners who did not have the great fortune to be born British.

Bad Homburg was a great step up from the little town they had been in, much more sophisticated, with large hotels, beautiful parks, tree-lined avenues, and everywhere the carriages of wealthy families. A lot of foreigners too, French, Russian, a large number of English, and even an American family. Everyone seemed immensely rich and determined to let everyone else see they were, so that there was a lot of very obvious competition to show off their shiny carriages, the ladies' elegant dresses, the diamond pins in the gentlemen's neckties, the number of servants, the sumptuous dinners and suppers that were served at all hours of the day, because no one appeared to pay much attention to normal hours here – it was a kind of perpetual carnival – and above all, the amounts they were prepared to lose at the tables in the casino.

They strolled round the town late in the afternoon of the day they arrived, watching the beautiful carriages sweep by them, and the august figures of the flunkeys on the boxes behind them.

They also saw certain ladies, dressed in the pinnacle of *haute couture* who rode in their carriages alone, except for some minute dog, and who stopped sometimes to talk to certain gentlemen who had an unmistakable air about them. It was a swaggering air, as Julia thought about it, compounded of the military, the race track, the hunt, and other elements to which she could not exactly put a name, but who in any case wore clothes that were *very* carefully tailored, hats that were *very* rakishly tilted, waistcoats that were *very* expensively embroidered, and trousers that seemed very tight, and smoked cigars, and leant on the edge of the carriage and made knowing remarks, and grinned and ostentatiously knocked away the ash of their cigar.

After she had seen a number of these ladies and gentlemen, Julia began to grasp the sense of a line in the handbook that had puzzled her: 'The only manufacture is of black stockings; articles in very great request no doubt by the gentlemen who most numerously resort hither every summer'.

She was already nostalgic for the pleasant little town they had been staying in, with its little streets and wine-gardens, its little opera house, and the castle on the hill, where they had lain one afternoon, and admired the view.

Peter however had perked up considerably.

'God, in that other place, I was falling asleep, Julia.' She felt this was a little tactless, because there had been herself too, doing her best to be entertaining, but she let it pass. Peter's eyes had lit up. He had taken a deep breath, looking about and taking it all in and pronouncing himself pleased they had come, and there would be lots more to do here. And there might even be someone they knew. Again Julia was slightly hurt because up till now it had been just themselves, with Becky and Franks, and it had very cosy and pleasant just the four of them travelling together.

The prices in the hotels were of course far higher than they had been in that sleepy little town of which she already had such fond memories. Peter had the money – part cash, and part Letters of Credit that could be redeemed in various banks and commercial offices in cities as they travelled along.

Since he was paying for all, she had not asked him about expenses, although she had had to ask for money occasionally, for the box at the opera for example. Still, the habits of a lifetime did not desert

133

her, and she was immediately conscious of the far higher rates in the hotel here in Bad Homburg. She had always been careful with money, and expected to get value for it, and it was a trial having to stand meekly back while Peter negotiated the rates, which seemed to her wildly extravagant, and grandly agreed terms.

They were shown to a pretty room with a painted ceiling, with rose buds and cherubs and romantic scenes of peasants merry-making. Outside the window they could hear the occasional rumble of carriage wheels passing, and the voices of people chatting.

They dined in the hotel restaurant; the food was rich and fussy, lots of fiddling little dishes, and thick sauces, and far too much of it, but she was hungry after the day's journey. Later, when it was dark, they strolled out to walk off the heavy dinner – and Peter had drunk the best part of a bottle of wine – and walked up and down the avenues, well-lit with gas lamps, as the carriages still clip-clopped past, and groups of people, all most expensively dressed, strolled past, all seeming to be hugely enjoying themselves, laughing, and calling out to each other.

Then they found themselves in front of a long high building set back in its own grounds, lights blazing at every window, and carriages constantly coming and going from the front entrance, liveried flunkeys coming down the steps to open the doors while women in great sweeping skirts stepped daintily on to the red carpet and went up inside.

They stood watching this spectacle for some time, and Julia thought this must be the residence of the duke, or archduke, or whatever he was here in Bad Homburg, until Peter laughed and said, 'It's the casino. Let's have a look in.'

'Surely it must be awfully expensive to go in.' She was judging by the appearance of those she had seen go in.

'Expensive? It's free, you noodle. They'll get your money out of you at the tables. I've heard of this place – fellow in college told me all about it. Come on, let's take a look inside.'

'Oh, Peter, I can't possibly! I'm not dressed for it.'

After a short discussion Peter gave in, not very gracefully, and they agreed to pay a visit the following evening.

The following morning they had to see the Kurhaus and take the waters. Everything was most elegantly appointed; it was set in the Kurpark, the most lovely gardens (laid out 'in the English manner' Julia read in Murray) and the buildings very spacious and pleasant, lots of glass and very airy. However, first of all there was the most awful smell which hung over the whole place, vaguely salty, and secondly it was full of invalids, and worse middle-aged men who had come to pay their annual penance for a year's over-indulgence. There was too a depressing sense of age trying in vain to recover lost youth, and Julia, on Peter's arm, feeling so very youthful and full of health, was faintly disgusted by the sight of so many human wrecks.

Nevertheless they took the waters.

Then, as they were leaving, they did indeed run into someone Peter knew; a young man accompanied by three ladies and an older man.

'Morley! By Jove!'

Peter was lit up with pleasure.

'Freddie Morley, you sly dog! Splendid to see you.'

Young Morley turned to the lady by his side,

'Mother, this is Peter Cunningham. We are – were, that is – at Oxford together. How are you, old fellow?'

Peter introduced Julia.

'Allow me to introduce my wife.'

'Your wife!' Morley was visibly taken aback.

'Don't look so shocked, old fellow. A chap's entitled, you know – free, white and over twenty-one.'

Morley recovered himself.

'Of course, crass of me.' And he bowed to Julia and they shook hands.

'Cunningham, my father and mother – my sister Grace – Mrs Bradshaw –' this was a woman a few years older than Julia, and an older lady '– My aunt, Miss Morley.'

Hands were shaken, but Julia could see that Morley was not keen to let the conversation develop, and was aware too of the young woman, Grace Bradshaw appraising her, and suddenly felt awkward and sensed that there was something in the air between them of which she was unaware.

'What do say we all go somewhere for a spot of refreshment, get the taste of the waters out of our mouths?'

'We are engaged, unfortunately, old fellow'

'Well, where are you staying? We could meet up later on, eh?'

'We are at the Quatre Saisons – it would be good to meet have a chat. Later.'

He was obviously in a hurry to get away.

'Well, if you have time, come over and find me – we're at the Hotel César.'

'Yes, I'll see if I can manage it.'

They moved off, and Peter and Julia continued their stroll, Peter

135

pleased with himself, swinging his cane and whistling for a few minutes.

'Capital fellow, Morley. We're – were – at Christ Church together. Quatre Saisons, eh? Supposed to have the best chefs in Europe, so they say.'

After lunch Peter suddenly announced he was going over to find his friend Morley. It was the first time since they had left London that they had separated and Julia was not pleased. She did not say anything, and tried to reassure herself that it would be nice for him to have a bit of free time with his friend – no doubt there were all sorts of things they could talk about together when there weren't females hanging around them. But still, whatever she told herself she was a little hurt that he could prefer his friend's company to her own on his honeymoon, even for so short a time.

'See you at teatime,' he said, kissing her on the cheek, and taking his hat from the hat stand.

Julia called Becky and told her they would go for a walk too.

It was a hot afternoon, but the town was criss-crossed by shady avenues and boulevards, and it was pleasantly cool to stroll up and down, or as they did later, sit in the shade of a tall tree in the park and listen to the brass band.

Becky was home-sick already.

'Don't get me wrong, Miss Stone – Mrs Cunningham I should say – I'm enjoying myself like anything, never seen such a place, and the carriages, and fine ladies and gentlemen everywhere. 'Tis like fairyland, so it is, and Annie won't ever believe the half of it if I was to tell her. But still and all, you can't beat England I say, and I won't be sorry to get back to Stallbridge and my own bed.'

'You know that Mr Cunningham and I will be going to live in London, don't you, Becky? Would you be willing to come and live with us, and be my personal maid?'

'I'll go wherever you want, Mrs Cunningham. Personal maid, eh? Oh, yes, and I'll do my best to deserve well of you.'

Julia laughed.

'You're a good girl, Becky, and I think we suit very well.'

Although she was only a few years older than Becky, who was fifteen, Julia felt she could almost be her mother.

She looked vaguely round the gardens, and then noticed not far away Mr Morley's sister, who had been introduced to her briefly that morning. At the very moment Julia saw her, she lifted up her head – she had been reading a book – and noticed Julia. She inclined her head in silent acknowledgement.

Julia and Becky went on talking in a desultory way, and listening to the band, and a little while later the young lady closed her book, rose, and came towards them.

'Mrs Cunningham.'

Julia looked up.

'Mrs Bradshaw, I think. We met very briefly this morning. Won't you join us?'

The young woman was undecided for a moment, then seemed to make up her mind.

'I think I will for a few minutes.'

She sat on a vacant chair beside Julia. There was something of a hard-boiled, mannish quality about the woman. Poor Becky had become for the purpose of this conversation invisible.

'Have you been here long?'

'Oh, no – we only arrived late yesterday afternoon. And have had time to do nothing yet. Well, we did take the waters this morning. As a matter of fact my husband has gone in search of your brother. You behold me here, marooned.'

'Yes.' Mrs Bradshaw studied the point of her parasol as she drew lines in the dusty summer soil of the path before them, then she said very softly, 'Send your maid away.'

Julia was surprised, but turned to Becky.

'Becky dear, Mrs Bradshaw and I are going to have a little tête-à-tête. Will you leave us for ten minutes? Here –' and she fished a coin from her reticule '– perhaps you would like to go and buy yourself an ice-cream?'

Becky went off very happily.

The two women sat silently for a moment, staring towards the band.

'Forgive my curiosity. I had to see Peter Cunningham's wife a little closer to.'

Julia looked sharply at her and waited for her to go on. She did.

'To tell the truth, I had not thought him the marrying type. Besides he's very young.'

Julia did not like this at all.

'Well, Mrs Bradshaw, it appears he is the marrying type after all. I hope you are not too disappointed.' This was designed to have a sting in the tail, but the other woman looked carefully into Julia's face with an amused smile.

'So long as *you* are not disappointed.'

Julia stood up.

'Mrs Bradshaw, I am not sure that this conversation is going to be of much profit to either of us.'

Mrs Bradshaw did not lose her composure.

137

'Don't go yet. I want to talk to you.'

'I am not sure I want to talk to you.'

'Why not? We may be able to be of use to each other.'

'What on earth do you mean?'

'I beg your pardon, but are you on your honeymoon?'

'Yes.'

'How long have you known Peter?'

'Peter?'

'Mr Cunningham if you prefer.'

'Mrs Bradshaw, perhaps I should begin by asking you a few questions. How long have *you* known my husband? You seem to have a deep interest in him.'

Their eyes locked and Mrs Bradshaw, who was still sitting, suddenly appreciated the force of character of the woman standing over her.

She looked down, and began to sketch patterns in the dust again with her parasol.

'Oh, don't misunderstand me. I have met him a few times, that's all, with my brother, you know. I've been up to Oxford with Mama once or twice, for eights week – that sort of thing. And you?'

Julia sat down. She wasn't sure she needed to talk to this woman at all. But after a moment she did.

'Peter and I have known each other all our lives.'

'Really? Well then, you must know him very well indeed. Obviously you know what you are doing.'

'I think I do know him – yes.' Though she was suspicious of that last remark. 'Mrs Bradshaw, you are hinting at something. What is it?'

'As I say, I did not think him the marrying type.'

'But since he has chosen to marry, what then?'

'You seem a capable young woman, I must say. I dare say you will be able to handle him.'

'You are impertinent. We have been married just under two weeks. I do not think the question of "handling" him comes into it yet – if indeed it ever will. At the moment we shall just have to rely on our love for one another to carry us through whatever difficulties we may face.'

'Bravo, prettily spoken. How charmingly naive you are.'

'Naive!'

'Yes, naive. Naive to think you will be able to handle Peter Cunningham for long. Why has he married you? I'll tell you. Partly to get away from his mother of course; she did not like him out her sight – in case he got into mischief. He's a naughty boy, is Master Cunningham, and needs a firm hand. Clearly Mrs Cunningham Senior thought that if she couldn't spare the time to watch him, she would find a nice sensible girl to do it for her – and it seems she has. She promised to double his allowance the day he married you, from five hundred to a thousand. I believe that is right? Or perhaps he hasn't told you?'

Julia did not believe this. How on earth could this woman know such a thing? But she kept a strong grip on herself.

'You are very bitter, Mrs Bradshaw. Why?'

'Not bitter. Clear-headed. Perhaps I know your husband better than you do – you see, I've seen him when he's away from his mama's watchful eye.'

'Well, do you know, Mrs Bradshaw, I think we've talked long enough, so I will wish you a good afternoon. And before I do, I will say this.' Julia stood up. 'My husband is not perfect, I am well aware of that, and no doubt he has come into contact with many young women of more or less respectable character before now. He has had plenty of time to look around, Mrs Bradshaw, and no doubt plenty of eligible young women have made their interest in him clear. I am not so naive as you think – and I can see that he is drawn to attractive young women, as any young man is. But, and this is the point, Mrs Bradshaw, he has chosen me. I do not presume to question his motives. He could have gone elsewhere but he has chosen me, and I shall do him the honour to believe that because he has told me he loves me and asked me to be his wife, he meant it. And I mean it too, Mrs Bradshaw. I have sworn to love honour and obey him, and am fully adequate to the task, I assure you, and do not need to listen to innuendo and tittle-tattle from vindictive and petty-minded women.'

As she walked away, Julia's head was buzzing. Where was Becky? she kept asking herself, trying to shut out of her mind the ugly and vile things Grace Bradshaw had said. Had his mother bribed him to marry herself? He was to inherit the property – what power had she over him, anyway? It was a malicious smear on his character, and left her feeling mean and soiled, as if she wanted to run home to the hotel and have a bath to clean off the impression that woman had made.

What could possibly have prompted her to it? Female jealousy? Love of gossip and speculation? Worse, a hatred of seeing anyone, seeing any young couple, happy together?

Julia walked quickly towards the booth where ice-creams were

139

dispensed, and saw Becky sitting very happily spooning up hers. Julia could have swept her into her arms and hugged her, she was so relieved.

Chapter Sixteen

She would dearly love to have questioned Peter about Grace Bradshaw, but couldn't see what it would achieve. Whatever there had been between them, if anything, he would still brush it aside, with a laugh. Better not to mention it.

Julia's feelings about Bad Homburg were not improved by this meeting, as may be imagined, and if it had been up to her they would have left first thing in the morning.

Peter however was agog to visit the casino. Clearly it exercised a potent influence over his imagination, so that evening after dinner, Julia went upstairs to change, and towards ten they walked to the great Palace of Chance.

'We'll just watch tonight, Julia,' Peter said as they walked through the park, gaily lit by gas lights among the trees.

She had not inherited any theological scruples against gambling as such but it was contrary to her housekeeping instincts. Still, men enjoyed these things, and one was entitled after all on one's honeymoon to a little harmless indulgence. No doubt real life would call them back soon enough.

The building was ablaze with light, the carriages swept past them and up to the *porte cochère*, and there was a festive air, pulses quickened, the senses sharpened, and excitement was in the air. As they went in, Julia left her cloak at the *garderobe* and they went up the wide staircase. On either side, twisting barleysugar columns soared to the ceiling, which was a swirl of elaborate cornices, gold leaf, and painted designs with a swirling mass of gods and goddesses, stark naked and enjoying an elysian feast on the clouds. The doors at the head of the stairs were wide, spacious and open, and inside was lit in such a way as to throw the light downwards, concentrating attention on the gaming tables. The walls were hung with a dark red silk which seemed to absorb the light and returned a deep fiery glow, dimming away towards the ceiling.

An intense atmosphere of excitement, a loud buzz of chatter, sudden shouts of excitement, and sudden cries of disappointment. The rooms – there were several leading off each other – were crowded, and as they first ventured in, they could not see the tables, as men and women pressed round, leaning in, gesticulating and calling to each other, or invoking the Goddess Fortune to their aid, and always in and among them, a constant movement to and fro between the tables.

At first it was bewildering, and they wandered among the tables together, taking it all in. Julia found in herself a healthy puritan streak, a frank distaste for this folly, and worse, this abandon as she saw it of human dignity and reason. The feverish gleam in the eye, the sudden cries of elation as someone scooped a handful of gold coins and paper slips to his place, the equally sudden curse, half stifled on the lips – it did not bring out the best in people, she thought. As for gambling herself, she had not the slightest inclination. She might win – what then, she had not earned it; she might lose, and then how could she face the consequences of her own folly? There were many worthy, honourable, and important courses in life, but as far as Julia was concerned, gambling was not one of them.

Such was not the case with Peter, however, as she had already guessed. He would not be happy until he had his flutter at the tables. They were standing at one of the tables, when a a middle-aged man, stuffing a cigar between his lips, swept up a handful of coins and paper slips, and rose to go. Peter slipped adroitly into his place.

Opposite him, a fashionably dressed lady smiled, and then noticing Julia at his shoulder, her glance dropped.

The game was roulette.

'Well, here goes. What's your birthdate, Julia? The twenty-eighth, isn't it? Here goes for jolly old number twenty-eight.'

Twenty-eight did not come up, but this did nothing to dampen Peter's spirits.

'Why don't we stick to the colours – stand a better chance – here's one for the red.'

Le Rouge came up, and he pulled in his winnings. About them, there was a continual leaning in, and a pushing of piles of gold coins and slips of paper across the green baise. A croupier with the sangfroid of an English butler called out with a monotonous chant, '*Faites vos jeux! Rien ne va plus!*' The wheel spun, and it was '*Le Quinze. Impair, Noir!*' and so on, in a dull repetition.

Watching the game it seemed to her the most futile thing imaginable. Almost anything would have been more interesting than this.

142

Another visit to the opera, for instance, would have been lovely, or even just listening to the band. Or best of all, to go back to their room and go to bed together.

Julia saw, however, that Peter's attention was now riveted on the wheel, and she resigned herself to enduring the game for a while anyway.

Sometimes he won, sometimes he lost. There was something endearing about his childlike enjoyments and disappointments. He would win – hurrah! – as if he had the been the first man ever to win a prize or open a present on his birthday, such was the novelty; he would lose, then the strained expression, the curling in of the lip, the quick drawn in breath. Julia watched it all.

Half an hour went by, and then he stood, up with a sudden, 'Well, that's me for tonight!'

'Had enough?' she smiled at him, teasingly.

'Broke, old girl.' He took a deep breath. 'But I shall return!'

'How much have you lost?'

They were making their way among the tables; Peter looked wistfully at the play going on still, as they passed by.

'Um? Oh, I don't know – fifty or so.'

'Fifty? What, florins?'

'No – pounds, you noodle!'

'Fifty pounds!' Julia stopped him. 'You have just lost fifty pounds – there, in that short time?'

''Fraid so.' Peter was unruffled. 'But I shall win it back – no fear!'

His confidence and good humour were invincible, but Julia was appalled. She knew exactly what fifty pounds was worth – in terms of servants' wages, household bills, joints of mutton.

Peter would have to be handled carefully. Lightly if possible. She had reclaimed her cloak and they were strolling back to the hotel through the park.

'I say, that was a bit of fun, though. I always knew I should like it here.'

'What do you mean?'

'Oh, you know fellows in college used to talk about it – the casino and so forth. This is the place. Why, some of the men at that tabie – crowned heads, Julia, grand dukes, archdukes, all sorts. The *crème de la crème* of Europe here, don't you know.'

Julia didn't know what to say that wouldn't hurt his feelings. There was silence between them for a little, as Peter swung his cane, and whistled.

'Yes, this is the life. Who'd ever want to go home? You enjoying it Julia?'

How could she say no? She snuggled in close on his arm.

'Where shall we go next?'

'Eh? I thought we were going to stay here for a while. Don't you like it?'

'Well, there's so much more – the Black Forest, or perhaps we could go to Switzerland, and walk in the mountains.'

'Um? Yes, dare say. Eventually. No hurry, Julia, we'll just stay on a while yet.'

When they reached the hotel, and it was after midnight, Peter was pleased to find his friend Morley waiting in the bar.

'You run along upstairs, Julia. Here's Morley, we'll have just a glass of this lager beer, and then I'll be up myself.'

There was nothing she could do, and so with a good grace she said goodnight to the two men, took a candle and went up to her room.

She had told Becky not to wait up, so she set the candle on the mantelpiece, and set about undressing herself.

The evening had gone all wrong. As she pulled the drawstrings of her petticoats, unthreaded her stays, piece by piece shedding her clothes and throwing them over the back of a chair, she ran through the evening.

Peter had been bored. That was the horrible truth. He had been bored with her. First he couldn't wait to get to the gaming tables, and then later, as she thought at last they would be in bed together, there was his friend Mr Morley, and without a thought they had gone for a drink. How long he would be, she could not guess. It would be no use waiting for him, that was sure.

As for the fifty pounds, she couldn't even bring herself to think about it. Fifty pounds! When she thought of what they could have bought with that money!

Pulling her nightdress over her head, she climbed into bed. For the first time since they had left England, she was unhappy. It was all this horrible Bad Homburg. She hated the town. Hated all its flashy glamour, its ostentatious money. But how long was Peter going to want to stay now that he had found it? Slowly she fell asleep.

In the morning Peter was there on the pillow beside her, and she immediately felt better. He was fast asleep though, and she didn't want to disturb him, so she climbed carefully out of bed, and went and opened the shutter a little. Another lovely day, the trees in the avenue smelled so fresh and inviting; she felt her fears had been foolish. It was a beautiful town after all, everywhere beautiful buildings and parks – why shouldn't they stay a few days? How foolish she was! If Peter wanted to lose a bit of money – though she still winced at the thought of the fifty pounds – well, it was his money after all. She could hardly tell him how to spend it, could she?

She sat at the little table and wrote a letter to Aunt Frances. Again, as in her first letter, she found she had to edit the contents for her aunt's ear. A pity she couldn't tell . . . she put down the pen, staring out through the gap in the shutters. If she were quite honest with herself, she had always known what Peter was like, hadn't she? He had done nothing yet that had taken her by surprise. Honestly? Of course he wasn't perfect. No man was. And even if Grace Bradshaw had made eyes at him once – it didn't matter, she had always known he had an eye for pretty girls; and she was quite strong enough to make up for his little weaknesses. Still, the gambling . . . that had been a shock, she had to admit.

Peter slept on and on, and in the end, she began to get hungry, so she left a note, and called Becky to come and dress her – there was a pretty little dressing room adjoining their bedroom. Then she went down for some breakfast. It was odd breakfasting alone, but that was too bad. There was a selection of newspapers hanging on hooks by the door – even a copy of *The Times*, three days old, so she took it and ate her *brötchen*, drank her coffee, read the paper, and really it was quite pleasant. She would look up every so often in case Peter came into the dining room, but he didn't, and eventually when she had read the paper as much as she had a mind to, and it was now nearly eleven o'clock, she returned to the room.

Peter was still fast asleep. The note she had written was untouched, lying where she had left it. She stood looking down at him, his beautiful face looking so innocent, so undisturbed, the hair untidy across his brow. And again the warmth of her love rushed through her, and she wanted to sweep him to her, and hold him and cherish him, and protect him.

Then he stirred, and after a moment, opened his eyes.

'Hullo, pretty lady.'

'Good morning, kind sir. I trust you slept well?'

'Umm? Yes.' He looked about. 'Is it late?'

'Half-past eleven.'

'Lord. You were asleep when I came up last night.'

'How was your friend?'

'Morley? Oh, all right, you know. We just had a chat, that's all. I say, Julia, ring for Franks, will you? Do you think you might tell them to bring me up a spot of breakfast here, hmm?'

145

'Whatever you command, O master,' she smiled, and rang the bell pull. 'It's a lovely morning out.'

'Have you had breakfast?'

'Yes, and read *The Times*. They have it here, only it's three days old.'

'Lord, last thing I should want to do, on my honeymoon. Lot of dreary politics.'

She went back and sat on the edge of the bed.

'What shall we do today?'

'Oh, I said I'd meet Morley after lunch – two-ish. Lord, don't leave much time, does it?'

'Oh. And what are we going to do?'

Peter was a little embarrassed.

'Well, actually Julia, Morley said he hadn't seen the casino yet, so I said I'd show him round, you see, so that's what we're going to do. Frankly I didn't think you'd want to come, not very interesting for you, I could see. Why don't you go for a walk with Becky – you like walking, don't you?'

'I like walking with you better.'

'And nothing I like better either, my darling. It's just – well Morley was badgering me to go with him to the casino, you see, and now I've promised.'

Again Julia felt she was up against some invisible barrier. Peter wanted to do it. Obviously. And equally obviously if he wanted to do it, there was nothing she could say. It would be futile and weak to start complaining. She remained bright.

'Very well. Have you any idea how long you will be there?'

'No idea. Couple of hours? Might have a tiny flutter – just a little one, Julia – got to win back back some of my money, after all.'

He laughed, and reaching across pulled her down on the bed beside him.

'Kiss me.'

Julia needed no second invitation. All her need, her mighty capacity for love was his, at a moment's notice; if he did but open his arms, she was there.

'Oh, I say, steady on, old thing! Let a man get his breath.' He laughed. 'I must say this, Julia, you really are a capital girl. Really, the best. And I think I'm the luckiest dog on earth to have got you for my own. I mean – you never nag a chap, or look down in the dumps.'

He kissed her again. Her love for him swelled within her, and she knew again that she had done the right thing; of course there would be difficulties, and of course she would have to bite back her words

146

sometimes, contain her feelings, but still, oh, it was worth it, everything, for moments like this when they were so close, so easy with one another.

'My darling.' She ran her hand across his face.

There was a discreet knock on the door.

They disengaged themselves.

'That'll be Franks. Come in. Now listen, old thing, I'm going to have a shave, get dressed, and then have a bit of breakfast. Then around two I'm meeting Morley, and we'll probably be back around five. All right?'

It was true what they said. Men could do without women sometimes – could switch them right out of their lives. It was harder for women. It was going to be an empty afternoon for her, whereas Peter, with his friend, at the casino – would he even think of her once?

Later she and Becky went out for a walk round the town; they chatted, admired the spacious buildings, Julia read bits out of Murray, they strolled up and down the Luisenstrasse, where the best shops were and looked in shop windows, and then, to her surprise, they found a book-shop. As Julia stared in through the window she saw they had books in French as well as German, so she thought she would perhaps browse around, and told Becky to come back for her in a quarter of an hour.

Many of the books were in French, she saw, as she began to look along the shelves. All kinds of titles, and in particular a lot of fiction. Of course in those days in England, the words 'French Novel' carried a heavy overtone of moral dubiousness, so she was especially curious. Some of the stories she recognised and had in fact read, *The Count of Monte Cristo* and *The Three Musketeers*, but there other authors she didn't know so well, Balzac and Zola, and she looked through them carefully; unexpectedly it seemed to her she was going to have time on her hands, on her honeymoon, something she had not anticipated. It might be a good idea to get something to read. Then further along she picked up another one she had never heard of, *Madame Bovary*, and opening it here and there, began reading at random, and thought it looked interesting, so she bought it. It would help to fill up the time, and keep her mind busy.

She and Becky went to the park, where the band was playing, sat as they had done the previous day, under a large lime tree, and Julia read her book. Becky fidgeted for a while, so Julia gave her the money to buy an ice-cream. Becky ran off, and then Julia became

147

quite immersed in her book. Her French was good, and she read it almost as fast as if it had been in English.

It was good, It was very good indeed. The author seemed to have a real understanding of what it was to be a woman. No English male author did – she found the women in Messrs Dickens and Thackeray wooden, melodramatic or caricatures – though she admired Mrs Gaskell whose stories were printed in *Household Words* which was read in the kitchen at Stallbridge, and which Julia used to look into from time to time.

But this – this was in a class apart; she became completely engrossed.

Eventually Becky returned, so Julia put the book into her bag, which could just about take it, and they walked on, and eventually arrived back at the hotel.

It was not yet five, so Julia ordered tea on the terrace, and let Becky go, and opened her book again. The tea was very refreshing – and drunk in the continental style with lemon, a nice change – and once again she became completely engrossed in the book, the story of the young farmer's daughter with her head stuffed full of romantic dreams. The author had such a sympathy for her, and yet such a clear understanding too, no trace of sentimentality, and he followed her through the trail of her follies and her evasions and subterfuges, as she sought romance in that little French town – as if she Julia, trapped in Stallbridge had sought happiness in an illicit liaison.

How different was her case from that of Emma Bovary. Emma had made a foolish marriage with a man who could never satisfy her cravings for romantic love, no, not in a thousand years, a man of very common clay indeed; whereas she – she set the book down on the table for a moment and looked across the park, not seeing the gracious carriages as they rolled past; she, well, perhaps she too had had romantic yearnings – had yearned to be loved and to be able to give love – but unlike Emma Bovary, the man she had loved, had by some miracle asked her to be his wife. And in that affirmation had come a great strength, and she had the confidence and the strength to go forward with Peter in their life together, whatever might lie ahead.

But it was a very good book. She read on, oblivious, and time passed, and suddenly she was aware that it was seven o'clock, and still no sign on Peter.

She shut up the book. Perhaps he had gone up their room without seeing her on the terrace?

She went up, but the room was empty. She kicked off her boots, and threw herself on the bed and closed her eyes.

148

Eventually he would have to come back for dinner. His stomach would bring him back if nothing else.

At eight o'clock there was no sign of him. She felt a little hungry so she rang the bell and asked them to send her up some sandwiches.

Nine o'clock, and no sign. She could not read, could not think, had got into a state of agitation she found it more and more difficult to control. Surely he couldn't still be at the casino? It was impossible. What on earth was he doing?

Every instinct made her want to dash out and find him, but every ounce of her training told her not to. He would come in, in his own good time. He was lord of his own life, and one thing he did not want to hear was recriminations from her. If he chose to stay out, that was his prerogative. Unfortunately for her.

Chapter Seventeen

At eleven o'clock Peter came in.

He seemed alert, not drunk, but elated. His hands were in his pockets, and his hair was untidy on his forehead.

'Well!'

He beamed at her. She sat at the table, and looked up at him. She didn't know what to say.

'That's torn it!'

'What?'

'Julia, my dear, I've blown the lot!'

She stood up. Better let him go on.

'Blown – the – lot.'

He sat on the edge of the bed and pulled his boots off, and sat there for a moment, holding them in his hands and looking up at her. 'You behold me – broke.'

This was almost outside the range of her experience.

'Broke?'

He threw the boots across the room, and took her hand as she came to him.

'Julia, old girl, my dearest, light of my life, steel yourself. We are – broke.'

'You keep saying that. What do you mean?'

'It's very, very simple. I have lost every last farthing.'

'You are joking? I beg you, Peter, don't –'

'No joke. It's all gone.'

'But – well, what are we – how are we going – well, how are we going to pay the hotel bill? Our meals – everything.'

'That's it. Tickler, isn't it?'

Suddenly a coldness came over her. She could no longer let things drift out of her control.

'Let me understand you correctly. You have gambled away all

150

your money.'

'That's right.'

'The Letters of Credit as well?'

'The lot.'

'Why?'

'Ah!' He threw himself back on the bed. 'Why indeed? The lure of the green baize.'

'And how are we going to finish our journey?'

'It's a question, isn't it?'

'Well, let me ask you another question. As you threw those notes down on the table, did you ask yourself how the hotel bill is to be settled? How we are to carry on? How we are to get home? Have you thought of that? How are we to get home?'

'I know – it's awful isn't it? What are we going to do, old girl?'

He didn't seem concerned in the least. Her patience snapped.

'Peter! How could you be so stupid?' He sat up as her voice lashed him. 'Did you think of me? You know we still have weeks left. We were going to go on – to the Black Forest, or Switzerland. How could you let yourself throw that money away – our money for our honeymoon?'

Peter was seeing this side of her for the first time. He was dismayed.

'I don't know, Julia. Don't nag, I beg you.'

'Don't nag? Peter, we are on our honeymoon, my darling, we are celebrating our marriage. Does that mean nothing to you? Does it mean so little that you could go off with your crony and lose *all* your money?'

She swung away from him and walked across the room, stood for a moment, staring unseeing at the wall, then turned and walked back towards him, still lying on the bed watching her. Her mind was a blank. She rubbed her hand across her chin, one hand on her hip, thinking furiously. But thinking or not, her mind was a blank. What were they to do?

Peter clearly had no idea. She went to the table and took up her reticule, took out her purse, and emptied it on to the table, and sat down to count her money. This was the remainder of Aunt Frances's gift.

She stared at the money for a moment.

'We have a return from Cologne booked, haven't we?'

'Hmm? Think so. Why?'

'Where are the tickets?'

'Oh – er –' He thought. 'Well, should be in the trunk somewhere, I think – or else in my coat pocket. No that one – in the wardrobe.'

151

Julia found the coat and pulled some papers from the pocket. Crumpled up among them were the through tickets from Cologne to London.

'Well, that's something. We just have to get to Cologne. And settle up here. But we've never enough. Never in a thousand years.'

She folded up the tickets and put them into her reticule. There were going to be no more accidents.

'There's no use crying over spilt milk. What's done's done. In the morning we'll ask for the bill, and see how much we are short.'

'What shall we do?' Peter watched all this with an almost polite interest, as if somehow it scarcely concerned him.

'It's possible Franks may be able to lend us something, though I don't like borrowing from servants. If we still haven't enough, I can pawn my jewellery. There's this locket . . .'

'No! I absolutely forbid you to, Julia!'

She laughed.

'Have you any other idea?'

'Why don't we just do a flit?'

'Are you serious?'

'Why not? What a lark, eh? Just vanish, like a puff of smoke!'

'Peter –' she drew a breath ' – I know you're joking, but just consider for one moment. I have a trunkful of clothes here. Are you proposing to leave them all behind?'

'Well, what are clothes after all? We can always get you some more.'

He still couldn't understand the seriousness of their situation. Julia looked down at the money on the table, idly pushing the gold coins about and realigning them into little groups as she tried to plan out their next movements.

'Did you ask your friend if he would lend you any money?'

'Ooh-er, rather not, Julia. I'm not in *very* good odour with that family. Freddie didn't have more than a tenner on him, and his pa is as tight as an oyster.'

'Well, there's nothing more we can do tonight. We might as well go to bed. Tomorrow we'll get the bill and see how much we need.'

'Rather. I must say, Julia, you're taking this very well. I'm most terribly grateful, you know. Some girls would have skinned me alive, but you – why you're as cool as a cucumber.' He was smiling up at her, still sprawled on the bed. She was standing looking down at him.

'Peter, I'd better be honest with you. I'm not pleased. It was downright stupid of you. You've ruined our honeymoon, quite simply. I must say, I cannot understand how you, how any sane

152

man, could go and lose *all* his money. But as I said, it's done, and we shall have to plan accordingly. Let's go to bed.'

Wearily she began pulling her clothes off, throwing items over the back of a chair, and now, at this most inopportune moment, Peter became amorous. He was extraordinary. His antics at the casino had temporarily killed any feeling for love in her. She only wanted to get into bed, go to sleep and forget.

'I'm sorry, I'm tired.'

'Sorry, old girl,' he cajoled, in her ear, running his hand over her back as sat on the side of the bed, pulling off her stockings. 'Who's a pretty lady?'

'Peter, all I want to do is go to sleep. It's past midnight. Come on, we've got to make decisions in the morning.'

'Oh, all right.' He bumped away. 'Where's Franks when I need him?'

'Franks has gone to bed hours ago, and we are not dragging him out now.'

'Well, I want him. What's he for, for heavens sake?' Peter was moving to the bell.

'No, Peter, just leave your clothes, you are not waking Franks now.'

'What?'

'Get into bed.'

He watched her for a moment as she turned down the bedclothes.

'Oh, all right.'

But it was a long time before she could get to sleep. At this moment she wasn't sure how they were going to get out of this hotel.

On the following morning the manager politely presented his compliments and the account. Julia scanned it, totted up her money again, had a private conversation with Franks, in which it transpired that he did have a little money which he could advance them, and by the additional means of selling some pieces of jewellery – not her locket, she was relieved to find – the account was duly settled, and that afternoon they were in the train for Cologne.

It was a strange atmosphere. No one spoke much. Becky was bewildered, Julia was light-headed with lack of sleep, but Peter appeared his usual nonchalant self, and whistled a tuneless sort of whistle as the porters loaded their boxes. Julia watched the porters. She wasn't trusting Peter to do anything from now on. No doubt in future they would be able to settle down together into some kind of routine, but at this minute she wasn't going to take any chances. She had the tickets, and what little remained of their money, just about enough to buy them all a couple of meals on the journey.

They reached London, and didn't have enough for a hotel, so she sent a wire to Stallbridge and they took the last train at night, when they had been travelling it seemed for ever, train, boat, train, and a carriage across London.

While they were all sitting together in the dark cab, rattling through the night street, Peter suddenly said, 'Now listen, everybody. Once we're back in Stallbridge there's to be no word of this to anyone. All right? If anyone remarks on it you can just say – oh, I don't know, tell them I changed my mind. Or just say you don't know why we're back early. All right?'

They were all tired, and no one spoke.

Then another train, and they finally arrived at the station at three in the morning, where Belton, the Cunninghams' old coachman, was waiting for them, yawning and half asleep.

They were half asleep themselves, and Julia was depressed but very pleased to be home. They arrived at the Old Manor House to find Mrs Cunningham waiting up for them, wide awake, and pleased to see them, and even a bit of supper laid out. None of them was in a state to eat, however, and they went straight to bed.

However, as they were just climbing into bed, Julia said to Peter, 'I am not going to tell any lies. I shan't say anything about it myself, and I shall try to shield you as much as possible, but if your mother questions me – as I am sure she will – I will not tell any outright lies. Not now, or ever.'

As soon as she woke, Julia knew that Mrs Cunningham was going to want an explanation of their curtailed plans. She wasn't very pleased with Julia as it was, because of the sudden and hasty way she and Peter had run away to get married – almost eloped, frankly, – and she had been deprived of a mother's right to weep at her own son's wedding. Still it was done – for good and sufficient reasons as far as Julia was concerned – they were back with a bump, and she must take a deep breath and start facing the world. There was much to be done.

She got out of bed and looked out of the window; it was a cloudy day, with a dampness in the air, but there came a heavenly scent from the garden, and there was something so English about the lush dampness and profusion of the flowers, something so simple and unspoilt about the garden, that she was thankful to be home in Stallbridge.

She drew a robe over her nightgown and wandered out and downstairs.

154

Mrs Cunningham was sitting at a table in the drawing room.

'Good morning, my dear. Recovered from your journey, I hope?'

'I am a little tired, I admit. Peter is still asleep.'

'Let him sleep, poor boy. Well, my dear, you can imagine when we had your wire, we were full of curiosity to know why you have cut short your honeymoon. Nothing too drastic, I hope? Homesick for Stallbridge?'

'I am afraid we ran through our money a little faster than we had anticipated.'

Mrs Cunningham didn't believe this. Peter had been given plenty of money, but it didn't take long to worm the truth out of Julia. She had no intention of becoming a shield between Peter and his mother.

'Lost it all?' She smiled. 'Well, that's Peter. I hope you weren't too shocked?'

'I was surprised, of course. We had planned to go on and explore southern Germany. As it is we have had to race home. Incidentally Franks had to lend us some money, and I should like him reimbursed as soon as possible.'

'Oh, Franks will get his money, never mind about that.'

Julia wrote a short note to Aunt Frances and sent Beckie over to the rectory with it. It was just to ask when would be a suitable time to come over to see her. Her father had forbidden her the house, but he did go out sometimes, and she wanted very much to see her home again. In any case she and Peter would be setting up home together soon enough, and she would eventually wish to have her things with her.

After breakfast Lizzie cornered her.

'I must say, Julia you took us all by surprise. I mean, running away to get married – you! Of all people! What a daredevil you are. I never imagined! And beating me to the altar too, and I was so congratulating myself on being first. But I don't mind at all, of course, and I'm so happy for you. Look, let's go and walk in the garden – more private. Now tell me –' as they emerged from the house '– between ourselves, of course, how did you get on? Are you going to be happy together?'

'Lizzie, of course we are. We love each other.'

'Oh, I know all that. But I mean to say, Julia – Peter's rather a handful, isn't he?'

'Lizzie, I don't mind that one iota. He's very good to me, and we are going to suit very well, I promise you.'

Lizzie gave Julia one of her shrewd glances, narrowing her eyes.

'Sure? Of course you're the very best thing that could happen to

155

him – just the girl he needs – but you know, you'd better keep a
grasp on the purse strings –'

'Lizzie, what Peter does with his own money is his business. I can't
run his life for him.'

'Well, dear, you're going to run his house for him, aren't you?
Comes to much the same thing. Just try and make sure you get the a
regular allowance out of him.'

Julia smiled.

'Lizzie – you'll just have to trust me. Ah, here comes Becky.'

The girl was running towards them up the garden path.

She had a note from Aunt Frances:

Julia, my dearest,
Your father is usually out of the the house – as I am sure you
yourself know – between three and four when he goes for a breath
of air. I shall look forward to seeing you then.

With warmest love,
Frances Maxwell

'I shall take Peter to meet my aunt, Lizzie.'

Peter eventually emerged at one o'clock, and they sat down to
lunch. It was an odd sensation for Julia not to be in charge of
arrangements, and she was conscious of being a guest in another
woman's house.

Peter showed no great inclination to visit the rectory, but Julia
insisted, and at three they were at the door. Annie opened it.

'Oh, Miss Stone – Mrs Cunningham, I should say – how lovely to
see you!'

Julia embraced her.

'Where is my aunt?'

'In the drawing room, miss – missis – oh, I don't know, I'm all
muddled up, but I'm that pleased to see you I can't say.'

Aunt Frances came out of the drawing room at that moment and
they embraced, and then Julia was introducing Peter, who was was
debonair, easy and charming, which came so easy to him, when he
chose.

'Come in, my dear – of course I want to hear all about your trip.
You are looking so well! Marriage is doing you good as I knew it
would! How do you do, sir? I am so pleased to make your acquaintance at last. I have heard so much from Julia about you. Do come
in. Annie, tea! Now, let us all be comfortable. Your father won't be
back for an hour – and – well, no matter. It can't be helped. Now,
my dear, tell me all about it.'

Peter sat patiently while Julia gave Frances an edited version of their journey.

Francis had had her letters, and was already well informed.

'Well, as I told you, in my letter Julia, he is not pleased, not pleased at all, there is no escaping the fact. Of course he won't allow me into his room, but from the glimpses I get it seems in an awful pickle, papers and books everywhere on the table, on the floor.'

Julia felt terribly guilty for that moment, looking at the floor, biting her underlip.

'I really must do what I can to find him a secretary.'

'I must say Mr Grahame has been *very* good. I believe he has been doing a lot for your father – not that he could ever take your place, of course. Since you went away, Dr Stone has not preached a sermon – could not bring himself to show his face in the village as you can imagine – but once you have been round and made your visits, and shown off your new husband, people will soon forget and I have no doubt things can get back on to an even keel.'

Julia smiled at Peter.

'Are you ready, my dear? We shall have to make our visits.'

'Yes, suppose so.'

'There is one thing – after you had gone I took the liberty of engaging another girl to take the place of your Becky. I hope I did the right thing, but I was assured she was a good girl, and so far she has given satisfaction.'

'Really, Aunt? And who have you chosen?'

'Well, a very pretty girl, Amelia Goodrich – your gardner's daughter.'

'Emmy! Of course, Aunt, you did very well, a very nicely spoken girl, and willing to please.'

'And by the by, my dear, that brings me to another question – I too shall have to take my leave, so we shall have to put our heads together and decide what is to be done.'

Annie brought in the tea tray, and Julia said, 'Annie, if Mr Grahame is in, will you present my compliments and tell him we would be happy if he would join us for tea?'

'Yes, Mrs Cunningham.'

And in fact in a few minutes there was a knock on the door, and Arthur was there. He did not smile, but came gravely into the room and shook hands with them, even Peter – whom he detested – felicitated them on their marriage and sat for a few minutes making very small talk, feeling constrained, and a little later got up and left again.

Soon after Frances said, 'It's getting on, dear – shouldn't you be thinking of going?'

And Julia said, 'I think I should wait, Aunt. I want Father to shake hands with Peter.'

Both Peter and Frances looked at her.

'Dear, is that wise?'

'I don't know, Aunt, but it is right. I have that right. He shall acknowledge my husband.'

Chapter Eighteen

Frances looked grave.

'You know best.'

Julia turned to Peter and reached out for his hand. 'You don't mind, dear, do you?'

'Goodness me, no. I'll shake the old chap's hand – why not?'

After this the atmosphere became strained and conversation was fitful, and then after another ten minutes they saw the figure of Dr Stone come past the drawing-room window, and open the front door, and Julia went quickly to the drawing-room door, opened it and met him face to face.

'Father.'

Stone was silent, looking at her.

'Will you not say how do you do?'

She held out her hand. He did not respond. Then he said in a low voice, 'We have spoken before on this subject, Julia. You have abandoned this house, and deserted me. The responsibility lies on your own head.'

He was about to make a move, but she would not let him.

'I should like to introduce my husband, Father.'

Peter and Frances were in the drawing room watching through the open door.

Stone muttered, 'I have no wish – or intention – of meeting your husband.'

Julia stood fully in front of him, face to face, and said quietly, 'Father, you shall meet him, and shake his hand.'

'Shall?'

'I say you shall – you owe it to me.'

'And what do you owe to me?'

Julia was silent and Stone went on, his voice growing in intensity, 'How is my work to continue? After so many years, it is at a standstill. How can I continue? You have abandoned your responsibilities in this house, run away – on the spur of an idle caprice – ruined the labour of many, many years. Julia, you have ruined my work! More then ten years work on the Commentary, and you have destroyed it. By this thoughtless and frivolous action –'

Julia, filled with guilt, became conciliatory.

'Father, I will help you. I mean – that is – I will help you to find a secretary. I am sure we could easily find a young graduate who would be most willing to share your work and do it far better than I.'

'You shall not buy your way into my favour,' Dr Stone went on implacably. 'You deserted me – deliberately deserted my work – knowing its importance, knowing how many years I have laboured on it, knowing how precious it is to me. Ran away with barely any warning, left me bereft, unable to continue. It is out of the question we can be reconciled, unthinkable. You have destroyed my love for you.'

'No!'

'Yes, I say,' and he was breaking past her towards his room, but she turned with him and seized his arm.

'Father! Do not say that! How can you cast off your own daughter?'

'You have cast yourself off. It is your own responsibility. I have disowned you.'

'Father, it was my right! It was my right to marry! You could not ask me to remain here all my life.'

'Away! I will not hear!'

He pushed her away so that she knocked hard against the door post, and a second later the door of his study slammed shut.

Julia shuddered into long heaving sobs. Frances put her arm round her and urged her into the drawing room, and made her sit on the window seat. The two women sat with Julia's head on Frances' shoulder.

Julia was incoherent but at last her words could be made out.

'He disowned me, Aunt. Oh, I can't bear it. He disowned me. How could he after all – after all those years that I worked and worked and wrote, every day, day after day, writing and translating for him? To cast me off! Oh, it's unbearable, and not even to shake hands with Peter. Aunt, what shall I do?'

'Hush, dear, you have Peter now to care for you. You have your husband, and you will build a new life together.'

Peter was watching all this, unable to see what he could do in the situation, waiting for Julia's weeping to subside, which it did gradually, until she pulled herself upright, dabbing at her eyes, sometimes heaving up a great racking breath, as if to reflate her whole body.

'Oh, I'm sorry, do forgive me, I shall soon be myself. Peter, what must you think? My dear, I am so sorry to have brought you into this. I should never have brought you what must you think –'

'Hush, dear,' Frances said, her hand on Julia's arm.

Julia looked up at Peter, her face shiny with tears.

'Hold me, my darling, just for a moment.'

Peter took her in his arms, difficult for him, not something that came very easily, and tried to make soothing remarks.

'There, there, old girl, not to worry. We'll get out of Stallbridge anyway. Who cares? And we'll just let the old boy go hang, what?'

'Aunt, I must make arrangements for a secretary – and a house-keeper. Oh dear.'

'Don't say any more now, Julia. I'll call on you this evening and we'll make plans when you are recovered. It's been a shock for you.'

Julia rose, and they were about to go out together into the hall when there was a timid knock at the door, and it opened. Emmy Goodrich was there, in a white pinafore, with a white cotton cap on her abundant chestnut curls, looking as pretty and sunny as she ever had.

'Beg pardon, ma'am, shall –'

She stopped as she saw Peter, and Peter stopped as he saw her. His arm was round Julia's shoulder. Immediately he looked back down at Julia, and Frances said, 'Yes, that's all right, Emmy, you can take the tea things.'

But once more, as they were going out of the door, Peter looked back at Emmy, and she looked up at him as she gathered the tea cups on to the tray. Emmy looked pretty in any position, and even in such a simple action as bending over to gather up the tea things there was a intrinsic charm and grace to her. Peter saw it, and saw the long look she gave him.

When they got back to the Old Manor House Julia went to bed and stayed there for the rest of the day, sleeping and waking, and then lying half awake and half asleep, sometimes dreaming, sometimes hearing again her father, and feeling again the horrible feeling of rejection, the coldness, as if she were nothing, as if all her pride in herself were annihilated, and she could be wiped out of account.

Peter came up and sat on the side of the bed.

'I say, Julia, can't have this, you know.'

'I'm sorry, my darling.'

'Listen, don't you think about it, do you hear? That's what we got

161

married for. Put all this behind us – get out of the village. God, I hate all this, this small village life – all the backbiting and tittle-tattle.'

She smiled weakly up at him.

'What do you mean?'

'Well, what I mean to say is, Julia, you and I, we'll go off and find ourselves a snug little place in London, and really start to live, eh?'

'Whatever you like, my darling.'

She reached up her arms and threaded them round his neck, and he leant over and kissed her, and then, before either knew it, he was in bed beside her, and they made love, and it was the best they had ever done it, she just opening and opening to him. And afterwards, lying side by side, she thought things were really going to be all right.

The following morning Frances came.

'I called last night, dear, but they told me you had gone to bed. It must have been such a shock for you, poor lamb. Of course, I expected it. But he must come round in the end. He must.'

'Yes. I shall write to Christ Church and make enquiries. There should be no difficulty finding a young man to act as secretary. As for housekeeper –'

'I have been thinking about that, Julia. And do you know, I think we might do worse than promote young Annie. I know she's only nineteen, but I have been talking with her, and she seems to have a very sound head on her shoulders. She knows the household back-wards, and –'

'That's very kind of you, Aunt. But I'm afraid Annie would never be able to control Mrs Oldham. Oh dear. I know I should be there.'

'Now, now, dear. We have been through that.'

Julia thought for a while, looking out of the window.

'Well. Perhaps we could try, just for a while. How is her accounting?'

'I've been giving her a try, Julia, letting her cast up the accounts for me – you know, as if I were too foolish to know how to do it, just to see how she got on – and she is a very quick girl. I do think you might do worse.'

'Aunt, you are very good to me.'

'Julia, there is something else, and I may as well mention it now.'

She looked round the room, which was empty at this hour of the morning. Lizzie was out and Peter was still in bed.

'Julia, my dear, you'll think me foolish but never mind that. You've always been my favourite niece. No, let me finish.' Frances

162

took Julia's hand. 'I want you to know that I have made my will, and have decided to make you my heiress. Now, don't say a word! I can't tell you how pleased I was when you wrote and told me of your intention to marry. There were five of us girls, and only two got married – and I cannot get on with Harriet's children at all. Horrible spoilt things they are. But I have always had a special affection for you, and I know you deserve it. You have had a lot to put up with all these years and if ever a girl deserved happiness it is you. So the thing is done, and I won't hear a word. Now, give me a kiss.'

Julia said nothing, only took her aunt in her arms and held her very tight for a long time.

That afternoon she and Peter went to tea at the Emersons'. On their way, with Mrs Cunningham in the gleaming black carriage, Julia debated how to tell Peter about Aunt Frances' will. Her great-aunt was reputed to be very rich on account of another legacy she had received, a sort of stray legacy which had gone adrift in the family and after being handed down through two generations, veering wildly from a branch in the west country to another in the City, where it had grown substantially, had unexpectedly come to rest with Aunt Frances in her house in Kent. Julia had no idea how much it was worth. Not that she was greedy to get her hand on the money; she wished the old lady many years of health to come.

The point, however, was that once that money came to Julia – in the fullness of time – it would automatically become Peter's. There was nothing any of them could do about that. And much as Julia loved her husband she could not easily rub out the memory of that night in Bad Homburg.

Anyway, it was all far away in the future.

The visit was made, other visits were made, Peter went to church with Julia and heard Arthur preach a sermon on the wise and foolish virgins. Julia wondered for a moment if there was some kind of ironic message in it for her. Peter fidgeted, and whispered comments under his breath.

Then two days later they went to London for a few days to look for houses. In the train, Peter made an announcement.

'I want control of the money, Julia. Father can't do it, and Mother's had the running of the property too long. I mean to take over the business myself.'

He paused to see if there were any reaction. Julia said nothing.

'Up till now, I haven't given it much thought. She's doled me out spending money and so forth now and then, but now I'm a married

163

man, and all that, there's got to be a proper settlement. Father's unable to think about anything, as we know, so it's time for me to take charge.'

'What does your mother say?'

'I haven't spoken to her about it yet.'

'What do you want?'

'I want control of the property. Entirely, the whole business. Of course I'll make sure Mother is comfortable and all that, and Lizzie gets her portion and so forth, do the whole thing properly. Naturally. But I'm not having to go to Mother any more for a hand-out. From now on, I want the whole thing in my hands.'

'Although your Father is still alive?'

'The thing is Father can't handle anything. Up to now, it hasn't mattered because Mother has effectively run it in his name, had her own way with everything. But it's time I took over.'

'What do you think she'll say when you tell her?'

He grinned at her.

'She may not be too pleased.'

'Was there not a settlement on you when you married me?'

Julia was thinking of Grace Bradshaw, and the thousand pounds. Peter was not conscious of anything odd about the question.

'Of course. Anyway, up till now it hadn't really mattered, I've bumbled along, and if I needed any more I've usually been able to get round Mother. But things are different now.'

'Do you think she'll agree?'

'She might. Or she might not.'

'And then?'

'Well, in that case, we might have to put the screws on.'

'What on earth do you mean?'

'Work it out for yourself. Look, my father's non compos mentis – hasn't had control of the property for years – so who has the natural right to administer it in his stead?'

Julia was silent.

'Well, who? Me, of course. Once we're settled in London, Julia, I don't want to be trailing off down to Wiltshire every five minutes, begging for money.'

'But you have an income already.'

'It's never enough. It can be confoundedly annoying to have to go cap in hand, believe me. Anyway, I've had enough. I want control, and I am going to get it.'

Julia said nothing. A thousand pounds a year sounded a great deal of money to her. She knew for a fact that Dr Williamson kept a very comfortable house in the village, ran a pony and trap and kept four children on three hundred a year. A thousand pounds was a fortune for two people.

As she thought of Mrs Cunningham, she thought there might be trouble brewing up. She was a woman who enjoyed her power, and was not likely to give it up easily. Did Peter really contemplate legal action against his own mother?

They went to the Charing Cross Hotel in Trafalgar Square, deposited their bags, and set out to look at houses.

'Got to be central, Julia. Somewhere snug and convenient – and not too pricey. Not going to go paying through the nose to some Jew of a landlord.'

Even so, the houses they began to look at were very expensive, and far too big for them – one in Mount Street, Mayfair, had six bedrooms, a room on the first floor big enough for a ballroom, and an enormous dining room on the ground floor.

'We'd just get lost, my darling. Not very snug.'

Then there was a house on Regent's Park that was also far too big. Another house in Lancaster Gate with six floors and an ingratiating young man, who bowed and simpered all the time, and told them what a very genteel neighbourhood it was, a very good class of people, and there was a dairy that delivered fresh milk daily, and the chimneys didn't smoke, and a lot of other useful information. But it still came to the same conclusion – what would they do with seven bedrooms?

At the end of the first day they returned to their hotel, and had tea, and were rather gloomy. Julia thought it all ruinously expensive, houses with three or four times the space of the rectory, and foresaw all kinds of extra expenses, in the form of servants, and travelling expenses, and the cost of food here in London, which was much higher than in Stallbridge. It was summer now, and the air was clear, but she remembered London in the winter from visits, and knew how depressing that pall of smoke could be and how difficult it was to keep clothes clean.

The next day they went out again, and on her advice scaled down their demands this time, something with three or four bedrooms, plus servants' rooms in the attic of course, and then found something in Ebury Street, just on the edge of Belgravia – in fact with a little imagination they could call it Belgravia – and Julia thought this seemed a reasonable compromise. It was still expensive – thirty-seven pounds a year and they would need at least four servants, including Becky whom Julia had brought up with her. They went back to their hotel, had lunch and talked and decided to take the house, and the following morning the man came round with the lease, it was duly signed and witnessed, Peter paid over a cheque for the first half-year, the keys were handed over, he took his leave, bowing his way downstairs, the door slammed behind him, and the house was theirs.

Chapter Nineteen

Arthur walked through the village. The deed had been done, and he had to accept it. He looked down, and realised as he walked how hunched his shoulders were and that he was staring moodily at the dusty track before him, not thinking where he was going, only turning over in his mind what he had seen that afternoon when Julia had been reduced to tears by her father. It had been a bitter moment. He had been in his room and had opened the door so as to hear the exchange between father and daughter. Bitter.

What was worse was the feeling of uselessness which sat on him. To watch that woman sacrificing herself, and be unable to do anything about it. Arthur drew a long breath, straightened his back, and walked on. In front of him he saw Emmy on her way down into the village.

He walked on, catching up with Emmy, and as he came up towards her saw that she was crying, her head bent over, sniffling as she walked.

'Emmy!'

She started at his voice, quickly wiped her face and stuffed a handkerchief into a pocket.

'Oh, Reverend, you gave me a shock. I didn't hear you.'

He came up to her and looked down into her face where he could see the evidence of her tears. She knew that he could see it.

'Is anything the matter?'

Emmy sniffed, lifted her head, and turned away.

'Thank you, Reverend, I'm very well.' They walked together down into the village.

Arthur tried to sound cheerful.

'And how are you liking it at the rectory? Getting on with Mrs Oldham, eh? She's a character, isn't she?'

Arthur was amazed at the note of quiet optimism and steady

confidence that he radiated, quite at odds with the mood within him.

Emmy seemed distracted. After a moment she looked away.

'Oh, yes, I'm doing very well, thank you, Reverend.'

Arthur, too preoccupied with his own worries, did not notice her mood.

They came to Granny Leggatt's broken-down little hovel in the middle of the village and Emmy ran into her own home next-door, which was not much larger.

Later, as he was about to set off back through the village for dinner at the rectory, Mrs Goodrich came darting out, and caught up with him. This was Emmy's mother.

'Reverend!' she said, in a loud whisper. 'I wonder if I might – could I be so bold – I knows you be a busy man, Reverend, and I don't like to be troubling you, and you such a good man, as all the village knows – but just now –' She bit back tears, and Arthur saw she was very agitated. ''Twill be the ruin of us, Reverend. I don't know what to do, and that's the truth.'

They were walking side by side.

'What's the matter, Mrs Goodrich?'

'I don't how to tell you, Reverend, and I do be so ashamed to say to you – a man of the cloth, a saintly man, that lives for others, as you be, but I don't know who else to talk to, and if it do be known, 'twill be a disaster for us – with George – and Emmy too – working at the rectory.'

Trouble was coming, and Arthur steadied himself.

'Is it Emmy?' he said softly.

'That dratted girl, Reverend, I don't know what's to become of her.'

Arthur waited. In a speech like this there was usually only one ending.

'I would never speak of it to you, only there's no one else! And once 'tis known –'

'Tell me, Mrs Goodrich. Emmy –'

'Oh, Reverend, she's expecting.'

Arthur was silent for a moment.

'Do you know who the man is?'

Mrs Goodrich stared up into his face. She was bitter.

'Who d'you think?'

Arthur looked into her face.

'Peter Cunningham?'

The woman nodded.

Arthur stared at the ground. He could not trust himself to speak for a moment, but at last he said, 'How long has she known?'

168

'What – that she was expecting? Only this last two days for certain, Reverend.'

'And have you any idea how many months she has been –'

'As far as we can make out, she's not past her second month.'

There was a bit of time. Something might be effected; nothing was going to show for several months yet.

But whatever he did, Julia would be there, would see everything, know everything.

Something must be done, though. Cunningham was not to be allowed to escape, and Emmy's good name must be saved, if at all possible. Arthur turned to Mrs Goodrich, looking down into the brown face lined with concentration from a lifetime of scraping and making do, now looking up at him, in the summer evening light.

'Just give me time, Mrs Goodrich. At this minute I can't think of anything, but I promise I'll think about it and see what is to be done. There's a little time yet; something might be done. I'll think.'

Mrs Goodrich was profuse in her thanks, and turned away back into the village and Arthur went on up towards the rectory.

Julia had never had the furnishing of a house. It was a novel experience. It was decided the house should be redecorated first, and a firm of painters and decorators were called in.

Peter was happy to lounge about for a while, then, growing bored with it, he went out 'to smoke a cigar' as he said, and Julia was left with the decorators, choosing designs and trying to think which colours would match with which. She suspected that a particular design of wallpaper the decorator was very enthusiastic about was in fact a job lot that he couldn't get rid of, and thinking she was a young newly-wed, which she was, and therefore green, which she wasn't, tried to foist it on her.

Politely she declined his suggestions, and looking through the pattern books and the books of wallpapers gradually came to some decisions, and after a very busy morning she and Peter departed and left the decorators to get on with it.

Next they went to Shoolbred's furniture warehouse in Tottenham Court Road and looked at beds and sofas and curtains, and Peter seemed to have no idea what he wanted and was very happy to let her decide. It was exhausting, but in the end decisions had been made, orders placed, and they emerged into the street again. That still left sheets, towels, household utensils . . .

Ten days later they were able to move in.

Julia had brought Becky, Peter had Franks, who was to double as personal valet and butler, and in addition they had a cook, Mrs

169

Standish, a housemaid, Mary, to do the cleaning, and a boy called Josh to run errands, clean boots, peel potatoes and make himself useful.

The furniture had arrived and Julia had watched the men carry it in, and told them there was to be a special bonus if *no* paint was chipped. The men, looking at each other, thought she looked a regular good 'un, and were careful, and she was able to pay them handsomely for their trouble, and they went off well satisfied, and wishing 'they 'ad a lady like that to deal wiv every day'.

Mrs Cunningham, Lizzie, Dolly, and Aunt Frances were invited to a housewarming party. Also, to her surprise, Julia found herself introduced to some of Peter's friends, who suddenly manifested themselves.

'Chums from the club, Julia.'

They were not at all like Peter. One of them, for instance, Sir Cosmo Whittington, was a baronet, and looked forty at least, a bachelor who kept three racehorses at Newmarket, and lived with his mother in Welbeck Street; he wore heavy whiskers, had a loud voice and a high colour in his face, although whether from an open air life on the race course or from a taste for claret, or both, she could not make out at first.

Then there was Jonathan Selby, the younger son of a Yorkshire county family, who had been at Oxford a year ahead of Peter, a slight, sallow, man with hunched shoulders and a way of looking at things from the corner of his eyes, who had a cold look and a cynical laugh, and managed to cheapen every topic of conversation with some snide or ironic comment.

Toby Holden was extremely dense, as far as Julia could make out, and seemed to go along with whatever the others were doing, but was reputed to be very rich. Morley was present, and there were two others, but Julia could not remember their names. In the middle of this family gathering, they introduced a boisterous note, and Julia was very surprised Peter had invited them, but he was reassuring.

'Wonderful to have one's chums round one, Julia. Now we'll have something to talk about. Something to do of an evening. Have a bit of fun together.'

They were all very attentive to her, but she hoped he wasn't planning to invite these gentlemen round too often. They were as far removed from what she was used to as she could imagine. She had supposed that Peter must have friends here in London, and had she put her mind to it, could have imagined they might be like this, but still it came as a shock.

Mrs Cunningham took her aside at one point, and they stood by the window, looking down into the street. They had dined in the dining room on the ground floor, and were now in the drawing room, which was on the first floor of the house, and stretched through two rooms, with a pair of large dividing doors, now folded back. The room, with windows at either end, and raised up above ground level, was light and airy. From the back window, you could look down into a pocket handkerchief of an unkempt garden.

'Well, Julia dear, do you think you'll manage?'

'Manage? Well, of course we've had a massive upheaval getting in – oh, you mean –'

She saw Mrs Cunningham's look, which was directed at the group of Peter's friends, standing together, glasses in their hands, and talking loudly together and taking little notice of the family group.

Julia looked back at Mrs Cunningham.

'Peter's friends, you mean?'

Mrs Cunningham looked at her. Julia thought.

'He's entitled to his friends. There's nothing I can do about it. Do you know them?'

'Oh, I've had dealings with some of them over the years. That one –' (pointing to Sir Cosmo) '– for example, owes Peter money. Though whether he'll ever get it back or not, we shall see. Peter does have a knack of getting through money. So do his friends. Some of them are especially good at getting through other people's money, too. Has he told you about his club?'

'Only that he belongs to one.'

'Hmm. Well, take a good look at them – they're all members, I think.'

'Do they have professions?'

'Not that I know of.'

'Has Peter ever had any intention of devoting himself to a profession?'

'Of course not, dear.' Mrs Cunningham laughed. 'Can you see Peter *working*? In any case, who would employ him?'

Julia did not like the way this conversation was going. She herself was so used to being occupied, and filling up every day with useful tasks, that she still had not really absorbed the fact that Peter did not actually do anything, and had not the slightest intention of doing anything.

'Of course,' she began hesitantly, 'in due course, he will take over the property. It will be a great responsibility.'

'In due course. And the longer I can keep him from it the better. I don't trust it in his hands for a moment.'

171

'What do you mean? He's in his majority. He is an adult, he is entitled to assume the trust – the responsibility –'

'I fear Peter may never be mature enough to assume the trust – as you very charmingly put it. He's hopeless with money – as I thought you would have found out by now. My advice to you, Julia, is to work out what you are going to need for your housekeeping, and make very sure you get it out of him, or he'll lead you a dog's life.'

Julia went pale. Mrs Cunningham smiled.

'Forgive me, my dear, I don't mean to depress you on such a day. Here you are in your new home, and such a dear little house – and I must congratulate you, by the by, on your taste in furnishings. Charmingly restrained. But, all the same, we both know Peter, and there is no harm in preparing for the worst. Forewarned is forearmed.'

'Mother!' Peter called her over, and Julia was left alone by the window, looking down into the street at a knife grinder who had just set up his little machine at the kerb, and at Josh, their new boy, who had just gone up from the area steps with a handful of knives to have them sharpened. As she watched the man sharpening the knives at his wheel, Mrs Cunningham's words ran through her mind. Of course Peter was entitled to his friends, and in any case there was nothing she could do about them, though she could have wished for slightly different sorts of friends, and of course he was entitled to have control of his own money. But Mrs Cunningham had been pretty brutal about the future. As if Julia were going to have problems with money – and she had always been accustomed to having absolute control of the household accounts.

And then there was his mother's very low opinion of his ability to control the family property – and Peter was preparing to seize it from her if he could. It was all food for thought.

Lizzie came across to her.

'Julia, you were going to show me round.'

'Of course, Lizzie.'

There had been a viewing when they had arrived, and the family had trooped round together, but Lizzie wanted to have a closer look and the chance of a private chat with Julia. The house was on five floors. In the basement was the kitchen. On the ground floor was the dining room at the front and a room at the back which Julia had proposed as a study. She already saw it lined with books, and with a large desk, at which she would sit and arrange her papers, as she had at home. What papers they would be, she was not yet sure. She still vaguely thought she might be of some use to her father. After all, with the penny post, there was no reason why they should not keep up a correspondence – a day's delay was nothing; she could work for him just as she always had done, and there would be nothing but a slight delay in the transmission of the papers back and forth. It ought to work very well. It only needed Dr Stone to unbend, acknowledge her husband, and accept the new state of affairs. She still had hopes.

The room looked into the little garden. Coming up to the first floor, where the party were all gathered, sipping Madeira and nibbling macaroons, this was taken up by the drawing room, their main living room. Going on up, there were three bedrooms, a large one and two small ones. Finally at the top was the attic with the servants' rooms. Franks had his own room, and Becky shared with Mary the housemaid. The cook did not live in, and the boy slept in the kitchen.

Lizzie was very pleased with Julia's arrangements.

'You've done it very well, Julia, I must say, and I honestly don't think I could have done better myself. And that's saying something. I always thought of you as so bookish and so on, quite a blue stocking, and me as the little home body, and here you are, all established. I'm quite envious, I assure you, and you make me all the more eager to get married myself so I can set up house. What fun it must be!'.

'You know,' Julia said quietly, 'Lizzie, all those years at home, I used to think I was destined to stay there for ever. Sometimes, I was quite desperate. You only saw me as father's secretary, but that wasn't all there was to me. You can't imagine how it feels to have this house now, and to be here with Peter. I'm very grateful.'

'Grateful? To whom?' Lizzie laughed, but Julia did not.

'I mean, I feel grateful – just to God, I suppose, that he has given it to me.'

'Oh, well, yes – and you jolly well deserve it Julia, and I am so pleased for you.' Lizzie kissed her on the cheek. Julia grew thoughtful.

'Of course,' Lizzie went on, 'living here in London, you'll have so much more to do. Down in Devizes, it is going to be rather dull for Dolly and me, I expect.'

'I would willingly exchange. I have no great love for London, and I would have been very happy to stay in Stallbridge.'

They were silent for a moment, leaning on the bedroom windowsill, looking out at the rooftops of the houses opposite, which hemmed in the view. It was a clear late afternoon of summer.

'When I think of the scents of the hayfields, the fruit blossoms, the smell of freshly turned earth, and the wild flowers in the lanes, I am nostalgic for Stallbridge already.'

'Yes, but you must admit, Julia, it is jolly well dull, too.'

An hour later the Stallbridge party declared they had to catch their train, and Aunt Frances said she too ought to be going, and everyone kissed everyone else on the cheek, and told Julia again what a lovely house she had, and how well she had it all fitted up, and they all eventually departed in cabs, and as Mary was clearing up the glasses and plates, Julia was able to turn her attention to the men, who were sitting round in the rear part of the drawing room, and had helped themselves to more Madeira.

They were effusive.

'Capital little house you've got, Mrs Cunningham!'

'And, Cunningham – you're a deuced lucky fellow, to get such a clever little wife – why look at you here in the lap of luxury. By Jove, an improvement on my miserable rooms, I can tell you.' Mr Toby Holden looked gloomily down at the carpet for a moment. Peter laughed.

'The solution is obvious! You should get married, Holden. Why be a bachelor? It's a dog's life – eating at the club, spending all your evenings in the club with a lot of bores, and then crawling home to some dreary rooms on your own. Get married, it's the only thing!'

'Dash it, think I might – if only I could find a girl who'd have me!'

'Mrs Cunningham must have some friends,' said Jonathan Selby, in his dry voice, 'isn't there any one you could find to take Holden – then we could all get some peace?'

'Well, I'm for the club,' Sir Cosmo said, rising. 'Mrs Cunningham, most pleased to have met you. Cunningham's a lucky dog, that's the universal verdict, and it's my belief you'll be the making of him.'

The others rose.

'Hear hear.'

They made their way down stairs to the door, where Mary was waiting with their hats and sticks.

'Hmm, you know, think I might stroll up with you fellows – get a bit of air. Julia, think I'll just stroll up to the club for a bit with the fellows. Hmm? See you later.'

She was surprised. 'Will you want any supper?'

'Oh, just tell the cook to leave a bit of cold meat and a glass of wine, will you?'

He gave her a peck on the cheek, and then they all ushered themselves out.

Julia returned to the drawing room, where Becky was helping to tidy the room.

'Good to have a bit of peace and quiet, miss,' Becky said.

Julia went over and opened the rear window. The men had lit up cigars after the family party had departed, and the smell hung in the air.

'It's a terrible thing for getting in the curtains, miss,' Becky said.

'Hmm?'

'I mean cigar smoke.'

Julia drew a breath.

'Yes, it is. I think I must ask Peter not to smoke in here.'

Chapter Twenty

Later Julia wandered round the house alone, as the light of the summer evening slowly faded. She stood in their new bedroom, looking down at the bed, covered with a flowery light cover, a summer cover which she had chosen specially and with care, thinking of herself and Peter there in that bed, and wanting everything to be pleasant for them. The curtains too. She wandered to the window and looked down into the street, deserted at this time of the evening, and heard not far away a church bell chime nine o'clock. How quiet it was here. Strange, being in the middle of a great city, she had thought it would be so noisy, and of course it was in Regent Street and Piccadilly, but here in Ebury Street there was very little traffic; the occasional growler would come clip-clopping past, and the sound of the hooves would recede slowly in the distance.

What time would Peter get back? She had thought of them together that first night here in their new home. Odd that he not understood; it was their first night here, that was special. She had imagined them in a sort of holy rite, turning down the covers of their new bed, and getting in together and making love – as it were, to christen the bed – how silly her thoughts were sometimes. It was just that she wanted him so much, often had trouble keeping her hands off him, but now always afraid in case he might think her forward. She was muddled.

She wandered away downstairs, to the ground floor, and to the back room. There was nothing here at the moment but some spare dining chairs. This should be a study. Yes, work. She should be busy. In all the upheaval of her marriage and moving in here, it had been pushed to the back of her mind, but now she was established, she could not bear to be idle. There must be work.

But what work? In rushing off to get married she had cut herself off from her work. She thought for a moment.

The only thing would be to write to her father. There was no putting it off. He couldn't hold out for ever. Sooner or later he must relent, mustn't he?

She went up into the drawing room and took her portable writing box, which opened back to reveal two surfaces of soft green leather forming a sloping writing surface, and sat down to write.

By the time Peter came in she had gone to bed. She heard him downstairs calling for Franks, and then stumbling on the stairs and cursing, and guessed he had been drinking. Finally he appeared at the doorway, a candle in his hand.

'You awake, Julia?'

'Yes.'

'Confounded stairs, nearly broke my confounded neck, why d'they make 'em so steep? Don't they know a fellow's got to get up in the dark?'

'Hush, come to bed, the servants will hear you.'

'Let 'em hear. What's it matter? Anyway Franks knows me of old – got no secrets from Franks.'

He lurched across the room, and fell heavily into a chair.

'Did you have a pleasant evening?'

'Hmm? No. Confounded luck, didn't have one decent hand all night long. Just pay, pay, pay. Really should give it up. Confounded waste of money.'

'Were you playing cards?'

'Of course we were playing cards. What did you think we were playing – hunt the thimble?'

He had succeeded in pulling his boots off.

'Oof!'

'Your mother seemed very pleased with the house, Peter,' Julia said quietly.

'Ah yes, Mother. That reminds me. We'll have to go down and pay a visit shortly. Have a word with my lawyer first, though. The old girl's as sharp as a razor, she won't be easy to fool. We need a watertight case, Julia.'

She did not think this was the best time to discuss the matter especially after all he had to drink.

'Let's discuss it in the morning. Come to bed now.'

'Eh? Rather. I'm dead on my feet, I can tell you. Just walked from the club. Hadn't a penny on me.'

He fell heavily into bed beside her and was asleep almost immediately.

Julia lay awake a long time. This was not how she had imagined the first night in her new home.

*

177

Arthur walked to the Old Manor House, and asked for Mrs Cunningham. The butler directed him through to the terrace at the back where she had entertained her guests at her archery party, and where, in the warm summer sunshine, she was now sitting at a table with correspondence before her, writing letters.

Nearby her husband was nodding in his wheelchair. She looked up, and a tiny expression of triumph and pleasure flitted through her eyes. But her composure was complete. Arthur took in her husband, half slumped forward in his chair, dozing.

'Well, we haven't seen you for a long time.'

Arthur arranged his thoughts.

'There is a matter of urgency which I must speak to you about.'

She raised her eyebrows.

'You alarm me, Mr Grahame. Not another of your rustic protegés, I hope?'

'I beg your pardon?'

'The last time we met, it was on the matter of one of my beggarly tenants.'

Arthur took a breath.

'It is on the matter of another of your tenants, Mrs Cunningham.'

'How tedious.' She looked down and shuffled the papers in front of her. 'Be brief, I pray you.'

'Mrs Cunningham, I should like you to pay close attention to what I have to say.'

She looked sharply up at him.

'It concerns your son.'

'My son? Really? And what concern can he be of yours, pray?'

'He has compromised a girl in the village.'

'Heavens, is that all?'

'Got her with child, if you prefer.'

'So?'

'*So*?' Arthur contained his anger with difficulty. '*So*, Mrs Cunningham, this girl will be ruined if something is not done quickly, and since your son is not here, it is your responsibilty.'

'Fiddlesticks! The girl has only herself to blame.'

'You are wrong, and it is shameful of you to say that. The girl has been seduced and abandoned by your son, and I insist on you playing your part in securing her good name.'

'My part?'

Arthur looked round at Mr Cunningham.

'Take no notice of him,' Mrs Cunningham said briskly, 'he's past all understanding. You could explode a cannon in his ear and it would make no difference. Go on.'

'Whatever you may say, you – or your son – have a responsibility here, and I intend to hold you to it, Mrs Cunningham. And you should not underestimate me.'

She smiled slightly.

'Oh, I do not underestimate you, Arthur. What is the girl's name?'

'Amelia Goodrich.'

'Really! The girl is notorious – why are you wasting my time like this? She deserves whatever she gets!'

'No! She was perfectly innocent until she met your son. Now listen to me. There is a young man, William Masham, her father's assistant. I know he's sweet on her, and I think would be willing to marry her – probably wants to very much. But there's the matter of the child. As things stand, once he finds out, he will repudiate her. However, I know the lad, I know his feelings for Emmy, and I'm pretty certain I can talk him into it. With one proviso – money. I propose to explain the matter to him and offer him twenty pounds to make an honest girl of her.'

'And how do you intend to raise twenty pounds?' she said looking up at him shrewdly.

Arthur looked down at her without blinking. They looked at one another a long time before she said quietly, looking into his eyes with an impudent smile, 'The story in the village is that it was you who was seen kissing – or should I say *compromising* – Emmy Goodrich.'

'The story in Oxford, Mrs Cunningham, is that your son nearly caused the death of a pot-boy at the Mitre, only a student prank of course, but I would not like it to come to the ears of his wife.'

Mrs Cunningham went white.

'How did you know about that?'

Arthur said nothing.

'You wouldn't dare.'

There was a long silence between them. At last she took a grip on herself, looked down at her papers, and spoke in a muffled voice.

'Very well. I can rely on you to be discreet. Masham need not know who the father is?'

'I will do my best to keep his name out of it, but I cannot answer for what may pass between William and Emmy.'

Mrs Cunningham looked up at Arthur. She smiled a little.

'I was not mistaken in you.'

'Really?'

'Come with me to my study.'

As they were walking through the house, she said, half over her shoulder, 'I once said you had the qualities a woman looked for in a

179

man. Julia Stone should have married you. Unfortunately she is besotted with my worthless son.'

'Do not underestimate your daughter-in-law.'

'Oh, I do not.'

They were in her study. She took a metal box from a drawer in her desk, opened it with a key on a chain round her waist, and took out some notes and gold coins.

'I know you will handle this matter discreetly, Arthur,' she said as she came up to him, closer than he would have liked, and held out the money. She was looking up into his face, straight, frank and inviting. Arthur was unmoved. He took the money and put it in his pocket.

'There is a faint possibility this may not work. William may repudiate Emmy despite everything I say. I don't know. In that case you will get your money back, and your son can face the consequences in the village as best he may.'

He turned and left the room without another word. Mrs Cunningham watched him, swinging the key on its chain from her hand in a thoughtful fashion.

Peter rose late the following morning. In fact Julia found that he rose late every morning. He would ring for Franks who would bring him a cup of tea about eleven. Then he would descend in a dressing gown, and lounge about drinking his tea, and staring out of the window, or flicking idly through the paper. Eventually he would go and get dressed, by which time it was nearly one o'clock, and they would sit down to a bite of lunch. Their first serious misunderstanding came about one lunch time a few days later.

'Peter.'

'Hmm?'

'There's something I want to ask you, my dear, a little request.'

'Hmm?'

'All our new furniture – these curtains, the carpets, everything we bought together –'

'Yes, my dear?'

'Well, cigar smoke – you know, it's very difficult to get the smell out; it hangs in the fabric and lingers in the room. It would be much nicer in here – sweeter, I mean if you wouldn't mind – if you could bear – not to smoke in here.'

There was a long silence, while Peter went on eating.

He looked away from her and at last said, in a faraway voice, 'You know, Julia, the thing I liked about you from the very first was the way you never nagged a fellow. It was so pleasant to be with

180

you. I could just be myself, we were chums, and could talk about anything we liked, do anything we liked. All free and easy.'

'We didn't have our own home then,' she said quietly.

'What's that got to do with it?'

'This is our house, all these things are ours – we bought them together. I want to keep everything clean and sweet for you.'

'Julia, what did I just say? Did I just speak, did I just say something about not nagging and criticising a fellow?'

His voice had risen.

'Yes,' she said quietly.

'Well?' he went on, still on a rising tone. 'I am in my own home. This is my home, Julia, paid for with my money. I believe that is right – correct me if I am wrong. Am I right?'

'Yes,' she said, knowing now what was coming.

'Well then, Julia, for the last time, I will not be nagged and criticised! If I wish to smoke, I will smoke. If I wish to whistle, hum, or twiddle my thumbs, I believe I enjoy the right to do so.'

Her patience snapped.

'And if you wish to remain a spoilt child for the rest of your life you have that right also!'

She got up and ran quickly out of the room, upstairs and into her bedroom. She was so full of irritation and frustration, that she could not trust herself to stay in control of herself.

Peter did not appear, and when three-quarters of an hour later she came downstairs, he had gone out. He did not leave a message, and did not reappear until midnight.

This was often the pattern of their life at that time. The novelty of marriage appeared to have completely worn off and he reverted to a bachelor existence as completely as if he had never been married.

Julia found it bewildering. She found herself left in the house day after day with almost nothing to do. She could not order meals properly never knowing whether he would be in for dinner or not. In the end she got tired of asking, and informed him coldly that cook would leave some cold meat and he could help himself if he wanted anything.

The issue of money was the next serious difficulty. Peter never had any. She got tired of asking him for money. 'Oh, sorry, must get to the bank. Cleaned right out last night.' But he was always getting cleaned out. Night after night, he would come home 'cleaned out'. She did not even bother to stay awake any more. At some point during the night she would be half-aware of his weight rolling into bed beside her, that was all.

When she got up, around seven-thirty, he was fast asleep. She would watch him then, often, look down on him, and could almost weep for the way their marriage was already coming apart, and the beautiful illusions that were already threadbare. He was still as beautiful as ever, though; the rackety life he led seemed to leave no mark on his face.

But the money. She asked for a regular weekly amount to cover her household expenses. She never got it. He would reach into his pockets, pull out a handful of notes and coins, and thrown them down on the table.

'See how much is there.'

She would count it. Sometimes there was more than she had asked for, sometimes less. But it was quite impossible to get a steady payment on which she could rely. Again, she could not restrain her temper sometimes, and would whip him with her tongue.

'You did me the honour of asking me to be your wife, and I gladly consented. Among other things that entails the duties of running your house, which I am happy to accept. But I must have a regular allowance to do it efficiently. It is no good throwing handfuls of change on the table every so often! We must get our finances in order.'

He did not like that. Peter seemed almost afraid of Julia; he would like to bully her, but she was the wrong girl. There was just too much of her. And all the time her exasperation grew. They could have been so happy, she wailed to herself. It was so easy. There was so much they could do together. They had plenty of money – where was the problem?

The problem however was very simple indeed. Peter preferred to go to his club day after day and play cards and drink with his friends. He could not bear the slightest infringement of his liberty. If he felt the merest breath of control, it irked him more than he could stand; he simply had to get out, and that meant the club.

Julia understood all this, saw through him completely. She had believed he loved her. And he did – in so far as he was able. But he was not able to love much; as soon as it clashed with his own convenience or caprice, as soon as he was denied the idlest whim, he bridled, sulked, huffed, and disappeared through the door.

Julia lay awake and thought all this through. She did not know what to do. As far as she could see there was nothing she could do. The money was all his; she had none of her own. The house was in his name, everything was in his name. Everything. She was in his name.

She hated to admit it to herself, but she was bitterly disappointed. She had abandoned her father, caused him great hurt, abandoned her work, run away to marry, with a man whom she was at that time ready to die for, and now she found herself here, and the marriage was already a meaningless facade.

Tradesmens' bills began to come in. A lot of bills: decorators, the furniture company, the people who had supplied the curtains, and then the butcher's bill, the dairy, the man who had replaced a cracked window pane, many more.

One morning Peter threw a tantrum.

'Another confounded bill! What do these people think? They're a set of regular blood-suckers, Julia! Look at this – the butcher wants eight pounds five shillings! How can he make that out? He's robbing us, it's obvious, thinks just because we're newly-weds, we're an easy touch, a sponge for him to squeeze. I know these characters of old. Well, he'll find out he's made a big mistake, let me tell you!' And more of the same.

'Let me see the bill.' Julia rang the bell, and when Becky came, said 'Run down to cook and tell her to let me have the house-keeping book.'

Peter puffed and fumed, his hands in his pockets, and stared out of the window. Becky reappeared with the housekeeping book.

'Now let me see.' Julia opened the book, and started going through the pages, running her finger down the columns and ticking off items on the butcher's bill. At last she closed the book.

'Thank you, Becky, you may return the book to Mrs Standish.'

She said nothing. Peter stamped about the room for a while, drew a deep breath, stared out of the window, and at last turned to her, and tried to look outraged.

'Well?'

'The bill is correct,' Julia said.

'I see. Well, then, madam, perhaps *you* can explain how a bill of this amount came to be run up? I trusted you to run this household, and it seems you haven't the faintest idea –'

'Faintest idea?' Julia flared up. 'Faintest idea? No, Peter, it is you who have not the faintest idea of how a house is run. Do you imagine I could run my father's house for so many years and not know how to run this house? Do you suppose I am so green as not to know how to deal with the butcher? There is nothing wrong with that bill, believe me. *Nothing* gets by me. No. But if I were to ask you how much you get through in one night of cards at your club . . . Come tell me, honestly now, how much did you lose last night?'

'As it happens I won last night, madam, thank you!'

'Bravo. And the night before, and the night before that? And many and many a night, when you've come home and told me you'd lost every penny in your pocket – and had to write out IOUs. Be honest now – if you can. This month, how much are you down?'

'Lord knows. And it's no business of yours in any case. My God, if a fellow can't go to his club and play a hand of cards without having his wife over his shoulder counting his winnings –'

'Winnings? If only it were. I want to know how much you have lost this month. Come, you must know. Why be ashamed? Tell me. Don't you trust me?'

'Eh? Of course I do. But –' Peter was taken aback. 'Off hand –'

'Peter, you must know how much you have lost. Come tell me.'

'Oh, for the Lord's sake, Julia, you'd drive a fellow to drink!'

'Peter, I am beginning to despair. Drive you to drink? You come home drunk every night as it is – of your own free will! How can I do more than you are doing already? Just tell me, how much you have lost this month. Come, sit down. Here is a pencil and a piece of paper. Write it down – all of it – you must know.'

'I swear I don't, Julia.'

'Well then, approximately.'

'Oh Lord. Julia, honestly you are a tyrant.'

'Approximately.'

After much more of this, and shaking his head, Peter finally put the figure at about eight hundred and fifty pounds.

There was a long silence. Julia sat down across the table from him, but could not bring herself to look at him. After a long time, during which Peter kept expecting her to say something, and she didn't, he finally came out with, 'Well, there's no need to look so solemn. Lots of fellows lose money it's not that much! Good God!'

He lapsed into silence. He was still watching her, and at long, long last she looked up at him. He was frightened at the look in her face. It was not anger; it was close to despair.

'How long do you think you can keep it up?' she said quietly.

'God, Julia, don't look so blessed solemn.'

He looked around the room.

'My God! I wish I'd never told you! Honestly, you give a fellow no rest. Always on my back. Eight hundred and fifty, that's not much.'

'Not much? Two minutes ago you were questioning me over a bill of eight pounds! Have you any sense of reality at all? We have an allowance from your mother of a thousand pounds a year – that is ample for our needs. Ample. We can live very nicely, very respectably on that; you can entertain your friends, pay visits, receive guests, pay our servants, make trips to the sea-side, and still have change out of that. What's the matter with you? Peter, how can you lose so much money?'

'Oh, hang it all! That's it again – nag nag nag, just like the fellows say at the club. Once you get married, you'll be for ever having your wife on your back – well now, Julia, just you listen to me. It's my money, every last penny, and I don't owe a farthing of it to anybody, and what I do with my money is my business, and I won't be dictated to by you or anyone else. So I'll ask you to keep your comments to yourself from now on! Anyway, a thousand a year is a wretched piddling little allowance, and it's time I took control of the property. I've been to the lawyer, and he's looking into the matter for me, and you'll see, I won't have my mother, or you, or any other blessed female tell me how to conduct my affairs. My God! It's no life for a man, to have women forever telling not to do this, not to do that!'

Julia said nothing. It was as if she were in some nightmare game, where everything had gone topsy-turvy, the ground was lurching beneath her feet. She was going to have to get a grip on the situation eventually, but at this minute didn't see how she could.

Chapter Twenty-one

Julia woke up one summer morning and realised she was pregnant. She did not know how she knew at that particular moment; it was just an accumulation of things, the cessation of her period over two months, and then the strange early-morning feelings, the occasional nausea.

In the uncertain way they lived, her feelings were mixed. Before she allowed herself to think, her reaction was one of joy; she remembered how she had envied Lizzie her announcement of her betrothal to Dolly back in March, and now Julia herself was here, it seemed such a short time, and how much had changed. Here she was in London, a married woman, in her own home, and now, lying in bed, looking at the sun peeping through the curtains, and knowing she had within her a child. It was a great change. And she knew she was equal to it, she could cope.

But then, turning her head, looking at Peter on the pillow beside her, and thinking of how much she now knew of him, and how little she had known when they had married, her happiness was dampened. How was he going to take the news? He must have an idea it was coming. They had used no contraceptives – at the time of her marriage she did not even know they existed – but in the short intervening time, she had learnt much.

As a matter of fact she had found out about such things overhearing a conversation between Becky and Mary one afternoon, when they were discussing Mary's sister and her problems, which Julia found were depressingly similar to her own. Money. And now a baby. Mary's sister had three, and was determined to have no more – and there were ways, she assured Becky. Julia, fascinated, listened through the half opened door.

In the future it might come to it for her too. What sort of a father was Peter going to make? Why had she never asked herself that question before? Why never thought of it in Stallbridge? She might be more mature than Peter, but in Stallbridge she had also been woefully ignorant of many things.

She must tell Peter soon. Today. Better get him prepared for the idea as soon as possible. What was his reaction going to be?

That morning she received a large envelope through the post. She did not at first recognise the handwriting. When she opened the it, she found inside the letter she had written to her father, unopened and readdressed to herself, and a letter with it.

It was from Arthur Grahame.

This was a gloomy letter. There had been communication with Christ Church, and a young clergyman, a Mr Crabtree, was now installed in the rectory and acting as amanuensis to Dr Stone. The Great Work was on the move again. Dr Stone was still implacably hostile to herself, and would under no circumstances consent to receive her. Julia sat at the table, and wept when she read these words. She could not restrain herself, one hand holding the letter, the other propping her head, and the tears streaming silent down her cheeks.

Arthur went on in his letter, trying to soften the news as well as he could, about how much she was missed by the villagers, and how changed the rectory was without her. He also offered to remove her books from her room to the Old Manor House if she would like. She must miss them. Julia was surprised by this letter; she had hardly expected such kindness after the last meeting between them.

Peter had news from his lawyer. The thing could be done, they said, but it was expensive and uncertain. Peter would have to have his father certified senile, and unfit to manage his property, and then apply for a court order to make him competent administrator of his father's property. The lawyer privately warned Peter that his mother would contest him, and it would make for a very unseemly wrangle between them, and was likely to be very expensive. He counselled Peter instead to have a talk with his mother, and ask her to increase his allowance if he wished. The funds would easily allow it.

Peter returned to Ebury Street, however, with but one thought in his head. The thing could be done. That was all he needed to know.

They would go down to Stallbridge, break the news to his mother, and ask her to cooperate. If she did, all well and good. If she did not, there would be a fight. He wasn't sure about the local physician, a man they had known all their lives, Dr Williamson; Mother might get at him. It was difficult to say. Might be safer to bring in a man from outside.

187

In the midst of this Julia sought with difficulty for the right moment to break the news of her pregnancy. It was obviously not the news he would wish to hear at this moment, yet she should tell him as soon as possible. It must affect his plans too. Was he to go launching into some lengthy and uncertain law-suit against his own mother, while she was expecting a child? Julia thought these things over.

The fact was, he had to know, and there was no good to be served by delaying matters. She decided to tell him after lunch, when he might be a little more relaxed and receptive.

'Expecting, eh? I'll be jiggered. Well, that's a stopper. Good Lord. Well, suppose I should congratulate you, Julia. Good news! A son and heir!'

'It might be a girl, Peter.' She smiled faintly.

'Don't you believe it! It'll be a boy, I feel it in my bones. Yes, a boy – hmm. You know, this is going to make a very great difference – all the more reason to make myself master of the estate, eh?'

'Peter, your allowance is adequate – more than adequate – for our needs, even with a child.'

'Julia, I've told you, that is not the point. I'm the heir, Father's past it, and it's time I took over.'

'Peter, I must say one thing. Like it or not, your mother is a very competent woman. She runs the estate very efficiently for you – you could not imagine anyone doing a better job than she does. Why change it? Ask her for more money if you must – though as I tell you, we have plenty for our needs – but believe me, you would be better to leave her in charge. In any case, even if you did get control, you aren't there. Either you would have to go down and live in Stallbridge and bother your head with all the problems of administering your estate or you would have to engage a steward to do it for you – and what steward could do a better job than your mother is doing already? And you would have to pay him.'

'Julia, that is not the point! I have told you a thousand times, I am entitled to have control of the estates. I am tired of being fobbed off by my mother, telling me everything is fine, and not to worry my head about it. Treating me like a child. Well, it won't do, Julia, and I tell you so.'

They travelled down to Stallbridge.

That evening after dinner, Julia told Mrs Cunningham that she was expecting a baby. Mrs Cunningham was very pleased indeed.

'My dear,' drawing Julia to her on the sofa where they were sitting. Peter was outside smoking a cigar, 'it's the best thing that could have happened to him. It'll be the making of him, I know it will – there's nothing like a baby to sober a man up. He'll be transformed, I promise you!'

Julia tried to believe her.

Lizzie too was very pleased. Her own wedding was fast approaching, and she was beginning to get nervous. She was being fitted for her wedding dress, and there were endless discussions about her wardrobe, wedding presents, the lists of guests to be invited for this was to be a full-dress wedding – choice of hymns, bridesmaids, and the menu for the wedding breakfast. Dolly and she had settled on a house in Devizes, and had been picking furniture and furnishings and deciding on how many servants they would need – and could afford. As a result, even though she had a month to go, her nerves were already stretched.

'Honestly, Julia,' she said, 'I wish we could do what you and Peter did – run away and get married on the spur of the moment. It was so romantic – almost like eloping!'

'It was eloping,' Julia said drily, 'and think what I sacrificed, Lizzie. No bridesmaids, no wedding breakfast, no wedding presents.'

'I don't know if it's all worth the candle, though. I'm so worried already I am sure I'm losing my bloom just worrying about it all, and by the time the day finally rolls round, I shall a perfect old fright!'

'There's no danger of that,' Julia said quietly, giving her a reassuring squeeze.

Peter had not said anything yet about his plans, and told Julia he was going to broach the matter the following morning. Julia said she was going out. Whatever he decided she would support him, and help him, but she did not approve of his decision, and he must speak to his mother on his own.

So after breakfast, she went out and decided, somewhat with her heart in her throat, to go to the rectory.

She went first to the churchyard and looked down at her mother's grave.

Her unhappy mother. She prayed that her mother might be looking down on her and would bless here in her own marriage. Would she have a happier marriage than her mother had done? Looking down, and thinking about her childhood, buried there with her mother, she wanted so badly to vindicate her, and prove to her, by success in her own marriage, that her mother had not suffered and died in vain. She so wanted to make it work, otherwise what was it all for?

Her mother had been unhappy; she had done all in her power to

189

bring up her daughter in the hope that she would be be happy and avoid the fate she had suffered. If Julia's marriage was a failure, it would be as if her mother had died for nothing. Biting her lower lip as these thoughts flowed through her mind, Julia determined that her own marriage should not be a failure if it were humanly within her power.

Churned up by these thoughts she was walking up the lane when she noticed idly that there were men hay-making in the meadow beside her, and then only after some time as she walked, thinking her thoughts, she noticed that Mr Grahame was among them. It was most odd; not only was he there scything away among the other men, but he was bare to the waist, and she was self-consciously aware of herself noticing his strong man's chest and his shoulders. It was more awkward because she wanted to speak to him to thank him for his letter. He saw her, however, and throwing down his scythe walked across to the hedge where he had left his shirt, and drew it on before he came to her.

'Mr Grahame,' she said, 'I scarcely recognised you. I think you – well, I think you will have set some new record in Stallbridge.' She was embarrassed.

'Are you thinking of the scything or the absence of a shirt?' he said with a smile. 'Whether it will bring the Church into disrepute?'

'I am sure Mr Trefusis must be very glad of your assistance at any rate. How is the hay this year?'

'Oh, good.' He said it vaguely looking away across the field. His face was flushed with the sun. 'To tell the truth, time hangs on my hands. Between Sundays there are still six days to fill.'

'I understand you have been taking all the services since I left.'

'That's right.'

'It would have been embarrassing for Father to appear in public when it looked as if I had eloped.'

He did not answer.

'Mr Grahame, there was something I wanted to say – that is, I wanted to thank you for your letter. It was very kind of you.'

'Well.' He paused, then looked at her. 'It was not very kind of your father to return the letter unopened. I only wanted to soften the blow.'

'I understood that.' She paused. 'You mentioned my books. You could not have named anything dearer to my heart.'

'I can easily move them to the Old Manor House.'

'If my father –'

'They are your books, Mrs Cunningham.'

'I know – still –'

'Do you want them?'

'Yes.'

'You'll get them.'

The atmosphere between them was strained, and it was difficult for her to go on, so after one or two more random remarks, she was about to leave him, when he said, 'Mrs Cunningham, there is something else.'

She turned back, glad to have an excuse to stay.

'Yes?'

'You will eventually hear this anyway, but I wanted to tell you myself. I have decided to leave Stallbridge.'

'Leave? Why?'

'The Bishop of London has written to me. Before I came here, as you know, I worked in the East End of London with a group of university friends. The bishop thinks – well, to put it simply there is a lot to be done. The fact is I could be more profitably occupied there than here, helping with the hay-making.'

He found it difficult to look at her. She too was looking down.

'I see,' she said faintly.

He turned to her more briskly, and held out his hand.

'So in case we do not meet again, Mrs Cunningham, I wish you well.'

'Oh, yes.' She took his hand readily, and they stood there in the corner of the field, holding hands, and looking into each other's eyes.

'Mr Grahame, you have taken me by surprise. Excuse me, I am in a muddle. But before we part I should like to say – I – I fear I was ungracious to you before.' She shook her head, as if trying to arrange her thoughts. 'There were one or two occasions when I wish – I wish it could have been otherwise between us.'

'I too wish it could have been otherwise, Mrs Cunningham, believe me.'

She tore herself away at last and went out of the meadow and at the bend in the lane she at last looked back.

He was there watching her, and as she walked away she was conscious that there had been something between them, that something, some great event, had nearly happened, as if at sea by night she had been in some tiny yacht or fishing boat, and had thought herself alone, but then suddenly some great ship had come upon her and passed her very nearly, some great clipper lofty with all sails spread, that had come right round the world, had very nearly hit

191

her, but just narrowly passed by in the night. And Julia was left in the lane like that, feeling that some great event had very nearly happened to her.

She met Annie in the lane.

'And how is everyone, Annie? Are you well, yourself?'

'Oh, yes, Mrs Cunningham. Very well, thank you.'

'And everyone – how is Mrs Oldham?'

'Same as ever, miss.'

'And – oh yes – I seem to remember Emmy Goodrich –'

'Lord, miss, Emmy's gone and got married! All of a sudden like, with no notice I mean one moment there she was going about the house, clearing the plates and sweeping the stairs, and the next – there she was – married!'

'Who is her husband?'

'William Masham, of course, that was always soft on her, miss.'

'And why were they in such a hurry?'

'No idea, miss. But they was married two weeks ago. Mr Grahame married 'em himself, one Saturday afternoon, with just their families and some folk from the village, quiet enough, but very jolly by all accounts, and had a bit of a wedding breakfast afterwards too. I couldn't go myself, but they do say Emmy looked very pretty in her bridal.'

'Is she still here?'

'Oh, yes, ma'am, she still works here, only now she lives in the glebe cottage, which Dr Stone let 'em have – along with her gran.'

'Where is she – could you call her? I should love to see her and wish her well. I wish I had known – I would have sent them something. Well, I will find something for them. I will come with you Annie, just to the door.'

Annie went in as Julia waited at her own door – it was an odd experience – and then Emmy appeared, wiping her hands on her apron. She was bashful with Julia, and bobbed a curtsy. Julia, even at her most relaxed, had a slightly awe-inspiring quality.

'Emmy, my dear,' she said, kissing her cheek, 'I am so happy for you! I had no idea you and William had made up your minds. I am sure you will be happy together – he is a very kind and hardworking boy.'

Emmy was awkward and embarrassed, and blushed.

'Thank you, Mrs Cunningham, you are very kind.' She smiled slightly. 'Yes, I never knew William was that sweet on me, but he just up and popped the question, and there weren't no call for us to wait, so we just went ahead and did it and got married – and Mr

Grahame, Dr Stone I should say, was so kind as to give us the glebe cottage, and we're as snug there as can be.'

There were tears in her eyes.

'Emmy, whatever is the matter?'

'Matter – oh nothing, miss.' And before Julia or Annie could say anything, Emmy turned and fled back to the kitchen.

'Emmy!'

'Whatever is the matter with her?'

'No idea, miss.'

Chapter Twenty-two

Julia walked back to the house, thinking of Arthur Grahame and their conversation. As she approached the house, she was startled by the sound of Mrs Cunningham's voice. She was in full flood.

Julia was about to pass the window when she heard her own name, and couldn't help stopping to listen.

'Even while you were paying your addresses to Julia, to go whoring with a common village trollop! Have you no taste? I will not say shame, for shame you have none!'

She could not hear Peter saying anything, and in a moment Mrs Cunningham went on. 'And if you imagine – if you *imagine* – I am going to tamely hand over the management of this estate, after all this time, when I have got it into such good order, so that you can simply go through it as your whim directs –'

Then she could hear Peter, quietly, as if he were further inside the room, or mumbling, and she could not make out his words properly.

Mrs Cunningham started again.

'What? Frankly I did not think you could be so stupid. Julia is worth a thousand of her! Have you no sense? Good God!' She drew a deep breath. 'You're not worthy of her. What can you have been thinking of? Emmy Goodrich – I give up. I wash my hands of you. Julia must do the best she can.'

Julia could not listen any longer. She walked away round the side of the house and through a brick arch into the garden.

Was it possible? Emmy Goodrich? Had she heard right?

She was looking down the path, and the glorious flowery borders on either side; the old elm throwing its shade further down on the right; the lovely old red brick wall at the end. She wandered slowly down and sat on an old rustic seat.

Emmy Goodrich? Of course. It explained the girl's strange behaviour to herself.

Suddenly everything seemed to descend on her at once, all the disappointments, the unpleasant surprises, the disagreements, the giant disappointment of their wedding night, it all came upon her. Red anger swept through her.

She stood up sharply, walked back round the front of the house, and into the drawing room. Mrs Cunningham and her son were there, though not speaking.

Julia stood in the doorway.

'I had better tell you straight away, Peter, that I have overheard your conversation about Emmy Goodrich. And since I have heard it, I do not think there is any thing we can say to each other. Alicia, will you tell Belton to have the carriage ready immediately? I am returning to London.'

Peter gaped.

'I say, Julia –'

Mrs Cunningham started forward.

'Julia!'

She walked quickly to the bell pull, and jerked it.

'I shall take Becky with me. I am going up stairs to pack my things. Tell Becky to come up to me.'

'I say, Julia, wait.'

'I will not hear you.'

He stopped her.

'Julia, don't be angry.'

'*What?*'

'You misheard.'

'I think not. I distinctly heard your mother's words – "whoring after a common village trollop." Don't touch me!'

'Oh, for heaven's sake, Julia – it was nothing!'

'Nothing? While you were paying your addresses to me, you were seducing Emmy Goodrich? You disgust me!'

Becky appeared.

'Come with me to my room. We are leaving this instant!'

Becky gaped as Julia swept past her, then followed her upstairs. Julia went into the bedroom with her, and slammed the door behind them. In a second there was a knock on the door.

'Take no notice, Becky. Help me pack my things. We are going to back to London now. If we have to walk.'

She started throwing things into a trunk, but in a moment, in a fit of anger and on the edge of tears, threw the shoes she was holding across the room.

'Oh, what does it matter? They can send them on after us. Becky dear, go to your room and pack your bag. We are going now. I will not remain here another second.'

195

She rushed out and up to her room, thoroughly frightened, and Julia pulled a cloak from the wardrobe, and threw a couple of things into a hand bag, and walked out quickly on to the landing. Peter was waiting.

'Julia, wait, for God's sake calm down. I can explain . . .'

'Calm down? Why should I calm down? What is there to calm down for? You have made a mockery of our marriage from the start. You can never have a cared a straw for me. Our marriage was a joke for you, wasn't it? Our honeymoon was a joke, or have you forgotten the night you squandered all your money? We have no home. What is a home if you are never there? It might as well be a hotel as far as you are concerned. Why did you marry me? You could satisfy your lust with Emmy Goodrich, what did you want me for?'

She thrust past him, went down the stairs two at a time, and walked quickly to the front door.

'Is Belton ready?'

Mrs Cunningham came out a second later.

'Julia, I beg you –'

'Is Belton ready?'

'Oh dear, yes, he's coming round.'

Becky came running down the stairs.

'Good. Tell him to catch us up in the lane. Come, Becky.'

She walked quickly out of the door and Becky ran after her, a bag in her hand, and fastening a cloak round her shoulders. Julia would not slow down, and Becky had to half run to keep up with her.

It was not until they they were halfway down into the village that they heard the carriage behind them. Belton pulled up.

'Thank you, Belton. Take us to the station, if you please.'

All the way to London Julia sat in the carriage alone with her thoughts. (Becky was of course travelling third.) It was not just the insult – the attack on her womanhood – his unfaithfulness comprised more than that. That she was made to seem shabby, cheap, to feel that she was of no account, as if he had toyed with her, treated her as something for a moment's distraction; worse, worse than that. It was not these transgressions – these "wild oats" – so much as the light it threw on him. How shallow, thoughtless, how callous, and unthinking it made him seem. His immaturity and thoughtlessness, which she had hitherto thought of as boyishness, something he would eventually grow out of, were far from innocent. He was a responsible adult, accountable for his acts, and the consequences of his shallowness and folly were hurt to others – they were moral blemishes, faults. It was shameful.

At last her eyes were opened. Their marriage was a sham, a hollow joke, a shameful mockery, and everything, all the love and devotion she had brought to him, offered to him, was thrown back at her, trampled beneath his feet, as he went on his careless way, a man incapable of valuing her, incapable of valuing what she had to give. She felt sick. How could she have imagined it would come to this? Her father had warned her – even Mr Grahame seemed to have known – how could she have been so blind? So foolish? How could she have been so carried away?

She stared out of the carriage window. She had had so much to give. Had wanted to give so badly; she would have done anything for him, would have died for him. And all the time, with Emmy Goodrich . . . she could not think. Her throat felt choked. She could not even weep. It was just such a rush of anger, of frustration, of disappointment, of shame and rage with herself, that she could have been so stupid – she, Julia Stone the calm, the rational, the wise young lady who was so collected and in control of her feelings. Oh!

She would not take his name. Hateful name. She would not sleep in his bed. It was over.

Oh God. But they were married, vowed to live together as man and wife. And she was carrying his child. Oh God.

Late that evening they arrived back in Ebury Street.

'Come with me, Becky.'

Julia went upstairs, past their bedroom, to the third floor and a little bedroom at the back which contained a spare bed, unmade, but with some blankets folded neatly on top of it.

'Help me make up this bed. I am going to sleep here tonight. And every night, from now on.'

Becky was too frightened to say anything, and silently the two women spread the sheets and blankets on the bed.

'Thank you, Becky. Tell Mary to bring me up some hot water then you can go to bed.'

She returned to the main bedroom and took some night things from the chest of drawers, went back upstairs and undressed. Mary came up with a can of hot water, then Julia took off her nightgown and washed herself all over, from her feet up, wanting to wash it all away, cleanse herself of him, of his touch. Rubbing the towel harshly up and down her legs, it was if she wanted to make herself new again, wholesome, as if he had never touched her. Then she went to bed. It was nearly midnight.

She could not sleep. It all came back, everything, all the disappointments, the frustrations, most of all the keen disappointment in him.

197

How could she not see that he was not worthy of her? A worthless, shallow, vicious, unprincipled, idle young man. What had she been thinking of? She was just so angry with herself. How had it happened? She thought back over the period of their courtship – if it could be called that – since March. She had been dazzled by him. So certain that such a glorious and beautiful young man could not conceivably be interested in her, that she had never stopped to think what he was really like.

That was part of it. But really it was her need to love which was at the centre of it all. Her overwhelming need to give the love she had in such abundance. That was what had blinded her. No good blinking at the fact.

Eventually she drifted into a shallow sleep, waking at intervals during the night, and then, in the morning, feeling drained and listless.

Becky brought her a cup of tea, but she left it undrunk, standing on the floor by her bed, while she lay staring at the wall, asking herself what she was going to do with the next fifty years of her life. She was married to him. He had absolute power over her. He could come or go, spend his money or not spend it, demand his conjugal rights if he chose. Suppose he demanded she should come back to their bed downstairs? She couldn't refuse. He would be within his rights to force her.

Well, he should never force her. She would kill herself first.

But then their child. He had an absolute hold over her there. Even with all her superior powers, all her strength of character – once their child was born, she was helpless in his hands. He could threaten to take the child away from her if he chose. Why had she got pregnant so quickly? It seemed madness now. And yet so recently, only a matter of a few weeks ago, the thought had never even entered her head. She had been giving herself to him, ready, willing, throwing himself at him. He had called her 'forward'! Oh God, she couldn't stand it. What had possessed her? But it was no good going on like this, she would go mad.

What was to be done? She would not go back to his bed. Never. She would keep house for him. Bring up their child when it should be born; maintain his dignity to the world, no one should know. But within – nothing. There should be nothing between them. That was certain.

All morning she lay inert, the thoughts following one another through her mind, repeating and repeating themselves.

And then, around five that afternoon, there was a step on the stair, and then a timid knock at the door.

'Julia?' Peter's voice meek, scarcely audible. She stared at the wall.
'Julia?' He scratched on the door.
She would not move a muscle, would not lift an eyebrow for him.
Slowly the door inched open.
'Julia?' He was whispering.
No reply.
'Why are you up here?'
She would not move, staring at the wall. Silence.
'Julia, for God's sake, forgive me. You can't imagine what I've been through. Honestly, Julia, we've got to – I mean, I know it's my fault –'
Silence.
'Julia, for God's sake, forgive me. It's all my fault, I know it – everything, but I swear I'll make it up to you.' Pause. 'Only say you'll forgive. me.' Pause. 'You've no idea, Julia, we can't go on like this, for God's sake.'
Silence. Nothing.
He came across the room, looking down at her, lying with her back to him. He knelt by her side.
'Julia.' In a whisper. Nothing.
He reached out tentatively to touch her shoulder. She shook him off violently. Now he seemed to be in tears.
'I don't know what I'm going to do, Julia, I can't go like this if you won't speak to me. For God's sake, I implore you, just say something, anything. Only look at me, I really can't bear it, honestly.'
Julia spoke so quietly that he wasn't sure he heard her.
'Go away.'
'Julia, I can't go away. I can't – not until you say you forgive me. I swear to you, honestly, on my honour, Emmy meant nothing to me, less than nothing. Honestly – it was five minutes, just – and anyway it was before we – you and I really got to be friends, I swear it, just a couple of evenings – and I just got carried away – believe me, I beg you, I can't bear you just to lie there.'
Julia rolled over and looked at him. Her face was very grave, and he could see where the tears had dried on her cheeks.
'Oh my God, you've been crying, I can't stand it. I'll do anything, anything, if only you will stop crying. I can't stand it.'
He tentatively reached out a hand to touch her face where the tear had dried. She pushed his hand away.
'Peter, we are married. Can you understand that?' Her voice was hollow, inert, strange and distant, as if she were speaking down a long tunnel, a voice drained of feeling.

199

'We are married. We have sworn to live together for the rest of our lives. Can you understand what that means?'

'Yes, oh yes,' Peter whispered fervently, grateful that at last she was speaking to him.

'It is the most solemn sacrament of our lives.' She was looking close into his eyes. 'Peter, it is the most important thing in our lives. We must take it seriously, we must give it everything we are capable of, otherwise –'

'I know, I know! And I will, my darling. Only say you forgive me? I swear it'll be all right from now on – all that, the club, the cards, no more, you have my word. We'll live within our income, we'll be a happy little couple, we'll have our little boy, we'll be a model couple, I swear to you.'

A bleak smile crossed her face.

'It may be a girl, Peter.'

'Nonsense.' He was alert now as he saw Julia thawing. 'I know it's going to be a boy – feel it in my bones!'

Suddenly something in her snapped, and she threw her arms round his neck and wept.

'There, there, old girl, don't worry, it's going to be all right, I know it is. Don't you worry.'

After a while, she lay back on her pillow and looked up at the ceiling.

'Peter, there is one thing, I must tell you. This talk of a law-suit against your mother. There must be no more of that.'

He hesitated and then, 'Quite right! Foolish idea. What was I was thinking of? Mother was a frost, I can tell you. Would have caused the most enormous ructions. And Lizzie – I could see she would have been pretty upset. No, bad idea, all buried. Tell you what though, Julia, Mother's upped the income – twelve hundred a year from now! We'll live like lords!'

She looked at him again.

'We are going to live within our income.'

'Quite right. Do the proper thing. After all, I am going to be a father. Got to settle down now you know, got to start acting the paterfamilias. Oh, and I say, Julia I've got a surprise for you downstairs.'

'Hmm?'

'Can't you guess?'

'No.'

'Why, I've only been and carted all your blessed books up from Stallbridge. Weighed a ton, I can tell you! Boxes and boxes of 'em. Can't think when you ever had the time to read 'em!'

Julia couldn't hold out any longer. She ran her hand down the side of his face, and he leant over and kissed her.

'That's better. I say, Julia, are you hungry – want to come down and have a spot of supper, eh?'

She smiled faintly.

'I'd rather not get up tonight, Peter. I'll get up tomorrow.'

'I say, tell you what – we'll have a picnic up here. By the by, you're not going to stay here, are you?'

'I will tonight, if you don't mind. I feel very weak.'

'Have you eaten today?' He looked at her suspiciously.

She smiled faintly again, shaking her head.

'No wonder! You're weak with hunger. We'll have a a nice little bit of supper together, just the two of us. My God, now you're expecting, Julia, I've got to start taking care of you.'

He was about to rush out of the room, but she called him back.

'Peter.' She smiled at him. 'Really, it's better not. Leave me now, I want to sleep. I'll be all right, and I'll be up again in the morning just as usual. Don't worry, my dear, just for tonight.'

'Eh? Oh, all right, if that's what you want.'

'Thank you, my dear.'

He came back and gave her a brief kiss then disappeared downstairs.

She lay staring up at the ceiling.

Had anything changed after all? It seemed they were reconciled. Could she trust him? He seemed the same as ever. How long would his reformation last?

She had to accept it, had no choice; and it was true, after all, she had felt a flicker of her old love for him, when she had heard that sad, pathetic note in his voice. It was true.

Chapter Twenty-three

Julia went off into a deep sleep, and woke the next morning feeling hungry. She came down and knocked on the bedroom door to find Peter awake, and sat on the side of his bed. They chatted, and then, after they had dressed, went down and had breakfast together, something they had not done for some time, just the two of them, and all the time Peter was attentive – laughably so sometimes – and when she teased him about it, said, 'God, Julia, you can't imagine how relieved I am. I thought you'd never speak to me again. What shall we do today?'

What Julia wanted to do was to unpack her books. She told Peter she wanted the little room behind the dining room as her study, with a desk in it and book shelves, and of course he was all agreement, and full of useful suggestions, and letters were despatched to a firm of joiners to install book shelves; then they went out to the furniture warehouse and chose her a desk, very nice, with a scroll top, and lots of charming little drawers, and Peter said, 'Can't think what you want so many drawers for Julia,' and she said, 'To keep all the letters from my lovers, of course,' and he said 'For the Lord's sake, don't tease me about it, Julia. I'm destroyed, I promise you!' and they were very jolly together.

That afternoon she unpacked some of her books and sat on the floor of the little back room looking through them. Books from her childhood, fairy tales, school books from when her father had taught her geography and French, and Latin, and then there were others, text books and dictionaries, relics of the work she had done for her father, and looking through them, she thought of all the years she had worked for him, all those days when she had sat at the desk in her room by the window, and would look down at Goodrich and William – now Emmy's husband – planting out vegetables and soft fruit. All gone, all behind her. Then she thought of her father, who had still not forgiven her for deserting him; and she grew sad, wondering whether he would ever do so.

As they were drinking tea that afternoon, Peter said, 'Tell you what, we ought to go out somewhere – do something together – would you like to go dancing? Why don't we? Let's go to Cremorne!'

She had never heard of it.

'Never heard of Cremorne? Julia, where were you brought up? Don't tell me – I know. My dear, Cremorne is simply the jolliest place in London, on my life! And we can dance!'

After dinner he told her to go and put on a pretty frock. So she put on a lovely lavender green dress, with a large paisley shawl in violet and mauve for the later evening – 'Can't have you catching a chill,' Peter said – and a new bonnet, trimmed with artificial flowers, they went out around eight, and took the omnibus down the King's Road and went into Cremorne Gardens.

There was a large illuminated entrance, and people were flocking in. Once Peter had paid and they were inside, Julia found herself in a fairyland of ornamental gardens, with gas-lights everywhere among the trees supported by garlanded statues, curious grottoes and tempting arbours, beautiful flower beds, little artificial waterfalls, a cafe all done up in the Moorish style serving suppers, little Turkish kiosks serving ice-creams, and the distant sound of a band. They strolled through the crowds, all high spirited, all out to enjoy themselves, and everywhere so many beautifully dressed women, and Julia felt almost ashamed, having had no idea it was such an elegant place, and wished Peter had warned her to wear something a little more showy.

They strolled along by the river, and the lights of Battersea gleamed across the water. It was lovely.

At nine there was to be a firework display, but first Peter said, 'You want to dance, don't you?'

'Oh, yes, please.'

So they went to the dancing platform, which was a most elegant construction, with a shining parquet floor and a fancy wrought iron fence round it, and lights over it on wrought iron hoops, and above them in a sort of oriental pagoda suspended in the air on graceful filigree screens, the band played. Dancers were hurling themselves into the festivities with great energy.

'Now, Julia, don't forget you're in a delicate condition, so we'll just take it gently.'

But Julia did not feel delicate; the spirit had revived in her, Peter was so attentive and pleasant and she felt such a desire to dance again.

They whirled about to a Strauss waltz among all the other merry folk, all laughing, smiling, everyone exuberant, elated, and the band above them sawing away, and as the summer evening slowly deepened into night, the lights stood out against the deep violet gloom among the trees, and Julia thought it all quite magical.

At nine everyone stopped to watch the firework display over the river, standing among the trees along the waterside, and there was a great chorus of 'ooh!' and 'aah!' as the rockets shot up into the dark night.

After that they went in to the charming little coffee rooms and had coffee, and nibbled a macaroon, and Julia couldn't help admiring the stylish clothes some of the graceful young ladies were wearing around them, and they way they were flirting and laughing with their friends. It all seemed very agreeable and refined.

Around eleven, as they were about to leave, Peter went off to spend a penny and left her alone for a moment near the entrance gate.

She was adjusting the shawl round her shoulders, and pulling on her gloves, when she was approached by a clergyman. He was a very respectable young man, impeccably dressed in a frock coat and silk hat with his dog collar. He held in his hand a small printed pamphlet.

'My dear young lady, I beg you to read this. It may yet not be too late.'

Julia was startled, and looked at the pamphlet in her hand. It was entitled *The Washerwoman of Finchley Green*. She knew what it was – an 'improving tract', a sort of low-church tale with a Biblical moral. Her father had been very scathing about this kind of evangelical missionary effusion.

'Thank you, sir, I don't think –'

She held it out to him.

'No, I beg you, take it! Take it, dear young lady, and read it diligently. It may yet not be too late to turn aside from the path of error into the way of righteousness! There is always a place reserved at the Lord's table for the penitent sinner; though ninety and nine be refused, yet through repentance –'

'I beg your pardon?' Julia couldn't help smiling at his exhortation. 'I assure you, I have no need of any such instruction. I am a clergyman's daughter myself.'

'Oh! And so fallen!'

'Fallen?'

'But the Lord is merciful. His ways are just. Oh, daughter, that we might pray together, and that I might be instrumental in leading you into a purer, better life! That you might yet be clothed in the shining garb of penitence!'

'I beg your pardon, sir, but I am a married woman.'

The man was not to be deflected. But before he could go on, Peter reappeared.

'Ready, old girl?'

The clergyman was startled.

'Here is my husband, sir.'

'Oh, I beg your pardon, I believe there has been some – I do most awfully beg –'

Looking between them, he was covered in confusion and hurried away.

'You forgot your pamphlet,' Julia called after him.

'What was that all about?'

They turned and made their way out into the King's Road.

'I really have no idea. He came up to me while I was waiting for you, and thrust it into my hand, and began babbling on about repentance.'

Peter looked at her for a moment and then began to laugh, and the more he laughed the funnier it seemed to get, until Julia was beseeching him to let her into the joke. Peter was doubling up with laughter.

'Julia, I can't – oh, wait till I tell the fellows! I've never heard anything so priceless, and you the rector's daughter too!'

'Peter, what is it? Tell me, for heaven's sake.'

'He thought you were –' He collapsed into giggles again.

'What?'

Peter stopped, wiping his eyes, and drew a breath.

'Well, how can I put it for your chaste ears? He mistook you for – ahem – a *fille de joie*. A Daughter of the Night.'

'No! How on earth – Peter – why should he have thought that?'

'Well, old girl, I didn't like to draw it to your attention, but – well, you remember how you admired all the girl's dresses and gowns, and how refined and beautifully turned out they were, and you said to me you wished you'd worn something a bit more showy?'

'Yes?'

'Well, I'm afraid, all those girls –'

'What?'

'Not quite what they seemed.'

'Peter –'

'The Great Social Evil.'

The penny dropped. She looked at him, wide-eyed.

'Really?'

''Fraid so.'

'Oh, what a pity. They seem so innocent, so charming.'

'Ahem. Yes, didn't like to tell you before – the place has got a bit of a reputation for that sort of thing, I'm afraid. Still, we enjoyed ourselves, didn't we?'

Julia was very thoughtful on the way home. She was a little aghast that she had been taken for a prostitute; and she was rather surprised that Peter had thought of taking her there. Even so, they had had a jolly time, it was true, but that was because she didn't know – no, it wasn't that. There was something else which rankled at he back of her mind, and she couldn't exactly locate it.

It was Peter. There had been something about his laugh, something cold, callous; it had struck a jarring note. No thought of the embarrassment caused to her. Her arm was in his, and he was whistling and twirling his cane, and she looked at his face half in shadow as they walked beneath the street lamps. It was true, there was a callous streak in him; she hadn't wanted to recognise it before.

It was only a matter of three weeks to Lizzie's wedding, but before that Peter, still solicitous for Julia's health, said to her next morning, 'What we need is some sea air! We'll go to Ventnor!'

Julia had never been to the sea-side so that seemed an excellent suggestion. Peter never waited about. He seemed to do everything on the spur of the moment. Boxes were packed, servants were instructed, and that afternoon they were on a train to Portsmouth.

'Are we going to find anywhere to stay? It's the middle of August. Won't it be awfully crowded?'

'Don't you worry, my darling, leave it to me.'

They arrived at Portsmouth, took the steamer across to the Isle of Wight, and a little local train carried them round to Ventnor.

It was half-past six. Julia and Becky were ready for some tea.

'We'll leave the boxes here. Franks and I will go and find somewhere, and you girls can sit and drink a cup of tea.'

So Julia and Becky sat in the winter garden of a seafront hotel, which was full, and drank tea, and looked out at the view. It was a bright afternoon, the beach was crowded, the bathing machines rolled down to the water's edge, and there were yachts out at sea.

'All taken care of!' Peter said half an hour later as he and Franks returned. 'Very nice hotel – cut above this place, just ten minutes from here, sea view rooms too. Last-minute cancellation! Is there any tea left in that pot?'

That evening they were installed. They had a suite of rooms, in fact the best rooms in the hotel, looking directly over the beach, the sea right beneath their window, and as she threw back the windows that first afternoon and heard the sound of the breakers, and the mewing of the gulls, and the sound of people talking outside, and walking up and down, it seemed a very good idea indeed to have come.

Peter was lounging in an armchair, while Becky and Franks were unpacking boxes.

'Think you'll like it? Sea air will soon put some colour back into your cheeks.'

'Oh – do you mean – was I looking pale?'

'Just a *leetle*.'

After dinner, they strolled along the promenade.

'Are you going to swim, tomorrow?' she asked.

'Certainly.'

And that night she fell asleep to the sound of the waves, and felt immediately better, and thought how sweet and good Peter could be when he chose.

The next day they walked along to a deserted part of the beach, Julia sat with a parasol, and with a shawl round her, and Peter took all his clothes off and went in for a swim. She thought how beautiful he looked naked, his slim white body, his slender hips, and he seemed quite fearless and just threw himself into the sea, fighting his way out through the breakers. Later as he came back out, all dripping, she couldn't help noticing that the beach wasn't quite so deserted, for there were now several other ladies behind her, also enjoying the sight of him naked. She turned round and gave them a cold stare, but they were quite unabashed and stared impudently at him.

'Oof! That's good. Mind you, colder than the jaws of hell.'

'Are the jaws of hell cold? I always thought they might be rather warm.'

Peter was rubbing himself vigorously with a towel.

'You seem to have gathered a little audience.'

'I know. Confounded shame, isn't it?' He looked up at them, and they promptly turned away. He raised his voice. 'Confounded shame when a fellow can't take a dip without half the old maids of the town turning out to gawp!'

The women now scuttled away in high dudgeon. Peter laughed, and threw himself down beside Julia, and began pulling on his clothes.

'What do you think, Julia? Capital place, eh? Live to be a hundred here.' He reached over and patted her belly. 'Good for the little fellow too, bound to be'

'Peter, it may not be a little fellow, I keep on telling you.'

'Yes, it is. My little son and heir. So we're taking care of you. Plenty of rest, sea air and all that.'

He looked about and drew in a deep breath.

'You can feel it doing you good, can't you?'

Away to their right, the cliffs beetled above the town, sheltering it from the westerly winds, and giving it generally a mild and almost un-English quality.

'Yes, nice little spot. Came here once before when we were little.'

'I wonder what you and Lizzie were like as children.'

'Don't you remember?'

'Hmm? In a hazy sort of way. You pulled my hair once, that I remember.'

'You probably deserved it.'

'I can't remember.'

He looked away thoughtfully for a moment.

'I wasn't a very gentlemanly little boy, I'm afraid.'

'No, your mother spoilt you. You needed a father to pull you up.'

Peter made a face, and stared out to sea. They sat in silence, each full of their own thoughts.

'Peter?'

'Hmm?'

'Have you ever thought of taking up a profession?'

'Profession? I am a gentleman.'

'Of course you are, my dear. But I mean to say, nowadays many gentlemen have taken up a profession, you know.'

'What? Do you see me as a grubby little lawyer? Or a quack? God, Julia, it takes forever to qualify as a medic. Can you see me burning the midnight oil for seven years, just so I can have the privilege of dosing old ladies and sticking on sticking plaster and pocketing guineas for the rest of my life? Are you serious?'

Julia was silent. The thought had popped into her head at that moment; and yet it had been the fruit of many months of thought, simmering in her mind. The trouble with Peter was very simple – he didn't have anything to do. He was naturally energetic, and without any aim in life he easily turned to dissipation, drink, cards, joking with a handful of friends as idle as he was.

The idea of a profession, a respectable activity to take up his energies, had naturally presented itself to her. In the world in which she had been brought up, men had duties, a calling, tasks ahead, they applied themselves to some cause or project beyond, and bigger, than themselves. It gave a focus to their lives. It also made them naturally more serious, more mature. But one had only to look at Peter to see that that was quite out of the question for him.

208

He had been staring away, silent.

'Oh, I know what you're thinking. I haven't the wit to run the family estate, and Mother does it far better than ever I could, and that's true, for now. But one of these days – I mean, Father's not going to last for ever, anyone can see that, and then I shall take over willy-nilly, whatever Ma says. We'll have to go back to Stallbridge, push mother out into some sort of dower house, and settle down to being the village squire. Can you see me? Hmm?'

He grinned at her, but there was a sardonic twist to his grin.

'You'll be all right. Why shouldn't you?'

'Don't know. I just can't see it somehow.'

'You won't have any choice, my dear.'

'I dare say. It's just that I often feel that somehow we're doomed, the family, I mean, got some sort of malevolent spirit that's going to pull us down.'

'Peter, whatever do you mean?'

'It comes over me sometimes. I just don't see a life stretching before me, like other fellows, all neatly ordered; somehow I'm rotten within, and it's all going to come to pieces, crumble, and decay.'

'You are in a strange mood.'

'Am I? Sorry, but you asked. Anyway, what about a spot of lunch, and then, you must rest this afternoon.'

'No, stop – tell me, why you said that. I want to know.'

'Can't explain it. Sounds silly, there it is. Come on, let's go.'

'Peter, I can't let you go until you have answered me. What do you mean by those words?'

'Oh, nothing. Really, come on.'

'It is important, my dear. Think of me for a moment, I am your wife, and everything which touches you, touches me too. Come, you must explain yourself.'

'I tell you, I can't. There now. Sorry, I shouldn't have spoken – it's frightened you.'

'No, it hasn't frightened me – I am not easily frightened – but I want to understand.'

'Well, since you insist, what I mean is – Father's ill, you have seen for yourself, and who knows, but it may be hereditary.'

Julia felt a shaft of alarm.

'Hereditary? Who says so?'

'No one seems to know what is the matter with him for sure. But sometimes I feel it may be in me too, latent, and then one day, when no one is expecting it, it'll come out in me too. That's all.'

She reached out and took his hand.

'Peter, listen to me. When that day comes – if it comes – we will

209

face it together. All the same, I don't believe what you say, you are a picture of health, and must not think these thoughts. It is just morbid. Come now, kiss me.'

They walked back to the hotel, and Peter shook off his mood and seemed cheerful again.

That afternoon she retired to sleep for a couple of hours while he strolled around the little town, whistling in his tuneless way, then on an impulse climbed the steep cliffs behind the town, and eventually came in around five o'clock as she was waking up.

He sat on the edge of the bed, and patted her belly.

'Have a nice sleep?'

'Hmm.'

'It's doing you good.'

Suddenly seeing him there, with his shirt open at the neck, and his face already brown with the sun, a flush of health on him, looking so impossibly handsome, she felt a great rush of love for him, and sweeping all the thoughts and scruples, all the memories of Bad Homburg, and his cards and drinking, all of it behind her, she reached up to him, pulling him down to her and kissing him, and felt they were on their honeymoon again, another better honeymoon, and had survived their first important test.

It was dark as Arthur arrived in Whitechapel, and made his way along the street in the yellow-green light of uncovered gas flares. Along the street, in the muddy roadway, stood stall after stall selling every imaginable thing. All kinds of cheap food – pig's trotters, tripe, calves' heads, home-made pies, sausages, hot chestnuts, rotting vegetables. There were stalls covered with old household utensils, bowls, cutlery, saucepans, cabbage strainers; and furniture dealers with arm-chairs of unimaginable antiquity, their stuffing on display, and broken-bottomed cane chairs; and then clothes stalls, too many to count, all overflowing with wretched threadbare cast-offs that had been cast-off so many times they had no longer any pretension to identity at all but partook of a general nameless old-clothesness; all stretching along the curb as he made his way through the crowd, with a hand in his pocket, his little bag slung over his shoulder and his long easy stride.

And the faces that passed him in the cold green light of the gas, the thin, the pinched hungry faces: the young, painted face of a girl offering herself for sixpence; a prematurely aged mother clutching a ragged shawl round her, and pulling a crying child behind her; an old man with a white beard, so weak and emaciated that he might just collapse in the street at any time; and all the loud young men

210

shouting their wares from the stalls, bartering with customers, haggling over a penny; a man who stumbled out of a public house and nearly knocked Arthur over, leering into his face and breathing stale tobacco and beer over him . . .

He turned off Whitechapel High Street into a narrow side street and so came to the Universities' Mission. Shambling, destroyed wrecks of humanity were already lining up to get in.

A young clergyman was at the door, attempting to organise them as they came in to the bare and gloomy hall.

'Take your time! There's room for all. No pushing at the back there!'

Arthur stood watching him for a moment, and then as the tide slackened for a moment went forward.

'Good evening. I wonder if you remember me? Arthur Grahame – a friend of Herbert's.'

'Arthur, of course! Welcome! We could do with another pair of hands. You'll find Herbert stirring something at the far end there.'

Arthur pushed his way into the long hall, where now, in the light of a number of wide circular gas rings which hung from the rafters, he saw what seemed like hundreds of the most ragged and abject mortals he had ever seen, the detritus, the veriest last off-scouring of the human race, more ragged and abject than ever he could have imagined, fighting and scrambling as they were each issued with a wooden bowl, and a spoon. The hall was set out with long collapsible trestle tables.

At the far end he saw several men and women standing round large vats and cauldrons from which steam rose. As he made his way through the crowd to them he recognised Herbert.

'Arthur! Just in time! I am fearfully short-handed this evening! Would you take hold of that ladle, my dear fellow?'

The pale face of his friend, the thin blond hair lying flat on his head and the neat neck-tie which was visible above the long apron, and above all the genteel accents of Herbert, all made him seem most out of place. Arthur smiled, threw down his bag on a step at the back, and grasped the ladle.

'Now, as they come past, one ladleful per person and no more – well, not at first any way. There is sometimes a little left over. Mrs Dickinson, will you take responsibility for the bread? Is everyone in, Hobson?'

'Not yet,' called a colleague, another dapper young clergyman, halfway down the hall. He held up his hands, and called out in a thin voice, 'Ladies and gentlemen, I beg you, please form an orderly queue.'

211

The whole hall was a seething mass of smelling humanity, and it never throughout the evening approached any kind of order, but by degrees at least the disorder was lessened. Over the babble of confused voices, the thin cultured tones of Mr Hobson were heard in a grace, and the doling out of the thin soup and hunks of bread began.

Arthur lent a willing hand, ladling soup into greasy wooden bowls, Mrs Dickinson beside him distributed the hunks of bread. Arthur's solid bulk encouraged a semblance of respect in the poor savages who shuffled past, holding out their bowls, and tearing at the bread even as it was put into their hands as if it were their first meal of the day – which for aught he knew it might well be.

On one occasion Arthur saw a burly fellow blatantly take the piece of bread out of the hand of the old woman in front of him, and gave him a a vigorous clout on the head with his ladle, which caused a roar of laughter all around him. The man swung round with a murderous look ready to tear in pieces the godly man who had dared such an outrage, but he found himself face to face with Arthur.

'Shame on you, friend,' Arthur said mildly.

To the amazement of everyone watching, this heavy thickset man took a closer look at Arthur and decided that it had in fact been an unchristian thing to do after all. He shuffled on and took a seat at the trestle table, to drink his soup. Arthur went on with his ladling.

Later the meal was over, the trestle tables were stacked away, and they made ready for bed on the floor, in a profusion of bits of ragged blanket and old overcoats; a constant sprawling, seething, boiling heap of life. Here and there fights broke out, shouts and cat-calls, and through them, with what seemed to Arthur saintly forbearance, the young clergymen went, lending a hand here, adjudicating in some dispute there, giving advice or counsel somewhere else.

Arthur had little time to observe it all since he had had been in the thick of it from the moment he walked through the door; the mission had developed out of all recognition since he had last seen it.

Much later that night, Herbert took Arthur to the house they had now acquired nearby and which he occupied with his companions and they shared a late supper – it was after ten by this time – and talked, and then later still Herbert took Arthur up to the garret room of Spartan emptiness and order where he had a narrow bed, a small dressing table, and a crucifix on the wall.

'Here we are, my dear fellow. I hope you'll find it comfortable.'

He went out and returned with a handful of blankets, and began to arrange them on the floor.

Arthur stopped him.

'Herbert, I shall sleep on the floor.'

'You have had a long day – besides I'm used to it.'

He was pulling off his shoes. Arthur stopped him.

'Under no circumstances am I going to turn you out of your own bed, Herbert. I admire the spirit of Christian renunciation you have shown, but enough is enough.'

He took the blankets from Herbert, and was soon rolled up in them.

Once Herbert had blown out the candle, they talked in the darkness, and Arthur told him about the Bishop's letter, and as they talked on more and more drowsily, confessed to his friend about the rector's daughter and why he had left Stallbridge.

Chapter Twenty-four

'And to think in twenty-four hours I shall be married! This time tomorrow I shall be Mrs Adolphus Emerson! Julia, tell me, I am doing the right thing, aren't I?'

Julia couldn't help smiling. They were in Lizzie's bedroom, the wedding dress was laid out on the bed, and everywhere clothes were strewn about, hanging over the backs of chairs, shoes everywhere, underwear, crinoline hoops hanging behind the door. Julia was a little tired from the journey but Lizzie had rushed her up into her bedroom they moment they had arrived.

'Well, Lizzie, there are an awful lot of people looking forward to their wedding breakfast tomorrow. I suppose you could always give them the *déjeuner* and cancel the wedding.'

'Oh, Julia, do talk sense! Is it right? Should I go through with it?'

'If you don't, poor Adolphus will go into a decline, I know it. He will never marry another and his life will just wear away in hanging round the village, a sad disappointed old man.'

'Really?'

'Or he might take to drink. Have you considered that?'

'Dolly? Don't be absurd! Can you imagine Dolly – oh, Julia, I do wish you'd take me seriously!'

Lizzie stamped with vexation.

'Julia, am I doing the right thing? Oh, if only I knew!'

Julia took her in her arms and held her tight.

'Don't worry. Everything will be all right, and you will look a picture in your wedding gown.'

Lizzie shed a few tears on Julia's breast, pulled out a minute lace handkerchief, and blew her nose.

She drew a long breath and hiccupped.

'Sorry, it's all getting on top of me. I'll be all right.'

She sat on the edge of the bed.

'It's just that it all seems a tremendous responsibility. All the guests, there's over a hundred you know, the arrangements for the *déjeuner* – the kitchens have been turned upside down, Mother's been screaming at the servants, and the bridesmaids' dresses . . . the dressmaker got the material wrong after all that I had told her, and written it down too. And then Dolly and I went down to the church yesterday afternoon for a rehearsal with your father and he went on at us about what a holy sacrament marriage was, and how we were making the most solemn promise, taking this great oath, to love honour and obey and all that, and he went on about the "for better for worse, and in sickness and in health" – I mean, I don't know what I'd do if Dolly got ill – until in the end I was in a perfect stew about the whole thing, and thought we'd better call it off while there was still time.'

Lizzie's mention of her father made Julia think. Tomorrow in church he would be there, and of course would be invited to the wedding breakfast. Would he come? Whatever the case, there ought to be an opportunity for her to try to speak to him. She was sure any move must come from her. There was no use arguing the rights and wrongs of the case; the fact was he was an obstinate man, and had been hurt, and she must do whatever she could to effect a reconciliation.

They had returned from Ventnor two days earlier. The day after Peter's swim, the weather had turned against them, and they had been confined to the hotel, where Peter had threatened to fidget himself to death until he found out the hotel had a billiard table, whereupon he was perfectly content and played billiards incessantly against all comers for sixpence. She had taken up *Madame Bovary* again, and determined to finish it. Peter had been very impressed.

'Reading it in French, eh? I say, Julia, you're a regular blue-stocking, in fact the most brazen blue-stocking I know.'

'What on earth do you mean?'

'Well, you remember I said you were a secret and confirmed brazen hussy, and now I find you're a blue-stocking as well. It makes a fellow dizzy, I can tell you. I never know which way to take you.'

'You can take me any way you wish.'

'Julia!' he giggled.

'I mean, you could if I weren't in this condition.'

'Sometimes I wonder about you. Did you have a secret life before we met? Sometimes I can't believe you were brought up in a rectory at all.'

In this happy way, two weeks flew by, and they travelled back to London, and then down to Wiltshire.

215

Julia was now about four months pregnant, and beginning to be aware of it; when she washed herself there was now a definite swelling, though of course her clothes easily swamped it.

Looking at herself that evening as she changed for dinner, she thought of Emmy. Poor girl, no wonder she had burst into tears that afternoon. Julia and Peter were staying on after the wedding for a month at least for the shooting, so she was bound to meet Emmy in the village. She could feel no resentment against Emmy. As for Peter, she had adjusted her expectations of him. After the first traumatic weeks of their marriage, she had had to scale down her expectations, and so long as he could keep on the rails she thought they could rub along together.

Lizzie got very little sleep that night and was up at six the next morning, and soon after Julia was in her room, and Watson – her woman – was ironing her gloves and petticoats, and Julia was doing last-minute repairs on her veil: Honiton lace with a chaplet of orange blossom.

At eight there was a knock and Mrs Cunningham was there with a tray.

'You must sit down and have something, dear, or you'll go completely to pieces.' She made her sit on the edge of her bed and sip a cup of tea, and eat half a piece of toast.

'To think I shall never sleep in this room again. To think by lunch time I shall be married. I shall be Mrs Adolphus Emerson. Watson, where are my gloves? Oh, you've got them –'

'Calm yourself, my dear, everything is going to be lovely.'

'It isn't going to rain, is it?'

'No, it isn't. There's not a cloud in the sky; now drink your tea, and finish that piece of toast.'

'I can't touch a thing. What time is it? Oh, is that all? What about the carriage? Hadn't I better start getting dressed?'

'There's plenty of time, just relax and calm yourself.'

'Julia,' Lizzie said timidly, 'when you got married – I mean, on the first night – did you, I mean you know – how was it? All right?'

Julia sat her on the edge of the bed again. Mrs Cunningham had gone out to supervise the preparation of the wedding breakfast, and Watson was at the other side of the room, arranging and laying out her clothes.

'Tell me, Julia, honestly – how was it?'

She thought of that night in London, and the smell of brandy on Peter's breath, the brief flurry, and then him fast asleep beside her. Could it be different for Lizzie? She doubted it. She wondered

216

whether she ought to try and have a talk with Dolly. Poor fellow, he would be as nervous as Lizzie. There was probably little Julia could do.

'I mean – was it painful?'

'Just a little – at first. Don't worry, Lizzie, everything will be all right. These things do take time to work out. You and Dolly will have to get to know each other. If it isn't everything you hope for at first, well, you have each other for the rest of your lives, and there is plenty of time for you to learn each other's ways.'

'You're not being much help.'

'No, dear. Frankly there's not much I can say. I only wish men had lessons in how to behave to a young woman. It could save a lot of embarrassment. Try not to let him drink too much.'

Lizzie perked up at that.

'Don't worry, I have him well trained already. Oh, and I say, Julia, the house has been beautifully furnished. As soon as we return from our honeymoon, you shall be our first guest. And the beauty of it is that being in Devizes I shan't have Mama breathing down my neck every five minutes.'

Lizzie was now more cheerful.

'Well, Julia, this is it. I think I may as well get dressed. Thank you, darling, for listening to my woes. You are my dearest and best friend.'

And on this happy note, she called Watson over, and Julia and she began dressing Lizzie.

At eleven-thirty Belton brought the carriage to the door. He was resplendent, with a large white rosette in his button hole. Peter, who was to give Lizzie away, helped her into the carriage, but the others were walking, since it was barely a quarter of a mile to the church.

Julia walked beside Alicia Cunningham. The lane was crowded with carriages, and the church had been decked with flowers and evergreen boughs. Adolphus and his family were all waiting inside.

As Julia took her place in her pew she couldn't help looking at her father, a few yards away, in his surplice and Oxford hood, avoiding her eye, and all the anguish threatened to well up in her again. She must make an attempt to speak to him today.

Next to him was Mr Crabtree, promoted to curate in Arthur Grahame's absence. Watching him she remembered Mr Grahame, and wondered where he was now.

Lizzie and Adolphus were married. The ring was produced, put on, the bride was kissed, the register signed, the new organ played. Lizzie, in her satin dress with its long veil of Honiton lace now

217

thrown back, and the chaplet of orange blossom in her hair, a posy of flowers in her hand, was glowing, smiling at everyone in spite of herself, and unable to stop her happiness and triumph from shining forth. Dolly was unaccustomed to so much attention from everyone but rather enjoying it.

Lizzie was helped into the carriage as Julia and the others threw rice over them, and soon they were all in the house. There was an uproar of chatter, champagne corks were popping, Lizzie was overexcited, laughing and chaffing everyone, Dolly was blushing while everyone heaped compliments upon him, and eventually they all sat down to the *déjeuner*, a long table in the dining room, and another in the hall, and a third outside for tenants and servants. Everywhere serving girls were hurrying about, glasses were replenished, and food was being served.

Dr Stone, still in his robes, said grace, looking solemn and grave – a man who did not unbend in company, and who made the slightest remark sound like a pontifical pronouncement.

The table was crowded with dishes – roast fowls, mayonnaises of lobster, garnished tongues, boiled fowls with bechamel sauce, collared eels, shoulders of lamb, raised pies, decorated hams, veal and ham pies – and these were followed by blancmanges, jellies, dishes of pastry, fruit tarts, cheesecakes, compôtes of fruit, hothouse pineapples and grapes, ices . . .

Dolly, bathed in so much good will, was more forthcoming than usual.

'We're going to Scotland for the honeymoon. Laidlaw has very kindly offered us the use of his hunting lodge in the Grampians.'

'*Where*?' Peter had been drinking champagne fast and had become lively.

'The Grampians. Well, what's so funny about that? Very fine scenery. I'll be able to get in some deer-stalking.'

'The Grampians!' Peter couldn't stop laughing. 'Oh Lord, Emerson, have you stalked before?'

'No, why? I mean to say, they have ghillies –'

'Ghillies! Ghillies in the Grampians!' Peter was becoming helpless with laughter, and Julia could see Dolly beginning to colour with embarrassment. 'You realise you'll have to wear a kilt?'

'What?'

'Assuredly. Can't go deer-stalking unless you wear a kilt; it would never do. The Scotch would be deeply offended. The ghillies would be offended. It would show a deep lack of respect, Emerson. You have to do these things properly or you shouldn't do them at all, isn't that right? Have you ever worn the kilt?'

218

'Now look here, Cunningham –'

'Problem is, have you got the knees for it? Many men haven't. Could spoil your honeymoon, if you haven't. I think you'd better show us your knees, to be on the safe side. I would hate you to make an ass of yourself on a point like this.'

Dolly was red with embarrassment. Julia was sitting away from Peter and there was no way she could shut him up. He seemed positively to enjoy Dolly's discomfiture. She remembered he had been the same at the engagement ball, only then she had been besotted with him; now she could see more clearly the callous streak in him. Lizzie also saw what was going on, and was about to intervene when Peter abruptly stood up and knocked a spoon against the side of his glass for silence. Julia knew he had been drinking yet it did not slow him or impair his movements; he seemed only more heightened, more effervescent.

He was making a speech on behalf of his father, who sat at the end of the table in his wheelchair. Peter's speech was extempore, light and witty, as if he had just thought of it on the spur of the moment, and watching him, Julia could see the qualities she had at first so admired and loved in him: his debonair easy manner, as if everything came effortlessly, and he could knock off a wedding speech – which would cost another man sleepless nights – with one hand in his pocket, and his mind half on something else.

When Dolly rose to speak, taking a handful of cards from his pocket on which he seemed to have prepared the headings of his speech, Julia could see the effort it was costing him, and could see too Peter sitting back with a conceited smirk on his face, obviously comparing Dolly's lame performance with his own. Yet Julia understood that Dolly, in the awkward way he mumbled the trite and traditional phrases, his gratitude to the bride's parents, his own great good fortune in having secured such a paragon as Lizzie to be his wife and so on, was far more touching in his sincerity than Peter with his easy superiority. Julia wished him well, and everyone clapped with warmth when Dolly at last sat down, covered with embarrassment.

Throughout the meal Julia kept an eye on her father, always hoping at last to catch his eye, to be able to smile at him, and hope for some response. He never looked at her, either concentrating on his food or staring away into the distance as he answered some remark from a neighbour at the table, not able to unbend even at such a moment as this. Julia bit her lip. There was nothing she could do, yet she tried and tried to think of some means of bringing them together again. Remembering that she was expecting a child, she thought that eventually that might be the means of effecting a reconciliation.

Later, after the *déjeuner* was over, as guests mingled and talked in the drawing room, Julia found herself in front of the wedding presents set out on a table at one side of the room.

There were a number of silver items including a splendid antique silver wine cooler, an heirloom of the Emerson family's; a Royal Worcester dinner service, a gift from Alicia Cunningham; a cut glass wine decanter; a pair of Sèvres vases . . .

A woman's proudest day, Lizzie's triumph; Julia's eyes wandered over the presents. Well, she had received some presents too, she thought; they had come in belatedly, in dribs and drabs, by post, as an after-thought. She had sacrificed a lot in running away to get married. All this – the guests, the ceremonial, the display, the glory – and yet she had had no choice. Her father would not give her in marriage to Peter, and how she could she be married in the village, if not from her own home?

After all, Julia knew that there was something more important; she did not regret the loss of all this, so long as she was married to the man she loved. She looked across the room to where Peter was chatting to Fanny Emerson, laughing, and teasing her, making her giggle and blush. The man she loved. The same man she had loved so intensely, and loved still, she told herself, yet in a way she could not quite explain to herself, now loved differently.

Chapter Twenty-five

Julia settled happily into domesticity, and began work on her baby clothes. It surprised her to find she had a taste for the quiet life, and she felt less and less inclination for any kind of intellectual pursuits. *Madame Bovary* lay by her bedside unread, and every night she went to bed more and more conscious of the growing baby inside her, which was now beginning to assert itself by little movements.

'Put your hand here, Peter. You can feel it moving,' she said one night as they lay in bed, and he put his hand rather tentatively on her swollen belly.

'Can't feel a thing. Dash it, strange to think there's a little chap in there growing bigger every day. Wonder of nature, eh? Shouldn't fancy being a woman all the same.' He rolled away.

'Would you mind awfully if it were a girl?'

'Eh? Well, never thought – I mean, I always assumed it's going to be a boy. Got to have a boy, Julia – always have, in our family.'

She sighed. 'We'll just have to accept whatever God sends.'

'Eh? Not much choice, I should think.'

Ten days after Lizzie's wedding came the first of September, and the pheasant shooting season opened.

That very afternoon the old black Hackney carriage rolled up from the station, baggage piled high on the roof, and a beautiful black horse tethered behind. With many a hulloo and cry of greeting Peter's cronies began tumbling out.

'Now then, you fellows, we're going to have some fun! Thank God you're here. Place has been like a morgue since Lizzie's wedding, I can tell you.'

'How is the married lady? Have you heard from her?' Sir Cosmo was opulent in a massive tweed Ulster, a cigar between his teeth. His dundreary whiskers were, if anything, more luxuriant than they had been before, his colour more purple.

'Lucky beggar whoever's got her, *I* say,' said Toby Holden, who had not yet shaken off the city air, and was in a tight black suit and a stiff silk hat, and holding a walking stick.

'She'd never have done for you, Holden; she's got too much bounce, too much snap. You'd have had a dog's life. You're more for the quiet life, now admit it. You're one of nature's bachelors.' Jonathan Selby was mousy and sallow, a lank lock of hair falling across his face.

'Well, I like my creature comforts as much as the next man, dash it. Why not?' said Holden, as Peter led his guests into the drawing room. Peter clapped him across the shoulders.

'Holden's in the right of it. A fellow is entitled to his comforts! What's life for otherwise?'

Julia was sewing baby clothes. Alicia Cunningham was in her office, busy as usual.

Julia rose to greet their guests, and saw to her astonishment that there was a lady in the party. Mr Morley had come, and brought his sister with him.

In the swirl of hand-shaking and greeting, Julia scarcely had time to adjust her thoughts, but Grace Bradshaw forestalled her in any case.

'Mrs Cunningham, it was *so* kind of your husband to invite me. I had wanted to see you in the family home.'

Julia allowed the woman to take her hand and shake it vigorously. None of the men noticed Julia's expression but she could scarcely bring herself to reply to the woman, who in any case had already turned to Peter.

'What a lovely house this is, Cunningham. You're a lucky fellow. By the by, I have brought my hunter down with me – can you get a man to see to him?'

'Do you hunt, Mrs Bradshaw?' Peter asked.

'Hunt?' Sir Cosmo interjected. 'She hunts, fishes, shoots – look to your coverts, Cunningham, she'll have 'em flushed empty.'

Julia regained control of herself.

'Welcome to Stallbridge, gentlemen. I'll ring for tea – or would you like to go upstairs first? Parker, have the gentlemen's – and Mrs Bradshaw's – rooms been prepared?'

'Yes, Mrs Cunningham.'

'Tell you what, old fellow, the thing we'd all like is a drink!' Sir Cosmo looked round to Peter and rubbed his hands in anticipation.

Peter made a face at him, signifying that he had said the wrong thing. Julia rang the bell, and as a maid appeared ordered tea to be served.

'Tea will be in five minutes, gentlemen. Why don't you go upstairs and wash your hands?'

'Have to mind your P's and Q's a *leetle* bit, old fellow,' Peter said to Sir Cosmo as he led his guests upstairs. 'Wine with dinner, a brandy or two afterwards – perfectly acceptable. But not in the afternoon. Ladies frown on it! Besides, have to be on your best behaviour; the little woman – ahem – in the family way.'

'Never! Cunningham, congratulations! A father to be! By God, it'll be the making of you!'

'That's what everybody keeps telling me.'

'Anything else we aren't allowed to do, while we're on the subject?' Sir Cosmo was crushingly ironic.

'Steady on, Whittington,' Holden interrupted him. 'Dash it, we're guests, don't you know. Another fellow's house . . .'

Sir Cosmo frowned but said nothing. Peter sighed, and then brightened.

'Still, one day I shall be master here – and then we'll see what the ladies have to say! Damme, things will be run my way! Anyway, don't worry we'll have a gay old time.' His tone picked up. 'Coverts are in tip top-condition Randall assures me, bursting with wildlife. We'll be out there first thing tomorrow, blasting away; they won't know what's hit 'em!'

When Peter returned downstairs, Julia was still agitated. He didn't notice and was rubbing his hands with glee.

'Now we'll have some fun, Julia. Wonderful to have one's chums round one!'

'Peter –'

'Whittington's a capital shot – and that Mrs Bradshaw, have to watch her. My God!'

'Peter –'

'Hmm?'

'I wish you had told me you were inviting her down.'

'Why?'

She drew a breath, and looked down at her sewing.

'If I had known you were intending to invite her, I would have asked you not to.'

'What? Why?'

'Well, when we were in Bad Homburg, that afternoon when you went to the Casino with Mr Morley, I met her in the park.'

'Yes? Well?'

'She was not very polite – in fact she was very rude to me.'

Peter looked at her for a moment, then laughed.

'She's very rude to everybody.'

223

'I would have preferred her not to be invited.'

'Whatever for?'

'I told you.'

'Oh, Julia, come. I know she's a little boisterous –'

'It isn't that. She said some things about you which I cannot forgive. I would prefer her not to be here.'

'Did she, by Jove! Well, what things?'

Julia looked down, studying her sewing and thinking over that afternoon.

'She said your mother had wanted you to marry me so that I could keep an eye on you.'

It sounded rather lame as she repeated it, and Peter burst into laughter.

'Priceless! She was pulling your leg!'

Julia was bewildered.

'In any case, isn't it it rather irregular to invite a single woman?'

'Single woman? It isn't her fault if her husband's on active service. In any case, the house is full of women, isn't it? You, my sainted mother. She isn't a leper – show a bit of charity.'

Julia felt on uncertain ground. There was something about Mrs Bradshaw but she couldn't say what it was. She felt an instinctive hostility towards the woman, and then suspected herself for doing so. Peter went on: 'She's a lot of fun – regular sort, believe me. Help to liven the party up a bit.'

Peter was determined not to take her point, and soon went off to arrange matters for the morning. Julia remained alone, her sewing forgotten on her lap. She was more agitated than she could account for. There was something – how could she put it? – the woman had intruded here where she was not wanted, and Julia was not free to ask her to leave. It was not her house. All her life Julia had been mistress of her own house, but here she was not. She had not been consulted in the list of guests – Peter had vaguely told her he was having a few friends down for a bit of shooting – and she had assumed it would be his usual friends, so had never thought to ask who they were exactly. Now this woman was under their roof, she could not object. She could not even walk out. She was in a position over which she had no control.

That evening dinner was more lively than it had been since Lizzie had left. The guests dominated the conversation, and were full of London news. Peter felt sadly out of the swim, and wished he were back.

Mrs Bradshaw held her own with the men, and to Julia's surprise, when she and Alicia rose to leave the gentlemen to their wine, Mrs

224

Bradshaw elected to stay with them. Julia had to take a grip on herself.

That evening again she felt at a disadvantage. When the party had all assembled after dinner in the drawing room, Mrs Bradshaw had a fund of stories, she laughed loudly, and was perfectly at home with the men. Julia saw it clearly; she understood them completely, and kept up the bantering conversation, the sporting anecdotes, the jokes, the gossip and tittle-tattle. She could also hold her liquor.

Julia felt sick. Worst of all, she hated herself for the feelings which the woman excited in her. Of course Mrs Bradshaw was not flirting with Peter. Not directly – not in front of Julia. But she understood him, and played up to him in a way that Julia could not. Julia was different from Peter but had believed that, different though they were, yet they could complement each other; bring different things to their marriage.

Watching Mrs Bradshaw, she saw a woman speak directly to Peter and his friends in their own language.

Julia was heavy now and the weight of her pregnancy debarred her from displaying herself as Mrs Bradshaw did quite openly, sitting there in an evening gown, cut low across the shoulders and emphasising her bust over a tight waist. Julia watched her playing with her fan, flicking it, tapping a man on the arm, looking into his eyes with an impudent smile, speaking boldly across the room, behaving as if it were *her* drawing room, and then calling on Julia to sing for them.

'That's a very nice piano, Mrs Cunningham. Won't you favour us with a song?'

Skilled as she was in many ways, Julia could not play the piano. Her father, in his obsession with his work, had neglected to teach her the various accomplishments thought necessary to a young lady's education in other households.

Sitting with her sewing, and conscious of her ungainly bulk, she was ill at ease.

'I am afraid I do not play.'

'Oh.'

Mrs Bradshaw looked round at the others. Sir Cosmo spoke up.

'Perhaps you could sing for us, Mrs Bradshaw?'

She needed no second invitation.

'May I?' She looked impudently at Julia.

'I beg you –'

In a moment the men were gathered round her at the piano, Mrs Bradshaw had struck into *Champagne Charlie* and the men were all roaring it out.

225

Champagne Charlie is my name
Champagne drinking is my game.
Good for any night, my boys,
Who'll come and join me in a spree?

Alicia Cunningham looked across at Julia with a raised eyebrow; with an effort Julia managed to look as if it were all greatly amusing.

'After all, Mrs Bradshaw is keeping the men entertained. We ought to feel grateful,' Alicia whispered.

Julia hated her. And hated herself for such a petty emotion.

Later the men settled to cards and Mrs Bradshaw came to sit with Julia and Alicia by the fire.

Julia took a grip on herself. This woman was a guest in the house – not even her own house, Julia reminded herself – and it was her duty to be hospitable.

'A most charming house you have here,' Mrs Bradshaw said to Alicia. 'My brother had told me about it; it has been a great pleasure to come down. Living at home with a pack of women, you know, it's the most tedious thing imaginable. It's such a relief to get some male company, don't you think?'

'I imagine it must be,' said Alicia.

'And to get a breath of country air too, of course. London's a filthy hole at the best of times. Impossible to keep anything clean.'

Julia concentrated on her sewing as Alicia Cunningham parried these questions. She still could not bring herself to be familiar with the woman.

Mrs Bradshaw turned to Julia.

'You have a capital hunt not far from here, your husband tells me. Do you think they would welcome an interloper?'

'I really have no idea,' Julia said faintly. She wondered what else Peter had told her.

'Do you hunt yourself?'

'I do not ride.'

'No! Really? Not ride? In the country? You astonish me. How do you get about?'

'I walk mostly.'

'Walk. Yes, I see.' Mrs Bradshaw shook her head, as if to indicate her opinion of such a dreary mode of locomotion. 'Well, I have brought Angelus, and I look for some sport, I assure you! Beautiful beast, best I ever rode. Picked him up when we were in Ireland.'

The following morning she appeared in a black riding habit, cut to fit her very closely, outlining and emphasising her figure as if

226

she were wearing nothing beneath it, and with a skirt which hung over her hips so as to show off every movement of her body. She wore a stiff black top hat, and a veil. The sense of modesty implied by the veil was impudently contradicted by the way she wore her habit.

They were all assembled in the hall, the gentlemen inspecting their shotguns, and slinging game bags across their shoulders, buttoning their jackets, and checking their shot pouches. Mrs Bradshaw came down the stairs to join them, and as the men turned, Julia saw Peter's frank admiration as Mrs Bradshaw displayed herself to their gaze.

She accepted their attention calmly as if she were entitled to it, the men crowding round her, and Julia, now visibly pregnant, was conscious of her manipulation of them.

She was confused. She didn't know whether she was entitled to hate Mrs Bradshaw outright, or whether she should take herself in hand in some way on Peter's account.

But she was aware too of Alicia's reaction, and wondered at the effrontery of their guest in displaying herself like this in another woman's house.

After they had gone and Julia and Alicia were in the drawing room together, opening windows to clear the air of the stale smell of tobacco which lingered, Julia asked her, 'Alicia, what do you know of Mrs Bradshaw? Peter said her husband is in the army.'

'I believe there is a Captain Bradshaw somewhere.'

'On some kind of active service overseas?'

'Presumably. Though I imagine a very long way off. I mean, Julia, a very long way.'

'What do you mean?'

'They don't live together any longer. The captain and his lady have agreed to go their separate ways.'

'I see. Presumably he sends her an allowance?'

'Does he? Either that, or she is "maintained" by various friends.'

'I don't understand.'

'She is a sort of charity with them, if you like.' She looked at Julia. 'There are times when I see that you are indeed the rector's daughter. I wish it was not I who had to enlighten you.'

'Don't go on, I think I understand. But why did you allow her to be invited here?'

'My dear girl, what choice did I have? Peter announced he was inviting down a few friends for shooting. *Et voilà!*'

227

Chapter Twenty-six

Dear Julia,

At last I have a moment to sit down and write! You can't imagine what a time we've had of it. I won't inflict everything on you – just give you the bones of it otherwise we'd both be up till the wee small hours (as they say up here), nodding over my prose.

Needless to say, the first problem was actually *finding* the place. Have you ever been to Scotland? It's much bigger than I expected. The train got us as far as Pitlochry, and there was supposed to be a carriage to meet us. There wasn't. So there we were sitting on the station platform with a mountain of stuff including all Dolly's equipment for deer-stalking – I thought Peter had been joking but he wasn't – and Dolly was fussing about like an old hen, counting the boxes, and watching the porters, and then tipping them a *penny*! Honestly, I thought, we're on our honeymoon, old fellow, I think we can afford to be a bit more generous than that. It might help to explain why they took so long to send a wire to the lodge.

Well, at last a *cart* arrived and all the stuff was piled on to it, and we were piled on top of that and we set off. The old fellow who drove us was no great conversationalist, but I prodded him a bit, and asked him about the lodge and how far it was and so on; frankly I needn't have bothered, because I couldn't make out a word he said! He would grunt out some guttural phrase and then lapse into silence. Anyway, it didn't matter because the road – track, actually – wound higher and higher up into the mountains, and everywhere the scenery opened out, and I must say it was quite magnificent, and Dolly and I were in high spirits, the sun was shining, and all the tiredness from the journey – needless to say we didn't get much sleep on the train, and I know what you're thinking and it wasn't that only I never could sleep on a train –

but as I say, up there on top of the world we revived. The moors stretched away, and at this time of year the heather is all purple with bloom, and it was wonderful.

Eventually when I thought we were never going to get there we came over the brow of the mountain, and the car-man pointed with his whip down into the valley at this enormous castle and said something I didn't understand, and I prodded him and asked what he meant, and he said "Yon's Castle Dreary!" and Dolly and I looked at each other, and thought, That can't be it! My dear, it is huge – it isn't called Castle Dreary really, the name's Gaelic and quite unspellable, something like Castlean na Dru-airaig, only it sounds like Dreary. By the way they're always asking "D'ye have the *Garlic*?" and at first I couldn't make out what they meant, and thinking it was a funny time to start discussing cookery, and then the penny dropped – he meant the *Gaelic*. Dolly and I laughed till we cried at the thought of all these highlanders with their garlic!

I must say it is typical of Beattie Laidlaw to talk of their "little place in the highlands" and when you get there it's about the size of Windsor Castle – and about as old too, fifteen foot thick walls, and corridors with icy draughts whistling down them, and windows about three inches wide. Anyway we were shown into the baronial hall and there was a fire burning – you can imagine, the sort of fireplace you can stand up in, together with all your friends – and I was thinking of a nice cup of tea, only forgetting where we were, because the old lady brings up a tray of whisky, "to keep oot the cauld" says she, so there's Dolly and me, toasting our toes in front of this inferno of a fire and sipping whisky, this is four o'clock in the afternoon, and laughing to each other about the accents, and "Castle Dreary", and "the Garlic" and then having another, and within half an hour we were pie-eyed. It was embarrassing; the old lady – or "auld leddy" as they say – comes to show us to our room, and we are weaving about, and falling over the furniture. Honestly, Julia, I'd never drunk whisky in my life!

The next morning and all Dolly can think about is the deer-stalking; an old fellow has arrived – he really is called a ghillie – and we can hardly understand him, but Dolly was there in his best tweeds and boots, and checking his guns, and I was looking around and thinking, Well, if Dolly's going out for the day, what am I going to do? Looking around the place I didn't fancy being left for a whole day on my own, so I decided to go with him. The old fellow draws in a sharp breath. "The deer-staukin's no furr the leddies," says he. "Well, I'm blessed if I'm going to be left here all day," says I. "I'm coming!"

Eventually we trudged off along a winding track up the side of a mountain, and after a while looking back you could see the castle down in the valley, quite alone in all this vast space of heather and bracken. It was wonderful. A clear sky, little white clouds high above us, a lark somewhere singing its heart out. At last, when we'd been tramping for ever and the sun was getting up, so I was quite warm, the old ghillie says "Shush!" and we all crouch in the heather, and he points, and Dolly gets out his little telescope, and there far away across the side of the mountain we see the deer. Dolly let me look through the telescope; the deer were all peaceful, grazing, and sometimes looking up and then moving a little – just like a herd of cows really – and then the old chap points again, and away further up the mountain side there were the males, with enormous antlers. We look at the ghillie; he touches his lips – "shush!" – and we started making our way up the mountain side, supposedly in silence. You'd have laughed, Dolly lumbering in all his tweed, and me having to heave up my skirts to get among the heather, and the old fellow looking back all the time and frowning at us to be silent.

Now I began to notice the midges. The sun had got warm and the insects came out, and I kept wanting to shoo them off but the ghillie was telling us to keep still, and we are crawling, tip-toeing supposedly, through the heather – and the deer still about a mile away, and I'm beginning to be *eaten* by midges. I had no idea, and I mean they were really large, man-eating midges, afraid of nothing, and ravenous for my blood. Dolly noticed them too, but for some reason they didn't bother the ghillie, and he kept on signalling to us to be still, and I'm whispering, "How can I keep still, you idiot, I'm being devoured by monstrous insects!"

I didn't know whether we could stand it for long, our arms flailing about as if we were semaphoring – which I think we were: "Message to deer begins: beware, Sassenachs approaching." Well, at last, after an eternity of this, and me at my wit's end, we seemed to be within range – frankly I'd forgotten all about the deer by now, but the ghillie thinks this it; so out come the guns, there's a lot of wriggling about in the heather, as Dolly checks the shot.

At last, my fingers over my ears, Dolly let rip. It was like an explosion, the noise echoing through this great empty space, birds fluttering up all round us and of course the deer flying for dear life – pardon the pun. They were out of sight within seconds. The

230

old chap stands up looking very displeased. "Ye've missed – well, that's it furr the day!" At last we can stand up, and it was a great relief to stretch our legs after all that crouching in the heather. Frankly I was glad Dolly hadn't hit anything, they looked so noble there on the mountainside. So the next thing was lunch – I was starving by this time. We sat down and took out our sandwiches, and then – you can imagine, I expect – clouds began to gather. The prophet of doom looked up with many an ominous shake of the head.

Of course it came on to rain. Not heavy English rain but a fine moisture that comes at you across the mountainside in great sweeping curtains, and drenches you. You can see it coming – very beautiful in a way, of course. Well, we pulled our hats down over our ears and turned to make our way home. What a trudge it was, we just got wetter and wetter until we were soaked. I mean, drenched through and through, our clothes got heavier and heavier, and more and more cumbersome, clinging round our legs so we couldn't walk properly, and the heavens simply closed in on us – couldn't see the other side of the valley, couldn't see the mountaintops, couldn't see anything, only the next five yards of the path – when there was one. Well, old Jeremiah earned his pay that afternoon otherwise there's no knowing where we would have ended up – probably our bleached bones would have been found years hence, picked clean by the midges. We finally dragged ourselves back to the castle. How I blessed that fire! The auld leddy brought us bowls of hot water and we sat in our dressing gowns with our feet in mustard baths, drying our hair by the fire, and steam rising from our clothes all round the room spread over the furniture. She also brought us hot whisky toddies, so we were soon giggling uncontrollably. Imagine the picture. What a country!

Next day Dolly had a streaming cold, and I was fussing about getting him potations and concoctions – as if we had been married forty years instead of forty-eight hours. I must say married life suits me; it's just so much *nicer* to have a man about, isn't it? Even the sight of poor Dolly in bed with a red nose and streaming cold didn't put me off. He's a dear sweet boy, and there's no harm in him, and I think we're going to rub along together very well.

After a couple of days he was about again, and we decided to leave deer stalking and try for salmon instead, so most days we've been along the river, and I wear a net over my bonnet against the midges, and we have dispensed with the ghillie, so it's just the two of us, and a very merry time of it we are having.

In the evenings we play cards. After hearing about you and Peter at the casino, Dolly wanted to try gambling too, so we play 'Old Maid' for money. At present Dolly owes me thirty-five million pounds!

Looking forward to seeing you again, my dearest,

Eliz. Emerson

Chapter Twenty-seven

Julia thought the guests would settle down into a comfortable house party and enjoy a quiet few weeks in the fresh air. Peter was of a naturally delicate constitution, and she was happy to think that long days in the open air would fill him out – give him a healthy appetite, and make him sleep soundly.

It turned out differently. The shooting gradually took second place to a nightly round of drinking and cards. The games went on later and later, the drinking became deeper and deeper. Julia saw the old pattern beginning to reestablish itself. Peter no longer came up to bed at eleven with her.

'You go to bed, Julia – got to think of the little fellow,' he would call, as he sat with Sir Cosmo, Holden and Morley at their cards. On a small table to one side the brandy decanter stood open. Mrs Bradshaw would be reading a magazine, and showing no sign of moving. Selby would sit alone by the fire. What was she to do?

'Good night, gentlemen,' she would say, as brightly as she could, and take her candle up to their bedroom.

At some time during the night, Peter would join her.

It was London all over again, only now the club had been imported into their house.

Apart from Jonathan Selby, the men were not interested in a formal breakfast, He would sit with Julia and Alicia in the dining room at eight o'clock, and though his conversation was monosyllabic, Julia believed that he was making an effort to be sociable.

On the sideboard a row of chafing dishes stood loaded with a breakfast that the other men were unlikely to come and eat. They would reappear at some late hour and order a light snack.

Occasionally Mrs Bradshaw joined them for breakfast. She seemed to have a constitution of steel. Julia had no idea what time she went to bed, but it was certainly much later than herself, because their rooms were next to one another, and Julia was never aware of her entering.

On Sunday Julia went to church with Alicia Cunningham. None of their guests made an appearance. The men were all in bed, except for Selby who had taken out a gun, and Mrs Bradshaw had gone out for a ride.

It was now late-September and the old beech trees in the church yard were in wonderful shades of gold and russet. There was an agreeable nip in the air too, and they had put on warmer coats this morning.

They walked up the lane to the church behind a groom who pushed Mr Cunningham in his wheelchair.

Julia could not help remarking to Mrs Cunningham, 'This is exactly as it was when we first moved into our house in Ebury Street. I felt I was running a hotel.'

'You'll get used to it. He was just the same when he was an undergraduate.'

'I will not get used to it,' Julia said warmly. Alicia raised an eyebrow. 'It is no way for a gentleman to behave, or a husband either. We are entitled to more. You are entitled to more. It is insulting to you as their hostess.'

'Ah yes,' Alicia said, 'their hostess. We must take the men in hand. What do you propose we do?'

'I shall not stand it much longer.'

'Exactly. And what will you do?'

Julia was silent.

'My dear, there is nothing you can do. They are men, you see. They are free to do as they please. If they cannot be shamed into civilised behaviour, we are helpless. Men have the power – all the power, Julia. I have a little power at the moment because my husband is senile. But once he has gone, I shall be helpless. Peter will have everything, and then we shall see the sparks fly.'

Julia was silent.

'You walked out on him once,' Alicia went on. 'He was really frightened, and I admired you for it. But you took him back.' She sighed. 'You had to. Don't misunderstand me, my dear. I am not belittling your motives – I am sure you love my son – but actually you had no choice. There was nothing else you could have done.'

Julia stared down at the ground in front of her as they walked side by side, and bit her lip. No choice? They should see about that! And yet some voice within her told her that Alicia was telling the truth. After a while Alicia went on, 'I lose my temper with him from time to time – just to relieve my feelings. I expect I shall again, before too long. Of course in the long run it doesn't make any difference. He does exactly as he pleases. Men do.'

In church Julia was pleased to see Lizzie sitting in the Emerson pew. It was odd how they had moved about in the church; Lizzie gone to the Emerson pew; herself now in the Cunninghams' – which incidentally was more comfortable than the bench on which she had been used to sit. Here Mrs Cunningham had really made herself cosy – ostensibly in the name of her husband; there was a tiny stove, which the groom lit before retiring to the back of the church, there were foot-stools to keep their feet out of the draughts, and the pew was heavily upholstered. Julia made herself comfortable, and smiled again across at Lizzie. Mr Cunningham nodded.

Dr Stone took the service. Sitting at the front now, and only a few feet from him, she watched him, hearing again the familiar voice. Julia was depressed. They were as far apart as ever.

Her father took care not to see her, though she never took her eyes off him during the service. It was still as if she did not exist.

Afterwards as they came out of the door, Julia found herself face to face with him, and before he could turn away, she smiled at him.

'Hullo, Father.'

His face was rigid. Not a flicker of a muscle. He stared at her as if she were some stranger who had impudently intruded herself on his attention.

'I hope the work is going well,' she went on hurriedly. 'I believe Mr Crabtree is an able assistant – much better than I ever was, I am sure. I wrote to Christ Church about it, you know.'

He had turned away even as she spoke, and addressed Mr Emerson, Dolly's father, and Julia was left staring at his back, her heart beating painfully and tears smarting at the corners of her eyes. Among the crowd of people coming out of the church there was nothing more she could do. She took a desperate grip on herself, and turned away. Alicia was beside her and saw her agitation. She looked up at Dr Stone's back, and understood what had passed.

But now Lizzie was before her, taking her hands in her own and kissing her on each cheek. Julia drew a deep breath.

'Lizzie, how lovely to see you. How long have you been back?'

'Got back the day before yesterday. The weather held out almost every day, Julia, I never would have believed it. These last few days the highlands were just beautiful, weren't they, Dolly?'

He had just come to join them.

'Rather.'

'Lizzie told me all about your deer-stalking efforts, Mr Emerson.

235

I'm glad you didn't manage to hit anything.'

Lizzie laughed.

'He couldn't have hit a deer if it had come up and posed for him, could you, darling? Still, we caught plenty of salmon. We had salmon for breakfast, dinner and tea. I thought if I ate any more salmon I would start to look like one.'

Julia smiled.

'Peter has some friends down for shooting at the moment. I'm sure he would be very glad for you to join them.'

'Oh, yes.' Dolly coughed. 'Actually, we're very busy at the moment. Got the house to sort out, haven't we, Lizzie?'

'And Dolly's very busy at the brewery. Besides, we're having some work done, Julia; needs all Dolly's concentration. But I shall come over, and you must come and have dinner with us – soon. I'll write and suggest a date.'

She and Dolly went off arm in arm. Julia felt a slight pang at their evident happiness, and the way they had already blended into a couple.

As they returned to the house, Alicia looked at Julia beside her, withdrawn into her own thoughts.

'Thinking about your father?'

Julia nodded.

'He'll come round in the end. He must. What else can he do? He's getting older, and once your child is born he's bound to want to see his grandson.'

'Do you think so?'

Alicia laid her gloved hand on Julia's arm, looking into her eyes.

'I'm sure of it, my dear. Sometimes grandchildren are more precious than one's own children.'

Something in Julia snapped, and she could feel tears in her eyes. She looked down as she touched the corners of her eyes briefly.

'I do hope so. I know I betrayed him, left him –'

'Stop it. Julia, it was your right. It was, and you know it really. He should not have opposed you. Never reproach yourself.'

After a moment, Julia took a deep breath. Still without looking up at Alicia, she murmured, 'Thank you'.

Alicia was staring forward, and after a moment she said in a faraway voice, 'I wonder if I should speak to him . . .'

Julia looked round sharply.

'It is very kind of you to think of it, Alicia, but I fear you would have little success.'

'Perhaps.'

*

236

It was only a few days after this that Mrs Cunningham fulfilled her promise to lose her temper with Peter. It was after breakfast and the two women were sitting in the drawing room. Julia was sewing as usual, and towards eleven Peter made an appearance in his dressing gown, yawning.

'Any chance of a cup of tea? I rang but nobody seems to have heard. Servants in this house have all gone deaf.'

'I told them not to.'

'What?' Still half asleep, Peter turned towards his mother.

'We expected you at eight to breakfast. If it is too much trouble to join us, you had better get your own tea. The servants have plenty of other work to get on with.'

'What? I say, look here, mother –'

'No, don't "look here" me. I shall also be grateful if your friends could bring their own supply of brandy in future. We are running low.'

'Dash it!'

'And the scent of cigar smoke does nothing for the curtains. In the morning it smells like a tavern in here. I've had enough of it.'

Peter had by this time woken up. Julia looked down at her sewing.

'I see.' He walked up and down for a moment, his hands in his dressing gown pockets. 'The old song. Has Julia been on at you? She's always so concerned about her precious furnishings. What I should like to know is what matters most – the master of the house, or the blessed curtains? Blow me, Mother, you'd be the death of a fellow! Hang it, if a man can't take a glass with his friends and smoke a cigar in his own house, what's life for? You're a thorough-going misery – and Julia's no better. Always whine, whine, whine!'

This was what Alicia Cunningham had been waiting for. She stood up.

'Master of the house? You are yet not the master of the house – thank God! And I only pray your father has many years of life in him, because it will be a sorry day when you do become the master of this house! Then we shall see Liberty Hall indeed. You will have no curb or bridle, my young master, you will be able to have your fling to your heart's content.'

'Thank you, Mother! You never could abide the idea of giving up the house, could you? You've got to have everything under your own control. Well, once I come into the property, out you will go! We'll find some nice *little* place for you in the village, out of sight where you can't interfere any longer. God, I'm sick of being lectured by women! A man would suffocate in this house from petticoats. Always women about to nag nag nag!'

237

Mrs Cunningham had turned pale. Peter had got into his stride.

'Ah, that's got you, hasn't it? Can't bear the thought of giving it up, can you? You just love running this place, don't you? Can't bear the thought that your little boy has grown up and become a man, and is going to take over.'

'Grown up?' She turned to him with a look of contempt. 'If only you had. As for taking over, what do you know of your estate? Eh? What do you know of it? I doubt if you have the faintest idea of what's involved. Who's the lessee of the Home Farm? How many years are left on his lease?'

Peter was silent.

'Well, come on, since you're so keen to take it on. What's his name? Surely you know that? Good God, he lives not three hundred yards from here.' Silence. 'Well then, tell me the names of your three biggest tenant farmers? When did you last –'

'All right, what does it matter? I don't have to bother my head with all the piffling details; there are people to do that – I can get a lawyer.'

'A lawyer! Oh, yes! Oh, yes, Peter, you'd get a lawyer, wouldn't you? You were at the lawyers when you had that scheme to take over before, didn't you? Do you know what that little scheme cost your estate in lawyers' fees alone? My God, I tremble for Julia and your child once you're in charge.'

Peter seemed to degenerate into a child now. He screwed up his face, and would almost have stamped his foot. Julia was appalled watching him.

'Mother, I will not be talked to like this! You never let me have my own way! Always interfering! I won't stand it, I tell I won't. I won't! I'll make you pay for this! Just you wait till Pa is dead, and then you'll see – I'll make you pay for this, you see if I won't! You'll wish you hadn't crossed me!'

His face was bright red. Mrs Cunningham did not move. She was pale but perfectly controlled.

'You had better go and get dressed. Your cronies will be making their appearance soon, I dare say. It's nearly midday.'

'See? You won't take me seriously! I warn you, Mother – you'll regret this! I'll make you pay, you see if I don't!'

He rushed out of the room, and they could hear him on the stairs.

Julia rose and went after him. On the stairs she met Franks who was also going up.

'It's all right, Franks. Come up in ten minutes, please.'

As she entered the bedroom, Peter had opened the wardrobe doors and was flinging clothes on to the bed.

'Where's Franks?'

'Franks will be up in a few minutes.'

'I want him now. We're going back to London.'

'Peter –'

'Damn it, I won't be lectured by my own mother.'

'Peter –'

'She's sent you, I suppose. Well, you can just go and tell her we're off. Tell Belton –'

'The house is full of your guests. There is no question of returning to London.'

'I won't –'

'What will you tell your friends? You're running out because you have had a row with your mother? What will they think of that?'

Peter was still flinging clothes on the bed, but now he slowed down.

'I won't be talked to –'

She placed her hand on the coat he was about to pull from the rail.

'What did we say?'

He looked down at her.

'Wat do you mean?'

'What did we say? You remember, Peter, don't pretend. We will leave your mother in charge of your estate. She does it best.'

'Oh, yes, and I'm supposed to knuckle under all the time?'

'It's not a question of knuckling under, Peter, only of recognising other people have their rights too.'

'What? I'm damned if I'm going to say I'm sorry.'

'No one's asking you to.'

He had stopped taking out the clothes.

'All right, what am I supposed to do, then?' Now he was petulant.

Julia drew a breath.

'Your mother is the hostess here. She is entitled to respect.'

'Huh!'

'It is not an infringement of your sacred rights; it merely means behaving like any civilised gentleman – keeping regular hours, and not turning your own house into a tavern.'

Peter sat on the edge of the bed. He looked gloomy. Julia could see he couldn't accept what she said.

'Oh, yes.' He grunted. 'That's it. Can't have a bit of fun.'

'Peter, other people manage to have fun without behaving like drunkards and wastrels. It's only a question of keeping within reasonable bounds.'

'I'm hungry.'

He wasn't listening any longer.

'And where's Franks?' He crossed the room quickly and pulled the bell.

'Franks is on his way. I told him to give us a few minutes.'

Julia felt drained. They were no further forward. She could see he had calmed down, and probably would reform for a few days. But after that . . .

'You're looking pale. Why don't you all go out today? The fresh air always does you good.'

'Yes, I'd better do myself some good, hadn't I?' he said sarcastically.

There was a knock at the door.

'That'll be Franks. I'll leave you to get dressed.' Julia returned to the drawing room.

Chapter Twenty-eight

It was if there were some thick stone wall which she could not get past. Whatever she did, whatever she said, Peter was still the same. He simply didn't hear her.

She had frightened him once, and in her simplicity imagined that that had solved the problem, and everything had righted itself. And even for the few days they had been in Ventnor, it had seemed that everything was right between them. It wasn't. Oh everything would be right between them so long as she did not criticise him, or interfere in the slightest way with his pleasures, his idleness and shallow follies. So long as he was permitted to go on and please himself, come and go just as he liked, he was very pleasant, though she found his humour crueller and colder. It had been like that as far back as she had known him, but in her own folly she had not noticed it because she had been dazzled by his looks and quick wit.

That afternoon she retired to their bedroom to lie down for a couple of hours, and happened to notice *Madame Bovary* again where it had lain unopened for the past two weeks.

She still had not quite finished reading it. She seemed to have no energy, but now she turned to her page and began to read. Her thoughts soon strayed. She remembered the afternoon she had bought it in Bad Homburg; how she had sat in the park engrossed with the story of Emma Bovary and her daydreams. How she had smiled at poor Emma; how superior had she felt herself, so secure in her love for Peter.

And now. She laid the book on the bed beside her. What had her own marriage degenerated into, in how many short months? Did she still love him? She couldn't honestly say at this moment. Love seemed the wrong word for their relationship. It was as if it had become irrelevant. She was too taken up with the task of simply coping with him. She remembered what Mrs Bradshaw had said to

241

her – that Alicia had wanted a strong woman to keep an eye on him. How ironic. She remembered how scandalised she had been. Scandalised! How she had stood up, and given that insolent woman a piece of her mind! "They would just have to rely on their love for one another." Oh God!

Was Peter capable of love? She seriously wondered. She had upset him that one time, when he came up with the books. But was it love? She was in a muddle; perhaps he did love her, in so far as he was able.

She was in a pit, and there seemed no way out. At this moment she could see nothing before her but more of the same; years and years of it, and probably getting worse. Peter drunk; Peter in debt. What would happen to the estate when he got his hands on it? She dreaded to think. It was in good shape now – excellent shape; Alicia Cunningham was a first-rate woman of business. But things would change. How long would it all last?

She seemed to have no control over him, over their relationship, over her life, over anything. She was adrift with Peter in a rudderless boat and the seas were rising on all sides.

Something in her rebelled against her condition. Yet Alicia had spoken truly. What could she do? Nothing. She had better learn to make the best of it.

And there were his friends. Judge a man by his friends . . . what a crew they were. It was so depressing. She hated them all. One tiny crumb of comfort was that she had ceased to fear Mrs Bradshaw. Why had she feared her so violently when she had arrived? She now seemed to Julia perfectly uninteresting; just another "chum", a man who happened to wear a skirt. She was out all day in any case, riding, or shooting with the men, and in the evening she kept them amused. Thank God she did not drink too much.

Julia stared out of the window; perhaps it was her pregnancy that was getting her down. Perhaps she was imagining it all really, and everything was going to be all right. Perhaps they would go back to Ebury Street, have their child, and settle down into a nice hum-drum existence.

She fell asleep.

That evening after dinner she suddenly felt restless, and seeing that it was not quite dark yet, announced that she would go out for a little air.

Throwing a cloak round her shoulders, she set off down the drive and into the lane, and was about to walk down into the village when an impulse made her turn her steps towards the church and the rectory. She would go and visit her mother's grave.

She often thought of her mother. If only she might be looking down on her now. Would she be pleased to see her expecting her child, and yet so miserable? Julia had always wanted so badly to make a success of her marriage, to please her mother.

She was coming up towards the rectory gate when a figure appeared at it, came through and hurried on down towards her. In the half light of the late-September evening, Julia saw it was Emmy.

Emmy stopped abruptly.

'Oh. Mrs Cunningham. Good evening, ma'am.'

'Good evening, Emmy. I hope you are well?'

Emmy had been about to pass her, but stopped. She seemed uncomfortable, looking away from Julia's eyes.

'Oh, yes, very well, ma'am, thank you.' She bobbed a curtsy.

Suddenly Julia wanted very much to confide in another woman of her own age.

'Emmy.'

'Yes, ma'am?' Again Emmy had been about to go.

'Your husband – William – is he well?'

'Oh, yes, ma'am, thank you. Very well.'

'And your new house – you are settled in, I hope?'

'Yes, ma'am, thank you very much indeed. Mr Grahame –'

'Mr Grahame?' Julia took her up rather quickly.

'That is, 'twas through Mr Grahame we got the cottage.'

'Really? I thought Dr Stone –'

'Yes, ma'am – only 'twas Mr Grahame's idea.'

'I had no idea. Mr Grahame. Really.'

Looking into Emmy's face, she could not help herself thinking: This is the face Peter kissed. These the lips. And no wonder. Emmy was lovely, what man could resist her? How drab Julia used to think herself compared with Emmy's plentiful charms. And Peter, even as he had been so amusing with herself, had been meeting Emmy, kissing Emmy . . . As if to interrupt her thoughts Emmy pulled the shawl round her more tightly.

'Well, good evening, ma'am.'

'Good evening, Emmy.' The girl hurried past her.

Julia continued slowly up the lane and came into the church yard. It was almost dark now, but she made her way across the uneven ground; the old grassy humps between the tombstones, some upright, some leaning at crazy angles, and the tombs, the elaborate family vaults now falling into decay, some cracking open. How many

243

funerals had she attended as a child, watching her father, the wind blowing his vestments about him, flicking the pages of the prayer book as he stood at the graveside?

The tower was now a dark shape against the last vestige of the day. Nearby the old yew tree was another black shape.

It was too dark to read the inscription on her mother's gravestone. It didn't matter. She knew it by heart.

But now she couldn't think of her mother. Only one thought was in her mind. No wonder Emmy had been in such a hurry, so awkward. It was unmistakable, try though the poor girl might to hide it with her shawl: Emmy was expecting a child.

Of course. But why was Julia so agitated? She should have realised. Peter had been "whoring after Emmy Goodrich" – what else could it mean? Why had she not realised? The hasty marriage . . . Julia leant on the tombstone.

No wonder the girl was so awkward with her. She must feel ashamed. But if it were Peter's child, where did that put William? Did he know? Surely Peter had a responsibility? Never mind herself, she could cope; but Emmy – Peter must acknowledge his responsibility. And now she felt angry. She could no longer feel anger on her own behalf, but for Emmy . . .

She walked back down the dark lane to the house, and went in. As she came into the drawing room, the men were at their cards as usual, though as yet the brandy decanter had not made its appearance. Alicia was at the fire talking with Jonathan Selby and Mrs Bradshaw. The matter would have to wait.

'Did you have a pleasant walk?' Alicia looked up.

'Yes. I passed Emmy Masham,' Julia said lightly. 'Such a pretty girl.'

'Is it cold out?' Selby interjected abruptly.

'No. Why?'

'You look pale.'

'I expect I have been walking too quickly. I do, when I have things on my mind.'

'What things have you got on your mind, Mrs Cunningham?'

'Oh, women's matters, Mr Selby, nothing that would interest you.'

'I assure you, I find women's matters most interesting. Do tell us.'

'This is a new side to you, Selby,' Peter called across from the card table. 'Taking an interest in the ladies' gossip?'

'Since you are too busy yourself to talk to your wife, I'd better do it for you.' Selby seemed almost sharp with Peter.

'Steady on. Julia doesn't mind us playing cards, do you?'

'I dare say she'd be as happy to have you join in a conversation

244

instead of taking up every hour of every evening with your eternal card games.'

'Hoity-toity! Just because you don't play.'

'Quite right I don't. A more tedious and insipid waste of time never was invented if you ask me.'

'I say! Steady on!' The game had come to an end briefly as the players turned to Selby.

'Dash it – here are the ladies of the party having to make up an evening's conversation among themselves because you fellows are wrapped up in that interminable game. Whatever happened to the art of conversation?'

Peter turned to the card table again.

'Don't mind Selby – he's out of sorts. Probably something he ate. It's all right, old fellow, we'll leave all that to you. You do it so much better.'

As Julia well knew, Selby could often not get out two sentences in a whole evening – and when he did speak it often came out awkwardly and jarred on the others.

'I'm not out of sorts,' he stuttered, 'but if I were married to such a gracious lady as Mrs Cunningham, I'm blowed if I would spend every night at a stupid game of cards. It's shameful, if you ask me.'

Uproar. The men at the card table stood up.

'Look here, Selby, dash it! No call for that kind of talk.'

'About time somebody said it.'

Whittington came over.

'Another fellow's house, Selby. Have to mind your language.'

'Cunningham knows what I mean.'

Julia was watching in silence. She had not had the slightest hint of any such thoughts in Jonathan Selby's mind.

Selby was pale. He turned to Julia.

'Excuse me, Mrs Cunningham, so sorry to be disagreeable. Couldn't help myself, you see.'

He went out of the room.

'Well, there's one for the book!'

'What's eating him?'

'You see the effect you have on men, Mrs Cunningham,' Whittington said to Julia, but the joke fell flat. There was silence, and then Peter said petulantly, 'Well, I don't know, that's rather killed it for tonight. What say we leave it for this evening, you fellows?'

Shamefacedly the players left their table and came over to the fireplace, and after a few false starts a conversation of sorts got underway.

That evening Peter came upstairs with her a little before eleven. After they had got into bed, and blown out the candle, Julia stared up into the darkness. At last she said,

'I saw Emmy Masham this evening.'

'Yes, you said.'

'She is expecting a child.'

He was silent. Finally and with difficulty, she said, 'Is it your child?'

Peter was silent for a long time. At length she forced herself to say, 'Well, is it? You must know.'

There was a long silence until at last he muttered, 'You damn' well know it is.'

She felt sick. After another long silence, she had to go on.

'It doesn't matter about me. I don't think I expect anything of you now. But you have a responsibility to her.'

'Oh, don't worry. That was all taken care of long ago.'

'What? When?'

'Ages ago. When we were on our honeymoon.'

'What?' She was utterly mystified. 'How?'

'How do you suppose? Mother took care of it.'

'Well – but how did she know then, so early?'

'Don't ask me. She knows pretty well everything that goes on in the village. Anyway I expect old Goodrich came up pestering her.'

Julia lay in the darkness. Peter didn't seem in the slightest concerned. The Goodriches had been paid off, and he had put the matter completely out of his mind.

She could not sleep. As she lay in the darkness, the thoughts went round and round in her head. Peter appeared to be completely amoral. He had absolutely no comprehension that his actions could have any effect on anyone else, or what that effect might be. He had simply shrugged Emmy off.

Julia fell into a doze at last, but woke up during the night, and finally as the first light of dawn was barely making the objects in the room visible, found herself wide awake again. All the thoughts of the previous night returned and churned about in her mind. In a mood of impatience, she got out bed, pulled a robe over her shoulders and went down to the kitchen for a drink of water. She was neither awake nor asleep, but in a tired, low kind of doze, too awake to sleep but yet not quite awake, feeling depressed and down. She padded barefoot into the kitchen, empty and still in the dim light, and took a glass of water from the butt in the corner.

As she was returning to her room, climbing the stairs, and about to cross the landing, she heard the sound of a door, and stopped in the middle of the landing. As she watched, Mrs Bradshaw's door slowly opened, and a man came quietly out, turning to close the door carefully behind him, and then straightening up and turning again, and thus coming face to face with Julia.

It was Sir Cosmo. He was half dressed, in the evening dress of the previous evening, and holding his shoes in his hand. For a second they stared at each other, and then, without saying anything, he hurried past her in the direction of his own room.

It was the last straw.

As if by mutual consent the shooting party came to an end the following morning, and without anyone apparently saying anything, train timetables were consulted, the carriage was called for, trunks and boxes were packed, and the house was filled with the bustle of departure.

Mrs Bradshaw left before the others, briefly shook Alicia's hand, and thanked her in a few clipped and embarrassed phrases for her hospitality. Belton brought the carriage round, the beautiful black horse was tethered behind it, and Mrs Bradshaw was seen no more.

Peter wanted to go up to London with the men, but Julia told him they were staying in Stallbridge another day. There were two things she wanted to sort out before she returned to London. After their conversation in bed he was in no mood to argue with her.

Around eleven the men left. They appeared to be on on perfectly amicable terms with Selby again. Julia by now had come to realise that men didn't want the kind of intimacy she craved; they preferred to keep one another at arms' length. This "easy come, easy go" atmosphere left room for the occasional outburst such as she had seen the previous evening. They none of them seemed the worse for it.

It seemed very odd to her, however, as if they could never quite take themselves seriously.

As for Mrs Bradshaw and Sir Cosmo Whittington – she thought she must have been blind or stupid not to realise that something of the sort was going on, especially after the hints which Alicia had given her, but she had to admit she had never noticed a thing.

After they had left, Julia went to see her in her office. Alicia was already at her desk, papers before her, and a pen in her hand. She was dressed brightly and neatly as always.

'Alicia – Peter has told me you have made arrangements about Amelia Masham.'

She looked down, and rearranged her papers. At last she looked up into Julia's face.

'I had hoped to keep it from you.'

'You were very kind. But it was better that I should know.'

'You are a brave girl, Julia. I admire you. But I knew what you were taking on when you married my son. I wanted to save you as much pain as I could.'

'How did you find out about Emmy?'

'Can't you guess?'

'Her father?'

'No, my dear – our trusty curate, of course. He was the man they all went to in their troubles.' She smiled wryly. 'He drove a hard bargain, did Mr Grahame. He has been much missed in the village.'

'Mr Grahame? He negotiated a settlement between you and Mr Goodrich?'

'Not quite. It was he who persuaded William Masham to marry the girl.'

Julia was silent for a moment.

'And this was while we were in Germany?'

'About then – or soon after.'

'So Peter knew nothing of it?'

'Not until you overheard us having one of our charming tête-à-têtes.'

Again Julia was silent, as she tried to take in the import of it all.

'I'm sorry, Julia.'

'Well, I must admit it gave me a very strange feeling. I am carrying Peter's child, and now I find Emmy Masham is too. It is most odd. No wonder the poor girl was awkward with me in the lane.'

Alicia rose and came round the desk to take Julia's hand.

'My dear, you are carrying your own child. Once it is born it will be yours to care for and nurture.' She looked carefully into Julia's eyes and then went on, 'Poor girl; you lost your mother early, and all these years you have had to cope with everything on your own. Life has not been fair with you. You could have done with a mother's help. I hope – I hope you will let me be a mother to you, Julia, in so far as I am able?'

She smiled an oblique smile.

'Some people would say I have not been a model mother myself. But I feel a real mother's regard for you. We can help each other, you know.'

'How can I help you?'

'You are doing so now. You have taken on Peter, have you not? Can't you imagine what a relief it was to me to know you were to marry? Sometimes, I confess I should have been honest with you, and warned you what you were letting yourself in for. But I wanted you to marry so much.'

'I wasn't much of a catch.'

'Never say that. There is noone for whom I have a higher regard. Julia, you are – well, all I can say, is that Peter is a fool if he does not realise what a jewel he has in you.'

Chapter Twenty-nine

It was raining. Down in the hall the clock ticked, but otherwise the house was quite silent. As the afternoon wore away, Julia sat at the window and looked down into the street. It was comforting to sit here, nice to see people walking up and down. Gentlemen came down towards her, leaning forward into the gale and holding their umbrellas with difficulty against the gusts that threw them about. An old hackney cab rattled past throwing up water all over a gentleman's trousers; he looked back and shook his fist as the cab rattled on down the street. Josh came running along the pavement holding a package over his head against the rain, and then dodged quickly down the area steps beneath her. She had sent him out to the baker for muffins. A dog scuttled quickly along the gutter, oblivious of the water gurgling along it.

She looked up. There was a crack in the clouds towards the west; the rain should ease soon. With difficulty she rose and waddled across the room. She was great with child, expecting to give birth within a week. It would be a relief when the child was finally born. She had become progressively more bored with the whole business of pregnancy, and would be glad to be her old shape again, able to fit into her clothes, get back to normal life . . . except that once the child was born it would a quite different kind of normal life . . . except that she no longer had a normal life.

Great-aunt Frances should be here soon. Her train was due at Charing Cross at a quarter past three, and allowing a quarter of an hour in a cab . . .

Julia had tried to calculate the exact date of the birth. At one time she had thought the baby might be born on February the fourteenth, and it had seemed a happy omen to be born on St Valentine's Day. What a foolish dream. Happy omen of what? Restlessly she adjusted the lace antimacassar over the back of an arm chair. She stopped before the fire, looking down into it, then bent with difficulty and added a shovel of coal. The fire burnt sluggishly; if the wind were in the east smoke would sometimes blow down and fill the room with its acrid sulphureous smell. She poked the fire absent-mindedly, tried to stir a little life into it, then shivered and pulled the shawl round her shoulders. As she straightened up she looked at herself in the looking glass over the mantle. What did she see? An unhappy woman. Might as well admit it. She straightened her hair, pulling it back from her face and fixing the comb in it again. What else? She looked well enough, rather pale, but there was nothing wrong with her that giving birth would not settle. She was bored with being pregnant that was all, wasn't it?

No, it wasn't. She wandered back to the window and sat down to watch for the cab and Aunt Frances. The middle of February. The rain pattered against the window pane, smoke swirling and vanishing in the gusts. A man was pushing a cart along the street ... he seemed oblivious of the wet.

They had been back in London since the beginning of October, apart from a few days in Stallbridge at Christmas.

She had found herself back in the house in Ebury Street living with a man with whom she seemed now to have no sympathy whatsoever. It was as if they were just sharing the house. They slept in the same bed still, but there were no caresses, no touching, not even a goodnight kiss. Emmy's pregnancy had killed the wish in her. After they had been back a couple of weeks, Peter announced that he had received an invitation to go down into the country for a few days to see Whittington. Julia had wondered whether Mrs Bradshaw would be there.

He was away three weeks. When he got back she had expected to see him looking refreshed from the country air, but instead there was something sallow and unhealthy about him. Not difficult to guess why.

Then he had hung about the house, getting up late, going out every night, and getting back after she had gone to bed. She did not bother any longer to question him, or argue with him. It was his house, his money; he was free to do as he liked. That was how he wanted it, though it did not appear to do him any good; he often seemed out of sorts, under the weather, listless. So? Was she to fret about him? Tell him to see his doctor? He was a grown man, he hated to be told what to do. Very well, she would interfere no longer. She would not lose her temper; she refused to upbraid him about the aimless life he led. It was his life; she was only his wife, and it was not her place to tell him how to lead it.

251

There was an empty space between them, and in despair Julia realised she had no will to bridge the gap.

A few days after he had disappeared to stay with Holden, she had wandered into her study behind the dining room, looked down at her desk, and then up at the shelves – newly fitted, newly varnished, and with the few rows of her old books – and suddenly for the first time it seemed in so long, the old feeling took hold of her: she must work.

She sat at the desk, opened it, and looked at all the little drawers, and the pen rack, and the two neat ink wells. To work. Of course, she must give herself a task. She drummed her finger nails against the soft red leather surface, and then her eye caught the copy of *Madame Bovary* on the shelf where she had put it that morning. She had been reading it in bed, and had finished it at last. She took it up, and leafed through it again. A brilliant book. Nothing like it had ever been written in England, and there was no English translation that she knew of.

As a way of giving herself something to do, she began to make a translation, as an idle exercise, to fill a couple of hours of her empty days, something for her mind to chew on. And after the first few pages, as she read through what she had written, she was so pleased with herself, that she vowed to complete the whole book. There was no hurry, she had months – years – ahead, but it would keep her busy and that was what she wanted.

Now in February she was nearly halfway through, and a mounting pile of manuscript sheets was stacked neatly in her desk as she closed it every day. A thought had crossed her mind that she might even get it published. It was difficult to know. She was not acquainted with any publishers, but after all Mrs Gaskell was well known, and Julia thought the sort of people who read her books might be interested in *Madame Bovary*.

A cab was pulling up to the door. It must be Aunt Frances. Pulling her shawl up again, she went down to the hall. There was a jangling of the bell, and Mary came up from the basement, past Julia as she was half down the stairs, and opened the front door. A gust of cold wet air blew in, and shaking an umbrella, and exclaiming against the rain, Aunt Frances burst in, and immediately turned to shout to the cabbie.

'Yes, bring them in here – and be careful with that one, it's got some bottles in it! And do hurry – oh, everything will be soaking wet. Oh, drat this rain to be sure. Julia, my dear, how pale you're looking. Come give your old aunt a kiss – no, don't touch me for heaven's sake, let me shake some of the moisture off first – I feel like an old dog, got to give myself a good shake – yes –' the cabbie was coming in with some boxes and Mary was about to run out to help him, but Frances caught her arm '– no my dear, not like that – you'll get soaked, it's pouring cats and dogs outside, it's alright the cabbie can do it –'

And with much more of the same, Frances was in the hall, unravelling a large shawl from her head and shoulders, and unloosing the ribbons of her bonnet.

'Now, come let me give you a hug, that's better. Young lady –' to Mary '– as soon as the boxes are in, let us have some tea. Now, let me see,' fiddling with her purse, 'how much does that come to? One and ninepence? Are you sure? Julia, can that be right? Oh, very well, here's two shillings – no, no keep the change. One and ninepence – I'm sure it never used to be so much. Come let's get in front of a fire, my dear, you'll catch your death with that door wide open. We'll go upstairs.'

Then they had pulled two chairs up to the fire, and Frances had slipped her feet out of her boots, and was wriggling her toes on the fender as she set her boots to dry, and was running her fingers through her white hair, setting her lace cap straight, and rubbing her hands together, smiling at Julia, and exclaiming, 'Now a cup of tea, and I'll be as right as rain! My goodness, what a day of it! Julia dear. how are you? I was so pleased to get your letter, you can't imagine, and between us we'll make you so snug. Later on you can show me all your preparations.'

She rubbed her hands again at the fire.

'I think everything is prepared, aunt. It's lovely to see you.'

'And you too, my dear. Is London agreeing with you? I must say I don't see how it can agree with *anybody*. How is Peter?'

Julia looked down.

'He's quite well, thank you. He's not here at the moment – er – that is, well, he had an invitation from a friend, Sir Cosmo Whittington, to go down into the country.'

'Well, let's hope he'll be back soon. How long do you think you've got?'

'It's difficult to say; it could be any day.'

Frances smiled into Julia's face, and took her hand.

'So soon. I'm glad I've come then. I would have been devastated if I'd missed it. Have you telegraphed him?'

'What?'

'Well, he isn't going to want to miss it, is he? He won't want to miss the birth of his child.'

Julia tried to laugh. 'Men can be strange. That was why he went away. Anything like that makes him rather squeamish.'

253

Frances raised an eyebrow.

'Really, dear?'

The door opened, and Mary came in with the tea tray and placed it on a table beside Julia. She set the kettle on the hob at one side of the fire, where it steamed quietly to itself as Julia and Frances continued their talk.

Julia poured cups of tea, and uncovered a dish containing buttered muffins. Frances tucked in and there was silence for a few moments.

'Julia, my dear,' she said at length, 'is everything all right between you and your husband? You know I don't like to pry – well, I do actually – but I couldn't bear it if you were to be unhappy.'

Julia looked into the fire. What was she to say? She didn't want to admit the truth – even to herself it was difficult enough – yet who else was there in whom to confide?

'I'm sure there are difficulties in every marriage,' she began tentatively.

'Difficulties? What difficulties?'

Julia was silent as she thought. At last she said, 'Aunt, if I tell you, you understand it is in strict confidence. There is no one else almost – with whom I have talked about it. I found out that my husband had been deceiving me with a girl in the village – before we were married – and she is to bear his child. It has – well, it has made things difficult between us.'

'I see. And is that the real reason he has gone down into the country?'

'Probably.'

'Oh dear.' The old lady looked into the fire. She heaved a sigh. 'Well, dear, I don't know what to say. Young men aren't exactly paragons, even the best of them. They need time to settle. Of course they don't understand at first what's expected of them, and a wife has to make allowances.'

'Allowances?'

'I'm afraid so, dear.' Frances looked sorrowfully into Julia's face.

'I'm supposed to just bury it and pretend it never happened?'

'Well, dear, looking at it in the long run, what else can you do? You're married to one another now, and you're about to have your baby. There's not much else you can do, is there? I beg you, don't harbour a grudge. There's nothing worse in a marriage, than a wife who nurses a grievance. Better to put it all behind you and make a fresh start.'

She smiled, and patted Julia's arm. Julia took her hand.

'And you don't imagine I haven't already tried to do that? Aunt, I swear to you, I have done everything in my power to bring us closer

254

together. Nothing works. Peter won't adjust, won't adapt in the slightest degree. He's gone off now, you see? He won't even be here for the birth of his child. Sir Cosmo offered him the chance of some hunting, and that was enough. He was off. Told me to wire him when the baby was born. In any case, it's worse than that. It's not a question of indifference. We are utterly unsuited to one another; our tastes are different, our standards, our habits, we keep different hours. You have no idea. It is as if two complete strangers inhabited the same house.'

Frances looked dismayed.

'Forgive me, dear, but do you – er – still share the same bed?'

'For the time being.'

'Oh Lord, Julia whatever do you mean?'

'After the baby is born – if he demands his conjugal rights – at this moment I don't know what I am going to do.'

'Julia!'

'Aunt, I am not joking. I don't think I could bear him to touch me again!'

She looked desperate. Frances stared at her, with her mouth open.

'Julia, no!' she breathed.

There was a long silence between them as the fire crackled and the kettle on the hob whistled quietly. Julia absent-mindedly took up the poker and pushed one or two coals about, and there was a spurt of flame for a moment. She looked up into her aunt's face. Frances had adjusted to the situation.

'Well, dear, this is very serious.'

'I know. Don't you think –'

'Julia, forgive me, but I must speak my mind. Have you quite thought out your responsibilities?'

'What?'

'My dear, you are his wife, and like it or not, it is your duty to care for your husband. Now it may be he is not perfect –'

'Not perfect?'

'No man is, Julia, every woman finds that out. Nevertheless as his wife it is your duty to make allowances, and if necessary to suffer occasionally. I know it is not easy. No one expects it to be. But your husband comes first, and it is your duty to see to his needs, whatever inconvenience may be caused to yourself.'

'*All* his needs?' Julia said quietly.

'If necessary.'

'Even against my own inclination?'

'Yes dear.'

'Even if he disgusts me?'

255

Frances was silent.

'Even if I cannot bear him to touch me?'

'Well,' Frances was uncertain, 'we are taught, are we not, that the Lord set the husband over the wife –'

'Aunt, believe me, I have said all these things to myself. I have thought them all through. I have lain awake thinking about them. I know my duty, and I will discharge it to the best of my ability. But I fear that if he tried to – approach me, I could not stand it. I find him physically repugnant.'

There were tears in her eyes.

'I beg you do not criticise me. I have thought and thought what I should do. But now, having seen what I have seen and knowing what I know, I could not stand it.'

Again Frances reached out and touched her arm.

'My dear, I did not realise you felt it so strongly. Perhaps you are rather wrought up with the coming of your child. Perhaps later you will think differently.'

'I hope so,' Julia murmured, looking down.

'It's the waiting – it's been preying on your nerves. Come my dear, let us go and inspect your arrangements, and see that everything is as it should be.'

She stood up, Julia took a hold on herself and the two women went up into the bedroom above, where a cradle stood by the bed. Julia produced armfuls of baby clothes.

'I have been most fortunate. Many of these are gifts. Do you remember Lizzie? This was given me by her, and this is Aunt Esther's. You see, I think everything is ready.'

She held up a baby's rattle, and shook it, and smiled mournfully at Frances. The old lady took her in her arms and held her for a moment.

'We'll just take it one step at a time. First you must have your baby and then we can decide what to do about Peter.'

Chapter Thirty

Three days later her pains began. A nurse, Mrs MacGregor, arrived and Julia took to her bed. All day she lay enduring the pains as Mrs MacGregor established her rule in the house, ordering servants about, commanding various preparations, hot water, towels, while Julia lay staring at the ceiling and willing herself to relax and let nature take its course, and then being racked by another contraction, arching her back, and hoping and praying it would not last too long.

Frances sat near her, knitting, and making helpful noises, 'That's it, dear, it'll be all right, soon be over now. Try not not to struggle, just relax,' and so on; none of it meant anything, but she imagined it would help. To Julia whose whole body seemed about to split open, who lay bathed in sweat, racked to the very soles of her feet with pain, it was merely a vague background noise, and meant no more than the sound of rain on the window.

At about ten o'clock that night her baby was born. Mrs MacGregor took the child, shook it as the first little cries were heard, washed it, and wrapped it in a soft fleecy blanket. She laid it on the bed beside Julia where she lay, drained and inert, feeling only a huge relief that the pain had stopped.

'It's a girl, Mrs Cunningham,' she whispered.

'Oh, I'm so glad,' Julia murmured.

Frances leant over the child, and stared into the tiny face.

'Just like her father.'

'Is she?' Julia was too exhausted to think.

'Would you like to hold her?'

'Yes.'

They helped Julia to sit up a little, and placed the baby in her arms. Julia looked down into the tiny red face, screwed up as if in some great pain, clasping and unclasping her tiny hands, her eyes still tight shut.

257

Julia loved her at once. A great weight was lifted from her. Not merely that the pain had stopped, but that the cloud that had loomed upon her spirit, the problems with Peter, now seemed less important. Here was her real centre now, here was her new purpose.

'I'll send off a wire immediately. Have you his address?'

'Yes, if you would just pass me that bag – there should be a notebook inside.'

Frances brought it to her, and Julia found Sir Cosmo's country address. Her aunt hurried away downstairs to send Josh out with a telegram.

Later Julia looked up at Mrs MacGregor, who was tidying the bedclothes.

'Should I try to feed her?'

'Why not, Mrs Cunningham? You'll have to at some time.'

For the first time she loosened her nightgown and offered her breast to the child. The baby understood at once and began to suck greedily, clutching with her tiny hands at Julia's breast.

Mrs MacGregor watched with a professional smile.

'They don't take long to learn.'

Afterwards Mrs MacGregor took the baby and laid it in the cradle by the bed, and Julia lay on her side watching her for a while as she slept, and then rolled back and fell asleep herself.

During the following morning they received a reply to Frances' telegram.

'Congratulations. Returning soon. Will wire again.'

This puzzled Frances.

'I don't understand, dear. What does he mean?'

'He doesn't know when he is returning, that's all.'

'Surely he must want to see his daughter? Why isn't he coming straightaway?'

'Perhaps he will tell us.'

It took Peter a week to get back.

He looked off-colour and tired. Julia could guess why.

'A girl, eh? Hmm. Let's have a look. Funny little thing isn't she?'

'Would you like to hold her?'

'Eh? Oh, rather not, I should think. Shouldn't like to drop her.'

Julia was still in bed. She would get up for a few hours in the middle of the day, but preferred to stay in bed until her strength returned. She still felt tired. She was sitting up against some pillows, and the child was in her arms.

'Peter, she is your daughter. Take her.'

258

'No, thanks. Leave all that to you, Julia. I say, I suppose we'd better start thinking of a name for her.'

'I would like to call her Agnes. It was my mother's name.'

'Eh? Oh, all right. Why not? Agnes – good as any other, I suppose. I say, do you think I could get a cup of tea round here? Could one of the servants be spared do you think?'

'Of course. Pull the bell.'

Awkwardly Peter sat on a chair near her and watched as she nursed her child. Later he sipped his tea as Mrs MacGregor washed her; Agnes set up a loud bawling, and after a while he said, 'I say, does that go on a lot, eh? I mean all that racket? Could drive you to distraction, I should think.'

'It's usually when she's hungry.'

'And when's that?'

'Most of the time.'

'Lord. I say, Julia, where am I going to sleep? What with all this going on, you don't seem to have too much room in there.'

She looked at him.

'You could have the back room upstairs if you like.'

'Might be safer. Then I shan't disturb you.'

'And Agnes won't disturb you.'

'Look, what's the time? I promised I'd see Whittington this evening. Just time for a shave.'

'Do you want something to eat?'

'No, I expect I'll get something at the club.'

'Peter – before you go –'

He turned in the doorway. Julia looked across at Mrs MacGregor's back, and then, slipping out of bed, she came across to him in her nightgown, hair hanging round her shoulders.

'Come outside,' she said quietly.

Once they were outside she pulled the door to behind them. 'I shall need some money.'

'Oh Lord, not again?'

'What do you mean, again? You've been away a month, and I've nothing left from what you gave me.'

He drew a sigh, his hands in his pockets, looking away from her.

'Money. It's nothing but pay, pay, pay in this house. Have you got to have it this minute?'

'No, not exactly, but as soon as possible. I owe Mrs MacGregor.'

'Who is she anyway? What's wrong with our own servants? Couldn't Becky be doing that?'

'If you had been here last week you could have seen exactly what she was for. She delivered our baby. She is very helpful, and we can

259

easily afford her. But she hasn't been paid yet, and I want to keep her a while longer.'

They were standing on the landing whispering to one another as Franks came up with Peter's shaving mug.

'Franks, take that up to the back bedroom. That's where I'll be from now on!' He said it in a loud, offensive manner, which made Julia wince. Franks gave her a look as he went on upstairs.

'Well, upon my soul, I don't know, it's deuced inconvenient at this moment. The monthly allowance won't be through for days yet.'

'And you're broke?'

'Well, as it happens, madam, yes, I am. Do you have any comments? Any wifely remarks to make?'

'Do I have any comments? It's ten days to the end of the month. How are we supposed to manage? You gave me twenty pounds before you went away. And your allowance is a hundred a month – so what has happened? Oh, for heaven's sake, you don't have to explain.'

She was seething with irritation, and turned towards the door again. It was draughty here on the landing, and she was only in a nightdress.

'That's a relief anyway,' Peter said.

Without saying anything else he went upstairs and she returned to her bed.

'Aunt, you have been the soul of kindness to me, and it makes me quite wretched to ask you this. Can you lend me some money?'

Mrs MacGregor was out of the room, and Aunt Frances was sitting with her.

'Of course, dear. Now you have little Agnes, there must be so many things to think of –'

'It's not that.' Julia was sitting up in bed. 'We have plenty of money. It's difficult to get it out of my husband, that's all.'

The old lady laid down her knitting, and looked perplexed.

'Well now, let me see. How much do you want?'

Julia sighed, and looked down at the quilt as she thought. 'He has nothing until the end of the month. Could you manage twenty? I'll pay it back, of course.'

'No, Julia, that's quite all right,' said Francs as she opened her purse.

'I insist! It's shameful I should have to beg from you like this – especially after all your generosity to me. Aunt, we have plenty of money! We do! And yet we never seem to have enough. It is impossible to make him keep within his income. However much he had it would never be enough.'

The old lady had taken out some money, and set it on the table. 'There.'

'Thank you. I really must pay Mrs MacGregor.' She paused, thinking. 'There is something else. I hope you won't mind my mentioning it. Some time ago you very kindly told me that you had made me your heiress. I have been thinking about this. The fact is, Aunt, I simply cannot trust my husband with money. What I want you to do is to change your will. I should like you to leave the money in trust for Agnes, so that she will inherit it when she is twenty-one.'

'My dear –'

'Aunt, what use would it be to me? Don't you see? The moment your will is proved – and I pray that day is many years hence – my husband would be free to set his hands on every penny of it. I shall have no control over it, and it would go the same way as the rest of his money.'

They travelled down to Stallbridge for the christening. Peter didn't want to go, but Julia told him he had no choice. Stallbridge was the family seat, the Cunninghams had been baptised, married, and buried in the village for generations, and they weren't going to upset tradition now.

Besides she thought that her father must unbend as he christened his own granddaughter.

Julia had Agnes in the compartment with her. Becky and Franks were in the third class carriage.

When Agnes woke up and began to cry, Peter was exasperated.

'Oh Lord, can't you shut her up? Anyway, why do we have to have her in here with us? What have you got servants for? Why am I paying for all these spongers to eat me out of house and home, if we have got to take care of the baby ourselves?'

'You haven't got to do anything.'

'Haven't I? Well, I'm having to listen to all that blessed racket, aren't I?'

'She's hungry.'

Julia began to unbutton the front of her dress.

'I say, Julia, you're not – I mean to say?'

'Does it offend you? I'm afraid babies have not had time to learn their manners. She knows she's hungry that's all.'

She had opened her dress, and brought the child up to her breast. Agnes was immediately silent. Peter looked out of the window.

'My God, it's perfectly disgusting. In a public place too.'

'We have the compartment to ourselves. What are you complaining about? Did you want me to go on letting her cry?'

'Confound it! I could do with a smoke!'

He was still looking out of the window. He couldn't bring himself to look at Julia as she nursed his daughter.

'Dammit, it's downright embarrassing. Really, I'm surprised at you. I thought you would have had more sense.'

'You surprise me. I never thought you would have been so squeamish. Haven't you ever seen a baby before? How do you think they get fed? Sometimes I wish you would grow up a little.'

'Thank you very much! Much obliged, madam. Grow up? Well, I tell you what, I wish you would just learn a little decorum, and not go making a spectacle of yourself.'

'Spectacle? To whom? The compartment is empty.'

This was the kind of useless inconsequential wrangle that took the place of conversation between them now. No sympathy, no understanding, no tolerance, and she found it draining and futile. If it hadn't been for Agnes she would have despaired.

Fortunately for her, the child was dearer to her than her own life. There was something so infinitely precious in the little face, the soft hair, the little hands, their tiny finger nails – everything, every little detail, so beautifully fashioned, so perfect, that she sometimes simply gazed into the little face, even though she knew Agnes could not yet even focus her own eyes. All the time, she thought: She knows me, she recognises her own mother, she knows my voice; foolish thoughts, but there was such a wonderful outpouring of love to the little morsel in her arms, as she felt the tugging at her breast.

Across from her in the compartment, Peter sulked, scowling out of the window, crossing and recrossing his legs, sighing and fidgeting with his fingernails against the window pane.

On a chilly March morning, they gathered in the church, Julia with Agnes in her arms, wrapped in a christening robe given her by Mrs Cunningham – 'Peter and Lizzie were christened in it, my dear.' Mrs Cunningham was looking vivid in violet and cerise. Lizzie and Dolly were there; Peter was ill at ease, fidgeting and yawning. He had been dragged out of bed at the – for him – relatively early hour of ten o'clock.

With them in his vestments was Dr Stone.

As Julia had feared, he did not unbend. He took the baby in his arms, and touched her with the holy water. The family stood round the old mediaeval marble font in the echoing church, cold on this raw morning, all of them in thick coats and gloves. The child cried, and was baptised Agnes Elizabeth (after Lizzie, one of her godmothers), and Julia took her from Stone's arms, and even in that moment as he handed the child over and she looked into his face, there was not a flicker of recognition.

As they were coming out of the church door, ducking slightly – for the old Norman round arch was low, as if over the many centuries, the church had sunk by degrees into the ground around it – Julia was just behind Dr Stone who was behind Mrs Cunningham, and Alicia stepped aside to allow him him to come up beside her. They did not see Julia who was in the dark porch, and she distinctly heard Alicia say, 'You are too hard, William,' looking straight into Stone's face, and then, 'It will not do.' And then she walked on ahead, and he stopped and looked after her, taken by surprise. Julia watched him, as he stared after Alicia, until he gathered his wits, wrapped his vestments about him in the chill wind, and continued after her.

Julia saw him walking down the narrow path between the gravestones. 'William'? She had never heard her father addressed by his Christian name in her life.

Three days later a small package was delivered to the Manor House addressed to Julia, and she recognised Arthur Grahame's handwriting on it. She was about to carry it upstairs but Peter, who was at the breakfast table across from her, said, 'What's that?'

'I really have no idea.'

'Aren't you going to open it?'

'I suppose I may as well.'

'Suppose you may as well? What on earth does that mean?'

She slipped a knife under the string and pulled the package open. Her fingers trembled slightly.

'Were you expecting anything?'

'No.' She coloured slightly. He was thoroughly suspicious.

'By George, you were. You're blushing.'

'Don't be absurd.'

'Well, what's in it?' He reached across and snatched it from her. 'Let's have a look.'

The package contained something wrapped in tissue paper. Peter ripped it apart. Inside was a 'coral' on a gold stem; a little trinket for babies to teethe on. It had obviously cost a lot of money. She tried to reach across for it but Peter leant back and held it out of her reach.

'There's a note. Let's see. "My dear Mrs Cunningham, I hope you will accept the enclosed as a token of respect and admiration and in hope that your child may grow in love and affection through the years to come, and may one day be as beautiful and good as her mother. With sincerest best wishes, Arthur Grahame."'

Julia snatched the paper from Peter.

He sat back and whistled as Julia devoured the words with her eyes. There was a long silence between them.

'Well, well, our goody-goody curate, eh? Who'd have thought it? By Jove, if that doesn't beat all. "As good and beautiful as her mother".'

Julia was reading and re-reading the note.

'You're quite pink, my dear. Would you like a drink of water? Come as a terrible shock, has it?'

She reached across the table and took the coral from his hand as he was twiddling it in his fingers. She turned it over in her hands. It was beautiful, and the gold had been carefully chased. She saw that the name "Agnes" had been engraved on it.

'"The love that passeth all understanding." To think our curate was harbouring unclean thoughts about my wife. Tsk tsk!'

'Shut up.'

He sat up.

'Mr Grahame is worth a thousand of you. It is a very beautiful gift. I will not hear him mocked.'

'I see.' Peter stood up. 'There's something going on, isn't there? And all this time I never suspected. I'll be damned. He's in love with you, isn't he?'

'I really have no idea.'

'No idea?'

'What are you afraid of? That I might be unfaithful to you? As you were to me? Are you accusing me – you, who even as we speak have a woman nursing your son in this village? How dare you! No, Peter – have no fear. I swore to love, honour and obey, and when I give my word, unlike you, it is a solemn undertaking. If I say I am going to do a thing, I shall do it. You need not fear.' She looked down again at the coral. 'In any case I have not the faintest idea where Mr Grahame is – or indeed how he knew I had a baby.'

'Really?'

'Yes, really!'

'Well, I am not sure I want my child breaking her teeth on something from my wife's lover, thank you very much. Give it here.'

'Certainly not.'

'Give it to me, I say! How dare you! I won't have it in my house.

264

My God, to think that that – lout has had the effrontery to look at my wife. Hand it over, Julia!'

'I will not.'

'By God I will have it.'

He came quickly round towards her, and she retreated.

'Give it to me this instant or you'll regret it.'

'Regret it? How can I regret it more than I do already? I have born you your child, and you have not taken the slightest interest in her. If Mr Grahame wishes to offer a christening gift to Agnes, it is perfectly proper – and it is more than you have done! It is a very beautiful gift, and must have cost a great deal of money, and Agnes shall have it!'

'She shall not. Do you think every time my chums come to see my daughter I'm going to let them see her sucking on a present from that lout? Do you want me to be the laughing stock of the club?'

'The club? When are they ever likely to come and see your daughter? Have any of them come so far? They never come near the house – thank God! You're all busy drinking and playing cards. Or going to some music hall, no doubt.'

Peter took her roughly by the wrist, and snatched the coral from her hand.

'Be silent. It's time you learnt to know your place; you've been a sight too free of late. And you'll soon see what I think of your rustic lover.'

He walked quickly to the window and threw the coral out as far as he could.

'Peter!' She ran to the window. Beyond it lay lawn and beyond that a thick shrubbery. Before she could think what she had done, she had slapped him hard across the face.

'By God!'

She made for the door but he went after her and seized her by the wrist before she could get there.

Chapter Thirty-one

'You've got some explaining to do.' He dragged her across the room by the wrist.

'Don't touch me!'

'You'll damn well do as I say.'

'I will not!'

'Julia!' He threw her into an armchair. The force of it knocked all the breath out of her, and her wrist hurt painfully where he had grasped it.

'You are a coward and a bully to use force.'

'Shut up. Now, what's this between you and Grahame?'

'I will not speak a word until you apologise for your disgraceful –'

'Answer me, I say!'

'I will not!'

'Julia, if you do not tell me this instant what is going on, I will give you such a beating –'

'Beat me, coward and bully that you are! Summon your mother, call Lizzie, and let them be witness to your degenerate behaviour!'

'Mother and Lizzie can go to hell! If Grahame is in love with you, I want to know it. Have you been seeing him?'

'How am I supposed to be seeing him? I do not know where he is! I have not seen him since he left the village. I have no idea how he knew of Agnes.'

She leapt lightly from the chair and crossed the room to the door. She was still breathing hard.

'But, Peter, I want you know this – if you ever lift your hand to me again, I will leave you.'

'Leave me!' He attempted to laugh. 'Don't be ridiculous. Where will you go? No, madam, you will do your duty which you have been shamefully neglecting.'

'Neglecting? I have not been neglecting you. You are never in the house in any case so the question does not arise.'

'I would be, if you made it more welcoming.'

'You liar! I have done all I can to make it comfortable for you, and you know it.'

He was on the point of coming at her again, but she wrenched open the door, and had run out of the house, and on to the lawn and was staring into the shrubbery.

'Oh!'

She ran round to the greenhouses. The gardeners should be there at this time of day. She soon had them all searching through the shrubbery for the coral.

In her mind was a rage she could not confront; too black, too bitter for words. In that moment there had been something malignant, really evil, in him. She could not speak to him, and her heart was too full to be able to think what to do next.

She could weep with vexation.

She could not even write to Arthur Grahame to thank him for his gift. It had been such a lovely gesture, it showed such delicacy, such a deep regard for her; she honoured him for it. Besides it must have cost so much money – for all she knew it might have cost him every penny he owned. Perhaps all his savings had gone on that present.

Nor had it been found; Julia had given strict instructions that the search should go on until it were, and even as she sat thinking these thoughts the gardeners were still sifting through the leaf mould beneath the shrubbery.

She thought about Arthur Grahame. He had arranged Emmy's marriage to William. She understood now that he had tried to shield her, Julia, from knowing.

Why should he be do these things for her? Why? Then she remembered the last time they had spoken, in the corner of the field on that June day last year, and the feeling she had had of some great thing that had passed her by so closely.

Within a few days they returned to London. They had nothing left to say to one another. They never saw one another; never ate together; kept completely different hours.

Julia turned again to her writing, and the pile of manuscript on her desk mounted steadily; *Madame Bovary* came close to completion. There was a strong conviction in her mind: she could no longer rely on her husband for money. A restless urgency had taken possession of her. How was she to make any money that he could not get his hands on? And it seemed to her that there, within her own hands, lay a possible answer. Pen and paper, and her own brain. Could she live by her pen? Would anyone be interested in *Madame Bovary*? Being now so intimately acquainted with the book, she was conscious that some people might find it offensive. Publishers might refuse to handle it. There was no doubt that the author had been very frank about Emma's passionate nature: perhaps too frank. There was certainly no heroine in English fiction who came close to her. Were the English ready for Emma Bovary?

The translation would soon be finished. She would have to think of finding a publisher. Of course there were publishers, they existed. Their addresses were to be found. There was nothing to stop her taking it to one of them.

Days passed, and they drifted into summer. Julia received an invitation to stay with Aunt Frances, and took Agnes for a month. That satisfied Peter completely; he had his own life to lead. There was the club, there were music halls, he was invited to balls sometimes. No one asked where his wife was. And then as autumn came he was invited to Yorkshire to stay with Selby to shoot a few grouse. At other times he was down in the country somewhere with Sir Cosmo Whittington. He simply came and went as it suited him.

Sometimes Julia was in London, sometimes she went down to Stallbridge, sometimes she visited Aunt Frances.

They had separate lives. No one really noticed. Outwardly they were married; no one had the curiosity to ask why they were never seen together.

Through the autumn and winter that followed Julia took to going out alone, to meetings, and lectures. She read heavily, and worked at her German. A lot of her time was taken up with Agnes, whose first birthday passed that February, and the breakdown of her marriage was disguised for her by the love for her daughter. So long as she had Agnes, she could fashion a life for herself, a life of the mind. She would sit at her desk in the mornings writing letters, and then little descriptive pieces, wondering as she sat looking looking down into the rain-sodden garden, as the dreary winter days passed, what she was going to do with the rest of her life.

There had to be more than this. This was the thought that ran through her mind. She must make something of her own. But what it should be she still had no clear idea.

She must try to get *Madame Bovary* published. That would be a good idea. The manuscript lay in a large pile on her desk, and she would leaf through it sometimes, thinking over the ideas in it: how a woman could be driven to suicide, not merely by an unhappy marriage, but by the accumulation of foolish mistakes she made as a consequence of her unhappy marriage. Was she destined to make such mistakes by her own marriage? This was a question that used to run in her mind sometimes. Was she destined to end everything with a dose of prussic acid?

They slept in separate beds. When Peter was in town she sometimes heard him pass her door during the night. But he rose late in the morning, and she was often out, so they continually missed one another. Then he would be away staying with friends; his capacity as a billiards player stood him in good stead at many a country house party. Hosts were quite used to seeing him arrive alone. No one noticed or cared. Other men did the same. 'The little woman has the baby to think of' was sufficient excuse.

One day in early spring, a cold April day, she was walking down Regent Street when she saw a poster. It was advertising a public meeting, organised by The Bishop of London's Committee for the Relief of The Homeless. A number of speakers were named, including several titled gentlemen, the Bishop himself, and a Mr A. Grahame. She stood, on that cold morning, the pavement wet from the rains, the traffic passing behind her in the busy street, the carriage wheels sending up sprays of mud and water, all the dirty tired end of winter. Julia stood reading the poster.

Mr Grahame? She remembered at their last conversation together – it was nearly two years ago – he had said something about the Bishop of London, and it had been to do with shelter for the poor, or something like it. At last she tore herself away and went on thoughtfully down the street. There was something else about the poster that she could not at first identify, but then, catching sight of it again, she saw that he was now Mr Grahame, not the the Rev. Grahame. Was there any significance in that?

She spent the morning in the bazaar looking at things for Agnes, picking over baby clothes and then vaguely looking at clothes for herself. She had become lethargic about herself, as if she no longer cared about her appearance. What was the point anyway? She spent too much time in her study, too much time in her head, if the truth were told. Perhaps she should buy some new clothes and try to present a fresh face to the world.

And she should try to get *Madame Bovary* seen by a publisher. In her dilatory, dreamy state she had become neglectful and vague. It was time to ginger herself up.

As she was coming out of the bazaar she saw the poster again, and on an impulse took out her diary and noted down the address and date of the meeting. It was at the Exeter Hall in the Strand; a large and important place for a public meeting.

Something in Julia which she did not wish to examine too closely made her go to the meeting. Something else made her dress smartly too. It was still April and the weather was cold, so she wore a navy blue overcoat over her thick woollen dress, and a fashionable 'toque' hat and gloves. There might be woes at home, but on that cold, light April evening she wanted to present a bright confident front to the world.

The Exeter Hall was the principal venue in London for rallies and meetings with anything like a religious or charitable quality. The most fashionable preachers of the age appeared there, sometimes in the presence of royalty. It was eminently respectable. Over the road, by contrast, was "The Coal Hole", the most notorious song-and-supper dive in London, famous for its "poses plastiques", and other titillation.

The Exeter Hall was already quite full when she arrived, but Julia found herself a seat and sat down to wait as patiently as she could. Arthur Grahame had been in her thoughts all day.

What a strange man he was. When he had first arrived at the rectory he had seemed aloof and unpolished, as if all the formalities and niceties of civilised life were something of a veneer which he had only recently acquired and which he was not convinced had much value. Then over the few months he had been with them she had begun to perceive in him a certain rock-like quality, a sense that he had a path to tread and that nothing would force him to deviate from it.

And she had thought at the end, when it was too late to matter, that if they had known each other longer, had had the chance to become better acquainted, then something might have developed between them, which there had never been the opportunity for. And now there never would be.

She remembered their talk in the corner of the field, when he had been hay-making, and the feeling of something which had so nearly happened.

Then she thought of the coral which had never been found. He had remembered her, had been thinking of her, and there was a strange unsettling warmth in her as she thought of him buying the coral, having it engraved, and sending it to her; that he had sent it out into the world, knowing she could never find him to thank him.

Just as she was thinking this, she saw the man himself on the platform. It was him, yet he seemed changed. For one thing he was very well dressed, neatly, like a gentleman with nothing of the poor clergyman: no clerical collar, nothing clergyman-like about him at all. On the contrary, he had a statesman-like quality, gravely listening to an older man who was coming on with him. Other men were appearing too, including a bishop, presumably the Bishop of London, in his episcopal gaiters and purple apron.

These important-looking gentlemen took their seats, Arthur to one end of the table. Julia quickly glanced about her. The great hall was full and it was clearly a respectable event. The people sitting on either side of her were ladies and gentlemen, the men with polished top-hats on their knees, the ladies in expensive clothes.

The bishop stood up and addressed the meeting as 'My Lords, ladies and gentlemen . . .' before going on to identify the men on the platform. The man with whom Arthur had been talking turned out to be the Earl of Worcester; he was sitting next to Arthur, and from time to time they would confer with one another.

The Bishop launched the proceedings with a brief speech identifying the terrible problem of homelessness in London, how the extent of it was not even known and there were no statistics – no one had ever actually *counted* the homeless, how more poor families arrived every day, how families were fragmented, women were left with small children, and how, because of the absence of proper dwellings, were crammed twelve or more into filthy and rat-infested cellars. And so on. Things everyone knew, but preferred not to think about. But they were there tonight to think about these things and to do something about it.

He introduced the Earl of Worcester, a man perhaps in his forties with long side whiskers, slim, and with a pale christian look about him, a curate-like look, Julia thought, and who spoke nervously, and stuttered.

He told of his first visit to the rookery of St Giles, of the sleepless nights he had suffered thinking of the unimaginable suffering he had witnessed, the scenes of unspeakable degradation, and of his vision of a better way; how he had vowed to dedicate his life to bringing some relief to these unfortunate wretches.

After a short speech in which he referred to Arthur as the man who had been his principal guide and helper, he sat down and the bishop rose again to introduce Arthur, and it was clear in a moment that he was to be the principal speaker to the meeting.

It was the same Arthur she had known. He had that simple, concentrated manner, combined with a certain physical ease, quite unlike the gentleman who spoken before him.

When he spoke, his voice was strong, focussed and unforced. It carried easily though the hall, over the large number seated round Julia, and it gave her a physical thrill to think that it was Arthur, the man she knew, who stood quite easily and unself-consciously and within a couple of phrases had everyone in the hall concentrating on his words.

He had some notes on the table before him, but did not refer to them except sometimes to pick them up and quote figures.

The problem had so many aspects, he said: it was not merely the overcrowding, not merely the constant influx of new people with nowhere to sleep, not merely the spread of disease, and the lack of medical attention, not merely the lack of sanitation, of pure water, not merely the presence of rats; there were also the social problems, the extortions of greedy landlords, the exploitation of the poor and ignorant by unscrupulous employers in the sweated trades – and he went through every aspect of the situation, explaining, clarifying, in his measured voice, serious, putting the whole picture before them, as the audience sat tense with concentration.

And there was was not merely the humanitarian aspect – though that was the foremost – but also that even from a political point of view, it was not difficult to see that in the future it would be impossible for such a society as they all inhabited to hold together, and that unless changes were made they must expect not merely the sort of mass insurrections that they had seen with the Chartist Movement in the '40s, but perhaps the kind of revolution which had been seen in France, Italy or Hungary.

The whole fabric of society was imperilled unless something serious was undertaken.

Frankly, he went on, there was only one body competent to undertake the work on the scale which was needed and that was the government. But the government was apathetic, and preferred to ignore it.

So together with their own efforts, by raising money to begin to construct new homes for poor people at rents they could afford, they must begin to bring pressure to bear on the government – of whatever colour – to undertake the kind of large scale housing that was the only long-term solution to the problem.

Such was the substance of his speech. There was prolonged and hearty applause as he sat down, and again resumed his conversation with the Earl by his side. Julia sat astonished even as she joined in the clapping. It was extraordinary. How had this transformation taken place? Arthur was a statesman; there was no other word for it. He had taken command of the meeting, easily; he had his arguments clearly set out, did not hesitate, or stumble over his words, there was

272

a kind of quiet control in all his actions. When she tried to remember him, she thought, It is the same man. But here he has expanded into his proper sphere; he has room to act. It was if, in the village, he had just been biding his time.

Later, as the meeting came to an end, she suddenly wanted to speak to him. To thank him. Yes, to thank him for the coral he had sent for Agnes.

People were getting up and moving about, but quite a number were gathering in groups to talk and discuss what they had heard, and Arthur was in conversation with one man, and then another. Julia sat in her place and waited, and as the hall slowly cleared, and there were fewer and fewer people, he at last looked across and saw her where she sat, and there was a long moment as they both looked at one another.

She was glad she had dressed well; it was a terribly important moment, among all these rather grand people and Arthur so soberly dressed, and talking to an Earl, and – oh a hundred thoughts flashed through her mind as their eyes locked together across the hall, and he started towards her, turning and quickly excusing himself to the man to whom he had been talking.

For a moment he was looking down at her, as if neither could find words to say.

She stood and held out her hand.

'Mr Grahame, it was a very good speech.'

He took her hand gravely, and it was difficult for them to take their eyes from one another.

'It has been a long time, Mrs Cunningham,' he said softly, and let go of her hand, it seemed reluctantly.

'I remember you mentioned the Bishop of London's Committee when we last spoke.'

'What is it – nearly two years – since I left Stallbridge? From the moment I arrived the work has grown. It swallows up every waking moment. And there is no end in sight. I wonder if I didn't take on more than I can handle.'

'I think not.'

'To tell the truth, it will be the work of generations. All we can do is to get the movement started. I don't honestly expect to see very much change for a long time.'

He looked round at the other speakers who were standing in a knot talking. The he turned to her again.

'It would be good to talk. Are you alone?'

'Yes.'

'Perhaps you would permit me to escort you home?'

She looked down, and then nodded without speaking.

'Excuse me a moment.'

Julia sat again as he returned to his friends. She did not want to look at him for a moment, feeling suddenly exposed in the middle of the now-empty hall. Sitting and collecting her disordered thoughts: how much to tell, what he would want to know, what she wanted to know of his life, all these things running quickly through her mind in the minute before he returned to her chair.

Together they went out into the cold night. He offered her his arm, and quite naturally she took it; after all a gentlemen could offer a lady his arm, and it might not mean anything. And yet for her it did mean something, and she was conscious of some electricity between them as they turned along the darkened street, arm in arm.

They did not speak for a long time, and had walked down the Strand, crossed Trafalgar Square and were into St James's Park, neither looking at the other, before either could find words to say.

'I – I notice you are not wearing your clerical garb.'

'No. To be honest with you, going about so much in the poorest parts of London, I found it a hindrance. It set up a barrier immediately. So long as I was a parson, it was difficult – or more difficult – to be taken seriously. I dropped it. It doesn't matter. The work goes on, and that is what matters.'

'Mr Grahame, I am very glad to have met you again because there is something I want to say. You sent a christening gift for my daughter last year. It was a very beautiful gift.'

'Thank you.'

'Oh no, it is I who wish to thank you. I have wanted to find you again, to tell you –'

She stopped.

'I mean, to thank you – I did not even have an address to write to.'

'It was better that way.'

She understood what he meant.

'Won't you tell me more about your work? It seemed so interesting.'

'Interesting?' He laughed. 'I suppose you could call it that. Hmm. Interesting? Necessary, essential. It isn't very pretty.'

'I did not imagine it would be. But I should love to see it.'

'Would you?'

'Oh, yes. Very much. You cannot imagine –' She drew a breath. 'Well. You cannot imagine how stultifying, how futile my life has come to be. I envy you more than I can say that you have thrown yourself into something of such great value.'

274

She looked up to his face, and looked hard into his eyes, just visible by the light of a street lamp as they passed under it.

'I will take you – you shall see our first new building. The Bishop's Fund has been able to complete our first block of houses, and they have been occupied a month.'

'Will you take me to visit?'

'With great pleasure.'

They shook hands on her doorstep, and again seemed at a loss for words.

'Is there any way I can contact you to arrange a date?'

He took out a card case, and drew out a card. She could not resist a smile.

'A calling card. Welcome to the respectable classes, Mr Grahame.' She turned it over in her hand. It contained an address in Marylebone.

'It took a little getting used to. Like so many other things. But I have adapted, as you see.'

'I will send you a note, then.'

Again she held out her hand.

'I am so glad we have met again.'

'And I. More, perhaps, than I can express.'

He turned away.

Chapter Thirty-two

A few days later Peter returned to the house, and she was uncertain whether to write to Arthur Grahame and, if she did, how to arrange it, so nothing was done.

Julia and Peter had nothing to say to one another, he always rose long after she had breakfasted.

Three days after he had got back she still had not written to Arthur. She got up feeling curiously restless, depressed, and more uncertain of her life than ever, and having had breakfast went out to walk about the streets and do some shopping.

Was she to start a clandestine correspondence? Make a secret rendezvous with a man not her husband? Should she write to Arthur at all? Yet beneath her doubts a deeper certainty told her that having found him again she was not going to let him go. She would write that letter, but must think out the problems first.

When she got back to the house, it was midday and she found Peter sitting in the drawing room sipping coffee. She said 'Good morning' but he ignored her, and went on reading a newspaper. She took off her coat and hat and went down to her study. It was dark inside as she opened the door. The shutters had not been opened. As she crossed to the window, something rustled about her feet.

She pushed up the bar, threw back the shutters, then turned to see papers, everywhere in the room: papers scattered, burnt paper stuffed into the fire place, half burnt papers strewn about the hearth, others torn and shredded, yet others crumpled, and many more just thrown at random everywhere. Everywhere paper. The room was full of paper.

It was *Madame Bovary*.

She threw herself on to her knees, snatched up sheets, flattening them out. It was utter chaos. Page 163, page 208, her neat handwriting, Emma and Leon just coming out of Rouen Cathedral, the farmer's daughter in the orchard, Monsieur Bovary in his pharmacy, fragments of her work, fragments of Emma. It was hopeless.

She knelt dazed in the room in this sea of paper. Was it possible? All her work, eighteen months of her spare moments, destroyed? A moment of childish petulance, and everything destroyed?

She picked up another sheet, and another, gazing about her in amazed disbelief. All of it? All gone?

She got to her feet, went out of the room, up the stairs, went quickly into the drawing room. Peter was across the room, the newspaper still held before his face. In one simple movement she dashed it to the floor, leaving them facing one another.

'You blackguard,' she said, a whisper of hatred. 'There was nothing – you could have found nothing to hurt me more, could you?'

Peter did not move a muscle.

'I should have seen it before.' He was calm, looking her steadily in the eye. 'It was disgusting. A degenerate vile book; obscene.'

'It was a great book. It could perhaps have made a real impact!'

'It could have brought me into ridicule and contempt! Do you think I am going to permit such a book in my house – to allow my daughter to be polluted? You're not fit to be a mother. There'll be no more of it.'

'It is not degenerate, neither is it vile – it is a work of great literature.'

'Humbug!'

'It is! And I have never made any secret of it! The book has been here; you have seen me reading it, a dozen times. You could have spoken at any moment. But to let me go on so long – it has taken me eighteen months to translate that book – to let me go on so long, and never say anything to my face, and then to go behind my back and wantonly destroy it, was the most foul contemptible thing –'

'Hold your tongue! How was I know what it was all about? I can't read French can I?'

'Don't boast of your own ignorance!'

Peter got quickly to his feet.

'Give me the key to that study.'

'What?'

'Give me the key, I say. From now on it will be locked. I'll have no more of your depravity. From now on you will confine yourself to activities proper to my wife – to your needle and your child, who you have been neglecting!'

'I have not been neglecting her!'

'Give me the key, Julia.'

277

'I will not.'

'Give me the key! Or shall I take it from you?'

'What I do in my study is my own business.'

'Are you mad? This is my house – and every room in it. Now give me the key.'

'No!'

'Give it to me this instant, or you will repent it.'

His face was white, blanched, with little red spots in his cheeks; his eyes enlarged.

The blood was thudding in her throat.

'Never!'

He came quickly at her, seized her by the shoulders and thrust her into a chair.

'Give it to me, damn you!'

'No!'

He looked around.

'It's in your bag, isn't it?'

He lurched across the room, snatching it from the table where she had put it when she came in, and began to ferret in it. She rushed at him, and tried to drag it out his hands. They wrestled with it for a moment, then he thrust her violently away, so that she lost her balance and fell on her knees, but a rage seized her now and she came at him again, refusing to let him go, twice as strong, and they wrestled a second time for the bag, and as they did so, he slipped on a rug, lost his balance and fell heavily at an angle against the front of an arm-chair, a violent blow against his ribs, knocking the wind out of him.

He was about to rise but there was a strange haunted look in his face; he stared away from her, he was in pain.

He stopped, half-risen, looking about, and reached a hand for the table to steady himself, looking down,

'Oh God.'

He began to double up, slowly at first, then sinking on to his knees, on the disarranged carpet, clutching his ribs and groaning again.

'Oh God!' He slipped sideways on to his side, still grasping himself.

She ran to him.

'Peter!'

His face was contorted with pain; he could scarcely breathe.

She leapt to her feet, rushed to the bell pull, tugging at it violently, and then ran out of the door and shouted down into the basement.

'Franks! Mary! Becky! Come quickly!'

She ran back to Peter. His face was deathly white, still gasping for breath.

Mary came into the room.

'Mary, send Josh for the doctor, immediately!'

'Yes, miss.'

Franks was behind her with Becky.

'Franks, your master has had a seizure – help me make him comfortable.'

The three of them now attempted to lay Peter out on his back with cushions under his head. His eyes were closed and he could scarcely breathe.

'Becky, fetch a glass of brandy!'

Mary meanwhile was bringing up a bowl of water, and bathed his face.

The doctor came an hour later. Peter was much the same. Julia had removed his collar, and the doctor opened his shirt and examined his chest. He opened Peter's eyes and examined them. He took his pulse.

At last he stood up.

'We must get him to bed at once.'

Between them Peter was half carried, half supported up to his bed, and settled in.

Afterwards the doctor took Julia out on to the landing.

'What has he been doing? He is wrecking his constitution. His heart and lungs are gravely weakened.'

Julia was silent for a moment.

'I imagine you can guess. It's not difficult. But, doctor, before you go on any further – there is nothing I can do to stop it. Believe me, I have tried.'

'Hmm. Well, it's got to be rest. Rest, and more rest. No alcohol, no tobacco, light food. You understand well enough?'

'Yes, doctor, thank you.'

When she returned to the room Peter had fallen asleep. She had satisfied herself that he was likely to sleep for a while yet. She went down to her study, and together with Becky and Mary cleared up the mass of charred paper and cleaned the room.

Peter was confined to bed for a week. There was nothing specifically wrong, but he was very weak.

Julia brought him food, sat with him, looked into his face and saw he had been frightened. He lay, white-faced, his eyes large, looking up at her. He seemed delicate, frail.

He wanted her there by him; seemed glad to have her with him. His need for her, paradoxically summoned like this, was touching, and she was confused. In his need for her, she suddenly again found a role for herself. And his destruction of her book was forgotten in this calamity.

She wrote a note to Arthur explaining what had happened and saying she would write again. She and Peter travelled down to Stallbridge a few days later, and he sat very quietly in the train, a thick tartan rug wrapped over his legs. He stared out of the window and did not say much.

At Stallbridge he spent a lot of time in bed, calling for her, and at other times sat on the terrace in the summer sunshine.

It was good to be wanted, but it seemed strange that their marriage only functioned when he was ill. As his health began to improve, and he regained his old boisterous manner, his need for her correspondingly diminished and she felt herself kept more at a distance.

He would sleep in the afternoons and she would go for walks with Alicia. She could not mention Arthur, yet he was in her thoughts all the time. Anything would serve as an excuse: a corner of the lane where they had met and talked, the church yard where she had seen him in his clerical robes one Sunday, the smithy where she had watched him once helping the smith shoe a horse. He dominated her thoughts, and she asked herself constantly what implacable fate had decreed that at the moment when she and Arthur had met again, Peter should reassert his hold over her in this unexpected manner.

A month later they were back in London. It was summer, the Season was on, and Peter was once more in demand for balls and soirées. He hired a horse and used to ride in Rotten Row with friends and titled folk. He seemed to regain all his bounce, all his glamour, and looking at him, it would be difficult to believe this was the man who had seemed at death's door in April.

Julia was once again relegated to the side-lines, and they carried on as if his illness had never happened. She thought it likely that this episode might be repeated; it might even develop into a habit. She would be required only when he was ill; at other times they would go their separate ways.

But as summer flourished, as the air was clear of fog and smoke, as the trees were once again in leaf, and there was the heavenly fragrance of the limes, still in her heart there was no lightness.

Arthur was in her thoughts all the time. She could write to him, yet – she didn't like to express it too exactly – writing in secret to another man was like a frank admission, on paper, of the wretched state of her marriage, and she could not repress a sneaking feeling of guilt, even as she read through the few blameless lines she put down. That her husband was now recovered, and was off to his usual haunts. That she would like to take up his offer, and make a tour of inspection of the new model homes he had promised.

The answer came, and a date was appointed.

'Wear your oldest clothes.' With this strange injunction in mind she prepared, and put on her old blue-grey dress and borrowed a shawl of Becky's and a battered straw bonnet.

She met him at the Exeter Hall and they made their way up Bow Street, and across to Seven Dials. He was in a blue reefer jacket, and his trousers were tucked into long boots.

It was a summer afternoon, and the narrow mean streets were crowded. The little houses all had their windows open, and everywhere people lounged. Old clothes shops had their wares displayed out on the street and ancient men in ragged long coats with scanty grey beards, fingered change in their thin hands. Nobody seemed to buy anything, but women sometimes pulled things down from racks and turned them over in their hands.

Then there were gangs of girls in thin gaudy shawls and short skirts, with bright scarves, gold, and scarlet and purple, wound round their heads, who talked and chattered together in strange accents; sometimes she thought they were Irish, but at other times, she could not make them out at all.

Young men, with flashy cravats linked arms and sauntered along the street, and old women would hurry by with jugs in their hands. Openings in walls led down into cellars, and children scrambled in and out. Or she would catch a glimpse of a cobbler hammering down there in that dim light, or a tailor cross-legged on a table working at a pair of trousers. On one corner was a butcher but she scarcely recognised any of the cuts of meat on his stall; they must have been the cheapest off-cuts and species of offal that even she was not familiar with. Ash-heaps crowded the street, washing hung in lines over their heads, window panes were missing; on one corner an Irish fiddler was playing and two little girls were dancing an impromptu gig.

All the time this tide of ragged humanity ebbed and flowed round them as they passed through the narrow streets. As before, she unconsciously took Arthur's arm, and felt a comfortable sense of his strength and nearness, as if so long as he was there nothing really mattered.

He would look down at her sometimes, smile, make a comment or point out something. He knew exactly where he was going.

281

After they had made their way through this Rookery for some time, they came out in Drury Lane and found that here some of the old houses had recently been demolished and a new block had gone up. It had a shiny newness, was built of yellow brick, with open staircases and little balconies at each landing, everything regular.

'We opened it last November. Our first building. But there will be more. And others are getting the same idea.'

He led her through an arch into the courtyard within. The court was asphalted and completely surrounded by the buildings, five stories high, and on this summer afternoon, women and men were standing about in the sunshine chatting, the men smoking short pipes. Lines of washing hung everywhere, and little children played a game with a long rope which two boys were swinging as the girls came into it and skipped through.

One of the pipe-smoking men noticed Arthur and nodded and touched his forehead. Arthur nodded back.

'There's a laundry on the top floor – and a drying machine for use in wet weather. Also a library.'

'How do the people like living in apartments?'

'The great advantage of apartments is that they can't be divided up. Those streets we've come through – the houses have been divided and divided until often you get several families in one room. But here it's one family per apartment. It's got to be the way of the future.'

Later he led her through into Clerkenwell, through foreign quarters, and here everyone was speaking Italian, and shop signs were in the same language, the women wore outlandish clothes, and at a corner a man was selling ice-cream from a cart.

Later still they had a cup of tea in a little cafe.

She wanted to know all about him, what he had been doing and how this amazing transformation as she saw it, had come about.

'When I first left Oxford I went to London with a group of friends, and we set up a refuge for homeless people where they could get a roof for the night, and a bowl of soup. We funded it by charitable donations. The Bishop of London was interested, and used to visit us. He could see how valuable the work was, and how it could be expanded. But then I was offered the place in Stallbridge – the last thing I had expected, it was through connections in Oxford, and of course your father's reputation is immense – and although it was a diversion from what I had been doing, I thought it was worth taking. I didn't like to admit to myself how ambitious I was. Some voice inside me told me it might be a useful step; it was just that – I'm not proud of it. As soon as I arrived I realised I had made a mistake, but I was there and I stuck it out. Later, when I had the letter from the Bishop saying he had the interest and backing of the Earl of Worcester and why wasn't I there to get things started, it was time to get back.

'The Earl has made an enormous difference. For one thing he is very rich. It was mostly his money that put up the buildings you saw in Drury Lane, and then again he has all sorts of connections in Parliament.'

Arthur smiled.

'I'm going into Parliament myself, you know.'

'You?'

'The Earl wants me to stand. He's prepared to pay all the costs – which by the way are considerable. The electors of Chelsea are a thirsty lot.'

'I don't understand.'

'It's quite simple. When the election is called, I shall go down to Chelsea to canvass for votes. This will consist of offering to every publican to underwrite the cost of free beer to any elector who promises to vote for me. Not very dignified but until we have secret ballots there is no alternative. It will certainly cost several thousand pounds.'

'Goodness.'

'Goodness, as they say, has nothing to do with it.' He laughed.

'So you will be in Parliament.'

'The struggle has to be carried right into Parliament itself. Otherwise it's simply groups of well-meaning and generous people making all the effort they can, but with almost no voice at the highest level where it really matters.'

'I see.'

Later she said, 'I must get back soon,' and the atmosphere became tense between them.

By this time they were not far from Smithfield and it was too far to walk back so he called a cab and then they were sitting in the darkness together, as if by prearrangement, as if the whole afternoon had been leading up to this. It became more and more difficult to talk, as if there was an atmosphere of unspoken thoughts which must be spoken – only who was to speak them? Who was to open the conversation, and how far should it go, and how was it to end?

She wanted to tell him how much she admired him, but he would never let her begin that sort of remark, but then he asked her about her daughter and she told him, and then he asked her about Peter who had not been mentioned so far, and she had to make evasive replies, and he could easily see that she was avoiding a straight

283

answer. At one point she mentioned Agnes, and then said, 'He always wanted a boy.'

And Arthur said straight out, 'Are you going to give him one?'

It was a very odd, very direct question, and she had no idea how to answer it. But he went on, 'I mean, are you going to let him into your bed again, Julia?'

This was even harder to answer.

And then he said, in a strong concentrated rush of thought and feelings, 'It is all I think of. I could stand anything, so long as I thought you were happy. But to think of you with him –'

'Hush,' she said.

'To think of you, wasting your life, wearing out your life with that man, it is more than I can bear.'

'Arthur, I beg you, my dear –'

'Why do you think I left Stallbridge? Oh, yes, I had the letter from the Bishop, that was part of it, but only part. If things had been different, I might never have left. It was a bad time. The worst time of my life.'

'Oh no –'

'Julia, I think of you night and day. Not very good of me, is it? Breaking the Seventh Commandment with every breath I draw, and yet I could bear anything so long as I thought you were happy.'

'Oh, I beg you, don't go on.'

But he had taken her in his strong arms and was kissing her in the half darkness, and there was nothing, nothing in the whole world she could do about it. She felt such a rush of joy through her, such a wonderful completion of herself, as if this was right and should be so, and they were together rightly, and his kisses strong, urgent devouring her, swallowing her up, so that she surrendered utterly to him.

Afterwards he held her, his arm round her.

'For years and years I worked, first at Oxford, then in London. Everything else I put aside, put away anything that might hinder me in my work, always a goal ahead which I worked towards; I never deviated, never was distracted. All those years, and slowly I passed the markers I had set for myself. I got in to Oxford. The humiliation I underwent that afternoon, I could not even begin to tell you – when their lordships of the college deigned to admit me as a humble servitor – then when I saw all the other students enjoying themselves, spending their money getting drunk, I worked steadily on, never going out, consumed with ambition. For so long, going to the East End to set up the mission, and then the offer of the place with your father, and then' – he paused, and his tone softened, 'and then, after

284

all that, it was just one little thing, one thing I had not foreseen, and I was lost, all my plans thrown into the air.'

He paused again. His arm was still round her. She sensed his body beside her, the warmth of him, as she drank in his words.

'It was just one thing. It was at Lizzie Cunningham's ball. I had never been to a ball in my life, didn't know what to do, was feeling very awkward, and then I saw you dancing. I shall never forget it all my life through. It is impossible to describe how you changed. In the rectory you were quiet and controlled, and so – shall I say? – in possession of yourself, nothing ever seemed to be spontaneous. And then watching you dance, it was as if it was another you. You were transformed. Your face lit up with a flush of pleasure, your eyes – I can't begin to tell you – but you were just so beautiful, I couldn't take my eyes off you. But then, – I think you were dancing with an old gentleman – your shawl fell to the ground, and in one second you changed again. I saw a look pass over your face, I don't know – half terror, half awkwardness. And you were looking back over your shoulder even as he swept you on in the dance. And in that moment, seeing your helplessness, your vulnerability, I was lost. In one little moment I knew that I would love you all my life.'

She reached for his hand.

'I picked it up, and brought it to you. I thought we could talk – I wanted to speak to you more than anything on earth, and here was the perfect excuse. But at that exact moment he – your husband – came up, and I saw the expression on your face as you saw him, and understood everything. The man I detested more than anyone alive, and you were smiling at him.'

He paused.

'I believe I may have appeared a trifle brusque.'

He was silent. She could not stop the tears on her cheeks. But he sensed it, and took her face in his hands.

'I don't care for myself, honestly. It is only you. If you are happy, I can bear anything.'

'Don't say any more. I cannot bear it. I beg you. You have torn my heart.'

She reached up to him just once, pulling his head down and kissing him hungrily. Then she pushed him away.

'Arthur, you must let me go now. Don't you see? I mean – oh, my darling, it never can be. There is nothing we can do. Whatever my husband is, he is still my husband; there is no way I can leave him. And besides, you have your career. Let me go, I beg you, or you will kill me.' She pulled away from him. 'Cabby! Stop!'

They were in Grosvenor Place. The cab pulled up, and Julia

wrenched at the door, throwing it open, and almost fell out into the street.

'No, Arthur, go on. Go on, cabby. Drive on.'

But Arthur was out behind her. She clung to the railings, her head bent as she tried to wipe away her tears.

'Arthur, no. I beg you, how can it –'

He threw a coin to the cabby who drove on. Arthur tried to pull her to him, but she clung a moment to the railings.

At last he was able to take her into his arms and hold her to him, in the street on that summer evening, the quiet street, with the tall empty-looking aristocratic houses staring down impassively, as if they would not condescend to notice the doings of these puny people below them.

'I will not let you you go. Not now.'

She tried to push him away again, tried to wipe the tears from her eyes.

'Arthur, you must. Don't be cruel. It cannot be, you know that.'

'Never.'

She was silent, trying to still her tears, drawing a deep breath, and then, at last looking up to him, pulling herself away, she said, 'My dear, you know what I mean. Take my hand – there. Now say it with me. Goodbye. Perhaps sometimes we may be able to see one another – perhaps meet now and then. But more than that there never can be, so goodbye, my dear. Now shake my hand, I beg you.'

For a long time he was silent. Then he said, 'You have my address. I will be there, ready at any time.'

'Yes. I know you will be there – that will comfort me, my dear.'

He saw the look in her eyes, took her hand, and there was an awful, awkward moment as they shook hands. Then she said, 'Now go, my dear and God bless you.'

And with a last look he turned away, and she watched him as he went from her along the street, and at last, unable to restrain herself, turned to the railings again and clung to them, her head bent as she wept helplessly to think that such a beautiful thing as their love must be for nothing.

At last her tears drained to a hollow finish and she turned and made her way along the street, and at first it was as if she were quite empty. She looked up into the sky, still seeing nothing, but slowly, slowly, beginning to feel a strange transcendent feeling, an exaltation, a feeling which she did not at first recognise, but only after a while understood, that this was what it meant to be really loved by a man.

And everything that had happened to her until this moment had been nothing, had been as smoke blown in the wind, and all her life until this moment had been a shadow on the wall, a groping in the half light, until suddenly someone had thrown open the door and a light had shone on her, and the whole world had been revealed to her as it really was.

She had to acknowledge this, and could not acknowledge it. No, she Julia Cunningham, could not. She had her path and she must tread that path. All the force of her mind told her this. But it could not cancel the transcendent feeling, the exaltation. All her thinking, all her reasoning, could not cancel that.

Chapter Thirty-three

As soon as she got into the house she told Becky they were going down to Stallbridge. Peter was out. Agnes was prepared, they had a cup of tea, packed some bags, and sent for a cab. Within an hour and a half, they were on their way to Paddington.

In the train, she could think only of Arthur's words and of the huge injustice of life; of the useless waste of human affection; how qualities like goodness were so capriciously distributed; of the great urge to goodness; how it was rebuffed and abused, how it was frustrated. And of human folly and waste; of the power which some men wielded over others; of how people could surmount that power, or be crushed by it.

Sitting there as the carriage rocked and jolted through the summer countryside, and the evening faded, listening to the distant sound of the engine, the thoughts went round and round in her head. What was the point of it? That she should be married to Peter, and that Arthur should love her with such a heroic, such an utter and selfless love, and all to no avail. Oh, the pity of it.

She looked down at Agnes beside her asleep. She kept the child with her almost all the time. Agnes was sixteen months now. Studying her little face, framed in its bonnet, the doll lying in her lap, Julia was thankful again for her. It was Agnes who would keep her sane. So long as she had Agnes, she had a purpose and her life had meaning. She moved the child slightly to make her more comfortable.

But for Arthur – she must not think of him. He had spoken his love to her and torn the heart out of her in one burning speech. She could not, must not think of him, yet how could she not? How could she forget that look, those words?

No good thinking of it. She watched Agnes sleep. She was a delicate child. Julia must be ever on her guard.

They reached the country halt and settled themselves into the old station fly.

Julia remained a month in Stallbridge. It was a strange period of hibernation. A time of waiting, of suspension, as if her feelings had been for a moment cauterised, so that she did not want to feel any more, but just went through the days of summer, sitting in the garden watching Agnes crawling on the lawn, going to tea with Lizzie and Dolly, and admiring little Jeremy, Dolly's son; a strange time, with no contact with Peter at all, never hearing from him, never wanting to. Not writing either.

Alicia watched her, knowing that something had happened, but not knowing how to unravel it; Alicia who usually was so capable in these things.

It was almost the middle of August when at last Julia decided to return once more to her home – except that it was not her home. She did not feel that she belonged there in any way, but that it was only some kind of temporary lodgings. She had a strange feeling that something must happen to change everything, her whole life.

It was late when they reached Paddington Station. Becky found them a cab, the boxes were stowed on the roof, and the two women climbed wearily in. Agnes continued to sleep on Julia's lap.

When they reached the house, she was surprised to see the lights on in the drawing room upstairs, and as they rang the door they could hear voices.

Franks opened the door.

'Good evening, Franks. Is Mr Cunningham in?'

'Yes madam.'

'Give the cabbie a hand in with the boxes, please. Becky, take Agnes upstairs will you and then wait for me in my room.'

Wearily, Julia pulled off her bonnet, and went up to the drawing room. There were voices, the sound of the piano, and then someone began to sing.

She opened the door.

All Peter's usual friends were in the room and the air was thick with cigar smoke. Mrs Bradshaw was seated at the piano. Holden was standing at the fireplace a glass in one hand, the other raised as he began to sing. He stopped as the door opened. The men looked round.

There was a moment's silence.,

'By Jove, it's my blasted wife.' Peter was lounging in an arm-chair. 'What are you doing here?'

289

'You knew we were returning today,' she said quietly. 'Good evening, gentlemen.'

They had pulled themselves together. Some had stood up, on their best behaviour. Peter and Sir Cosmo remained deep in arm-chairs. Mrs Bradshaw sat on the piano stool, looking at Julia with a cool stare.

'Blessed if I knew anything of the sort. And what a time to walk in – spoilt the fun. Just like you. Well, run along off to bed, that's the best.'

'Are you going to be up long?'

'What's that to you?'

'I was thinking of Agnes, that's all.'

'My God, trust you to walk in and start ordering us about! The brat won't hear us, will she? Her room is two floors up – next to my little hidey-hole. Isn't that typical? A fellow can't have a bit of fun without you throwing cold water on it.'

He threw himself from his chair, and lurched across the room. The others were silent, waiting for a cue from either Peter or Julia.

'Gentlemen!' Peter took her wrist and held it up in a violent jerk. 'Anyone want a wife? No, come on, I'm serious. Who'll take her off my hands, eh?'

Julia wrestled to get her hand free, but he held her tight, even as he swayed slightly. A glass was in his other hand.

'Well, come on! Who wants her? She's no blasted good to me; regular blasted blue-stocking. Look at her fingers – see – covered in ink, aren't they, my dear? Useless. Can't play the piano, can't sing. No good to cheer a fellow up, but very tight with money. Oh yes, no problem there. She'll keep your accounts in apple-pie order. So come on, any takers?'

He swayed again. Julia couldn't get free.

'Peter,' she whispered.

The others watched in fascination and discomfiture.

'Well, come on!' he roared at them, lurching slightly, his eyes bloodshot.

'That's enough, old fellow,' Holden muttered.

'What? Holden – you want her?'

'Mrs Cunningham, perfect lady, dash it –'

'What? A lady?'

'Peter, – will you let go my hand!' Julia was struggling now to free herself.

'Shut up. Come on, she's a perfect lady, Holden says so – must be true.'

'Yes, she is. And too good for a cad like you!' Selby suddenly spoke up. He was white. 'Let go of her.'

'Selby! Always knew you had a soft spot for her. Right, let's start the bidding. What'll you give me for her? A fiver?'

'Let go of Mrs Cunningham!' Selby shouted at him.

The room was frozen at this moment. Peter's grip seemed to be of steel. Julia could sense the alcohol in him, the heightened expression, the manic look.

'Holden – Selby's made an offer. You want to raise your bid?'

'Cunningham, this is disgusting. Let go of her this instant!'

'Cunningham's got a perfect right to do whatever he likes with his wife,' said Sir Cosmo, still leaning back in his arm-chair, and drawing on a cigar.

'See – Whittington's a man of the world, he knows what's what. So come on, let's hear you. Holden, you want to improve on five pounds?'

Selby lunged for Peter to wrench his grip from Julia, and as he did so Peter hurled his brandy glass at him. It missed but smashed a framed painting on the wall, and there was a loud splinter of glass.

'You swine!' Selby now had Peter by the throat, and he had to free Julia to defend himself. Selby was a small man, but wiry and fit; he threw Peter to the floor.

'You disgusting degenerate!' He breathed heavily, looking down at Peter. Julia was rubbing her sore wrist. Peter sat on the ground, dazed. He glanced up.

'Thank you, Selby. Nice to know who one's friends are.'

'Matter of fact, Selby's got no business interfering between man and wife,' Sir Cosmo drawled.

Selby turned on him.

'Hold your tongue. I won't stand for it, Whittington, from you or anyone.'

There was a moment's silence as everyone seemed to wait for someone else to make a move, then Cosmo gave a sigh of impatience and got out of the arm-chair.

'Well, Selby, I should say between you and Cunningham that's it for this evening, and just as things were livening up. Are you coming?' He looked at Mrs Bradshaw, who also rose.

'See you in a day or two – or whenever you've sorted out your marital differences, old fellow.' He looked at Julia. 'Would you mind ringing for your man and telling him to bring our coats?'

She pulled the bell-pull by the fireplace without speaking. Peter had got up and lurched into a chair. Holden was rooted to the spot in a stupor of amazement.

291

'Well, I'm not waiting,' said Selby. 'Cunningham, we shan't meet again. Mrs Cunningham, I'm truly sorry you should have been subjected to this. Good night.'

He went quickly out of the room, and a moment later they heard the street door slam beneath them.

Franks came in and Julia told him quietly to fetch Sir Cosmo's and Mrs Bradshaw's coats. There was a frigid silence as they went out of the room and down into the hall. Holden looked uncertainly between Julia and Peter.

'Er – most awfully sorry, Mrs Cunningham. Most regrettable.'

'Good night, Mr Holden.'

He sheepishly edged out of the room. Julia was left alone with Peter, sprawled in an arm-chair.

'Well, pleased with yourself? You have succeeded in chasing all my friends away. Caused uproar in my house. Come in here, broken up a very pleasant party. Satisfied?'

The street door opened and closed beneath them. A moment later there was a knock on the door, and Franks came in.

'Will there be anything else this evening, sir?'

'No, Franks, you may go to bed now,' Julia said.

'Are you telling my servant what to do? Bless me, you really are impossible. Do you pay his wages? Did you engage him? I can't do anything in this house, without your coming up behind me and correcting me. Get out, madam. Take yourself up to bed. Your presence offends me. You're a bore, do you understand? Tiresome, a nuisance, a pain in the neck, a frost. Franks – first of all fetch me another bottle of brandy – because this one appears for some unaccountable reason to be empty – and when you've done that you can get one of the women, if there's any still awake, to clear up that glass which I was *provoked*' – and he shouted this at Julia '– into breaking!'

She could not speak to him or look at him. In a low voice, looking down, she said, 'Very well, Franks. Do as your master bids you.'

He went out of the room without speaking.

'Well, go on. Go away, Julia. Can't you understand English? I do not require your presence in this room. I wish to be allowed to get drunk in peace.'

She stopped by the door and turned slowly.

'I will keep house for you,' she said softly, still unable to look at him, 'I will bring up your daughter, and I will uphold your name before the world. But that is all. There is nothing more between us. Our marriage is over.'

She turned and went upstairs to her bedroom where Becky was sitting on the end of the bed.

'All the gentlemen gone, miss? Sounds like they was having a regular party, very jolly.'

Julia turned as Becky began undoing the hooks and eyes of her dress and helped her out of it, and then undid the drawstrings of her crinoline so that it fell to the ground about her. She did not dare to think. She sat at her dressing table and Becky pulled her boots off, then turned as Becky began to take the pins from her hair, and brush it. Julia sat staring into the mirror as Becky brushed, then the girl caught her expression in the mirror.

'Lor', miss, is anything the matter? You look like you've seen a ghost.'

Julia had no words to say. Becky stared into her face for a moment, then embarrassed went back to her brushing. There was an awkward silence between them, Becky brushing, Julia staring into her own eyes, unnaturally enlarged, staring; her face blank white, drawn, tight.

Becky finished brushing her hair, and fetched Julia's nightdress and helped her into it.

At last Julia rose, and without looking at Becky said in a whisper, 'Thank you, you may go to bed.'

She could not sleep. She seemed confronted by a blank wall. There was no going forward. Only the rest of her life stretched before her, like some book full of blank pages. What was she to do? He would not permit her to write. She could not go to Arthur. Only Agnes remained to her, her beloved daughter; so long as she had her Julia could hold on to her sanity.

It must have been half an hour later, she did not know, she was still awake, still thinking her futile thoughts. She heard Peter on the stair, as she had so often heard him, stumbling, cursing under his breath as he went up to his room.

Her door flew open, and he was there, a candle in one hand, a brandy bottle in the other. He stumbled across to the mantelpiece, set the candle and the bottle on it, then turned to her, drawing off his jacket as he did so with a drunkard's deliberate movements.

'Our marriage is over. I see.' Pulling his arm from one sleeve of the jacket, he spoke almost to himself. 'My wife tells me our marriage is over. She dictates to me. She lives in my house, eats my meat, drinks my drink, and she tells me our marriage is dead.'

He flung the jacket on the floor with a sudden lurching movement, uncertain on his feet, and then came towards the bed, beginning with awkward fingers to unbutton his trousers.

293

'Well. Let's see. Let's see what my wife has to say about this. She'll keep house for me. Very well. We'll try her; try an experiment. See what she'll do.'

She was watching concentratedly, knowing he was drunk, knowing instantly what was on his mind, her own mind clear as ice, calculating his strength, his weight, against the alcohol in his blood.

He was standing over her; she cowered in the bed looking up at him in the half light.

With one sweeping drunken lurch he ripped away the bedclothes, leaving her in her nightgown huddled beneath him. He swayed a moment.

'Get it off.'

She did not move.

'Get it off. You're my wife. Wife's duty. Get it off.'

She began to pull herself away from him now, but the instant she moved he moved too, a sudden violent movement, seized the front of her nightgown and simply ripped it right away. She was naked in front of him, and terror seized her. She sprang back.

But again in his heightened drunken state he was too quick for her. He threw himself across the bed, and pulled her shoulder, tugged her back in a strong violent movement that had her on her back, sprawling beneath him, as he was now on one knee, holding her with his hand.

With his other he fumbled with his trousers.

'Yes.' He seemed collected, meditative, as if he were speaking to himself. 'Yes. A wife must do her duty. When the husband requires, she will comply. It's the law.'

She smacked him hard on the cheek, and wriggled away, and leapt over the other side of the bed, and would have been out of the room but he caught her wrist and threw her back on the bed, and this time struck her a violent blow on the face.

'Wife's duty,' he said again, quietly, and then he struck her again on the face. For a second she lay quivering with shock and terror as he once more fumbled with his trousers, opening the front. Watching him, a last inner impulse prompted her.

She brought up her foot and drove it in to his chest. He flew backwards and fell heavily to the floor. She raced to the door.

'Becky! Franks! Mary!'

The rags of her nightdress clung round her shoulders. Behind the door was a dressing gown, and she snatched it and pulled it round her.

There were footsteps on the stairs. Julia wrenched the door open, even as Peter was stumbling to his feet.

294

It was Franks.

'Your master is going to bed now. Please help him to undress. Then you may go to bed yourself.'

Peter swayed in the centre of the room, as Franks stood in the doorway.

'Blast you!' Peter mumbled, snatched the brandy bottle and lurched past Franks and up the stairs to his room. Franks followed him.

In bed in the darkness, the tears began to flow, the tension to be released, until Julia's body was heaving, shivering with sobs, as if she would never stop shaking.

In those few minutes she had been confronted with the fact which she had tried and tried to keep out of her thoughts, the reality of their marriage.

Even as her weeping at last subsided, and she felt deathly weak, exhausted and shivering, alone in the darkness, staring up, unable to sleep, shuddering suddenly with the after-effects of hysteria, with the effort of controlling herself, she was seized with a horrible freezing fear that she was in a situation now which she could not control, bound to a man whom she could not even say she hated – because mere hatred was not the case, that was something human, almost warm – whereas what lay between them was something in a nightmare, beyond reason, beyond discussion or compromise, a struggle in which one or the other must be destroyed.

I must leave him. The simple words were repeated over and over in her mind, I must leave him. I must get out of the house, get out of his power, or he will destroy me. I must go. In the darkness, staring and staring, the words going round and round in her brain. I must get away.

And seeing no way to leave him, having no money, unable to return to Stallbridge. Father will not receive me. What would he say if I were to stand on his doorstep, Agnes in my arms? Father, I have left my husband. Unthinkable.

The Manor House? Alicia, I have left Peter. Unthinkable.

Arthur? For a moment she saw herself on his doorstep with Agnes in her arms. Arthur ... But she imagined a carriage drawing up as she stood there, the Earl of Worcester getting out, or the Bishop of London. He had his important work to do – his whole life to live – was she to stand on his doorstep with Agnes? Impossible.

Aunt Frances would take her.

Julia became frantic, thinking out her plans. It must be in deadly secrecy. If Peter should get wind, oh God, he would take Agnes for a certainty. It must be in deadly secrecy. He's out a lot of the time, isn't he? I must write to Aunt Frances first. That would be the first thing. And I must plan it very carefully, decide what things to take, just a few things, the bare essentials, just Agnes' things.

So her thoughts ran faster and faster through her brain. Unable to sleep, tired to death, frantic, possessed by one certain thought: I must get out, I must get out.

The dawn grew slowly in the room, the shape of the window behind the curtains. Objects began to be visible, the dressing table, the wash stand, as Julia lay dazed with tiredness waking from a shallow sleep with a startling realisation, Oh! I am here, it is true. She turned her head on the pillow, full of violent restlessness. I must do something, now, must get started now. She lifted herself from the pillow, then fell back in exhaustion. Rest, for God's sake, the servants won't be awake yet. You can't do anything, rest. Everything will be all right. Will it? How can it be, how can anything be all right ever again? What was the future to be? She could see nothing; she was on the brink of a void, and about to cast herself into it.

Restless, she pulled herself out of bed. I must begin, I must make my plans. Now, what shall I take? Pulling drawers open, in the half light. Oh, this is madness. Wait for Becky to get up. Poor girl, it was late last night when we went to bed, I can't disturb her. Opening and shutting drawers, then standing and having to steady herself against the chest of drawers, dizzy with fatigue.

She pulled her dressing gown round her and ran upstairs. Outside Peter's room she stopped and listened. She could hear nothing. He would be fast asleep. She ran on up to the attic, to the little room which Becky shared with Mary.

She shook her maid gently.

'Becky,' she whispered.

The girl stirred, and her eyes opened.

'Becky, it's me. It's very important. Listen carefully. I am leaving.'

Becky started up.

'Leaving, miss? When?'

'Now. I am going to my aunt's. Will you come with me?'

'What? Yes, miss, if you say so.'

'No, Becky – no – only if you will.'

'Yes, miss.'

'Hush. The master is still asleep. Get dressed.'

Becky was alert, and got out of bed.

'When you are dressed, bring your things and come down to my room. I am going to see to Agnes.'

296

Julia stopped at the door. Mary was stirring in bed by now.

'Oh dear, I have not even had time to write or anything. No matter, I cannot remain one second longer in the house.' She looked at Becky again. 'You are a dear, dear girl.' Julia couldn't help sweeping Becky into her arms. 'Now we must lose no time. I am going down to pack a few things, and get Agnes. As soon as she is dressed we are leaving.'

Julia went back to her room, took a grip from a cupboard and began packing clothes into it – nightclothes, several spare dresses, underwear – thinking all the time. What do I need, what does Agnes need?

Money. In her purse, four pounds. It wouldn't last long. So – Peter's pockets. There must be something – if he hadn't lost it all gambling.

She tip-toed back up to his door. She opened it. He was deeply asleep. She crossed silently in the dim light to the door of his dressing room, and ferreted through his pockets, through betting tickets, music hall programmes, restaurant bills. At last some bank notes, screwed up amongst the rest. Twenty pounds.

Well, she would have those.

Now, no more time to lose. As she passed through the room again she looked across at the outline of him asleep in bed, and paused for a moment. But only for a moment. This was the end. She was filled with determination.

She ran into Agnes' room. Becky was pulling on her bonnet. Agnes was lying in her cradle, but dressed.

'Are you ready?'

'Yes, miss. Are you sure?'

'Becky, believe me, there is no choice. Bring Agnes.'

They went down into the hall. Julia took her mantle, but then there was a jangling of the door bell. The two women froze. They looked at each other.

'Look out of the window,' Julia whispered. Becky ran into the dining room. In a moment she was back.

'It's the postman.'

'Open the door.'

She took Agnes in her arms as Becky opened the door. It was nothing, a parcel for Peter.

'Put it on the hall stand. Now are you ready? Becky, have you got whatever you need? Once you leave here you will never return.'

She looked bleakly into Julia's face.

'Never, miss?'

'Never, Becky. Have you everything?'
'Yes, miss.'
'Then let us go.'

PART THREE
August 1864 –
September 1865

Chapter Thirty-four

Julia hurried along the street clutching Agnes to her like a thief. Behind her Becky was carrying two small grips.

'We'll get a cab at Victoria Station.' She did not dare look back or aside but stared at the pavement ahead of her. No one looked at them, on that sunny quiet early morning, the two women hurrying along the street. People passed them, a family on their way somewhere; a nursemaid with a perambulator; a servant girl with a can of milk. Julia ignored them, did not dare look in their faces. Did they know her? Did they know she was running away? Would they stop her, report her to the police? Would she be hauled back to Ebury Street in shame? She hurried on like a thief.

They turned into Grosvenor Gardens and Victoria Station. A row of black cabs stood outside. Thank God. Already the station was busy, another day was beginning and people hurried past her on their way to work.

'To Charing Cross.' She wrenched open the door. 'In you go, Becky dear.' She clambered in, and deposited her bags on the seat beside her. 'Here, take Agnes.' They were all in. The cabby clicked the horse into motion. Safe. Here in the dark, dank, cab, smelling of rotting leather and straw. Safe.

Her mind was racing. Did they have all Agnes' things? Agnes struggled a little in Becky's arms. She was sixteen months now, a weight for a woman to carry. Julia smiled into her little face.

'Are you well, darling?' Agnes had not yet begun to speak. She was a contented child and made little trouble. She gurgled at the two women. Julia was thinking: Agnes' clothes, her napkins, her little cup and plate, her rattle. A terrible guilt seized her. So many of the child's things they had had to leave behind. There was no question of going back for them.

'Where are we going, miss?'

301

'To my aunt's – first.'

Julia leant back in the carriage and tried to relax. At least Peter couldn't find her for the moment. She had a little while, a breathing space.

At Charing Cross she paid off the cabby and took seats for them on the Maidstone train. They had half an hour's wait; it was a very slow half an hour in which she bought a sandwich and a glass of milk, and fed little pieces of bread dipped into the milk to the little girl. At every moment she turned her head, expecting to see Peter accompanied by two policemen come striding in, demanding the return of his wife and child. If anything should happen to the little girl; if Peter should take Agnes from her . . .

The train came in, they boarded and left on time, with no sign of Peter. Julia tried again to relax. Agnes was awake and looked out of the window, wriggling on Becky's lap as Julia tried to work out a plan for the future. Her mind would keep on flying away at tangents; she kept seeing Peter coming after her, accusing her of stealing his daughter. Stop; think. Outside the train little dreary houses, in rows black with soot, slid by beneath them. Sudden glimpses of a street corner, a little shop, a woman coming out; another woman, another life. And how different must that woman's life be from her own – and yet her own life was going to be different from now on . . .

She had walked away from Ebury Street. Nothing, nothing, nothing, would drag her back. Her marriage was over. And what was to come? Would she be going in and out of a corner shop like that woman?

She was adrift, and there was twenty pounds at this moment in the world to keep Becky, Agnes and herself from disaster.

Aunt Frances would take them in. Oh, but what if Peter came after them? She couldn't remember whether Peter knew Aunt Frances' address. Biting her lower lip she tried to remember. Did he know it? Surely when she had visited Aunt Frances before she had left the address? Anyway, he had only to ransack her desk, and he would find her letters, with their distinctive letter-head – a little woodland scene with nymphs and shepherds, and the address: 'Elm House, Streete, near Maidstone'.

She reached across and adjusted the shawl wrapped round Agnes in Becky's arms.

'Becky, I must tell you, I am deeply grateful to you for coming with me. I shall see that you don't suffer by it.'

'What are we going to do, miss?'

'I haven't made up my mind. I want to talk to my aunt first. I was

302

going to ask her to take us in for a while, but I am afraid my husband may discover the address. Oh dear.'

She looked out of the window. And if they could not stay in Streete? Her mind at this moment was a blank.

'I will talk to my aunt.'

How much time did she have? Was Peter already on the way after them? She did not know what she would do if he were to take Agnes from her. He had never shown the slightest interest in the child, but she knew he was quite capable of taking Agnes simply to hurt herself.

'I will kill him rather than let him take Agnes.'

'Pardon, miss?'

'Oh, forgive me. I did not realise I was speaking. Oh, Becky, do you trust me? Will it be all right? I don't know . . .'

'There, miss, don't take on.' Julia was leaning forward, rigid with worry and indecision. 'I expect you'll work something out. And Miss Maxwell is bound to take us in, ain't she?'

Julia threw her head back against the seat and stared out of the window in silence.

'Lor, miss, I've just realised!' Becky exclaimed after a while.

'What's that?'

'We're travelling in the same compartment, miss.'

'So we are.'

In her hurry at Charing Cross Julia had purchased two first class tickets. Up till then, she had always travelled first, and her servants third.

Becky beamed at her.

'It's nice, ain't it, miss? Never travelled first before. More cosy like. And having little Agnes too.'

When the train drew in to Maidstone station Julia looked out anxiously for any sign of Peter. There was none. But there was no sign of a cab either, and a boy had to be sent to rouse the cabby from the nearby inn, where he was at the moment enjoying his morning refreshment. They had to wait as a horse was harnessed into the fly and brought down to the station.

In the fly her spirits rose a little. They were nearly at her aunt's and so far there was no sign of Peter. Perhaps it was going to be all right . . .

Streete was a pretty little Kentish village, with two straggling rows of cottages facing each other, of red brick or white clapboard. Hop fields surrounded it, and there were two oast houses with their characteristic conical red roofs and white weather vanes. The village appeared deserted apart from a dog asleep in the middle of the road who rose slowly at the cabby's shout, and grudgingly made way for the cab as it approached.

Elm House was a pleasant gentleman's residence set in its own large garden back from the road with two bay windows on either side of the door, white stucco walls and a low slate roof. A large kitchen garden stretched away to one side and as the fly drew up to the gate a sharp little terrier came barking down the path as Julia and Becky were getting out and Julia handed the cabby his fare.

She turned to greet Tib who quickly recognised her and then Frances appeared from the kitchen garden, a large apron wrapped round her, leather gloves on her hands and holding a small garden fork. She stared for a moment. Tib had stopped barking.

'Who is that? Tib, down! Down, I say! Who's there?'

She saw Julia.

'My dear!'

Throwing down her fork, and dragging off her gloves as quickly as she could, she came hurrying down the path and took her neice in her arms. Julia had dropped the bags.

'Oh, Aunt!'

'My dear, what a wonderful surprise! I was only thinking of you this morning, and saying to myself what a nice thing it would be to have you here, and here you are! Hullo, Becky!'

'Morning, ma'am.' Becky curtsied.

'Well, my dear, come in, come in. You'll be ready for a cup of tea. Is that all the luggage you've brought? Never mind. Becky you know your mistress's room, it's always kept ready, you may take up the bags. Then you can tell Mary to bring us tea in the drawing room. My dear, you look pale. Have you had any breakfast?'

Aunt Frances was escorting Julia into the drawing room. Even on a bright summer morning it was cool and dim. Heavy swags of plum-coloured velvet kept out most of the light. On the mantelpiece a stuffed magpie perched eternally under a glass dome. Julia remembered it from her earliest childhood visits. A parrot on a perch, brilliant blue and yellow with a long tail, screeched at her as they came in.

'Jacko is pleased to see you.'

Julia, still enveloped in her bonnet and shawl, sat on the edge of a chair, clutching the shawl about her.

'Aunt, I have left my husband.' With difficulty she lifted her eyes to Frances who was just settling herself in an armchair. Frances looked shocked. For a moment there was silence between them.

'Oh dear.'

304

'I beg you, Aunt, please don't blame me! If you knew – I will tell you everything. I swear I had no choice.'

'What did he say?'

'I don't know. That is, I didn't tell him. Well, I did. That is, he knew. What I mean is, Aunt, I had told him that if ever he used violence against me again I would leave him.'

'I see.' Frances said softly. The two women looked into each other's face for a moment. Then Frances snapped, 'Where's that tea?' She jangled a bell which stood on a table beside her. 'Julia, my dear, are you sure you won't have something to eat as well? No? A boiled egg?'

'Perhaps I will, Aunt. Thank you. And do ask Mary to give Becky something.'

'Mary! Where's that tea? And bring Mrs Cunningham a boiled egg. And don't forget that Madeira cake I made yesterday.'

The girl hurried out.

'Now first things first. We'll have some tea, and when you've eaten something you'll be in a condition to think. I can see you've been under a strain.'

'Thank you,' Julia said faintly. She sat silently staring down at the carpet, violent red and gold patterns, jarring against the pale jade green of the Chinese-style wall paper.

Tea was brought in. Mary set a cloth at the table and Julia ate her boiled egg, her bread and butter, her piece of Madeira cake. Frances sat across from her watching her and keeping up a running commentary on the contents of her garden, the condition of her chickens, one of whose eggs Julia was eating; the problems with a fox; the excellent prospects for her runner beans; how her gooseberries were coming on. As Julia finished her tea, the old lady got up from the table, and opening a low cupboard beside the fireplace, took out a bottle and glass.

'This is a cordial I made. Blackcurrants from the garden. I think you could do with a nip.' She poured out a tiny glassful. 'Go on. It'll do you good.'

The cordial was thick, dark, sweet, and very warming. Julia gave a little gasp.

'Oh, thank you. Yes, I did need it.'

'Now then, tell me all about it.'

Frances' house radiated comfort, stability, order, and sanity. It was such a relief to Julia who had felt for months that she no longer had a home but had been lodging precariously in someone else's house, living with a man who was unpredictable, erratic and hostile, a complete stranger. Sitting here now, twisting the stem of the little

305

glass between her fingers, Julia recounted the scene of the previous night. Frances listened in silence, watching her closely.

'Mind you,' she said, when Julia had finished, 'your going off like this will have given him a shock. He may change his ways. Is there any chance of a reconciliation?'

Julia looked down.

'I don't know. I doubt it. He doesn't regard himself as in the wrong. I can't imagine him changing. Oh, he may, for a week or so. But he always reverts to his old character. I know him. But in any case even if he were by some miracle to reform himself, it wouldn't make any difference. We have such utterly different characters and interests. We are strangers to one another. I could not bear to think I was going to pass the rest of my life with him.'

'Many couples do, I believe,' Frances said sadly.

'Aunt, I will not be sacrificed to his selfishness, his egotism, his random, futile existence! I want to do something with my life! I do! Ever since I married I have felt my life slipping through my fingers, frittering away day by day in useless fragments.'

'But your daughter –'

'Agnes is more more precious to me than my own life.'

'Perhaps if you had another child? A woman finds her true fulfilment in her children – that is, so we are told, are we not? I must say, from my experience of Harriet's family, I sometimes have my doubts. A wretched, ill-disciplined brood, and Harriet, poor dear, worn to a shadow.'

'I love my daughter! And I would love to have another child, Aunt. But not by him. I couldn't!'

'Julia! What are you saying? If you do not have your husband's children, there is no other way. I mean to say, dear, what on earth do you mean?'

'Nothing, nothing, I swear.' She recovered herself. The image of another man had at that moment risen unbidden into her thoughts. 'Only that I could never allow him near me again.'

There was silence between them.

'Well dear, you know you are welcome to stay here as long as you like. You know that,' Frances said eventually.

'You are the soul of kindness. I knew the moment I decided to leave my home that you would take me in. But, Aunt, I dare not stay. It will be easy enough for Peter to find out your address and I think it will not take him long to guess that I have come to you. I cannot return to Stallbridge. Father will not have me. And of course I cannot go to the Old Manor House. So he will guess I have come here.'

306

'What are you going to do?'

'I must return to London. Don't you see? It is the one place he will never find me. I must take lodgings, and then –'

She looked into the old lady's kindly face, puckered with concern.

'Aunt, I don't know how you will take this. I'm not even sure of it myself. But I mean to make my own living. I will not be beholden to others for my bread.'

'Heavens! But how? Julia, my dear, there is no shame in being a wife, surely? You run the house, you offer a warm family home to your husband and child. What a strange thing to say, that you are "beholden" – you might as well say your husband is beholden to you for giving him a daughter, and for keeping his home warm and bright.'

'As you say, Aunt,' Julia said sadly, 'his home, his daughter, his wife.'

Chapter Thirty-five

Julia need not have worried about Peter chasing her down to Kent. When he awoke it was eleven o'clock, and when Franks mentioned Julia's name, Peter brushed him aside and rushed out to catch his friend Morley at home while his mother was out. Morley owed Peter money.

Having given him the money, Morley suggested going out and spending it. Why not ride down to the Star and Garter at Richmond for a chop and a bottle of claret? So they had hired horses in a mews near Hyde Park Corner and ridden off. Peter had completely forgotten Julia.

It was after midnight when he returned home, ready to drop into bed, and when Franks told him the mistress had bolted with Becky and the child, he grunted, sat on the side of his bed as Franks pulled off his boots, pulled the bedclothes over his head and fell asleep.

Even the next day when Franks brought him a cup of tea and told him there was still no sign of the mistress, Peter did not really register the fact. She had gone back down to Wiltshire, to see his mother or Lizzie; or maybe to Kent to see her aunt. Peter did not greatly care where she had gone so long as she did not interfere with him or ask him for money.

But as the days passed, and letters arrived from Wiltshire – so it was clear she wasn't there – and there was no sound of the baby, to which in a perverse way he had become accustomed; as the house now had a different atmosphere, a somewhat neglected, deserted air; and as the servants whispered among themselves, it slowly dawned on him that his wife had actually run away from home.

At first he couldn't believe it, because all her things, all her clothes, her bits and pieces, her books, were still in the house, and all Agnes' things too; and he couldn't imagine she would have gone without them. But one afternoon as he stood in her study and remembered destroying *Madame Bovary*, the result of a moment of drunken petulance, and as he recalled the 'auction' and what followed, the penny finally dropped.

He felt at first alarmed – she really had gone. Then aggrieved – dash it, she had no right to walk out like that. Then angry – well, she should jolly well be brought back, pronto. How dare she? My God, who did she think she was? She had abducted his child!

This was a matter for the police. He stalked out of the house and down to the police station to register two 'missing persons' and gave descriptions, though he could not describe Becky very well. For the life of him, he could not remember what she looked like. A rosy-cheeked, apple of a face, two blue eyes – or were they grey? – and a good-natured, somewhat idiotic, manner. It didn't add up to much of a description.

He could hardly tell the police sergeant that he had been far more interested in her buxom figure, and had seriously tried to rearrange her clothing one night when he had come in drunk from the club, when it had taken all her strength to fight him off. Becky had never mentioned this incident to Julia for fear of hurting her feelings.

As he walked home he began to take the matter really seriously. If she had gone, it would have to be explained to his family and friends. He was going to look pretty silly. He wouldn't be able to walk into the club without remarks being passed. 'Any sign of your wife, Cunningham?' Or 'Think I caught sight of your wife this afternoon, Cunningham; couldn't make out the fellow she was with, though . . .' He could become a laughing stock.

But it would be worse in Wiltshire. What reason was he going to give for Julia's disappearance? He knew his mother and Lizzie both worshipped her; they would be satisfied with nothing less than a full explanation. And what explanation was he going to give?

At this point Peter lost his temper. God damn them all! He wasn't going to be questioned by a parcel of females. If Julia had deserted him that was her affair, but woe betide her if she ever tried to come crawling home, that was all ,. . Oh yes, he would just like like to see her on the doorstep begging to be let in; that would be a sight to see.

On this note of self-righteousness he himself knocked at his door and as he went up into the drawing room ordered coffee to be brought up. Having the house to himself certainly had one advantage. He could light a cigar without any nagging female to remark on it. He lit one. Nothing he like better than a cigar with his coffee. The first cigar of the day was the sweetest – though it turned his bowels to water. Still, it kept him regular, God damn it! And why shouldn't he smoke in his own house? Peter stalked round the

309

drawing room in an orgy of irritation, drawing harshly on his cigar, and staring out of the window. Damn it all, he was the injured party! She had deserted *him*, don't forget. And by God she would be made to pay! He was going to have his daughter back here if it was the – well, he would have her back, that was all.

Julia stared up at the house.

A dog-eared notice in a corner of the window read 'Rooms to Let'. It was a shabby street just off the Tottenham Court Road, and a dingy, grimy house of red brick. Becky was down in Kent with Frances and Agnes, and Julia was in London for the day to find lodgings. She had started over in Bloomsbury in the streets round Russell Square. It was more respectable, but also more expensive. Julia was not going to depend on Aunt Frances, though the old lady would have given her whatever she asked. But she had most of Peter's twenty pounds, and it should last until she found some way of making her own money. In Bloomsbury they were asking thirty shillings or two pounds a week for lodgings, though with coals included, and she couldn't go that far at the moment.

She knocked. As she waited she studied the peeling paint on the door. A distant shout, the pattering of feet on the staircase, and the door opened. A girl, twelve, fourteen maybe, thin, stunted and consumptive, stared up at her. As the door opened, a nauseating smell, partly sweet, partly boiling cabbage, wafted out.

'I should like to see the rooms.'

The girl turned and called out, 'Party to see the rooms, mum!'

A shout came up from the basement.

'Show her the first floor front!'

Julia was led upstairs. It struck her that this house was the same size and design as her own in Ebury Street, though in ruinous condition. The girl opened the door and Julia walked in.

It was uncannily like her own L-shaped drawing room, the same three long windows looking out on to the street, and reaching to the floor, the same corniced frieze round the ceiling, the same rose in the centre, and then the folding doors opening to the back half with another fireplace and a window overlooking a dingy, weed-infested garden. There were two beds in the rear half. In the larger front part there was a table, two chairs, and a brokendown chaise longue, its horse hair stuffing apparent through a long tear. The walls were bare and grimy and there were pale squares where paintings had once hung. A piece of carpet was so thick with dirt and grease that it was impossible to make out whatever pattern had once been woven into it.

310

Over everything there was a layer of dust.

'What are your terms?'

'Seventeen and six a week with coals and gas. Meals is extra.'

'We shall cook for ourselves.'

Julia looked round the rooms again, seeing the likeness to her own drawing room, comparing in spite of herself this slovenly, greasy, dusty, brokendown, smelly room to the graceful airy elegance of her own, where everything had been chosen and thought out, selected and arranged by herself. A wave of depression swept over her. What was she doing here? She must be mad. Why wasn't she at home where she should be? And her daughter too, and Becky – what right had she to take them away from that, and bring them to this? What would people say, what would Alicia and Lizzie say if they could see her here? What would Aunt Frances say?

Taking a grip on herself she followed the girl down into the hall. A plump middle-aged woman was coming up the stairs wiping her hands on her apron.

'I have a small child. My servant will want to do some washing. Is there a copper here?'

'Servant? We ain't got no servants' lodgings. The attic is took.'

'I should have said, my companion. She will of course share the room with me.'

'Suit yourself.'

'And washing –'

'Washing's extra.'

'I see. There is a broken pane in the window. Can it be mended?'

'Is there? Who done that? Mary, was it that Mr Weller? Did you collect from him afore he went?' She clipped the girl round the head. 'What do I keep you for, you lazy slut?' She turned to Julia. 'I'll get it mended.'

'Very well, I will take the room from today. I will move in tomorrow afternoon. I will pay you the first week's rent tomorrow so long as the pane is mended and the room cleaned.'

Julia had been thinking it out. She needed two rooms so that when Agnes was asleep she would have somewhere to work. The position was good too. She would be able to walk everywhere and that would save money.

'My name is Mrs Julia Cunningham.'

On her way to Charing Cross she stopped at a newsagent's stall.

'Have you the *Church Times*?'

'Yes, madam.'

'Oh, and I see – let me have the *Athenaeum*, the *Leader*, *All The*

311

Year Round, and – what is that one? – the *New Monthly magazine*. Give me that as well.'

In the train she went through the magazines slowly. Her first thought had been the *Church Times*. It was the one she knew best. They had book reviews. For years she had sifted through articles in learned journals for her father, boiling down the essence of a twenty or thirty-page article to half a page. It was a kind of reviewing. It was a pity she couldn't lay her hands on any of the things she had written for him. No matter. She could reconcoct, if that was the right word, some specimens to show an editor.

She remembered how once her father had asked her to make a study of James the Just, said by Josephus to have been the brother of Christ, and she had gone through Josephus' *History of the Jews* comparing it with some references in St Paul and Origen's Commentary on Matthew, and writing up her findings for Dr Stone. She could do it again. She would go to the British Museum, conveniently close, and rewrite her article. And one or two more. It would give an editor an idea of her talents.

She turned to the others. The *Leader* was a serious, intellectual journal. There were articles on prison reform, the situation in Schleswig-Holstein, recent advances in geology, reviews of plays running in Paris, the opera, book reviews of philosophical works in foreign languages. Was there any room for her here? All these writers had specialist knowledge. She was not a geologist; nor had she been in Schleswig-Holstein.

She turned to *All The Year Round*. This was much more accessible, much more popular. Could she fit in here? There was a cookery column. She looked out of the window. Well, she could certainly write one of those. What else? An amusing account of a walking holiday by two men in the Lake District, their triumphs and disasters: how they had reached the top of the Langdale Pikes, the glorious view, how the mist had come down and they had got completely lost and ended by tumbling straight down the fell-side until they were both soaked to the skin, and one had sprained his ankle. And so on. It was very light-hearted and required no effort to read. Could she write anything like that? What amusing experiences had she had lately?

She rested the magazine in her lap. Only the very amusing experience of being auctioned off by her husband and afterwards nearly raped.

She thought about the book, too, and the effort she had put in to her translation. Could she do that again? Retranslate *Madame Bovary*? The trouble was that it would take months, and no one would give her any money until it was finished – if they liked it. She realised by now – and Peter's reaction had confirmed her view – that it would in fact be very difficult to find a publisher. The book was too explicit, too honest, about human nature, for British tastes. It was not an 'uplifting work'; it did not preach a sermon, nor point a moral. It would be widely attacked if it were published in England. Better to put *Madame Bovary* behind her for the time being.

She picked up the magazines again. The *Athenaeum* was another heavyweight magazine with a literary bent.

She took a deep breath. She must be prepared to attack on as many fronts as possible.

Chapter Thirty-six

'Lor miss, are we going to stay here?'

Becky looked about her with dismay.

'For the time being, Becky.'

The room had not been cleaned, nor the window pane mended.

'Mrs Troughton, I have the rent here as agreed. But the window must be mended first. If you could see to that immediately. In the meantime my companion and I will clean the room.'

Mrs Troughton went out.

'Come, Becky, be of good cheer. Let us the give the room a good clean at any rate. Then we can organise ourselves.'

'But why can't we stay in Streete, miss? Miss Maxwell would have you, wouldn't she?'

'Becky, it is impossible. I cannot take the risk of my husband finding us and demanding Agnes. Come, set a kettle on the fire and let us get started.'

Becky went down to the pump for water while Julia laid a fire and once the water was boiling the two women set to work to clean the room. They took down the dingy curtains and gave them a shake out of the window. They had been thick with dust. The carpet was beyond redemption, but Becky took it into the garden and gave it a beating. They washed every surface including the floor, and as evening drew on sat down to survey their work.

'It's just temporary, Becky, while I get started. As soon as I make any money we'll find something nicer.'

'Make money, miss? What are you going to do?'

'I am going to write for the magazines. I am sure it must be possible. They do employ women, I know.'

Becky looked doubtful.

'What do you want me to do, miss?'

'Why, look after us, of course, and take care of Agnes while I am out.'

'I can't cook, miss.'

'Don't worry, we'll do it together. You'll soon learn.'

Becky thought for a moment.

'Maybe I could earn some money too, miss?'

'What do you mean?'

'You know – maybe needlework?'

Julia hugged her. 'Becky, you are a friend.'

Letters were piling up for Julia on the hall table. Peter regarded them suspiciously. He did not know what to do with them. They nagged at him; reproached him. He would burst out petulantly to himself that it was no business of his and if she wanted her blessed letters she had better come and collect them. But still they lay there, inert, mute, accusing.

Damn it, it wasn't his fault! Let her come and get them, if she wanted them! But she didn't come and get them.

He turned them over. He recognised his mother's hand, and Lizzie's . . . but there was another letter in a hand which he did not recognise, franked in London. In which case, perhaps it was urgent? An illness?

He ripped it open and read it.

Julia,

I have thought and thought about our conversation. It was wrong of me to say what I did, I see it now. God knows, I saw it then, yet could no more stop speaking than I could stop thinking of you. What must you have thought? Yet I know, by some kind of telepathic sympathy which connects us and by which we communicate in unspoken messages, that all is not well with you. God forbid I should ever bring you harm but it is my duty to show you that I am your friend and that you have but to utter a word, and I will serve you to the utmost of my power.

No more now – and no need to reply to this. God bless you, my dear.

A. Grahame

Peter slowly crushed the letter in his hand. It explained everything. That blasted curate had enticed her away. If that didn't beat everything. Run away with the curate!

God, if this ever got out – if it got round the club – he'd look the biggest fool in London. It had to be settled quickly. He must go down straightaway and drag her back. He was halfway up the stairs when it occurred to him – he didn't know where they were. They

315

wouldn't be in Stallbridge. They could be anywhere. They may even have gone abroad. God damn it! She had no right!

No, wait. This had to be thought out. He went into the drawing room and rang for Mary. As he waited he took out a cigar.

'Bring me some coffee.' She went out. What the hell, he might as well have a brandy with it. He had only just had breakfast, but no matter for that.

He threw back a tumblerful of brandy and drew on his cigar. He was in a fix, that was a fact. Mary brought in his coffee. He kicked some newspapers left lying on the floor where he had thrown them the night before.

'And what are these doing here?'

The woman mumbled something, gathered them up, and took them out of the room. Look at it! The place was going to the dogs, confound it! Damn it all, Julia had no right walking out on him! My God, just let him get his hands on her, that was all!

Oh God, and with the curate! He'd thrash him till he howled for mercy.

Peter drew savagely on his cigar. This was getting him nowhere. She was gone. The question was – how was he going to find her? Go down to Wiltshire? That would mean telling his mother. Hmm. He'd better have a good story ready for *her*. Anyway, what was the point in going down? They wouldn't be there, for heaven's sake!

He wandered about the room, drawing on his cigar. He had another tumbler of brandy. He didn't know whether to go out or stay in; whether to go to Stallbridge or stay in London. Confound it!

He threw himself into a chair. It was too bad, it was downright rotten of Julia. He wasn't that bad, after all; he had treated her well enough, hadn't he? If only she wouldn't nag him. Why couldn't she understand that? They could have rubbed along well enough. That was the trouble with women – they never knew how to treat a fellow. He poured another tumbler of brandy. The house was like a morgue – look at it. Servants couldn't be trusted to do the simplest thing. It was going to the dogs; it was no place for a fellow; no fun at all.

He stubbed his cigar out and stared across the room at a picture on the wall. Where had that come from? He studied it minutely. He had never noticed it before. It was a nice picture: village scene, cows and milkmaids. Reminded him of Stallbridge. Julia must have chosen it; she had very good taste. Oh God, why wasn't she here? It was so damned unfair!

There was a jangling at the front door. Peter noticed it vaguely. Franks opened the door. Some chat. Peter wasn't listening. Then steps on the stairs. The door opened.

316

It was Lizzie. Dolly was behind her.

'Peter! Phaugh! What a stink! It's disgusting!'

She waved an arm to dissipate the fug of cigar smoke.

'Open a window, for heaven's sake. How can you sit here like this?'

She crossed the room briskly, threw up a window, and then another. Peter took her in slowly.

'Lizzie? What are you doing here?'

'What do you mean, why am I here? You're expecting us to dinner, or had you forgotten? I wrote to Julia on Monday.'

'Dinner?'

'Peter.' She came closer and looked down at the tumbler on the table beside him. She stared into his face. 'You've been drinking!'

He looked blearily up at her.

'Is it any business of yours?'

'A bit early isn't it? What's the matter with you? And the place looks like a pig-sty.'

She crossed to the fireplace and tugged at the bell-pull. Peter swivelled round in his chair.

'Hullo, Dolly.' He waved vaguely.

Dolly coughed. He was dressed smartly, buttoned up, gloved, holding a shiny top hand in his hand.

'You're looking smart today, Dolly. Quite the toff. How's marriage suiting you?'

He was about to mutter something when Mary appeared at the door.

'Tell your mistress that Mr and Mrs Emerson are here.'

Mary looked at her, then to Peter, then back to Lizzie.

'That's all, Mary,' Peter said, 'you can go. Julia's out, Lizzie.'

'When's she coming in?'

Peter looked away.

'Not sure exactly.'

'What's she gone out for? She knows we're coming. I said in my letter we'd catch the early train.'

Peter's mind was a blank. Lizzie pulled on her gloves.

'Well, I'm not sitting here in this thieves' kitchen. We'll go along to the Army and Navy. Let's see. Half past eleven. Tell Julia –'

Peter attempted to get out of his chair which was rather low; but as he reached for the little table on which his brandy tumbler stood to steady himself he sent it flying, stumbled across the room, tripped, and fell headlong at Dolly's feet. Dolly bent to help him up.

'Are you all right, old fellow?'

'Peter!'

317

Lizzie came quickly to him.

As Dolly helped Peter to his feet, she reached down to assist.

'You're drunk! Peter, you're completely drunk! What on earth's going on?'

He wheeled on her, uncertain on his feet.

'Why don't you ask her that?'

'What do you mean?'

'Anyway, dinner's off.'

'What?'

'No Julia, no dinner.'

'Peter, I don't believe I'm seeing this.'

She set his chair on its feet and steered him back into it.

'Let's start again. Where's Julia?'

'Not here.'

'I can see that.' Lizzie stood over him. 'For the third and last time, where is she?'

'I told you, Lizzie, blast it! I don't know. Haven't you got ears?'

'Peter, in a minute I am going to lose my temper. If you don't explain all this to me now I'm calling Franks to ask him.'

'All right, if you want to know, she's left.'

Lizzie stared into his face. 'Left you? Left home?'

'Yes.'

'Why?'

Peter stared stolidly up at her. Lizzie was trying to fathom it all out; she had become very serious. Dolly watched her.

'We must find her.'

'Hear hear.'

'When did she leave?'

'Thursday morning a week ago.'

'Have you reported this to the police?'

'Of course I have.'

Lizzie turned away for a moment, thinking.

'If anything has happened to her I shall never forgive you.'

'Oh, you needn't worry about that. She'll be quite safe. She's run off with the blasted curate.'

'Mr Grahame?'

'Yes, and if you –'

'That's impossible. I saw Mr Grahame yesterday in Stallbridge.'

'What? But he wrote her a letter.'

'What letter?'

'Eh? Well, hold on.' He thought for a moment, 'I screwed it up. Probably down in the hall somewhere.'

'What did it say?'

318

'Lot of confounded lovey-dovey nonsense. Don't remember.'

'Mr Grahame?' Lizzie was astounded.

'Oh didn't you know? Our worthy curate has been in love with my wife for years.'

'Peter, I can see you're drunk –'

'Ask him! Let him deny it! Damn it, you shall see the letter, bound to be there somewhere!'

He lurched to his feet again, cannoned past Dolly, wrenched the door open and stumbled downstairs into the hall. Lizzie followed. In a moment he had retrieved a crumpled piece of paper, flattened it out and thrust it at Lizzie.

Lizzie read it.

Julia stared up in the darkness. A faint glow from the fire threw an orange light on the ceiling. The clothes horse hung with Agnes' napkins cast an exaggerated shadow on the far wall. Becky lay near her asleep. Their beds stood at right angles along the walls in the smaller of the two rooms. Agnes was asleep in bed beside Julia. The clothes horse was one of a small number of purchases Julia had had to make. Another was the rush matting on the floor. Mrs Troughton's carpet was beyond redemption; Julia could not endure the thought of Agnes crawling on that grease and dirt encrusted relic. She had also bought a couple of saucepans and a bowl at a junk shop on the corner. What little cooking they could do would be done on the parlour fire, pans of boiling potatoes balanced awkwardly on the coals, supplemented with pies and bits of roast meat from the cook-shop down the street. Small items of washing were done in a basin in water carried up from the pump in the yard behind. Mrs Troughton did the larger items for sixpence a week. There was a water closet in the yard at the back.

Julia lay and stared up in the dim firelight. It was a terrible thing she had done. What right did she have to take Agnes from her home and her father? By this step she had cut herself off from all properly regulated society. She could never see Lizzie again, nor Alicia, nor her father, nor Mr Grahame. She was cast adrift from all normal civilised life; a vagabond, a gypsy.

For herself, well, that was her own responsibility. But what right had she to inflict this on Agnes? What would her daughter say when she grew up and found out what Julia had done? Would she not curse her? How could she ever justify her action to Agnes when she should be old enough to understand? Surely any sacrifice, any misery, was worth it to give a child a secure and happy home?

The thoughts turned and turned in her mind. And how long

would her money last? Perhaps they should go back and throw themselves on Aunt Frances' generosity; and if Peter came – but no, that was impossible. If Peter came and demanded Agnes, Julia had no power to refuse. Agnes had the right to be brought up in a decent home with pleasant, respectable surroundings, but what sort of a father was Peter? It was impossible she should resign Agnes to his charge.

The thoughts continued to revolve in her mind, with all the time a hideous cold feeling of guilt that she was responsible for her daughter and had failed her.

And Alicia and Lizzie. They must know by now. She must write tomorrow and tell them Agnes was safe and well.

It was August and dawn came early. At half-past five she rose quietly, taking care not to disturb Agnes, raked the fire, added some coals and stirred it into life. She drew back one of the thin ragged curtains to let in a little more light and sat at the table. Here stood a ream of blank foolscap paper, a bottle of ink, and some new steel-nibbed pens, bought the day before. The five hundred sheets stared at her. Five hundred sheets – somehow out of them she had to fashion a livelihood.

She began a letter to Lizzie. She must at least let her know that she, Becky and Agnes were safe. Then she must give some account, some excuse for what she had done. She knew Peter would justify himself and very likely exaggerate what had happened. She wrote as far as she could a restrained and balanced description of events. When she had finished and was addressing an envelope, it occurred to her that she could not give this address, nor any other. She must give a Post Office box number.

She set the paper on the mantelpiece, took the kettle and went down to the pump for water. Agnes would wake soon. Becky was still asleep as she hung the kettle over the fire. She stood for a moment looking down at the sleeping girl. Poor Becky, dreaming of Stallbridge very likely.

Agnes stirred and Julia sat beside her, moving the bedclothes round her, settling her. Again the terrible gripping hand closed on her heart as she gazed down into her daughter's face. Her little darling: why had she brought her to this shabby lodging? What chain of misunderstandings, mistakes and failures had brought her from the rectory in Stallbridge to this slum?

She roused herself. No good thinking like this. The kettle was warm and she poured some water into a bowl on the table, slipped off her night gown and washed herself. As she dressed she thought of all her clothes, her dresses, blouses, skirts, coats, jackets, under-

320

wear, stockings and shoes in Ebury Street. She had brought two dresses with her and a change of underwear. Why had she been in such a terrible hurry – she should have brought more clothes, especially as autumn would be approaching in a few weeks. All those clothes, there, hanging in rows, and she unable to get at them.

Enough. It was done. She emptied the bowl of water into the bucket and carried it down to the water closet.

After Agnes and Becky had woken, after Agnes had been washed and they had all eaten a bowl of porridge, Julia set out to earn their living. She walked first to St Martin Le Grand, to the General Post Office, and requested a Post Office box number; then having written it in, she sealed up her letter to Lizzie and posted it off.

Next she walked to the British Museum and spent the morning with Josephus' *History of the Jews*, recreating the article she had written for her father on James the Just as best she could. Whether Christ really *had* had a brother could ultimately never be known, but her father inclined to the belief, which she shared, that it suited St Paul to think that James was rather his *spiritual* brother.

There was also an anonymous *Life of St John of Patmos* which her father had been interested in and which she had read and made notes on. She stayed in the reading room until it closed at seven and walked home with her roll of papers.

That night, after they had settled Agnes to sleep and she and Becky sat by the fire, Becky became fretful.

'I don't see where it's all going to end, miss, that's all. How long have we got to stay in this horrible room?'

Julia took her hand.

'I won't let you down, I swear it. Just let me get started, Becky, that's all I ask. If you left me I should have to return to my husband. You know what that means. I depend on you Becky, absolutely. I could not have contemplated leaving that man if you had not offered to come with me.'

'Offered, miss? Don't recall as I had much choice.'

'Becky, don't say that! I should never forgive myself if I thought I had dragged you away against your will! Would you rather still be in Ebury Street?'

'Well, I don't know, it was better than this.' Becky looked gloomily round the room.

Julia looked down thinking.

'You see, Becky, I have no money of my own. My only chance of escaping from my husband is by making my own living. I can *only* do that if you stay with me to look after Agnes.'

'Yes, miss, that's all very well, but it ain't a lady's place to earn

321

her living, is it? Your husband has the money. It's your place to be a mother to your child, ain't it, and keep house for Mr Cunningham. It's all wrong you going to work and then keeping me to take care of little Agnes. It's all topsy-turvy like, as if you was the husband and I was the wife. It ain't natural.'

This struck Julia very forcibly. She might achieve her own independence – but only at the cost of another woman's service. Becky's servitude negated her own freedom. Yet there seemed no way out. Someone had to care for Agnes.

But in the midst of her confusion there stood one sure rock of certainty. She would never return to Peter. And that meant she must somehow make her own way. And that meant Becky must stay with her, at least for the moment.

'Becky, I would rather die than go back to my husband! I beg you! Stay with me, just for now, just for a short while until I see whether I can make any money.'

She gave a grudging assent. Julia took her in her arms, clasped her, stroking her back, trying to soothe her. Becky calmed slowly.

'Sorry, miss, I ain't much help, am I?'

Julia held her tight.

'Becky, you are my true friend, believe me.'

Chapter Thirty-seven

Julia was in Little Queen Street, outside the offices of the *Church Times*. She had given her grey dress a thorough brushing and blackened her boots, but she was conscious of how difficult it was to keep neat and clean when she no longer had the assistance of the staff in Ebury Street.

In her gloved hand she held the roll of manuscript of her two articles, on *St John of Patmos*, and *James the Just*. She went in.

A gentleman would have sent his card in to the editor. Julia had no card.

She was in an outer office. The walls were lined with bound volumes of the *Church Times*, row upon row of black spines with faded gold Roman numerals on them. At two desks, crowded with papers, middle-aged men in frowsy black, buttoned-up coats were writing. Gas lighting made the room stuffy and airless. No window was open.

A man stood up, smiling.

'Good morning madam, can I be of service?'

'I should like to speak to the editor.'

'Very good, madam, who shall I say is calling?'

'Mrs Julia Cunningham.'

'Mrs Cunningham, if you would care to take a seat?' He was shifting papers off a chair, and wiping dust off with his hand. 'May I tell him in what connection you have honoured us with your visit?'

'I wish to propose some articles for publication in your paper.'

The man's eyebrows rose. He bowed without saying anything and went through to the next room. She glimpsed man another a large desk. A moment later she was ushered in.

A slender ascetic man with sandy hair and of uncertain age, but perhaps about forty, dry and unworldly, with an unfocussed gaze, extended a lifeless hand towards her.

323

'Mrs Cunningham? My assistant tells me you have something for us?'

'You will not know my name sir, but perhaps you will know that of my father, the Reverend Doctor William Stone?'

'Dr Stone? Of course. You have brought us something from him?'

'No. But I – er – I should be grateful if you would consider these two articles for publication.'

She offered the roll of papers across the desk with an almost perceptibly shaking hand. The editor took them, and began to unroll them.

'These are by Dr Stone, you say?'

'No sir, I wrote them.'

'You? I beg your pardon, what do you want me to do with them?'

'I would be grateful if you would consider them.'

The editor was unfurling the sheets and flattening them with his palms on top of the other papers already crowding his desk.

'*A Comparison of Josephus and St Paul as touching James the Just; A Reconsideration of the Anonymous Life of St John of Patmos.*'

'These are revised versions of essays I originally wrote for my father,' Julia said quickly, 'I used to help him with his studies.'

'You wrote them with your father's assistance?'

'Not exactly. He asked me to prepare them. They touch on various aspects of his own work.'

'Did he correct them?'

'He has not seen them.'

'Why have you brought them to us? Surely Dr Stone could have sent them himself if he had wanted them published?'

'I want them published, sir.'

He pursed his lips, sat back in his chair and placed his finger tips together.

'The *Church Times* is happy to publish anything by your father, Mrs Cunningham. But we could not consider these without his authority.'

'I was hoping you could find time to read them,' she said uncertainly.

'My dear lady, I am a busy man. If you had brought me something by Dr Stone that would be different. Now look here –' He held up a sheaf of handwritten sheets. 'I was in the middle of a piece by the Bishop of Worcester when you called. The refutation of an article we published five months ago by the Bishop of Bechuanaland questioning the consistency of certain passages in Genesis.' He leant forward. 'These gentlemen write with the authority of many years behind

324

them, Mrs Cunningham. What is your authority for these articles? Hmm?'

There was something spiteful, almost womanish, in his manner.

'It is not the policy of the *Church Times* to publish pieces by ladies. You appreciate that, I am sure. We do have a very high reputation, Mrs Cunningham. But if Dr Stone would send us anything . . .'

She stood in the street, the bundle of papers in her hand. Her heart was beating painfully, and she could feel the heat in her face. If he had read her articles, she could have accepted any amount of genuine, scholarly criticism. But his waspish, patronising manner, as if it were quite inconceivable that she, a woman, could write anything that could interest him . . . of course she wasn't the Bishop of Bechuanaland; that was obvious. The 'authority' that he had harped on lay in the writing if it lay anywhere, and if he had taken the trouble to read them he could have discovered for himself exactly how much 'authority' she had.

She walked quickly northwards towards the British Museum. It was no use crying over spilt milk. She must try something else. But she could only quiet her agitation by hard walking.

They travelled down by the afternoon train. Peter felt ill; he had a raging headache and would speak to no one. He knew he had to have a story ready for his mother, but his brain refused to help.

'You've got to tell her the truth,' Lizzie said.

Yes, at one moment, he thought why not? He had nothing to be ashamed of. At the next he shrank from facing her. Anyway, who said he wanted Julia back? Let her go off with her rustic paramour and leave him in peace. When he tried this tack, however, Lizzie got angry.

'We are leaving no stone unturned to find her. And you're starting with Mr Grahame. Tonight.'

'Oh God, not tonight, Lizzie. I feel like death.'

'Tonight. By tomorrow it may be too late. How would you feel if you went round to the rectory in the morning and they said he'd left? You'd never see her again. And she would be ruined for life.'

'Good riddance.'

'I shall lose my temper with you. You're going to find her, you're going to beg her pardon for your unspeakable behaviour, and you're going to beg her to return on any terms she chooses.'

'Eh?'

'Julia is my dearest friend. I don't care what Mr Grahame said in that letter. I don't care how he tempted her. I want her back. You're going tonight.'

Eventually he fell into a doze. Lizzie had wired home and Belton was at the station to meet them. In the carriage nobody spoke. Peter stared out of the window. His mouth tasted disgusting; his head was splitting; he wanted to die. And once they got home – oh God, Lizzie was a tyrant!

As the carriage drew up to the house he said, 'Now listen, Lizzie, I tell you straight, I'm not having any fireworks from Ma, and you'd better tell her so. And I'm not going to see Grahame until I've had something to eat. I'm starving.'

As they went in to the house Lizzie strode forward, took Alicia by the arm and whisked her away from the others into the dining room.

'Mama, a teeny word . . .'

Peter and Dolly went in to the drawing room and Peter slumped into an armchair. Dolly fidgeted, sitting down, standing up, staring at the long portrait of Mrs Cunningham on the wall, picking up a newspaper, putting it down again. Peter lay stretched out in the arm chair, his eyes closed.

'Oh, keep still, Dolly, for heaven's sake,' he muttered in the end.

When Lizzie told Alicia of the letter she gave a small sigh.

'What is it?'

'Oh, I think I had expected it.'

'Never!'

'To tell you the truth, Lizzie dear, there had been little straws in the wind. Still, the letter doesn't say anything about running away. Grahame appeared a few days ago. He's been staying at the rectory. As you say, he's our best chance. Peter must certainly go tonight.'

After dinner, fortified by food and black coffee, Peter set out to the rectory. In a way he was looking forward to this. It was something he should have done years ago. There was something about that man that cried out for a thrashing. It would be a real pleasure. He had a good thorn walking stick in his hand. His brain had cleared, though he still felt a trembling in his limbs.

He knocked at the rectory door.

'I'd like to speak to Mr Grahame, Annie – ask him to step outside.'

It was dusk, and the light was fading. As he waited Peter took a couple of steps back and forth and cut the air once or twice with swishes of his stick.

Arthur came out of the door, took him in, and closed the door behind him. The two men faced each other. Arthur's instincts told him immediately that this man's presence signified some difficulty, trouble or danger for Julia. Before Peter could say anything Arthur said brusquely, 'Not here.'

He waved them down the gravel path and ignoring Peter he walked a few yards away to where a cluster of laurels screened them from the house. Peter came after him.

'Listen to me, Grahame. I won't waste any time. I've seen your letter. Where is she? And speak out quick if you want to keep a whole skin on your back.'

Arthur's mind raced. What had he said in his letter that might harm Julia? And what did that second question signify? He needed to know more.

'Who gave you leave to open my letter?'

'Confound your impudence, answer my question!'

'Are you telling me you don't know where she is?'

The very sight of Arthur infuriated Peter. He tightened his grasp on the stick.

'Listen to me. I know you've induced my wife to run away. Tell me this instant where she is or you'll get the beating of a lifetime.'

He flourished his stick, but Arthur was too quick for him. Before Peter had even realised what was happening Arthur had rushed at him, seized him by the lapels, forced him to his knees, and was shaking him until his teeth rattled.

'She has left you?' Arthur spoke through clenched teeth in a quiet fury. 'Where has she gone? Tell me where she is, tell me!'

'I don't know, you idiot. That's why I'm here! Let me go!'

Arthur had him in an iron grip shaking him about like a doll. His eyes burnt as he spoke in a quiet hissing voice.

'You're lying! What have you have you done to her? Tell me! If you have harmed her I'll kill you.'

'Let me go for God's sake, I can't breathe! I tell you, I don't know!'

'You scoundrel! You shameless, worthless, idle, vicious scoundrel! You don't deserve her. If any harm has come to her –'

'Let me go, for God's sake!'

'Tell me what you've done to her!'

'I haven't done anything!'

'Why did she leave you?'

'I tell you I don't know!'

Arthur abruptly let go of Peter and he fell with a sudden bump backwards, sitting on the ground at Arthur's feet. He felt his head, looking about him as he recovered. Then he looked up at Arthur.

'Anyway, you should know that.'

'I never asked her to leave you.'

'You liar.'

Arthur loomed big over Peter as he sat in an undignified position at his feet.

'Get out. But take warning. If any harm comes to that woman I hold you responsible, and I will come after you.'

He turned away and strode back to the rectory.

Peter staggered uncertainly to his feet, retrieved his hat and stick which lay nearby, and stood for a minute, trying to get his breath back. He was trembling. Who would have thought the man would have been so quick? Peter had not even seen him coming. One moment he was threatening him with his stick, the next he was on his knees being shaken to a jelly.

As he turned in the drive, he stumbled; he couldn't keep his balance. He staggered about, and at last had to stop at the gate and rest as he tried to recover himself.

As Arthur let himself into the house he was trying to reconcile two very different emotions. One was a raw, primitive joy: she had left that man! The other was its opposite: where was she? Was she safe?

He had come down to Stallbridge on an obscure hunch, partly with the intention of looking for a way of bringing Julia and her father together again, and partly, as he confessed to himself, as a way of maintaining a contact with her, however tenuous.

His mind ranged about, trying to see if there was anything he could do. Cunningham didn't know where he was. That was good and bad. Because if he didn't, then how could Arthur find her? That was the worst of it. How could he find her?

Peter was leaning over the gate, feeling his heart pounding, and seeing little sparks of coloured lights whirling before his eyes. His head was throbbing with an agonising pain. The coloured lights grew more intense, the pain was throbbing, and darkness swam over his gaze. He collapsed on the path by the gate.

When he opened his eyes, he couldn't think for a moment where he was. Was he at home, still in the arm chair where he had been lying? What was the hard painful surface beneath his back; the dark shapes above him?

Those were trees above him, those dark shapes. Why were there trees in the drawing room? He was on the ground; why was he on the ground? There was an agonising, splitting, pumping, throbbing in his head. He tried to move his head, but a horrible pain darted through his neck. He fell back, staring up at the night sky.

This was absurd. He had fainted. That blasted curate had been too much for him. He tried again to move, trying to haul himself on to one elbow. He could not manage to. He didn't have any strength.

He couldn't even lift his head off the ground. He lay again staring up into the dark sky.

You certainly got a different view of things from down here. All those stars, look at them. Shouldn't like to have to count them; you'd never know where to begin. Funny how some were brighter than others. He just felt like going to sleep. Have a little sleep, he'd feel much better.

He was awake again. This was absurd, he couldn't lie here all night. What time was it? Anyway he was cold. He'd catch a chill if he stayed here. How long had he been asleep? He shuddered. He must get home. He'd look a terrible fool if anyone found him.

He pulled himself slowly to his feet, stumbling about as he tried to gain his balance, and shuddered again. He was cold. It must be late. It seemed to take all his strength to pull open the gate. What was the matter with him? He didn't have any strength. He was weaving all over the lane in the darkness. This was ridiculous. He stumbled into the bank. What would Julia say if she saw him? But she wasn't going to see him. She wasn't going to see him ever again. It was so unfair, how could she be so cruel? He crashed into the bank again, stumbled and sat down heavily in the grass. He shuddered. God it was so unfair, Lizzie nagged him, his mother nagged him, and Julia had left him. What was the point of it all? There were tears in his eyes. Oh God, life wasn't worth living!

He pulled himself to his feet, wiping the tears from his eyes. His brain felt like scrambled egg. Who would have thought Grahame would have been so quick? He couldn't think straight. Where was he going? But his feet were carrying him slowly back home.

When he stumbled in at the door, it was half-past midnight, and Alicia darted forward as Peter appeared, looking like a ghost, swaying about, with a dazed, crazed look, and marks of mud and grass on his jacket and trousers.

Franks got him into bed.

The next morning he had a temperature and was feverish.

329

Chapter Thirty-eight

In Peter's condition, rambling and confused, it was difficult to make sense of what he said, so during the morning Lizzie herself went over to speak to Mr Grahame.

He was polite but distant; so was Lizzie, but she did at least find out that Mr Grahame did not know where Julia was.

Then Lizzie questioned him about his conversation with Peter. What had they been talking about for so long, and why was Peter so shaken up and feverish when he returned? Arthur was mystified. They had only spoken for five minutes.

She questioned him further; yes, he gruffly conceded, he might have laid hands on Peter briefly but it certainly had looked as if Peter was about to strike him with a stick. Lizzie knew that Peter had gone out with some such intention. There was not much to be said on the subject; that side of male life was a closed book to her. Why men thought it necessary to start beating each other with sticks she had never understood. It was one of the signs that they were the inferior sex.

As she walked back to the Old Manor House, Lizzie was very thoughtful. Arthur Grahame was desperately in love with Julia, in a way that Peter could not have even understood. Although her loyalty was solidly with Peter, she was perturbed by her talk with Arthur, confused as to the rights and wrongs of the matter.

For four days Peter lay in bed, while Lizzie and Alicia tended him. He made a slow recovery, but Dr Williamson told him that his constitution, which was not robust, had been undermined by his way of life and if he didn't want a repetition of this he should stop drinking brandy, start going to bed at night, and get more fresh air. The shooting season was about to start; why not go out regularly with a gun for the next six weeks? Peter had been frightened by his

330

experience, the feeling of helplessness that had gripped him that night in the lane, and promised the doctor and everyone else that he would turn over a new leaf, and be a reformed character from now on.

As he sat up in bed eating his breakfast, and his valet was fussing about the room he would say, 'I've turned over a new leaf, Franks! You behold in me a new man. No more of that roistering from now on. I'm cutting Whittington and Holden and the rest of that set; lot of idle thriftless beggars! No! From now on, you're going to see, I'm going to start taking things seriously, got to get down and study how the estate works, go through the books, all that.'

'Yes, sir,' Franks would say, as he folded shirts and laid them neatly in a drawer.

And to Lizzie: 'Confound it, the house was so empty without Julia! What did she have to go and bolt for? Couldn't she have made allowances? I tell you, it's no life without her . . .'

A week later, when she returned home, Lizzie found Julia's letter waiting for her. Everything about it alarmed her, but especially the Post Office box number. 'I beg you to forgive me, Lizzie darling, for not giving an address, but I could not bear it if by any chance this should fall into my husband's hands. I cannot and will not return to him; the very thought of it induces a cold dread in me. I could not even speak to him.'

The intensity of Julia's feelings was frightening.

When Lizzie sat down to reply to the letter she found it hard to decide what to say. Julia had been under great provocation, but on the other hand Peter was her brother, and Julia was after all married to him. Wives weren't supposed to run away. You didn't do it. All right, if things were sticky, you made arrangements, you kept out of each other's way. It didn't matter what you did frankly so long as the proprieties were observed. But if people just went spinning off whenever they felt like it, society would fall to pieces. And think of the children.

Lizzie wrote her letter.

Julia, it won't do. Forgive me for speaking frankly. I know my brother is difficult and I'm not excusing him; but you are married to him. That's the point. You just cannot take it into your head to run off when things are bad between you. Your vows included the words 'for better or worse' and that can mean *much* worse. I agree that violence is intolerable and Peter must never attempt it again. From what he's told me I don't think you have anything to fear. But you *must* come back. You are married, and marriage is

331

forever. You have no more right to desert your husband than he has to desert you. How is Peter supposed to carry on without you? You should have seen him when we came up last week, expecting to have dinner. He was completely drunk and the house was in a mess. You cannot let this continue.

And, Julia, you have no right to take Agnes away from her father. How will you justify this to her when she is old enough to understand? She will never forgive you.

And think of your own position. You have forfeited your place in society. You have thrown everything away. No one will receive you, Julia. You have become a castaway; you will be friendless, and no door will open to you. How will you live? Think very seriously about this. You have many years ahead of you to repent of what you have done.

I beg you to return as quickly as possible. Come back tomorrow. I swear no one will say anything about it and Peter will be a changed man. You have my word.

Eliz Emerson

Julia read this letter as she sat in the British Museum reading room. She just could not stop the tears. At one point she had gathered her things and was halfway down the steps fully intending to take the train down into Wiltshire before she was able to get a grip on herself.

But even after she had returned to her seat, set out her papers and opened Murray's *Handbook to the Continent* again, the tears would keep coming. She stared at the page through a film of water, she sniffed, she wiped the tears from her cheeks; sometimes unexpectedly she would heave up a great racking sigh that would shake her whole body as if she were about to split in two.

Even then, even when a man to her left had given her suspicious looks as if she were disturbing his important cogitations, and she fought to hold back sobs which would have drowned her in a pool of tears, she would not draw back.

Feeling her hands shaking, she straightened the papers in front of her and opened her ink bottle. She nearly spilt it. Then taking another huge breath she turned over the pages of Murray until she came to the section on the Rhineland, and tried to focus her gaze.

The *Church Times* had rejected her. Very well, she would try an article for *All The Year Round*; something along the lines of the amusing piece about the two men falling down the Langdale Pikes. Two articles actually: one to be called Castles of the Rhine, an impressionistic piece, drifting down the river, watching the castles floating past and dreaming of all the stories, the wars, the loves, the thwarted ambitions, the triumphs they had seen. The other was to be amusing. She was to try to describe the night when Peter had gone with his friend Morley to the casino at Bad Homburg and lost all Peter's money, only as seen from their point of view.

She opened Murray and began to read. But as she read, it began to come back to her. She remembered it all, and when she read about the little town where they had climbed the hill and lain in the shadow of the ruined castle and lazily admired the view, it came back in such a terrible rush, that the tears would start again as she read. She fought to hold them back, but it was too painful to remember her happiness.

'Is anything the matter?' the gentleman to her left asked her, and all she could do was shake her head, burying her eyes in her handkerchief, and hunched over her desk.

There was a tap on her shoulder. It was a librarian.

'Are you all right, madam?' he whispered.

Julia nodded silently, looking down.

'I beg your pardon, but I fear you are disturbing other readers. Perhaps you would like to go outside for a few moments to compose yourself?'

Without looking at him, she rose and crossed the wide space under the great dome, thinking that everyone's eyes must be on her, and so out into the museum. Still shaking, unseeing, clasping her handkerchief, she wandered up down among the great Egyptian statues in their pink granite and black basalt, a dull light reaching down from the windows, alone in the great echoing hall, alone among the statues, looking up at them without seeing them, breathing slowly, trying to calm her nerves. The fact was there was no reply she could send to Lizzie's letter except 'Yes, I will return.' Lizzie was not ready to hear any reasons, excuses or exculpations. Julia must return, that was all.

The great statues gazed across at each other above her head, eyeless, unseeing, a blank stare of granite and basalt, strange, foreign, obscure, that had nothing to do with her, could never have, forty centuries old, and beneath them, Julia walked back and forth, breathing deeply, trying, trying, to take a hold on herself, trying to believe that what she was doing was right, but now not knowing anymore, not knowing anything anymore, except that deep deep inside her there was a blind instinct that drove her on.

She took a monstrous grip on herself, and returned to her place in the reading room. She focussed her gaze on the page. All day she wrote. Lizzie's letter would keep intruding, but she pushed it from

her thoughts, and went on with her article. By the evening she had
finished a first version of Castles of the Rhine.

Arthur knocked on the door.

'Come.'

'Dr Stone, I have received some news.'

Dr Stone looked up from his writing, questioning, the searching,
harsh gaze of a bird of prey, one eyebrow crooked.

Arthur came in to the room, and closed the door behind him. He
turned again to Stone.

'Well?'

'This may distress you –'

'You alarm me, Grahame. What is it?'

'I have news of your daughter, sir.'

'Julia?'

Arthur clasped his hands behind his back, looking into Stone's
face.

'She has left her husband.'

Stone stared at him, taking in the import of his words. For a long
time he said nothing. Arthur was uncertain whether to go or not. At
last in a low voice, he said, 'I take no pleasure in these news,
Grahame. I could have foreseen such an eventuality; I warned her.
But I take no pleasure in it. Unhappy girl.'

He looked away. For a long time he did not speak, and Arthur
was unsure what to do. But just as was about to take his leave,
Stone went on in that low monotonous voice, 'She was my right
hand. My hand maiden. Grahame, we thought as one; everything I
did, I did through her and with her. I had but to think of a thing and
it was done. Julia was everything to me in my work. Many, many
times, I can remember, she would bring me something, some suggestion, would point out some article in a journal, would draw my
attention to some passage I had overlooked. I cannot tell you,
cannot even begin to tell, what she was to me. And then, to be
seduced by such a one as Peter Cunningham . . .'

He passed his hand over his face.

'It was a bitter blow.'

There was silence.

'I had hoped –' Arthur began uncertainly '– I had hoped to bring
about a reconciliation.'

His words were left hanging in the air. Stone was still looking
away from him.

'Everything broken,' he said at last. 'Everything. She ran off,
without giving me a thought, without a thought for our work, left

334

everything at a moment's notice, left me bereft, floundering. Grahame, you cannot understand: it was as if I had been struck blind! Everywhere I turned, I was unable to continue. I reached out my hand – she was not there! I sought a book – there was no book. Julia was gone. My notes – look at them. Julia would order them. I was helpless without her.'

Again Arthur began softly, 'You had become over reliant on her.'

Stone did not answer, still staring at the books ranged along the wall.

'Ten years' work, it was to have been my greatest achievement; the definitive commentary on St John. It was my ambition to have been remembered ever after for this book.'

His hand strayed across the papers.

'You are too pessimistic. The work goes forward; Mr Crabtree has been invaluable.'

'She deserted me,' Stone muttered.

Arthur leaned forward, resting his hands on the desk, urgent, certain.

'Dr Stone, you must be reconciled! You must! I do not know what has happened between her and her husband, but you and I both know her. And we both know him. There must have been great provocation! Don't you see, at this time most of all, she will be in need of comfort and support? You must let me bring you together! You must!'

Arthur's vehemence caused Stone to look closely into his face.

'Let her take her own path, as she left me to take mine.'

'I will find her, I will bring her to you.'

'Let her go her own way. I have no daughter.'

Stone looked away. The interview was over. Arthur stood looking down at the rector, but Stone had turned from him again.

'You must be reconciled.'

Still Stone said nothing.

At last Arthur went out into the hall, and as he closed the study door he turned and stood where the sun shone in on that September morning, across the chequered floor.

335

Chapter Thirty-nine

Mr Cunningham died.

It happened quite suddenly. A servant girl found him dead in bed, lying there as he had done every morning, just as usual, his eyes closed, but when she moved him gently to wake him, he did not wake.

The family quickly assembled in the bedroom around the body, silent, uncertain what to say. No one was particularly upset. They had all expected it so long that it came as no surprise.

Arrangements were made for the funeral. Undertakers called, the body was dressed, laid out in the coffin in the drawing room. Everyone wore black. All the family were assembled for the funeral, except Julia.

On the day a horse-drawn hearse arrived, the horses dressed with black plumes, the men wore black crêpe round their tall hats, Mrs Cunningham looked superb in a long black veil. She did not weep. Nobody wept except an old woman servant who remembered Mr Cunningham as he had been before disease struck him.

It was a beautiful light autumn day, the beech trees in the grave-yard glowing in exquisite shades of green, russet and gold, as the sunlight glanced down through them. The air, cool and crisp, was clear, as if there had never been such a clear day. After the service, the coffin was brought out of the church to where a grave had been dug; everyone stood around, the atmosphere a queer mixture of the solemn and the exultant, that it was such a glorious day.

Lizzie watched the coffin as it was lowered into the grave. She had no feelings about it except a vague curiosity. The grave was deeper than she had expected; she thought what a labour it must been to dig out all that chalk. Her father had been such an invalid, it was as if he had been dead for years, only by some misunderstanding, some bureaucratic oversight, he had been kept waiting before being dispatched to heaven.

As Lizzie stood listening to Dr Stone's words, words which she knew well enough from other funerals, her attention wandered across the valley to the woods climbing up and along the downs, the view heightened with a clear lightness which stuck vividly in her memory so that years afterwards though she could remember nothing else of the funeral, she never forgot her exultant feeling in the air, and the colour, and the view across to the downs.

Afterwards the family and others mourners partook of a funeral breakfast at home. Cold meats and port were served. Peter and his mother had not spoken much but there was a certain gleam in his eye of which she was aware, and each was inwardly preparing for the last great confrontation.

At the moment of her husband's death Alicia knew that the bell tolled also for her. Her reign was over. The anomaly was rectified; her place henceforth was a woman's place once more; to do as she was bid, to fit in to the convenience of others. She had been lucky that her reign had gone on as long as it had. She had ruled well, she had improved her property, and everything was in as good a state as it could be. Now it was over and she would have to step aside.

She watched Peter across the table. He seemed to have recovered from his fever, was lively, speaking quickly to a neighbour. He was helping himself liberally to the port too. In the few weeks since his fever, the night when he had been so frightened, he had actually mended his ways. He had gone out shooting, he had gone to bed at a civilised hour, and he had drunk nothing stronger than Hock and Seltzer. But now . . .

Now Peter had come into the property, and she did not trust him to consult her in anything, nor to yield to her convenience in any particular. He would please himself. Absolutely. She would have to leave this house; he had threatened it often during their nerve-shredding rows. It would require all her strength of character to stand by in silence and watch him have the estate to himself.

There was one thing for certain, however; he should never rejoice in his triumph over *her*. He should see no mark nor sign of her humiliation on *her* face. Her husband's will allowed her a dignified competence. She would find a house in the village; she would keep herself busy. Whatever follies Peter committed he would find no opportunity to crow over her.

But she knew he was itching to begin; looking for an opportunity to get at her. He had waited so long; haggled with her so long for money. Now it was all his, he was going to make the sparks fly.

Lizzie watched him go at the port. There were important words to be said between the three of them; it would be wise to start while he could still hear sense. She signalled to her mother, and nodded towards Peter.

'Peter, come with me.' She took the glass from his hands. 'And you should keep away from this stuff. You know what Dr Williamson said.'

Peter was taken by surprise.

'Lizzie!'

'There are things we have to talk over.'

'Give me that glass back. You are the limit. It isn't every day a fellow comes into his own, and the event must be celebrated properly.'

'Not by getting beastly drunk.'

'I *never* get beastly drunk. A certain elevation perhaps, proper to a gentleman and a landowner, and entirely acceptable in the circumstances. If you don't like it, you know what to do – there's Dolly, you're neglecting him. Go and do your duty and keep your husband company.'

Dolly was standing alone looking forlorn, an empty glass in his hand.

'Dolly will keep. But you and I and Mama must have a conference.'

'Now?'

'Good a time as any. I will have to get home soon.'

The three of them went into the conservatory. It looked deserted without Mr Cunningham in his wheelchair. But that had disappeared to a distant shed at the moment the old man died. Alicia had also taken the opportunity to rearrange the plants and furniture, as well as ordering the room to be repainted. Even though she knew she must be out soon, she wanted to give the place a new feel.

'Well, here we are, all nice and cosy. What is it you ladies have so pressingly on your mind?'

'You must write to Julia and beg her to return,' Lizzie said.

Peter looked into the faces of the two women.

'I must, eh?'

'She's bound to come back now you'll be moving in here. She hated living in London. It was part of the reason why she went off. Now you're going to be living here, she's bound to want to come back. She'll have to take over the running of this house. She must return. Besides, your daughter has the right to live here. You must tell her all this, and tell her to come back now.'

'Oh!' Peter drew in his breath. 'Do we have to talk in here? I

338

detest this hot house atmosphere. And being pestered by two females makes it ten times worse.'

He got up to leave.

'Peter!' Lizzie was quick to cut him off. 'Sit down and listen to me. You are now master here.'

'Oh I am, am I? Nice of you to notice.'

'You are master,' Lizzie went on slowly and carefully, 'and naturally you have responsibilities. It is necessary that your wife should be here too –'

'I am quite capable of taking care of my own responsibilities, thank you, Lizzie, but I'm not at all sure I want to live here. Never liked the country. Deadly dull. Lot of boring business about cows and sheep.'

'It may be boring,' Alicia put in, 'but it is your business now.'

'Oh, thank you, Mother dear.' Peter spun quickly round. 'I wondered when you were going to open your mouth.'

Alicia said nothing.

'You have an estate bringing in more than three thousand a year, Peter,' Lizzie went on. 'That is a lot of money.'

'Isn't it just?' he said with a wicked grin.

'It is a lot of money,' she repeated, 'and it will need your attention. You can't just go off to London, and pretend it isn't there. You have got to settle down and think very seriously about the future.'

'You know,' he got up again, 'I think I've had enough of you two. It must be galling to see me in the driving seat at last. Especially for you, Mother!' He spat this at her, but she remained immobile. 'Deeply galling that the young master is in charge, and won't be pushed about and dictated to by the womenfolk. So let me tell you just a few things to be going on with. If Julia thinks just because I've come into the property that she can come worming her way back in, she's got another think coming! She can starve for all I care! God damn it, she deserted me, don't forget. Secondly, I am now the owner of this estate, lock stock and barrel. Every last barrel, Mother! Every plough, cow, sheep, chicken, every blessed ear of corn, every brick and beam in this house is mine, and I intend to do just as I like with it, without any assistance from you or anyone. And I shall particularly resent *any* attempt to assist me in my *duties*! Thirdly, I am now going to get beastly drunk, as you so charmingly put it, Lizzie, in my own home, with my own wine, without any assistance or comment from any nagging females!'

He walked out. Lizzie looked at Alicia and reached out for her hand. Her mother had been watching Peter, white-faced, with a strained staring expression.

*

339

Later, when she had recovered a little, Alicia said, 'Lizzie darling, I don't think I can remain here tonight. Peter is quite unspeakable at the moment. Once he gets drunk – I don't think I could stand it. Would you mind awfully if I came home with you for a few days?' She straightened her back, and looked straight before her for a moment, thinking. 'I shall never sleep in this house again. I shall start looking for somewhere else to live in the morning.'

There was no point in attempting to say goodbye to Peter so the two women called for their coats and gloves, adjusted their hats, Lizzie sent Dolly off to get the carriage brought to the door, and the three of them departed.

Lizzie and Dolly lived in Devizes, twelve miles away, to be near the business. Lizzie had at first complained of the smell of malt which seemed at times to pervade the entire town, but she said now that she had grown so used to it that she no longer even noticed it.

'You know, Lizzie, I have been thinking,' Alicia said as they were driving through the lanes, 'I think I shall come and live in Devizes. Would you mind awfully? You needn't worry, my dear, I swear I shan't pester you. I shall keep myself fully occupied. The town has its fair share of the poor and needy upon whom to inflict my charity.'

She tried to sound bright, but Lizzie understood what she was feeling.

'Stay with us, Ma,' she said, 'as long as you like. Anyway, there's something I meant to tell you. I'm expecting again, so it would nice to have you in the house.'

Alicia reached over and kissed her on the cheek.

'I'm so glad.'

Lizzie's son, Jeremy, was now a little over a year old.

That night when Lizzie and Dolly were in bed, Dolly spoke to her. It was unusual for him to offer an opinion, but he said hesitantly, 'You know, Lizzie, I've been thinking. I know it's a long way off, but now that Julia has left Peter, I mean, and supposing they are never reunited, that would make Jeremy the heir to your father's property.'

She said, 'It's too early to say. Anyway, I'm going to move heaven and earth to bring them together again. He'll kill himself if she doesn't come back. The doctor has warned him off the drink, but he just doesn't seem to care.'

'No.' Dolly was silent. 'Still, it would be rather nice for Jeremy – unite the two fortunes.'

'Dolly, never mention it again! There's no question of it! Julia must come back!' She thought. 'I shall go and see her. In any case, if she doesn't come back, very likely there won't be any property to inherit.'

'Mrs Cunningham, do come in! Malone, a seat for Mrs Cunningham!'

Mr Wills rubbed his hands together. As she took a seat, Julia noticed her manuscripts on his desk.

'We have had a chance to read your two articles, and we are very pleased with them, Mrs Cunningham! Very pleased indeed! My colleague Mr Malone and I have both read them, and we like them very much. Isn't that so, Malone?'

'Quite so.'

'Very colourful, most romantic, your piece on the Rhine; you have a delightfully light touch, Mrs Cunningham, most imaginative! And the one on Bad Homburg – we laughed heartily, did we not, Malone! Most amusing! And to think it was written by a woman! How did you get such insights, Mrs Cunningham? One would have thought you were there yourself!'

'Thank you,' she said faintly, her heart beating.

'Reading it, I could verily hear the click of the ball in the roulette wheel, I believe! Two gay young bachelors on their travels! It had a wonderfully infectious freshness about it. Ah what it is to be young Mrs Cunningham! Without a care in the world! It made me want to throw my cap in the air and take the first boat train to Dover.'

'You are too kind,' she muttered.

'Yes! Well, to business! We pay a guinea a page. Will you take a cheque?'

Julia thought for a moment.

'Thank you. Ordinarily that would of course be acceptable, and in future I will be perfectly happy to take a cheque. I wonder, though, on this occasion, whether you could make it cash?'

'Cash, no difficulty, I assure you. Mr Malone, if you would oblige? Now, Mrs Cunningham, what else have you got for us, eh? Hmm? The magazine is an insatiable beast, I am afraid, it gobbles copy. We are all its slaves, toiling to feed it. We await your next contribution with eager anticipation. What is it to be, eh?'

'I am working on various pieces at the moment, Mr Wills. I will let you see them as soon as possible.'

The other man had taken a metal money box from a safe.

'Fifteen pages.' He counted the money out on to the desk. 'That makes fifteen pounds and fifteen shillings. Shall we say sixteen pounds, Mr Wills, in honour of Mrs Cunningham's first appearance in the magazine?'

She put the coins into her purse and slipped it into her reticule. A complete stranger had just handed her sixteen golden sovereigns; it was a dream, and she would wake up soon, but for the moment she enjoyed the sensation.

'As a matter of fact,' she said, 'I have written a number of articles on sacred topics. I wonder –'

'Sacred? Ah. To be honest, Mrs Cunningham, not in *All The Year Round*. I'm sure you could place them elsewhere, mark you – have you tried *Macmillan's* or the *Leader*?'

'The other thing is,' she formed her words carefully, 'whether I could make myself useful in any other way – book reviews, that kind of thing?'

'Yes, by all means. We shall certainly bear you in mind, Mrs Cunningham, if anything should come along in the female line. Cookery, household topics and so on – ours is a magazine for all the family.'

As she descended the stairs, Mr Wills' words went through her mind. 'Delightfully fresh'; 'most amusing'. She had sat up till two in the morning, writing the Bad Homburg piece. She had reread the article in *All The Year Round* on the trip to the Lake District, trying to absorb its atmosphere of irresponsible gaiety, and had made five versions of her own first paragraph before she felt she had caught the right tone. By the dull light of the dying fire, and the uncertain flickering of her candle she had looked across to where Becky and Agnes lay asleep, as she crushed another sheet of paper into a ball and threw it on the floor. 'Fresh' and 'amusing'! She took a deep breath. She felt a hundred years older than when she had left Ebury Street. Was it possible that it had only been a month ago?

A month, and at last she had made some money. Sixteen pounds. At one stroke she was afloat again. One ten-minute interview in an editor's office, and the worries had for the moment slipped from her back.

But she had to do this again. And again. Every month she had to have this success; stretching into the future she foresaw a succession of months, and in every one of them she had to sell articles that were 'fresh' and 'amusing'.

Chapter Forty

'Mrs Cunningham!'

Julia turned. It was Mr Malone, the editor's assistant, running to catch up with her. He was a young man – perhaps her own age – with a rather unmanageable, leonine mane of hair, cleanshaven and slim but perhaps a little dark under the eyes, as if he spent too much time reading by candlelight.

'Mrs Cunningham!'

He caught her up. 'We clean forgot to tell you. Mr Wills would be most gratified if you could come to dinner next Sunday. He keeps open house on Sunday afternoons, and it would give you an opportunity to meet some of our other contributors, not to mention other friends. We usually make a jolly time of it, I promise you.'

He proffered a card. Julia read it. Mr Wills lived in a house on Regent's Park.

'About twelve-thirty?' He smiled down at her.

'Thank you. Tell Mr Wills I should be most happy to accept his invitation.'

Malone turned back, and she continued on her way. Sixteen pounds *and* an invitation to dinner! It was a red letter day! Suddenly her heart lifted. Perhaps things might yet be well. Perhaps she might be able to establish herself as – what? – well, as independent, at any rate. At least, at the very least, she had not had to go begging to Peter for the sixteen pounds – that was quite a triumph, was it not? The sixteen pounds were hers as of right. She stopped in the crowded Strand, as the traffic rattled along beside her, and the foot passengers swirled back and forth about her. She looked up. A church clock had just struck half-past ten in the morning. The realisation grew and grew in her mind, it expanded like a great balloon: the money was hers. No one had given it to her or begrudged it her; she was beholden to no man's generosity or charity. She had

343

earned it entirely by her own unaided efforts. She stared up at the clock face and the thought filled and filled her, until she smiled spontaneously.

She went in to Handley's Bank. She had to open an account. She disliked carrying cash about with her. It was simply asking for trouble.

However opening an account was not so easy as she had expected; which address was she to give? Then it was explained to her that the bank's usual practice in the case of married women was for their husbands to open the account for them.

Standing in the crowded banking hall, it was embarrassing to have to explain out loud to the smooth and self-important young man behind the wide polished counter that her husband had a bank account of his own, and that it was *she* who was opening the account. The young man then had the impertinence to ask whether it wouldn't be simpler to deposit her money in his account?

'I am opening my own account,' Julia said carefully, 'I have the money to deposit, and I am not getting my husband's signature on anything! Or would you rather I took my money to another bank?'

She fought to maintain a moderate tone.

'I may have to consult the manager –'

'I will wait.' Her expression was calm.

She waited a long time, standing in the crowded banking hall, as the morning's business went on around her. She was the only woman in the building. From time to time she looked up at the clock. Eventually an older man came out of an inner office.

'Mrs Cunningham? What appears to be the problem?'

'Surely your assistant has explained it to you?'

'Ah hem. Yes. It is the policy of the bank for the husband to open an account in his wife's name.'

'Why?'

'Why?' The old gentleman was lost for words. 'Well, er, naturally, as head of the household, the husband should be aware of his wife's assets. He is the responsible agent.'

Julia fought to remain calm.

'My husband is a drunkard and a libertine. As for responsibility, he has not the faintest idea what the word means. I have no intention of letting him know how much I may or may not possess.'

The gentlemen behind the counter were deeply upset at this turn in the conversation. Julia did her best to maintain an equable temper.

'Perhaps I may remind you gentlemen of the situation. It is very simple. I have at present some money in my purse. I wish to deposit

344

this money in a bank account. I have no wish to borrow any. I wish to deposit it. May I do so or not?'

Again, they seemed to be struggling to grasp the nature of the situation. Eventually, however, the elder of the two made a decision.

'With gravest respect, madam, I fear that the rules of the bank do not permit us to accept deposits by a lady in the absence of the husband's –'

'Thank you,' Julia said crisply. 'You have said enough. I will not take up any more of your time.'

She walked out.

Walking up the Strand she could not believe it. Was she living in the middle ages? Was she some sort of chattel? Irresponsible? Unable to decide what to do with a few miserable pounds of her own money? It was simply monstrous that she did not have the right to dispose of her own money! She strode on breathing deeply.

She, like everyone else, had always thought of a married couple as a single financial unit. There was no earthly reason why a wife should want a bank account of her own. What for? The household duties and responsibilities were divided up between the husband and wife, and as it happened the financial side fell to the husband's share.

Only in her case it didn't anymore. In her case, she was a free agent acting on her own responsibility and by her own initiative. And the world, and in particular its banking system, did not make allowance for this eventuality.

She could just imagine what Peter's reaction would have been if she had told him she wanted a bank account of her own. In the meantime she was free to go her way, free to lose her money, be robbed of it . . . she walked faster.

She had recovered a little of her composure when she reached St Martin Le Grand where she found a letter waiting for her. It was from Lizzie, and was very short. Lizzie had some important news to impart and must meet her urgently.

This threw Julia into a terrible state, as Lizzie had intended it should, and it took Julia more hard walking as she made her way back to her lodgings to clarify in her own mind the probable event behind it all. Peter was not ill, as she had at first feared; if that had been the case, Lizzie would certainly have said so, and would have ordered her immediate return to Stallbridge.

Lizzie was coming up to see her. So the matter was not very urgent, however mysterious Lizzie contrived to sound. It could wait the time it took the letters to pass between them and Julia to fix a meeting. At the same time if Lizzie wanted to talk to her it must mean an intensification of her campaign to get Julia to return to Peter.

Of course there was no question of refusing Lizzie's request, however painful the meeting might turn out to be. Lizzie was her dearest friend, now and forever.

But Lizzie must not see her lodgings.

'Lor, miss, you're back early!'

'Good news, Becky dear! I have sold two articles! And they have paid me, in cash, on the spot! Sixteen pounds!'

'Sixteen pounds!' Becky stopped where she stood and looked at Julia with her mouth open. It was exactly Becky's annual wages. 'Sixteen pounds!' she breathed again. 'Does that mean we can move?'

'Yes, of course we are going to move.' Julia was thinking, as she took off her cloak and hung it on a nail behind the door. 'But I think we should celebrate first, don't you? What would you like to do? Go to Astley's? Or the zoo? And let's get in something from the bake-shop for supper. What would you like? Oh, Becky dear, you can't imagine what a relief it is!'

She threw her arms round Becky and swung her round. Then she bent and swept up Agnes who had been crawling slowly across the floor towards her. 'And Agnes shall come too, my darling! We'll all three go together, and be ever so merry!'

She sat on one of Mrs Troughton's rickety chairs, and dandled her little girl on her lap. 'You can't imagine – they didn't haggle, they didn't ask me to change anything. They just said they liked them very much and here's the money, thank you! Becky, I thought I must be dreaming! The man just placed sixteen sovereigns on the table in front of me! And they've invited me to dinner next Sunday to meet their other contributors!'

'To dinner. Lor!' Becky sat on the chair opposite her watching her as she played with Agnes. The baby was on the verge of speaking, but as yet still contented herself with gurgles and shouts. Julia was lifting her up and down, rubbing her own nose against that of Agnes, and bouncing her on her knee, all of which was highly pleasing to Agnes.

'And we can leave this place, miss?' Becky repeated tentatively.

Julia thought for a moment.

'We are going to leave here, of course –'

'I hate it here, miss!' Becky burst out at her across the table. 'It's all very well for you, you go out all day. But I'm here all the time! I

346

don't know anyone, except that idiot Mary. I hate this street, I hate the noise, I hate the dirt, I hate that Mrs Troughton, always spying on me in case I do anything she don't approve of. I hate the smell, I hate not eating properly. We had a lovely warm kitchen in Ebury Street, and real proper food that Mrs Standish cooked, not trying to boil potatoes over the fire, and eating bits and pieces from the shop, and I had my room I shared with the other Mary . . .'

Julia was stunned.

'And, miss, it ain't right for us to be here! Look at Agnes, how pale she is! How can you do it to her?'

'Pale?'

'It ain't good for her to be in this room all the time.'

'But Becky, you – we both – we take her in the park sometimes.'

'It's not like at home, miss! Think if she was in Stallbridge living at the Old Manor House! Or even in Miss Maxwell's in Kent! They're nice houses, proper run, with proper food, and Agnes with her own room, and all her clothes and things! How can you bring her to this horrible, hateful room, I don't understand it at all!'

Becky burst into tears and threw her head on the table. Julia still holding Agnes in her arms had listened in stunned amazement. Her mind was a blank, but she was filled with that horrible guilt again. She looked into Agnes' face. Was she pale? What sort of a mother was she if she had not even noticed her own child's health?

She was so obsessed with her own independence and getting free of Peter that she was prepared to sacrifice her daughter's health! What kind of a woman was she? Tears started into her own eyes, and she clutched Agnes to her.

'Becky, I had no idea – do you really think –'

'We should never have come here, miss. It ain't right!' Becky's voice was muffled as her head was buried in her arms on the table. Julia stared into Agnes' face. Was she pale? Was she ailing? She looked well enough, didn't she?

'Becky, don't say those things, I can't bear it! You know what my husband is like – he wouldn't care for Agnes! You've seen him. How could you leave Agnes with such a man? And I can't take her down into Kent in case Peter comes and finds her! I told you this before! How do you think I feel? Oh God, and I thought we were going to be so jolly today!'

Becky looked up at her.

'All right, all right, we will move, I swear, I promise. And if you think it right I will get a doctor to see Agnes. Look, Becky dear, please, please bear with me. I have earned us sixteen pounds today. There will be more, I know there will. But I have got to get

347

established. The money is very good, and once I am established we may do very well. But I have only sold two articles! I beg you, stay with me; we will move soon, I swear to you. Once I am a little more certain of the money, that is all.'

That afternoon they went to Astley's circus, and on their way home, had supper in a chophouse near their lodgings, with a glass of gin toddy.

'Here's to us, Becky dear. You have been a true friend to me, and you shall not repent of it, I give you my oath.'

'Here's to us all,' Becky joined in. For all her efforts Julia had not been able to cheer Becky up. Every time Becky looked at her, Julia thought, Am I doing the right thing? Is Agnes well? Should I take her to Stallbridge and hand her over to Peter? Should I take Agnes and Becky to Kent, and hope that Peter doesn't come looking for them?

She gave Becky four pounds, her quarter year's wages. But Becky didn't know what to do with the money, and asked her to keep it for her.

Once more Julia was sitting in a train. During the night she had thought it over, and had decided: they must move. Even with sixteen pounds in her purse, she didn't feel confident enough yet of her own earning power, so there was nothing for it but to go to Aunt Frances again.

She knew what Aunt Frances would say, remembered the conversation they had had, the facts which Frances had pointed out clearly, facts which Lizzie had spelt out too. But they could not remain in that room any longer. Becky had said that Agnes was looking pale; there was no helping it, she must throw herself on her old aunt's mercy and trust to her generosity. After all, the money was in trust for Agnes – surely the old lady would let her have a little on account – for Agnes' sake?

It was a beautiful clear autumn day, and as the train cleared the suburbs of London and snaked through the countryside, Julia's spirits lifted. After all, it was not for herself. Aunt Frances could not refuse her something for Agnes' sake. The trees were the most beautiful shades of gold and russet, with glimpses of green still on the beeches, and the fields already ploughed. Her thoughts wandered. How beautiful the countryside was and how she would have preferred to be back in Stallbridge, except that she did not think she would ever see Stallbridge again. But then perhaps when she was better established she could move out into the country, somewhere else. She could easily correspond with Mr Wills by post; nothing easier.

Her thought floated on like this until she reached Maidstone, and she felt more and more and more cheerful with every mile she drew nearer to Streete.

But when she reached the village, and the fly had deposited her at the gate of the house, she saw the blinds down in the windows of Elm House. She hurried to knock at the door. There was no sound of Tib, no sound of Jacko.

She knocked. It seemed a long time, until at last she heard a bolt being drawn back, and the door was opened by a middle-aged servant woman whom she did not recognise.

'I have called to speak with Miss Maxwell.'

'She ain't here, miss.'

For a moment Julia's mind was a complete blank.

'Not here?' She stared into the woman's face. 'Well – may I ask where she is?'

'She's gone away, miss, and the house is let.'

'Gone? But ... well, where has she gone? I should explain, she is my great-aunt.'

'I'm afraid I don't know where she's gone. If you would like to step inside I will call the master.'

It was a most odd feeling to be shown into the drawing room which she knew so well; to see everything – except the parrot on his perch – exactly as she knew it, and yet feel herself a stranger.

A moment later a pleasant-faced, middle-aged gentleman came in.

'Can I be of assistance?'

'I beg your pardon, sir, but I was hoping to speak with Miss Maxwell.'

'She's out of the country.'

Julia felt dizzy.

'Excuse me, but I wonder if I might sit down?'

'Of course. Are you unwell?' He quickly pushed a chair forward for her. 'Would you like some water? You look rather pale.'

'I think I would – thank you.'

Mr Roberts – that was his name – explained briefly that Miss Maxwell had been feeling poorly, the doctor had advised a change of air, and she had taken herself off on a sea voyage for the winter. He had the house until April.

It seemed incredible that her aunt should have gone away without telling her. And yet she could not help remembering the coolness between them that day when she had come from London; generous as she was, Frances could not bring herself to accept Julia's desertion, as she saw it, of her husband.

As Julia sat, huddled in her shawl on the chair, the thought sank in: this was worst of all. Her mind spun round, and she could not seem to get a purchase anywhere on reality. She felt dizzy and her mouth was dry. Then as the housekeeper returned with the water and she drank it greedily down and asked for more, as she tried to steady her thoughts, she understood that now she was truly on her own. The money in her purse at this minute: this was truly all that she had, all that stood between her, Becky and Agnes, and absolute disaster.

Arthur stooped as he came out through the old Norman porch of the church. The parishioners shuffled past him, nodding or touching their foreheads. It was odd to be back in Stallbridge, but it touched him to see so much goodwill among the villagers.

He looked round the churchyard, thinking. It had been strange not to see any of the Cunningham family in church this morning. He could not work it out. As he waited for Dr Stone to unrobe, however, he noticed Mrs Anderson the housekeeper from the Old Manor House, and instinct made him touch her sleeve.

She wore a long white apron and had a grey woollen shawl wrapped round her shoulders crossed over her breast and tucked into the apron strings. Her steel grey hair was drawn back under a cotton cap. She was not given to smiling much and was known not to suffer fools gladly.

'Morning, Reverend.'

'I was beginning to think there was no one here from the Manor House, Mrs Anderson.'

'There ain't exceptin' only me.'

'What?'

'They've gone.'

'All of them?'

'Every last one. Mrs Cunningham's gone over to Devizes to her daughter's. And Mr Cunningham's gone to London and sacked everybody.'

'Do you mean it?'

'I said it, didn't I?'

'I don't believe it.'

'Believe it or not as you like.'

Mrs Anderson moved off along the narrow path between the gravestones, and said almost as an afterthought, 'Morning, Reverend.'

'Mrs Anderson – sacked everybody you say?' Arthur was behind her. 'So it looks as if he doesn't intend to come back?'

'There's talk he might sell the house.'

350

'Sell it!'

'Mind, I don't say as he will. 'Tis only talk.'

'So you've been left all alone, Mrs Anderson? I bet you never expected to see this day, eh?'

'Didn't I? 'Twas as plain as the nose on your face! Once let him get his hand on the property he'd go through it like a dose of salts. 'Tis said he holds court at Liberty Hall in London.'

Arthur thought for a moment.

'And never a word of Mrs Cunningham – Julia Cunningham, that is – I suppose?'

'Not that I heard tell of. Mark you, I don't blame her, leaving him when she did. She's well rid of him.'

'You're not so well disposed to your master, by the sound of it.'

'Should I be? What good's he ever done me, or any of us? We shan't see him again till he runs out of money. Then he'll come down here: first off he'll drink the cellar dry, then sell all the timber; the next thing is he'll be selling the land – mark my words, 'twill come to it. All Mrs Cunningham's work gone for naught. This family's finished if you want my opinion, Reverend, though I don't suppose you do.'

'It's really his wife I'm thinking of, Mrs Anderson. Her father misses her dearly. I want to track her down for his sake.'

I'm lying, he thought. Lying palpably, blatantly, shamelessly.

'You could try Mrs Loveday. Her daughter Becky went off with Mrs Cunningham. I heard the other day she'd had a letter from her, to let her know she was alright.'

'Did she? Well, maybe I'll stroll down and have a chat with here Mrs Anderson.'

' 'Tis your best hope.'

Chapter Forty-one

With some misgivings, Julia bought a new gown for her dinner invitation. She chose it in the bazaar in Regent Street, and had it altered to fit her. It was difficult to know what to choose; she had no idea what sort of people to expect at this event, and eventually decided that all she could say for certain was that they were friends of Mr Wills and Mr Malone, and thinking of these two as hard as she could, she tried to fathom what kind of women they associated with – or were married to, for that matter. In the end she had chosen a silk dress in silver grey trimmed with russet brown. Some alterations were necessary, a little taking in – she was not surprised to find she had lost weight since leaving Ebury Street.

In the looking glass she thought her face looked sharp and pinched, and she was frowning. She tried to breathe into herself some good cheer. She looked older than her age she decided. Difficult to get much cheer from that.

In the train on the way home from Kent she had counted her money. Apart from the sixteen pounds she had earned, she still had eight pounds left of Peter's money. Once she had absorbed the shock of her aunt's disappearance, a hardness had gradually settled in her. She would survive, and she would look after Agnes and Becky; it would be by her own efforts but she would do it, and it was in this frame of mind that she had spent seventeen shillings on her new gown. As she explained to Becky, it was very important to make contacts – she might meet editors who would buy articles from her. And as soon as she had sold one or two more articles, they would move to somewhere nicer. Becky said little.

Fortunately, Regent's Park was only a short walk from the Tottenham Court Road. At twelve she set off through the park to Mr Wills' house, on the far side – not one of the great Nash terraces, lofty and aristocratic, but a pleasant villa set in a garden on the fringes of St John's Wood.

A servant girl answered the door. Inside, the atmosphere was pleasantly informal. The girl took her bonnet and cloak, and Julia had a moment at the looking glass to arrange her hair – which was always very severe, very simple, and taken up behind her head.

Mr Wills was there, lively, cheery, his spectacles glinting in the morning sun which streamed across the room and lit up an exotic rug which was thrown across the floor in front of the fireplace. There were glass-fronted book cases, and a lot of paintings on the wall. A potted palm stood in the window bay, and another in a far corner. There were a number of wide easy chairs, and five men already present, all strangers to her, of course.

'Mrs Cunningham! So pleased you could be with us!'

The men all stood as she entered, and Wills introduced them. Mr Malone was there – his first name was Edward, and it turned out he was Irish, though she hadn't noticed his accent before. A short plump man with a beard and tiny gold spectacles and a merry lively expression was introduced as Mr Yately – but he said immediately: 'Call me Willie, I beg you, everyone does.' He was their champion serial writer, Mr Wills told her, and Julia realised she knew the name William Yately, and had read one of his books, and here he was before her, this lively little man. Next was Professor Thornton from the University; he was a biologist, but when they talked later it was all of music. In his spare time he wrote music criticism for the magazine. A middle-aged man with a broad beard streaked with grey, and smelling of cigar smoke, was Charles Sullivan who wrote theatre and opera reviews. What a life it must be, she thought, to spend one's entire life attending the theatre, and only be required to jot down a page or so of impressions to make your living!

As she was being introduced to these men, there was a ring at the door and a lady and gentleman were introduced soon after.

The lady was Miss Georgina Morton, and again Julia recognised the name. This lady was very famous indeed. She was an authoress whose books were on sale everywhere, and she was often mentioned and discussed in the newspapers. She was tall and large, with a grand, imperious, condescending manner, and a ferocious intelligence. Intellectually speaking she could have eaten them all for breakfast. The little man with her was shorter than herself and she was excessively fond of him, forever threading her arm through his or touching him in all sorts of little wifely ways. This was Mr Robertson, editor of the *Mercury* – another of the magazines on Julia's list. She was slightly puzzled by this couple; they certainly behaved in every respect as if they were married, but as far as she

353

could make out, they weren't.

Dinner was announced, but there was no ceremony about who went in on whose arm. They were all extremely lively, everyone talking at once and crowding into the dining room. Mr Wills called out: 'Robertson, why don't you sit by Mrs Cunningham – only mind you don't poach her! She's mine, you know!' And no one stood on any kind of ceremony but were delightfully informal.

Julia was staggered too at the level of talk that flew round the table as the dinner was served. At one moment the Professor of Biology was talking of deep water crustacea which appeared to contradict all previously held theories of the classification of species and a paper which had recently been read on the subject by a colleague from South Africa who had been collecting samples from the Malabar coast; the next moment Mr Sullivan was keeping them in fits of laughter with his description of a play he had seen three nights before, in which the acting was so bad it had to be seen to be believed, and the play was utterly unconvincing, and had only been mounted at all out of sheer desperation because there was such a dismal lack of anything else to put on.

'Look at the Parisian stage!' he exclaimed. 'The acting! The wit! The sheer subtlety! You have never seen such superb acting as I saw last month – Lemaître, quite simply the finest actor alive'

Then the talk got round to French literature, and Julia found that everyone at the table seemed to be not only familiar with the latest French novels but had read them in the original language. At last when they had discussed the subject for some time she tentatively mentioned that she had made a complete translation of *Madame Bovary*. This was greeted with considerable interest.

'Have you, by Jove!'

'Where is it? I should very much like to see that,' said the diminutive Mr Robertson.

Julia looked down at her plate.

'I – I am afraid it has been destroyed.'

'What? All of it?'

'Yes.'

'You translated the entire book, and it was lost? My dear Mrs Cunningham, months of work, what a tragedy! Good Lord. How did it happen?'

'By accident,' she said faintly. 'In any case, I am afraid it would never sell, you know.'

The table agreed with her.

'The French you see,' Mr Sullivan interrupted, 'years ahead of us; England won't be ready for that book for a generation yet.'

It was impossible for Julia to express to herself the gratification she felt, that all these people had not only known about *Madame Bovary* but had actually wanted to read her translation of it.

'Hmm,' said Mr Robertson, 'so you do translations? I may be able to put some work your way, if you're interested.'

At this the celebrated Miss Georgina Morton cut in.

'Don't you find it a thankless task? One can never be sure one has found quite the right expression; I never finished a translation but I was left with that sneaking suspicion that I had missed something; some shade of meaning had eluded me, and I never handed over the completed manuscript without a guilty feeling that it might contain some ghastly mistake. I was so glad when I was able to give it up.'

'Was there any work which caused you particular unease?'

'Lehrer's *Geschichtliche Grundfragen des Lebens Jesus.*'

'How interesting. My father wanted me to learn German to translate religious works. And that book was on his list. He has been working on a Commentary on St John's Gospel for many years. But my German never advanced to that level. I am afraid the only use I ever made of it was in ordering coffee and cakes in a cafe!'

After dinner was over and they were once more in the drawing room, other visitors began to arrive, and throughout the afternoon men and women came and went.

What was so amazing, so astonishing, was that no one seemed to think it odd that a woman should be invited to dinner without her husband. No one asked her where her husband was, nor what he did. And whenever she offered an opinion, heads immediately turned and people listened carefully to what she had to say. They liked to hear people's opinion on things, not only hers but anyone's, and would listen attentively and then sometimes agree, or disagree, and sparks of conversation would flare up and drive along for a while, then veer off at a tangent.

It was very lively, and although they often disagreed with one another there was never any rancour; they disagreed, but they respected each other's right to an opposing view, and every one had an equal right to an opinion. No one tried to pontificate, or patronise her; and as far as she could judge no subject was taboo. It was riches to her; food for the soul.

They also talked about professional matters; they all had the same preoccupations as she did – what am I going to write about for next month's issue? – and threw ideas at each other, weighing them up: would it go, or had it been played out? Was the public ready for such and such an idea, or was the market too specialised? During this part of the conversation Julia felt a novice, and listened carefully.

As she was leaving Mr Wills reminded her that he kept open house every Sunday afternoon, and she would welcome at any time. In the meantime he was looking forward to seeing her next piece!

As she was going down the steps, she heard the door shut behind her, and a moment later Charles Sullivan was beside her.

'Are you walking through the park, Mrs Cunningham? Do you mind if I join you?'

'By all means.'

'At last I can light a cigar. It's been killing me! Foolish habit, I know.' He lit one. 'Was this your first time?'

'Yes.'

'How long have you been writing?'

'I have scarcely begun, Mr Sullivan.'

'Didn't you say you had made a translation of *Madame Bovary*?'

'Yes.'

'And it was destroyed? That was bad luck. How did it happen?'

Julia looked down for a moment. Then out of her loneliness, out a need to confide in someone, she said what otherwise she would not have said, 'My husband destroyed it.'

Mr Sullivan said nothing for a moment.

'Didn't approve, eh? Bit too advanced for his taste?'

'If I remember correctly, he described it as a "disgusting, degenerate book".'

'Just about hits the mark, I should say. What made you want to translate it?'

'Partly to give myself something to do. My husband was out a lot; time was hanging on my hands. But also – I thought it unlike any book I had ever read. It was as if the author was a scientist, exploring the rock pools on the sea-shore, observing the creatures scurrying back and forth, and noting down what they did, what they liked and what they didn't like, but also able to see into their hearts, and understand what they sought in life, what they hungered after, and how they were driven along. It is a great book.'

Mr Sullivan smoked his cigar.

'You and your husband differed on your views of the book, it would seem?'

'You could say that,' she said faintly.

'Or was the book merely symbolic of other things?'

'What do you mean?'

He shrugged, then spoke looking away, 'Differences between a man and woman often come out over a relatively small thing.'

'We had our differences.'

'That's why he's not here?'

'I am separated from my husband.'

'Legally?'

Julia thought. 'Not so far.'

'Are you going to apply for a legal separation?'

'I haven't yet thought of it.'

'So you've only recently left him?'

'Yes.'

'You should take legal advice, Mrs Cunningham.'

'I suppose I should. To tell the truth, I have scarcely had time to think of it.'

'Are there any children to the marriage?'

'One – my daughter.'

'Did you bring her with you?'

'Yes.'

'Hmm. Well, if you applied for a judicial separation, you might be able to get some maintenance out of him. On the other hand, he could demand the return of his daughter.'

'I will never hand over my daughter.'

'Hmm.' Charles Sullivan smoked his cigar.

'And I will not be dependent on his charity.'

'He'll come after you.'

'That's what I fear'

'Where does he live?'

'He has houses in London and Wiltshire.'

'A man of means, eh?'

'Oh, yes.'

'Servants, and all that?'

'I presided over a full complement of staff, Mr Sullivan.'

'And you left it all, eh, just walked out? Where are you living now?'

'I have lodgings not far from here.'

'Hmm. Well, I'll give you the name of my solicitor anyway. It might be wise to talk to him. Clarify the legal position for you, eh?'

He took out a morocco card case, drew out a calling card, and wrote an address on the back.

'Lincolns Inn.'

'Thank you.'

They had reached the Euston Road. Julia turned. She didn't want him to see where she lived. She held out her hand.

'Thank you for listening to my woes, Mr Sullivan. Not a very uplifting topic, I am afraid.'

'I'm separated myself.'

'Are you? I'm sorry to hear it.'

'In a manner of speaking – my wife has had to be confined to an asylum.'

'Good heavens! I had no idea. And she is still there?'

'Yes. I go down to see her of course, though she doesn't recognise me.'

'She doesn't recognise you – yet you continue to see her?'

'Yes.'

Julia reached out her hand.

'Mr Sullivan, I do most strongly sympathise with you. You must find it a fearful strain?'

He looked away, thinking. 'I did. I'm used to it now. Part of one's life. And it gets me out of London from time to time.'

'Well, perhaps we shall meet again next Sunday?'

'Mrs Cunningham, it occurred to me, I have a pair of tickets for the opera on Tuesday – *Rigoletto*. Is that your cup of tea?'

'Oh, let me see.' But even as he spoke, the image of Becky was in her mind. 'That is most kind. Indeed it is. But I fear I must decline. I cannot be out in the evenings. Besides Mr Wills is such a tyrant – I have nothing prepared for him yet. It would be impossible to enjoy the music, I should be thinking of that deadline all the time!'

She tried to make a joke of it, and on this pretext took her leave of him.

As she walked home, she thought that of course it would be lovely to go the theatre or the opera. But it would also be unpardonably disloyal to Becky who was enduring so much for her sake. If only she could have sent Becky along in her place.

Chapter Forty-two

Julia had arranged to meet Lizzie in the Great Western Hotel at Paddington. It was anonymous, and easy for Lizzie, who could then take her train home. Julia had arranged the meeting for the afternoon. This was partly because she was now in the habit of trying to write every morning, and partly so that Lizzie would not come charging at her full tilt, but by the afternoon would have slowed down a bit.

The Great Western Hotel was (and is) a large classical building standing in front of the station at Paddington. Julia sat waiting for Lizzie in the ladies' waiting room. Julia had decided it was better not to have tea together – it would be sending out all the wrong sort of signals to Lizzie; that there was room for compromise, for instance, when there wasn't. It would make matters worse if one or the other were to storm out in the middle of tea, as if either had made a diplomatic opening, or offer, and then been rebuffed. Keep it simple. This way Julia showed she meant business.

She sat in the waiting room. Two other women sat in silence. A low dismal fire burnt in the grate. Outside it was a cold raw October day. Julia was swathed in a cloak and bonnet. She felt pinched, tight, closed up, and tired.

Lizzie came in. As Julia saw that she was in mourning she started up from the bench. Lizzie came quickly to her, and they threw their arms round each other. Lizzie noticed Julia's changed appearance. They looked at each other in silence.

'Lizzie darling –'

'Father died. I wanted to tell you myself.'

'I'm sorry.'

'It's all right. He died in his sleep. No one got very upset. I mean to say, no hysterics or anything. But of course, it means –'

'Peter has inherited.'

359

'Yes.'

There was a silence.

Lizzie tentatively reached out a hand for Julia's.

'I wish it didn't have to be like this.'

'Like what?' Julia was expressionless.

'Well, here,' Lizzie looked vaguely round the cheerless waiting room.

'Perhaps it is better for the moment, Lizzie.'

'Well, let's sit down anyway.'

They sat side by side on the wooden seat, Julia looking down, and both of them finding it difficult to look in to the other's eyes, or to know how to begin.

'I went to Ebury Street this morning, Julia,' Lizzie said seriously. 'I don't have to tell you what it's like. Of course the staff are there, but without you it's –' She paused. 'Peter's away. Gone off to Paris with Morley, they said. They have no idea when he'll be back. I had a look round. Without you it seemed empty.' She looked down. 'I can't tell you what a shock it was when Dolly and I arrived expecting to have dinner with you and a good chin-wag – and there was Peter in this fug of cigar smoke, dead drunk at half-past eleven in the morning, and you nowhere to be seen.'

'I'm sorry,' Julia said softly. 'I would do anything I could not to hurt you Lizzie.'

'I know!' She was unexpectedly vehement. 'And so would I for you, Julia! You must come back! I'm sorry if I'm not very subtle, and I'm not as clever as you but it's the truth! You've got to come back. He'll kill himself, I know he will.'

'He was killing himself very well before I left. There is nothing I can do to control him. Your belief in my powers is very flattering, Lizzie, but I have seen on too many occasions that my influence over him is negligible. Oh, I may have frightened him once, but he got over it quick enough, and was soon in the saddle again. He wants me back, I expect – for five minutes. But as soon as I disagree with him in any particular, however slight, he'll be off again. He'll fly at me, or sulk, or get drunk, or go off for a month with one of his cronies.

'How can I make you understand that we have no life together? A man and his wife, Lizzie, are supposed to share things. They're supposed to have interests in common, to like doing things together, to take an interest in what the other does, to give and take, and make allowances for one another. But Peter is impervious. His egotism is absolute. He allows no interests, no pleasures, no tastes, but his own. As soon as I cross him in anything, however minute, he

360

is off. We do not actually have anything in common, at all. Can you understand that?'

Lizzie was silent.

'And, Lizzie, even if I were to make the sacrifice you ask of me, to submerge my own self in his service – which, by the way, is impossible – what of Agnes? Can I allow her to be brought up in that house, to be the witness of his debauchery, his folly, his vices?'

'Julia,' Lizzie began tentatively, 'why did you marry him?'

'Why?' She gave a little cynical laugh. 'Because I was in love with him. You went into your marriage with your eyes open, Lizzie, but I rushed into mine blinded by Peter's looks, his wit, his easy manner. You think of me as being so rational, so intelligent, so controlled. I was besotted with him. If I were to tell you the dreams I had of him, shameless, wild dreams, dreams I cannot recall without a blush – Lizzie, I wanted him so badly, I would have died for him.'

'Well, I don't know, Julia, whatever I say you have an argument, and you're so clever, you always muddle me up. But all I know is that married couples are supposed to stay together, for better or worse, otherwise what's the point of getting married at all? You have made a mockery of your vows, Julia – as if you didn't care at all.'

'You think I don't care?'

'You should stick to your post, whatever the circumstances, that's what it's for. Otherwise how will society survive? Julia, do you realise, if we can't come to an agreement, we may never meet again? Have you thought of that? How can I ask you to visit me? How can I introduce you to anyone? This is my brother's wife – only they don't live together? Think of it.'

Julia was silent.

'And there is something else.'

'What?'

'Are you sure you are entirely innocent?'

'Lizzie, it isn't a question of innocence or guilt; we are completely unsuited, that is all. I am not saying that Peter should not lead the life he does – if that is what he wants, though I cannot respect him for it. I am only saying that I cannot live with him, or allow Agnes to be brought up in his house.'

'I saw a letter,' Lizzie began tentatively, 'which had been sent to you. Peter had opened it – I believe his motives were honourable – he didn't recognise the handwriting, and thought it might be something urgent – someone ill or something –'

'What letter?'

'From Mr Grahame.'

Lizzie saw a blush rise on Julia's cheek.

361

'Of course, I had no idea what might be in it, when Peter showed it to me.'

'And you read it?'

'I didn't know what was going to be in it till I read it – but that's what I mean, you are not entirely innocent in the matter!'

Julia had drawn herself up and was looking into Lizzie's face with restrained dignity.

'I have no idea what there might have been in that letter, Lizzie, but you have my word of honour that Mr Grahame has always behaved towards me with absolute propriety.'

'And have you behaved with propriety towards him – if he's told you he's in love with you?' Lizzie said sharply.

'What do you think?'

'Julia, I don't know! I mean, I never thought you would leave Peter – but you did! I never imagined Mr Grahame might be in love with you and write you letters – but he does! I'm completely muddled. Anyway, have you thought what Peter might do with the letter? Suppose he decided to divorce you and use that letter in court to suggest you had been unfaithful!'

'What did Mr Grahame say?' Julia said quietly.

'Oh, I don't remember exactly. Nothing very specific – only it was downright obvious that he was heart and soul in love with you.'

Julia looked down. Yes, Arthur Grahame was in love with her. She had not dared to think of him. If once she allowed herself to remember their ride together in the brougham, his words to her, his kisses . . .

And paradoxically, since she had left her husband, she was further from him than ever. The one thing in the world which was absolutely barred to her now was to stand on his doorstep with her daughter in her arms.

At last she said, 'You have my word of honour that Mr Grahame has nothing to do with my decision. You know your brother, Lizzie and you know me. There was no dealing between us, that is all. I would give anything not to hurt you, or your mother, but I cannot change my mind.'

Lizzie could not look at her. She began pulling on her gloves, and was about to start up.

'Well, it's a bad business, that's all.'

They both rose and walked out of the waiting room. The great railway station was alive with the noise of steam whooshing up into the gothic vaulting. Passengers hurried through the arches and up and down the platforms. Porters bustled past with their barrows loaded with boxes and parcels. A whistle blew.

Julia and Lizzie embraced in silence, then Lizzie turned away.

'Lizzie!' Julia called. Lizzie turned. 'God bless you, my dear.'

The two women stood facing each other for a long moment. Julia's eyes filled with tears, and then as if both thought of it together they flew into each other's arms, sobbing, hugged tightly, then Lizzie turned without a word and hurried away.

Julia took the omnibus back to the Tottenham Court Road. The dank grey autumn afternoon was closing in, darkness was hovering in the air, and as she sat in the omnibus, huddling in her cloak, she remembered all the times she had been with Lizzie, all the things they had done together, their girlhood, Lizzie's wedding, holding herself in, not allowing herself to feel any more, and thinking that a great door was closing, and there was nothing she could do to stop it.

She was very sober when she arrived at her lodgings, but Becky was there with Agnes, toasting bread in front of the fire.

'Oh, miss, I just made a cup of tea!' And Julia was so glad to be there. She picked up Agnes and swung her in the air, and thought, She is my home. Wherever Agnes is, there I am at home.

In the train Lizzie was subdued. She still couldn't really understand what had happened. Had they parted for ever? Would she see Julia again? Would they be able to write? What was one to do? Were she and her mother going to have to cope with Peter on their own?

And Mr Grahame. Was Julia in love with him? Could it be possible? He certainly wasn't the sort of man to appeal to Lizzie herself; for one thing, he wasn't really a gentleman, was he? His father was a labourer. Perhaps somewhere Mr Grahame had a family, living in some little cottage. How could any woman marry such a man? She could never introduce him to her relations.

In a way though, dimly, Lizzy could see what a woman might find to love in a man like that. There was no doubt that Mr Grahame was a formidable man, a passionate man; to be loved by such a man ... well, at least a woman would know all about it. She wouldn't be able to rule him the way Lizzie ruled Dolly; but on the other hand, with a man like that in her bed – Lizzie blushed as the thought popped into her mind – perhaps she wouldn't be so bothered about who ruled whom ...

When she got home her mother was waiting, and Lizzie sat down and told her everything that had happened. Both women were subdued. Everything seemed as unresolved as ever. Peter had gone off, had not even waited for probate to be completed on the will; the Old Manor House was shut up; Julia adamant. It seemed hopeless.

For three days Alicia wrestled within herself as to whether to go. Every morning she woke up, here in Lizzie's house, heard the movement of servants going about their morning business, smelt the malt on the morning air – Lizzie had been right about that, incidentally. Alicia was still waiting and hoping that she would cease to notice it.

Every morning as the housemaid brought her a cup of tea and she pulled herself up in bed, sipped her tea, and stared out of the window, she ran the thoughts through her mind.

On the third day she made up her mind. Julia must be brought back, let the cost be what it might. She called for hot water, and told the girl to stay and help her dress. Today she was going to dress to the very height of her powers; widow or not, today she was going to summon every allurement of which she was capable.

In any case she had made sure that mourning should become *her*. Some women no sooner went into mourning but they looked twenty years older. No sooner in black but they seemed to disappear socially. Men no longer noticed them in the street, as if they had ceased to exist.

Not in her case. She had prepared for her mourning long in advance – had her mourning clothes made very carefully to ensure that they became her to to the full. Alicia Cunningham should be as elegant, as stylish, as desirable in her widow's weeds as she had ever been in her brightest silks.

Once dressed, she dismissed the girl, and sat at the looking glass. She opened the sandalwood box, and took out her magic arts – those aids purchased in Bond Street, about which she was so discreet. A *little* shadow over the eyes; a *little* black liner along her eyebrows; a *blush* of rouge to the cheeks; a dusting of rice powder and a touch of carmine to the lips. As delicately understated as she could make it.

She stared into the looking-glass as the thought came to her – there had been a time when such aids were not necessary – then took a deep breath.

Today. It must be.

At breakfast Lizzie noticed her preparations immediately, though she said nothing; Alicia saw that she had seen and afterwards, when Dolly had gone to the brewery, and Jeremy had been removed to the nursery, she said quietly, 'Don't be too surprised, darling. There is

364

one other possibility. We must try every avenue to get Julia back, must we not?'

Lizzie said nothing. Alicia's gleaming black carriage was called round, and resplendent in black, a long veil over her bonnet, she ascended like a queen.

It was an hour's journey to Stallbridge. She was thoughtful, running the story through her mind, thinking of him, thinking of what he might say, how he might respond. She could safely say she knew him better than he knew her – or himself, for that matter.

The carriage rolled up through the village, past the long low rows of labourers' cottages, past Trefusis' farm, and already Stallbridge seemed like somewhere she was visiting for the first time; odd how in a few days she had lost the habits of a place in which she had passed a quarter of a century.

As the carriage turned into the rectory drive, the sound of the gravel beneath the carriage wheels changed, and she was alert.

The old man lowered himself to the ground, and rang the bell. As Annie opened the door, he growled, 'Mrs Cunningham to see Dr Stone.'

He opened the carriage door, lowered the step, and Alicia descended with gracious dignity.

Annie was mystified. It was a long time since they had seen her at the rectory.

'Is he expecting you, ma'am?'

'No.'

Annie opened the drawing-room door.

'I'll fetch him straightaway, ma'am.'

Alicia still had her veil down. She looked round the room. It had not changed. Still the old paintings on the walls, the marble fireplace unlit, the leather armchairs, the same cheerless, friendless air it had always had.

There was a long wait. She smiled to herself. Dr Stone had been taken by surprise; he needed a little time to gather his wits. Poor man, it was rather hard on him, to be disturbed in the midst of his labours . . .

The door opened, and Stone stood there, his hand still on the handle. They looked at each other for a long moment, then Alicia very slowly lifted the hem of her veil, lifted, lifted, and slowly revealed the little smile playing on her red lips. She looked into his face.

'I have come to talk to you, William.'

Stone could no more speak, than a rabbit could escape the snake's gaze.

'Come in. And close the door.'

He did as he was bidden.

'Sit down. Come. Here.'

They sat in chairs opposite one another. Alicia's back was upright; her hands calmly folded in her lap, the little smile on her lips.

'To what –' Stone began.

'I have come to forgive you, William.'

He said nothing, straining to catch her intention.

'I have often felt that I have been a *little* unfair to you,' she went on.

'What do you mean?' he said hoarsely, staring into her face.

'It is so long ago, and yet – even after all these years, you know, you have a right to justice. I mean to say, you have a right to know the truth.'

She paused.

'William, you know you were very much in love with me once, were you not? And there was one afternoon, which we both remember very well –'

'Oh God!' Stone groaned, and rested his head on his hand, looking down.

'William.' She reached over and rested her hand on his. 'I said I have come to forgive you. Perhaps you will understand better what I mean if I say I have also come to make a confession to you.'

'Confession?'

'Let us remember, I was eighteen. Not so young as you might think, and not as young as you thought me then, I assure you. I was already married, and I had made a very great decision in my marriage, William – to marry a man old enough to be my father, not out of love but out of ambition. I was old for my years, William, I knew what I was about. You need feel no guilt on that account. And if I could not love my husband that is not to say I could not love anyone, is it? You must not think that although you loved me, I was incapable of returning your love.'

She was saying all this very quietly, aware of the impact her words were having on him, and choosing them with care.

'I saw your feelings, I knew everything in your mind.' She paused. 'Do you think I could not reciprocate at all?'

'But you never –'

'William, I was a married woman. And being so much younger than my husband, I was especially open to suspicion; especially the target of innuendo, and prying eyes.'

'What are you saying?' he said again in a low voice.

'I told you, I forgive you.'

She smiled her sly smile.

'But more than that, I have to make my confession. After all, you are a man of God – and who better to confess to?'

'Oh Alicia –'

'You see, William, on that afternoon – which, I may say, my dear, I remember in *every detail*, it would be quite wrong to think that you were *entirely* to blame.'

He was staring into her face again.

'I don't understand.'

'It was a warm afternoon – June as I remember. I had been taking a walk when who should I meet at the gate, but the Reverend Dr Stone, a strong, handsome, and I may say virile, young man. A man very attractive to a girl not twenty. And that young Dr Stone was attracted shall we say, in spite of himself? Hmm?'

'Don't go on,' he groaned.

'My dear, I want you to understand. This is my confession, you must hear me.'

He looked away.

'So what I am saying, William, is – that if that strong young man, had taken the young girl into the field, in the shaded corner – and it was such a glorious afternoon, I remember it so clearly, and the hills a distant blue in the summer haze – and if that young man should have been carried away by his feelings – William, should have been overmastered – in spite of himself – done what he should not have done, in the force, the urgency of his strength –'

She paused.

'Well?' He looked at her, his face haggard. She reached out again for his hand.

'My dear, can't you understand? Don't you see? I could have got up at any moment. I could have walked away from you whenever I liked. Why do you suppose I stayed? Lying there, among the buttercups, the long lush summer grass.'

'But I forced you! Ravished you! I shall never forgive myself!'

'No, my dear,' she said very softly. 'You did nothing of the sort. It was I who followed *you*, I who sought you out, who brought you to that field. It was *I* who gave myself to you.'

There was a long silence.

'Alicia.'

She smiled into his face. 'There. It was a very long time ago. But you had the right to know the truth.'

'It's impossible – I remember it so well –'

'Impossible, but true. Oh William, you are so learned, so mightily intellectual – and yet what do you know? You who could not see what was so obvious!'

'Alicia, it was I –'

'It was both of us, William. Both. You wanted me, I could see that the first time we met. But of course you were a man of God, an upright man, strict, I could see that too. But you see, William, I wanted you too, and it was up to me to place us both in a situation where your scruples and principles would give way before your real feelings. I succeeded.'

'That is not true!'

'It is my dear. True as we sit here.'

'Oh –'

'I was a horrid little flirt, if you like to put it that way. I didn't want to take you away from your wife, of course, but I did just want you – once. I could see how upset you were and I must confess to you, William, I didn't care. I wanted you; I had you; then I sent you back to your wife. The last thing I wanted was a scandal.'

'Oh God, and all these years –'

'Yes. It was rather naughty of me, I see that. That is why I have come today. Incidentally, one other thing which might have been preying on your mind, William. Peter is not your child.'

'You are sure?'

'Oh, yes. You need have no fear.'

'Oh, Alicia!' The tears fell freely down Stone's face. 'I can't tell you, what this means to me. After so many years, it is as if a great cloud has been dispersed. You have freed me –'

'I owed it to you, William. Perhaps I should have said all this before but it is not easy. William, can we be friends again?'

'Friends? Oh, my dearest, dearest woman –'

'You see, William, there is, as you know, a terrible weight hanging over us at the moment.'

'Julia?'

'William, we must get her back! We must! *You* must!'

'I?'

'You must be reconciled! And you must make her come back to Peter!'

'How can I do that?'

'You must do everything in your power! Surely you more than anyone will be able to find her?'

'Alicia, I would do anything to bring her back. If only I knew –'

'Calm yourself, my dear. We will work together. We will each of us think of anything, any way, any channel –'

368

'Alicia, I cannot tell you what this means to me.' He stood up. 'You have removed such a weight from my mind.'

He took her hands and lifted her from the chair.

'Such a weight –.' He looked up, and smiled. 'Such a weight! But why did you not tell me before?'

Alicia, still holding his hands, looked down.

'It was not easy,' she murmured.

'Oh, I understand, I understand! Of course, poor dear creature. What a burden for you to carry.'

As he watched the carriage turn out of the gate into the lane, and heard the clatter of the horses' hooves die away as the carriage rolled down through the village, William Stone walked thoughtfully after it, across the lane, through the gate and into the church yard. On that autumn morning, still, silent, a faint mist in the air, the beech trees hanging above him still glorious in their russet and gold, he picked his way over the uneven humps and hummocks, between the grave stones at their strange uneven angles, through the long thick grass glistening with the dew, not looking, only thinking of his talk with Alicia Cunningham, and so coming to the grave of Agnes Stone, his wife, and throwing himself onto his knees, he clasped his hands in prayer.

His heart was opened. For so many years he had been haunted by the memory of that afternoon; for so many years, the memory of Alicia there in the grass yielding herself to him, had burned in his memory. That he, a man of God should have so transgressed! The memory of that hot afternoon, of the blind need in him, the overmastering desire, and of her, Alicia – was it possible that in some way that he but imperfectly understood that he had been relieved of his burden of guilt, that he was after all innocent?

And that Peter Cunningham was not his son – that that vicious young man was not after all the fruit of his sin? He closed his eyes, clasping his hands tightly.

Oh Agnes, how had he used her! So young, so pure, so unfit to bear the weight of his gross worldliness – Agnes, a child, untainted by the world and its impurity, of which he carried such a heavy burden. She had suffered most of all.

Was she looking down on him now? Could she see him? Agnes – would she forgive him the years of neglect? The years when he had spurned her? Could she see the contrition in his heart?

Was there room yet in her heart for forgiveness?

In her carriage Alicia was rather depressed. She had left William

Stone elated, twenty years younger. Yet as she looked down at her gloved hands, turning the one over in the other, and examining the stitching – what a schemer she was, what a manipulator. Even when she had confessed the truth to him so fully, told him to his face that she had arranged it all, even then he could not grasp the fact that as she spoke to him, watching the shifting emotions in his face, she was in control of him still, shaping every thought in his mind.

It didn't matter; she had been doing it all her life, no doubt would continue to do so. The important thing was he might be able help get Julia back. Without Julia to help her, she feared Peter would get completely out of control.

Chapter Forty-three

'You have placed yourself in a very weak position, I fear.'

The solicitor sat back in his chair, and placed his finger tips together. Julia had a pad of paper on her knees and a pencil. She wanted to make sure she understood everything he said; yet even as she concentrated, she was aware that the lawyer was taking a certain relish in what he was saying.

His face was in shadow. Behind him, outside the grimy windows in the dull light of the November morning, the bare branches of the elms reached up.

'You have deserted your husband. You will have to show first of all good cause. Can you bring witnesses to your husband's behaviour?'

Julia thought of the servants. Their wages were paid by Peter – would they go into a witness box and give evidence against him?

'If your husband had abandoned you then you would have some grounds – not sufficient, but something. But in abandoning him, you forfeit sympathy at once.'

She was dismayed.

'It will be easy for counsel to portray you as irresponsible and feckless. You are on very shaky ground, Mrs Cunningham. First of all, for you to divorce your husband it will be necessary to show not only that he has been unfaithful to you but that he has also used cruelty that endangers life or limb. On the other hand, if he wished to divorce you it is only necessary to demonstrate that you have committed adultery.'

Adultery. What an ugly word. Yet, with a letter from Arthur Grahame in his possession, what might not Peter do to hurt her?

'I need hardly add that an action for divorce would be very expensive, and that you could not expect to gain a penny from it. Nevertheless, so long as you continue to live apart, though still

371

married, he has sole legal right to the custody of your child, and also a right in law to any money you may possess now or in the future.'

'What?'

'Did I not make myself clear?'

'Any money?'

'Any money.'

'I mean, that is – you mean – if for example I were able to earn money by my own efforts at some future time, he would have a right to that?'

'Mrs Cunningham, you do not have any right to any money on your own account. All monies owned by either you or your husband are his in law.'

'That is outrageous! Are you telling me that if I am able to earn some money by my own efforts, he is within his rights to demand it from me?'

'Yes. You may call it outrageous, Mrs Cunningham, but the collective wisdom of many centuries has decreed otherwise. In law the husband and the wife are one flesh – they are also one bank account.'

'Thank you.' Julia stood up, and stuffed her pad of paper into her reticule. 'You have been most informative. Perhaps you would be so good as to tell me what I owe you? My present address is only temporary – I do not know how much longer I may be there, and it would be simpler if I were to pay you now.'

The lawyer's eyebrows rose. His dignity had been touched.

'My clerk deals with all matter of costs.'

Julia went out, into a shabby dusty outer office, where an out-at-elbows elderly clerk with fraying cuffs was writing in a ledger. He charged her three guineas for her interview.

Julia walked back through Lincolns Inn Fields, and up towards the British Museum seething with anger. It was outrageous! Monstrous! The idea that Peter could come and take her child at any time. That he could demand all her money from her – and wouldn't he just love to do that! She stopped in the street as the thought cleared in her mind: she did not have any rights at all! She was nothing! Before her marriage, she had been her father's daughter, and was known as such, lived in his house, ate his bread, obeyed his wishes. After her marriage, she was her husband's wife, lived in *his* house, ate his bread, obeyed his wishes. But once leave her husband – what was she she? Nothing. Quite simple. No money, no child, no right to anything. Nothing.

As she went in to the reading room, sat at her place, and unpacked her things, she thought, I cannot leave it here. The law of the land

372

does not want me to exist – not as myself. As my father's daughter, as my husband's wife, as the mother of my husband's daughter – but not as myself. There was behind all her thoughts a terrible fear that Peter would take Agnes, and it was this terrible fear that was her emotional driving force.

What could she do about it? Well, one thing she could do was to write about it. In fact, it was the only thing she could do. Would any magazine take an article on her woes? Without thinking, she opened her ink bottle, dipped her pen and wrote down the words: A Lady's Cheque Book There was no point in getting irate. She would merely be dismissed as a ranting female; and there was nothing men hated worse, she well knew. She would have to employ wit and irony.

She fought to subdue her indignation, forced herself to calm down, to be witty, to be ironical. Oh, how 'amusing' her article would be – a lady's attempt to open a bank account in her own name. She would take those two pompous men in Handley's Bank, and she would skewer them on the steel nib of her pen. How else could she get at them? She would employ a delicate, ladylike, waspish irony, she would make them squirm! And all the time, a boiling murderous rage seethed within her, that no-where could she be received or treated as a human being in her own right.

'There's nothing I can do about it, Mrs Archer,' Arthur said. 'Except write a letter to Mr Cunningham. That's all I can do.'

'If you would, I'd be so obliged, Reverend.'

Autumn gales had lifted tiles from the cottage roof. Arthur was standing in the garden with the old lady looking up at the damage.

'It could take a long time though. He's away from home. Couldn't you get someone to fix it up for the time being?'

'Where am I going to get the money? Nobody's going to do it for nothing, are they? Anyway, he's the landlord. It's his responsibility.'

'I tell you what, Mrs Archer, I'll write to his mother in Devizes. That'll be better than nothing. If she was still here it would have been done soon enough.'

'Hmm.' The old lady grunted. 'She never let the grass grow under her feet.'

Arthur took his leave of the old lady and made his way back up through the village, past the gate to the Old Manor House, and on up the rectory. It was his last morning in Stallbridge, and he had been taking a stroll through the village before going to the station.

He had spoken to Mrs Loveday. She had shown him a letter from Becky; dictated by the girl, actually written by Julia. Arthur's eyes

373

soaked up the familiar handwriting. It said simply that she was well and living in lodgings with Mrs Cunningham on account of differences she had with her husband. 'Differences': what a world that one word conjured up for him. There was no address.

He rang at the rectory bell. As he waited he remembered the first time he had ever stood there, and the March evening when he had first met Julia. How still she had seemed, so proper, so reserved. He remembered her so clearly, upright, in her blue-grey dress, with its little white collar, her hands by her sides, her clear intelligent gaze, her dark hair neatly taken up. He remembered every detail. How little did he know of her then, how much was hidden, and how much had he discovered since.

Annie opened the door, and he was just crossing the hall when Dr Stone's study door opened.

'Grahame? A word with you, if you please.'

Arthur followed him in to the study. Stone waited until he came in, then closed the door behind him. He stood, uncharacteristically hesitant, his hand playing about his mouth, looking up at Arthur from beneath his strong eyebrows, then his eye flicking away towards the window.

'Grahame, I have thought on what you said; our last conversation together.'

He walked a few steps towards the window and stood looking out. The large desk stood in the centre of the room, covered as always with papers and opened books.

'Since our talk I have thought much about Julia. I see now that you were right, and I was wrong.'

He rubbed his hands together.

'Yes. I was wrong. Poor girl. Of course she was right to leave that man. This house should have been a refuge to her, Grahame!'

He swung suddenly towards Arthur.

'I have been remiss in my duty! My daughter sought a refuge – and I denied it her. We must find her!'

'I will do everything in my power, Dr Stone.'

'Yes. But time is pressing. We do not know what privations she may be undergoing. And her child –'

'I believe she is in good health at present, sir. I have spoken with Mrs Loveday, the mother of Mrs Cunningham's companion – '

Stone looked at him.

'Perhaps you remember, sir – Becky, who used to be with us?'

'Ah, yes.'

'Becky has written to say that she and your daughter are well. Unfortunately, she gave no address.'

Stone swung about at random, the picture of indecision and uncertainty.

'She must be found!'

'She will be, Dr Stone. I swear it. You can trust me. We know she is in London. It is a vast city of course, and it will be a long task.'

'I will cover any costs.'

'You need not trouble about the expense Dr Stone.'

'Are you sure?'

'I have sufficient. I shall return to London tonight.'

Dr Stone came round from behind the desk and took his hand.

'Only find her. I will be your eternal debtor.'

Arthur had never seen such an expression in the old man's face, such a look of desperation.

It was raining when Julia left the reading room, and made her way back through the wet shiny streets to their lodgings. Her cloak was thin; it was not a winter weight. As the days closed in, and the weather grew colder and wetter, Julia realised what a fool she had been not to bring more clothes from Ebury Street, and how irresponsible to Becky and Agnes.

Her thin cloak rapidly became soaked through, and she could feel the cold clammy hand of the wet night on her shoulders. She hurried through the narrow streets and came to their lodging. She had written her article on A Lady's Cheque Book; tomorrow she would write another, stronger, bolder: the inconsistency in the law of divorce. It was not sufficient that a man should be unfaithful to his wife – no, that was not enough: he must beat her as well! He must 'endanger life and limb'! Irony could only go so far; a light waspish wit could achieve only so much. When it came to wife beating her restraint gave way. Tomorrow she would write such a piece!

As she came into the room, she sensed something was wrong. The fire was low and dull, and Becky was sitting on one of the battered old chairs, with Agnes on her knee, in the firelight. Agnes was fretful; obviously Becky had not fed her yet.

As Julia greeted her, Becky turned only slowly, and grunted.

Julia hurried to her, and took Agnes from her, held her close to her, and smoothed the silky fine hair of her head, which had not been brushed.

'Becky dear, is anything the matter?'

Becky gave a sigh.

'Oh, I'm sorry, miss, I just couldn't get the fire to draw, it would keep blowing back down, and then, I don't know, it's been raining all day . . .'

Her words hung unfinished. Agnes squirmed on Julia's arm. 'Have you given Agnes her tea?'

'No miss.'

'Becky, why not? It's past seven o'clock. She should have been washed and got ready for bed by this time.'

Becky flung round at her.

'I'm sorry, miss, if I don't give satisfaction! It's been a horrible day, and the fire won't draw, and I don't know why we're here – and you said we'd move – and we still haven't. I get so low, miss, stuck in this horrible room, I can't bear it!'

Becky burst into tears. Julia went quickly to her, still holding Agnes, and put her arm round her shoulders, but Becky shook her off, and went and sat on one of the chairs, hiding her face in her hands.

'I hate it here! We should never have come! And you said we would move! And we haven't! I can't stand it!'

Julia stood in the middle of the room, her hair still wet, and feeling the clammy dress across her shoulders. Hearing Becky's crying, the child began to cry too.

It was a risk. Curious how she had become bolder – desperate, really. She stood at the door and gave the bell a good sharp pull. The bell jangled down in the basement; she remembered it well. At least it wasn't raining this morning. The previous evening she had had taken off her dress and hung it over the clothes' horse to dry, and cooked them all some food, and Becky had slowly cheered up, and Julia had sat with her arm round her shoulder and slowly stroked her hair, stroked her back, trying to soothe her. Eventually Becky had quieted and Julia had promised her that she should have all her things from Ebury Street.

So she was here now. Peter was in Paris, it was said. Even if he had unexpectedly returned, it made no matter, Julia would stand no nonsense from him or any one. She was only here to claim what was her own.

The door opened. It was Franks. He was surprised.

'Mrs Cunningham!'

'Good morning, Franks, is the master at home?'

She strode in as she had done so many times.

'No, Mrs Cunningham, I believe he is in Paris.'

'So I have heard. How are you?'

'I? Very well, thank you, ma'am.'

'And Mary, and Mrs Standish?'

'Very well, thank you.'

'Good. You have no idea when my husband is returning I take it.'

'None, madam.'

'Hmm. Well, I won't disturb you. I have only called to collect a few things – some clothes and things of my daughter's and Becky's.'

Julia started for the stairs. Franks, though, was in front of her.

'I beg your pardon, madam, but that won't be possible.'

'What do you mean?'

'I very much regret this, madam, but Mr Cunningham left very specific instructions on this point.'

'What instructions?'

Franks was embarrassed.

'Believe me, Mrs Cunningham – for myself –'

'What instructions?'

'He said nothing was to be touched and if you called you were to be denied admittance.'

'Nothing was to be touched?'

'He was very strict, madam. I fear it would be more than my place is worth if I were to let you take anything away.'

'They are my clothes, Franks. What possible use could they be to my husband?'

'I beg your pardon, madam,' Franks was deeply unhappy, 'I dare not let you take anything.'

Julia looked down for a moment in thought.

'Franks,' she began, in a different, quieter mode, 'you have from time to time no doubt occasion to go out of the house?'

'Yes, madam.' Franks did not understand where this was leading.

'Perhaps a stroll in the park during the afternoon, when things are quiet?'

'Yes, madam.'

'Or to a shop occasionally for some little item of a personal nature? Or during the evening perhaps, to the Coach and Horses, for a pint of beer with your colleagues?'

'Yes, madam.'

'You cannot always be in the house? It would not be good for your health. You have a right to get out from time to time – your master understands that?'

'Certainly, madam.'

'And if I or Becky had chanced to call while you were out, you could not be held responsible for that, could you? You do not have psychic powers, Franks. You cannot know what is going in in the house while you are absent.'

She had opened her reticule, extracted her purse, and taken out a gold sovereign.

377

Looking directly into his eyes, she took his hand and folded it round the sovereign. She smiled.

'Franks, I wonder, would you be so very kind as to call me a cab?'

He held her gaze for a moment. Then a fleeting smile passed over his lips.

'Yes, madam, by all means.'

He went out of the door. She ran quickly down into the kitchen. Mrs Standish and Mary were astonished to see her.

'I hope I find you both well? Mary, would you be so kind as to come with me – I shall need your assistance for a few minutes.'

The two women went up into her old bedroom, and Julia threw open her wardrobe. All her clothes were there, as they had been, all the clothes she had assembled during her twenty-seven months with Peter. She ran her hand along the things, feeling the different fabrics. Then, more briskly, she began pulling things from the rail and throwing them on the bed.

'Mary, would you take those down into the hall?'

Later Mary went up into the attic and brought down Becky's things.

Meanwhile Julia had gone into Agnes' room, and taken some few toys and other trinkets she thought she could use.

In the hall Franks was waiting for her, and she could see outside the door a cab waiting.

'Listen to me, Mrs Standish, and you Mary. Franks is entirely innocent in this. He never told you I was not to be admitted, as I'm sure you understand, and he was out of the house when I called. And in your ignorance, not knowing any better, you allowed me to take away some of my own clothes.'

'Yes, Mrs Cunningham,' they said quietly.

'You are both very good, and I should you like to you to accept just a little –'

She opened her purse again, took out and gave them half a crown each.

378

Chapter Forty-four

'All your dresses, miss! And your coats and mantles!'

They were scattered all over the beds, the table, the chairs.

'And you brought my things too! My winter coat that I needed, and my other dress. How did you ever do it?'

'How do you think?'

Becky stared into her face. Julia smiled.

'What a relief to be able to change into something warmer.'

She was already reaching behind her neck to undo the hooks and eyes of her dress. Becky reached up and was doing it for her. Her grey dress fell to the ground, and, shivering in her shift and petticoats for a moment, Julia rifled through some of the warmer woollen clothes scattered on her bed. She pulled out a thick woollen dress in dark brown. Becky helped her into it.

'We would all have frozen to death, I believe, if you hadn't gone, miss! What a risk – to think if you had met Mr Cunningham!'

Julia was looking into the little piece of looking glass propped on the mantelpiece, and arranging her hair. 'I cannot stay. Becky dear, be an angel and hang these things up.'

'Hang them up where?'

Julia looked round.

'I suppose we could ask Mrs Troughton if we could drive some nails into the walls.'

Julia pulled out a coat and was putting it on.

'Where are you going, miss?'

'The same as every day.' She smiled. 'I shall go to the British Museum this morning. And if I can get that article finished today, I shall go round to see Mr Wills.'

'What article, miss?'

'On divorce.'

'Divorce! Are you going to get divorced, miss?'

'I didn't say that, Becky. I want to write an article on it for *All The Year Round.*'

'What for?'

'Excuse me, Becky, I am in a terrible rush. I will explain to you this evening.'

She turned to Agnes sitting on the floor, and picked her up.

'Goodbye, my little treasure, be good to Becky while I'm away.'

'And you will see about moving, won't you, miss?'

'Becky, of course we are going to move, I give you my word. But it's been over two months now, and I have still only earned sixteen pounds. I beg you be patient with me.'

Becky stared into her her face, saying nothing.

All day Julia sat in the reading room, and wrote her article on the iniquity of the divorce laws. Wrote and then rewrote it. She had to be very careful to get the legal situation correct, and no doubt Mr Wills would want it checked by a lawyer. Her boiling anger had cooled. It was all very well to be hot-headed, but the enemy they were up against had all the ammunition, all the weapons, all the advantages on his side. There must be no mistakes, no foolish blasts of hot air, no ranting females.

The legislators must be made to see that they were in the wrong, and if they had fashioned laws solely for the benefit of men, it was time they were changed.

As closing time came, she had finished a first version of her article.

She packed up her papers her pens and and ink. What a relief to have warmer clothing, what a difference it made. As she walked back through the dark streets, it was a crisp November evening, and there was the acrid smell of smoke in the air. Lights were on in windows, and she caught glimpses of families sitting down to supper, by the fire. Shops were still open, and people were coming out of the bake-shop as she passed it with tasty things to take home. What should they have tonight? She was hungry. As she was crossing the road to the house she looked up at the windows and saw that they were dark.

For a moment she thought she had mistaken the house. But no, this was her door. She went quickly up, threw open the door and ran in. The room was in darkness. There was no fire lit, and the windows were still uncurtained. A dim light filtered in from the street. It was strange, unfamiliar, in the dim light, and the silence, with only the faint noises from the street.

She stopped herself from panicking. It was all quite simple. Becky had run out for something, gone to the shops. She would be back soon. Nothing to worry about. She made her way to the table, and set her things down.

Odd that Becky had not lit the fire. Well, she could soon do that herself.

She felt along the mantelpiece for the candlestick, and then ran her hand along, feeling for the box of lucifers. They weren't there. She took a breath. No lucifers. Becky had left them somewhere. Perhaps in the hearth where she had lit the fire the evening before. No. Annoying, the silly girl must have put them somewhere. She was always leaving things where Julia couldn't find them. No matter, Julia would have to go down and get a light from Mrs Troughton.

She ran lightly downstairs into the basement, into Mrs Troughton's kitchen in all its usual squalor, the piles of washing, the heaps of unwashed plates. Mary, the diminutive skivvy, was standing on a box at the sink with her arms in a mound of washing up.

'Mary –'

Julia stopped. As in a dream, she saw Agnes playing in a heap of dirty laundry. She snatched her up.

'Mary, what has happened? Why is my daughter here?'

'Becky's gone home, miss.' The girl looked round at her over her shoulder, her thin waif's face, the greasy hair lank across her forehead.

Agnes was quite happy. Julia clutched her tightly to her, as she took in Mary's words.

'When was this?'

'Today, miss. This afternoon.'

'What – well – did she leave a message?'

Mary looked at her expressionless.

'She just said she couldn't take any more, miss, and she was going home. And she asked me to mind little Agnes for you. She said she was very sorry, miss. But she couldn't take any more.'

Julia tried to think but nothing came. Agnes squirmed in her arms, and she ran her hand over the child's head, fondling her hair, still staring at Mary. At last she said, 'Thank you,' quietly, and turned towards the door. 'Oh, have you got a lucifer?'

'They're by the range, miss.'

'Thank you, I will return the box.'

She took it, and went back slowly up the stairs and into her room. Her mind had still not absorbed the new situation. She set Agnes down on the bed and lit the candle on the mantelpiece.

Agnes must be fed. It was already nearly eight o'clock. This would

381

not do. She looked round her. It was cold. Light the fire first. Then think about something to eat.

She turned to the fire, cleared out the grate, swept out the ashes and put them in the ashcan by the fire, and laid a fire. She could take the ashcan down to the yard in the morning. She lit the fire. Agnes was calling for her, incoherent shouts and cries. Julia stood up. Her hands were dirty. Yes, she must wash her hands first. Water. The bowl was empty. She took the kettle and went down to the pump to fill it, carried it back and hung it over the fire. In the meantime she washed her hands in cold water.

'Now then, darling, what are we going to have for dinner hmm? What would you like? I think, some mashed potato would be nice, hmm? And let me see – some warm milk?'

There were some potatoes in a box by the fire.

As the fire caught, she set the saucepan on it to boil, and set about peeling the potatoes. And as she went about these everyday tasks her mind began to grapple with the fact of Becky's return home.

Poor girl. Why had Julia not seen how unhappy she was? The trouble was, she *had* seen it; had known that Becky was miserable. She had made it very clear. But as always Julia was so preoccupied with her own problems and priorities that she had too easily pushed Becky's to one side. Poor girl, Julia should never have taken her away from Ebury Street. It had been noble of Becky to have endured as long as she did. Julia could not blame her. And she had gone off without her arrears of wages – the four pounds which Julia owed her.

Well, she should have it. Julia would send her a postal order. Poor girl: she had been a saint to stay so long; it was a fact.

She set the potatoes on to boil, turned and wiped her hands on an old cloth.

'Now then, my darling, while the potatoes are boiling we must get you ready for bed, mustn't we?' Agnes was grizzling; she was hungry.

'Yes, I know you're hungry. So am I. The potatoes will soon be ready. And in the meantime we are going to give you a little wash.'

The kettle was warm. She ran some water into the bowl on the table, and took up Agnes to undress her.

'What a weight you are. You're growing so fast, aren't you? Hmm?'

As she washed Agnes she was thinking, This changes everything. I can't go out to the reading room without Becky here to look after Agnes. No matter, I shall work here. Still it was useful to be able to look things up, check facts and so on. Her thoughts ran through her

mind as her hands carried out the task of washing her child. I shall
have to adjust. I shall do whatever I can here. After all, I can take
Agnes with me when I go to see Mr Wills. For that matter, I could
post the articles. Why not? Simpler still. And I must work harder.
This is not good enough.

It was all very well to get hot under the collar about the rights of
women, but to be frank it affected only a small handful of well-to-do
ladies in easy circumstances. Most poor people were far too busy
keeping alive to worry about such things.

This had been brought forcibly home to her one evening in
conversation with Mrs Troughton. Her own husband had deserted
her long since. The idea of divorce had about as much meaning for
her as a visit to Buckingham Palace.

'Where am I going to get the money for a lawyer? And if you want
my opinion, half the families round here ain't married anyway, not
regular like, so it don't much matter, do it?'

And when Julia in her simplicity had raised the issue of a woman's
right to her own money, Mrs Troughton again set her straight.

'Right to her own money? Listen, Mrs Cunningham, let me put it
simple, so you can understand. First off, nobody's got any money
around here so it don't apply anyway. Second, if my good-for-
nothing husband was to come round asking for my money he'd get a
thick ear, and that's all there is to it.'

I must try to write some more "amusing" pieces; that will be a
more certain avenue, Julia thought to herself as she prodded the
potatoes. She put a little milk in a small saucepan to warm.

I could offer to write a column of household hints, too. If I could
get Mr Wills to give me a regular column, that would bring in a
steady income; better that way.

At last the potatoes were cooked, and she drained the water into a
bucket, and mashed them in the saucepan with some milk and
butter, and sat Agnes on her knee at the table. It was half-past eight,
and she still had not eaten herself.

'We'll share, shall we, darling? I'm too tired to go out for anything
tonight. I think I'll just have a little potato with you, then we'll both
go to bed, and tomorrow we'll feel better, won't we?'

So, wearily, as Agnes lay already tucked in, she pulled her clothes
off in the dim light of the fire, threw them over the back of the chair,
poured the last of the warm water into the bowl and splashed her
face. And pulling her nightdress over her head, she got in beside her
daughter, and with her arm round her, immediately fell asleep.

In the morning as Julia pulled back the curtains to reveal another low misty day, and looked round the room, she understood at once that everything would be completely different from now on. First of all there was no question of getting another servant. For one thing there was no girl who would put up with the privations that Becky had undergone. In any case Julia would never leave Agnes in the care of a stranger, not even that little slattern Mary.

Everything was going to be different. From now on she was going to do two jobs. She was going to work at home, here; and she could either post her articles off, or take Agnes with her when she called on editors. There was no other way.

She looked round the room, as she thought these thoughts. It had to be.

Yet even then, at that moment, she realised, every time she went out of the room, even down to to the water closet, even to empty the ash can or to fill the kettle, she would be leaving Agnes alone with boiling saucepans, with sharp knives, with the fire alight, with a hundred and one ways of doing mischief to herself. It made Julia shudder.

In the meantime, they had to be fed. She took the ash can and the kettle down to the yard, and brought up water for tea and porridge.

She washed and dressed Agnes as the kettle boiled.

You're my little island of sanity, you're my reason for being here, you're what I'm for, she thought, as she pinned the napkin round the child. But you're getting heavier, and heavier. And you need watching every second you're awake. You need washing, you need feeding, you need your clothes washing, you need entertaining, amusing, and very soon you're going to need educating. And I have got to do all those things, and earn us a living at the same time.

It was a sobering thought. She finished dressing the child and held her up in her arms. Was she pale? Julia studied the little face, the fine hair and eyelashes, the incomparable little rosebud of a mouth, everything about her so finely fashioned, a thousand times more delicate, more exquisite than anything could ever be done in porcelain. Her little jewel.

Chapter Forty-five

Arthur returned late in the evening to his rooms in Marylebone which, had he but known it, were a mere twenty minutes walk from where Julia was at that moment sitting at work in her room, looking up from time to time to see Agnes asleep.

His rooms however were large, comfortable, and clean, with pleasant, if old furniture, more than adequate for him, who was used to the spartan conditions he had endured at Oxford. There was a landlady who cooked his meals and washed his clothes. He paid her out of the salary he received from the Bishop's Fund, and which was paid indirectly by the Earl of Worcester. It was the Earl too who had insisted on Arthur dressing 'like a gentleman'. 'My d-d-dear man,' he had stuttered, 'you are representing the Fund to the w-w-world. It is imperative you should appear like a g-g-gentleman.'

He had paid for Arthur's clothes. When Arthur at first declined this offer, the Earl said, 'My dear Grahame – for g-g-goodness' sake, take it! It is for the good of the F-F-Fund. Besides I do not feel it is m-m-morally mine; I have no more earned it than you have.'

He had a meeting with the Earl in the morning on the Fund business. Over the ten days he had lingered in Stallbridge hoping to pick up clues as to Julia's whereabouts, his work here had been neglected.

The meeting lasted all the morning, then Arthur spent the rest of the day going to Police Stations and making enquiries. Through that week in his spare time he visited all the police stations of central London, asking diligently whether they had ever seen a lady of – he forced himself to give a prosaic and realistic description – a lady of medium height, of – ahem – full figure, of dark hair and dark brown eyes, with no mole or distinguishing marks, speaking with a cultivated and pleasing voice, of modest manner and genteel upbringing. As he spoke Arthur was in despair. Nothing of Julia was coming across to the bored desk sergeant who took down these particulars. Arthur wanted to go on – he wanted to say a woman of incomparable beauty, of sweetness of disposition, of patience and understanding, a woman of spirit and intelligence, but he contained himself, and finally left the police station, knowing that his description would be remanded to a file to gather dust along with thousands of others.

She was an educated woman, he thought, so it was possible she might get work in a bookshop, so he obtained a list of all the book shops, and branches of Mudie's Circulating Library, and intended to go through them systematically, making the same sort of enquiries.

It also occurred to him she might become a teacher, so he went into vestries enquiring about schools in the neighbourhood, and would take down particulars of "Select Academies for Refined Young Ladies" in the newspapers; it was possible she was in one such somewhere in Wimbledon or Norwood or some other suburb, teaching French.

As he walked the streets he would peer under ladies' bonnets, and get some strange looks for his trouble; sometimes he would see a woman on the opposite side of the street and think for an insane moment it was her, and run across, dodging between the carriages and carts crowding the street to catch her up, and find of course it was not her at all, and apologise to the young woman, lifting his hat.

It frustrated him more than he could bear to think that she might be there perhaps very near to where he was at that moment – perhaps only a few minutes' walk, and that he did not know it, and that it was quite possible they could both of them walk about London for the rest of their lives and never see one another.

The worst thing of all, the thought he tried not to dwell on, was that she had his address. She knew where he was, she could knock on his door at any time, she could write to him, and yet she had not. She knew he would want her to come to him if she were in trouble – which she clearly was – yet she did not.

There was no explanation he could think of, except one – that she was indifferent to him – and this, by some deep instinct, he refused to accept. He knew that deep in herself she loved him, he knew it, and it must be for some other reason she would not write to him. It must be.

The following week he would begin on the schools, but on the Friday evening as he took the train to Stallbridge to report to Dr Stone, he had to admit that so far he had drawn a complete blank. He would return on Monday to continue his search, but at that moment, as the train pulled out of Paddington Station, and he stared blankly out of the window at the wilderness of sidings, coal

386

trucks, and shunting engines, he had to admit that so far he had not had one single clue.

As soon as she woke, she knew something was wrong. The rhythm of Agnes' breathing had changed. It was coming with difficulty, and she was turning, wriggling in the bed with discomfort. At the second Julia was awake she had raised herself on an elbow over the little girl, looking carefully into her face.

Agnes was flushed, her neck was swollen, and there was a heightened brightness in her eyes. She was in discomfort, and as Julia moved in the bed beside her, she began grizzling. Julia watched her carefully, then saw that the child was wet with perspiration, everything, her little nightdress, even the sheet below her, soaked in sweat.

Agnes was ill. She felt her forehead. It was hot. She carefully got out of the bed, not to disturb her child, looking round her a moment, as if, madly, she might find some instructions what to do. What to do? Agnes was unwell. First thing: keep her warm. She was tucking her in but then thought, No, she is soaked in perspiration, soaked. Julia took up the squirming little body, attempted to wipe her with a towel, and resettled her in Becky's bed, unused last night. She dabbed delicately at the child's forehead as she thought, The doctor. She snatched her purse from the mantelpiece, and as she opened it was running two steps at a time down into Mrs Troughton's kitchen.

'Mary! Mary!'

Mrs Troughton was frying sausages.

'Mary's in the yard.'

'Oh, Mrs Troughton, my child is ill! Mary must go for the doctor!'

'We're just serving breakfast, Mrs Cunningham, you'll have to wait.' She turned over a sausage.

'Agnes is ill!'

'Yes – they all have their ailments, little darlings – but they usually gets over 'em.'

She took some plates out of the oven, and set them out on the table with a clatter.

'Mary!' she shouted through the window. 'Get out of that privy! Breakfast is ready – and that Mr Winthrop has got a train to catch!'

'Mrs Troughton, this is an emergency. If Mary could run *at once* to the doctor's. She must go at once!'

The girl came into the kitchen.

'What were you doing in there? Fall asleep? Get them breakfasts upstairs this instant, you lazy slut!'

The girl, who was hastily wiping her hands on her dress, snatched up the two plates of breakfast which Mrs Troughton had been doling from the frying pan, and disappeared up the stairs.

'Mrs Troughton!' Julia screamed at her. 'Agnes has a temperature! I cannot leave her! Mary must go to the doctor's this instant!'

'Yes, well, I am very sorry, Mrs Cunningham. It's a pity your servant run off, or you could have sent her! Mary will go when I tell her and not before. I've got paying guests in this house, what have got to be fed. Excuse me.' She pushed past Julia and took a loaf of bread from a bread-bin.

Julia spun on her heel and ran swiftly back up to her room.

Agnes was lying as she had left her, grizzling, squirming in bed, and staring about her, making incoherent cries, and disordering her bedclothes. Julia knelt by her, ordering the sheets and snatching up a towel to bathe her temples.

She must keep calm. Mary would go to the doctor soon. All she could do for the moment was to keep Agnes warm, wipe her face, tuck her in tightly and try to calm her. She looked about her. The room was cold. She had better light the fire. She settled Agnes a little, then threw herself down in front of the fire, scraping and riddling out the ashes, sweeping them into the ashcan, snatching up some old newspaper and hastily laying a fire. She ran down to the cellar for coal.

In the kitchen doorway, she stopped.

'Mrs Troughton – if Mary –'

'She's gone. I just sent her.' Mrs Troughton was impassive.

'Oh, thank you, thank you.'

Julia went through the area into the coal cellar and filled the coal scuttle and carried it back into the room.

Already Agnes had disarranged the bedding. It was agony. Julia seemed torn every way at once. She quickly added coal to the fire, turned – there was no water. She snatched up the kettle and ran down to the pump.

She washed her hands under the pump as she filled the kettle, carried it back up and set the kettle over the fire.

Already Agnes had disarranged the bedding, she was crying, grizzling, and writhing in her bed.

Chapter Forty-six

Julia watched over the doctor's shoulder. What delicate hands he had, long thin fingers, and how carefully he held Agnes as he lifted her, one hand behind her head, examining her face, looking carefully into her eyes then laying her down again. The moment he picked her up, Agnes was soothed and ceased grizzling. Julia said nothing, and the man continued his examination. He was a frail, tired-looking man, his eyes dark, the hair on his head thin and disordered. She thought, He ought to see a doctor himself. What else could you expect in a district like this?

He had made Agnes open her mouth, and was looking into her throat. Her tongue now had a white, furry coating. He undressed the child carefully and examined her chest which now also had the red flush. He took out his stethoscope, and placed it against her chest, listening, then took a thermometer from his bag, wiped it and slipped it under her arm pit. They waited in silence. It was morning now, and sunny at last after so many days of low dull cloud and fog. Sunshine was thrown across the room onto the wall. The doctor took the thermometer from Agnes' armpit. Still he said nothing. Julia watched, every moment of it burning into her memory so that ever after she would remember these minutes of silence as the doctor made his careful examination, unhurried, measured, his delicate hands so expert and reassuring to the child.

He placed Agnes back on the bed, and rearranged the bedclothes around her.

'She has scarlet fever.'

Julia could not think.

'It is a contagious disease. Do you know how she could have contracted it?'

Her mind was a blank. All she could say was, 'Will she be all right?'

'It is too early to say. She is a delicate child. With careful nursing she may pull through. I could not be optimistic at this stage. We must do what we can, and hope for the best.'

'What must I do?'

'Keep her warm and comfortable. She will not be able to eat, but give her plenty to drink. Inevitably she will lose weight. You must be prepared for that. She will be very uncomfortable, and unable to sleep. The crisis will come within three days.'

Julia sat heavily on a chair. The doctor did not look at her, but put his instruments into his black case.

'If there is a turn for the worse today you may send for me; otherwise, I will look in tomorrow.'

She saw him to the door, and heard his steps on the stairs, and the shutting of the street door. She turned in the room. It was light, the windows flooding the morning sunshine into the room. The fire crackled in the grate. Across from her in the back part of the room, Agnes lay on Becky's bed, moving uncomfortably, turning her head on the pillow, her face puffy and flushed, staring about her, and grizzling in a low continuous crying, which tore Julia in pieces, and made her want to scream with frustration and worry.

There was no certainty that she would be all right. It could get worse. It would get worse. There would be a crisis, and after that – she could not think. Was it possible Agnes was going to die? Julia stood looking down at her on that morning, in the room, alone with her child.

Her child whom she had conceived and brought into the world. Hers, the fruit of her body. How could she die? How could Agnes die, and Julia be left alive? What sense was in that? It would make a mockery of everything. There would be no meaning left in the world, if she could have borne her little girl, the most beautiful child that had ever been borne, and that child should die. It would wipe out all meaning.

Unless – she stared into Agnes' little face, grimacing and uncomfortable, wrenching her heart from her as she watched – unless this was a judgement on her. On her Julia Stone for deserting her duty. She Julia had taken her baby from her rightful place; from Ebury Street where she had had many pairs of loving hands to care for her; where many wise, intelligent and capable women had watched over her, where there had been a proper kitchen to cook her food, a proper laundry to wash her clothes and bedding; she had had a proper room of her own with her own proper bed, and careful women to watch her.

All this, Julia had deprived her of. What kind of unspeakable, shameful woman was she to do this? How could she ever face the world again if her child were to die as a result of her, Julia's transgression, her crime against her child?

The tears started into her eyes. She and no one else had done this. What did it matter if Peter had attacked her – what did it matter if he raped her a thousand times – so long as her child was safe? Lizzie had been right all along. She had sworn to stay with Peter in the house in Ebury Street, the proper home to which Agnes had a right.

Julia had betrayed that right, and this crime of hers was to be visited upon her innocent child.

She threw herself on her knees at the side of the bed, clasping her hands together tightly, and pressing her head against them on the side of the bed. Oh, please God, please God, let Agnes live. I will do anything, undergo any privation, return to Peter, anything at all, only let my child live. Unworthy as I am, hear my prayer and do not punish this innocent child for *my* sin.

This was no good; this would not help Agnes. She roused herself, took up a towel, and carefully wiped the perspiration from Agnes' forehead. Was she looking worse? Then to her inexpressible relief Agnes fell into a light sleep. Julia sat by the bedside in a chair, and watched her. She was exhausted; she had not eaten that morning. Suddenly she was hungry. She had a second while Agnes was asleep. She snatched up her purse and ran down into the kitchen in the basement.

'Mary! Mary! You must run out to the shops!'

Mrs Troughton was there.

'Must? What's this? What's must? She run for the doctor, didn't she? You might be used to having servants running after you, Mrs Cunningham, but you ain't paying Mary's wages, that I heard of.'

'Oh, I'm sorry, Mrs Troughton – you must think me very thoughtless. The doctor has examined Agnes and says she has scarlet fever –'

'What? In my house? You brought scarlet fever into this house?' Her voice was rising.

'I didn't bring it in, Mrs Troughton, I don't know how she contracted it.'

At this moment her eye caught the pile of dirty laundry on the floor.

'Unless – it is possible – Mary let her play on that laundry. She may have caught it from the bedding.'

'What? Rubbish!'

'How else could she have caught it, Mrs Troughton? She must have caught it from your dirty laundry! That stupid girl let my child play on dirty laundry!'

391

'Don't you go blaming my servants, Mrs Cunningham! Mary didn't tell your maid to run off home, did she? Not that I blame her, mark!'

Julia took a firm grip on herself.

'Mrs Troughton it doesn't matter now. It's done. But Mary must go to the shops for me – how can I leave Agnes?'

Mrs Troughton went quickly to the door, threw it open and shouted up the stairs, 'Mary! Mary! Come down here this minute!'

In a moment the bedragggled figure was at the door.

'You're to go to the shops for Mrs Cunningham, now.'

'Thank you,' Julia said softly. She gave a list of items and some money to the girl, and turned wearily up the stairs.

Agnes was awake again, crying. Julia ran to her, snatched up the towel, and wiped her face, wiped her nose.

She set a kettle over the fire, and waited as the water warmed, all the time trying to settle the child more comfortably. When the water was warm she poured out a little into the bowl, brought it to the bedside, and screwing up the corner of the towel, dipped it in to the water and carefully washed the child's face, then lifted her nightgown, and wiped her body as best she could, cleaning off the sweat. The bedding was wet beneath her, her nightgown was wet. Oh God, she must wash out her clothes. She had a spare nightgown. She changed Agnes' gown and her napkin, and changed the lower sheet on the bed too. She would wash out her clothes now. She went quickly down to the pump brought up some water and set it on the fire to boil.

During these operations, which gave her at least the feeling she was doing something for Agnes, something to alleviate the feeling of helplessness, Mary came in from the shop, with a loaf of bread, some butter and eggs.

Julia did not think she could ever forgive the girl for leaving Agnes to play on dirty linen, but was too tired to scold her. She thanked her softly for the shopping, and when she had finished washing out Agnes' things, and settling them over the clothes horse, she at last made herself some breakfast, and sat at the table eating eggs and bread and butter, sipping a cup of tea, and always watching Agnes, tossing and writhing uncomfortably on the bed.

At midnight she could keep awake no longer. She was in her nightgown in bed, and a few inches from her lay Agnes in Becky's bed, grizzling and twisting in the bed, disordering the bedclothes, so that every few minutes Julia must rearrange them.

She fell asleep, and then, she knew not how much later, started into wakefulness; listening as the child cried, and not knowing what to do, except to take her up again, and clutch her to her breast, and weep with tiredness, with fear, with anxiety, and then to lay her down again, and fall into a light doze herself, all night long, dozing, starting up, taking the child and trying to soothe her, and being unable to.

And so the bleak light of the November dawn came, and there seemed no change, and Julia wept and prayed that if only Agnes might be saved, she would ever after give thanks, and would do anything, anything, go back to Peter, endure his drunkenness, his violence, anything, only so long as her child should be all right.

Light-headed from lack of sleep, she staggered out of bed, knelt still in her nightgown at the fireplace to riddle out the ashes and put them in the ash can, and laid a fire, lit it, and then as it began to catch, went down and out into the yard, still in her nightgown in the damp dawn to fill the kettle at the pump, to warm some water, and wash her hands, then take up Agnes and change her nightgown – fortunately her other nightgown was dry by now – and strip the clothes from the frail body which seemed this morning in the half light ever more frail as if she was wasting away before Julia's very eyes, and would disappear slowly like some wraith vanishing in the morning fog.

She stripped the little body, washed her carefully, and dried and dressed her again, resettling her in the bed after changing the sheet. And as Julia sat beside her, the tears started again in her eyes at the sheer helplessness and utter frustration that she could not help the child, and that all this agony had been brought on her by *her* sin, by Julia Stone's sin, and that whatever torments, whatever agonies, she might volunteer to undergo, she could never make it up to Agnes.

She made a cup of tea and ate a piece of bread and butter and stared out at the foggy morning, feeling the huge weight of her utter helplessness and loneliness in this great city, among these thousands of strangers, all pressing and jostling past one another in their struggle to make their lives, make their marriages, have their children and bring them up, make their money and spend it.

The doctor looked in briefly and said little, but he thought the crisis might come within another twenty-four hours.

When he left Julia felt more lonely and helpless than ever, that this crisis was coming, and as it swept over her and her child, Agnes might be snatched from her embrace and she helpless to stop it or to intercede in any way.

The day wore away, and she felt ever more desperate, more helpless and useless, and could not see beyond this awful fact in this room, and thought seriously that if Agnes were to be taken from her she could not endure to live any more but must surely take her own life.

And as the evening closed in, early in the foggy afternoon, and Julia closed the curtains, the horrible weight of her loneliness and desperation pressed upon her until she thought her mind must be turning and did not know how she could live through another night.

Again, she changed Agnes' clothes, again she bathed her wasted little body, and the agony of seeing the transformation in the thin little limbs, and the difficulty in breathing, and the strain and incomprehension in her little face, was so awful to see that Julia thought she must scream – only it would not help Agnes, and she fought to hold on to to her own sanity for the sake of her daughter.

Again she settled her into the bed, and as the evening drew on, changed into her own nightgown, yet could not get into bed, but sat by the bedside, touching Agnes with the towel, moving her a little here, a little there. Oh God, but she must hold on to her own sanity for Agnes' sake, because otherwise she would utterly collapse and scream and cry and writhe on the floor at the thought of what was happening to her and she unable to do anything to change it.

She was dizzy with tiredness, she was afraid she would fall asleep on the chair, so she climbed into her own bed, reaching over to adjust the bedding round Agnes, and then she heard a foot on the stair, and there was a soft knock on the door. What could Mrs Troughton want at this time of night?

She pulled herself out of the bed, crossed to the door and opened it.

Arthur Grahame was standing there.

Chapter Forty-seven

Arthur stepped forward, took her in his arms, and folded her to his chest, the door still open behind him. She was almost too tired to be surprised, but at last she said, 'Arthur, Agnes –' and pulling from him gestured towards the back part of the room.

He released her a little, still with his arm round her, and together they went to the bedside and looked down at Agnes.

'How long has she been ill?' he asked softly.

'Two days. She won't get better, she can hardly breathe, her face –'

Her face had the red rash that Arthur recognised immediately as scarlet fever. He saw too the swollen neck.

'You poor soul,' he murmured.

He threw his little bag down on a chair, went back and closed the door.

'I had never guessed. You must be exhausted.'

'There's nothing I can do,' she said, staring up into his face, tear-stained, her hair streaming about her shoulders, looking defenceless in her nightgown, tired, dark under the eyes. Arthur took her hand; it was cold.

'I shall watch tonight,' he said. 'You must sleep.'

He looked around the room, thinking.

'I shall move your bed. You cannot sleep like this right beside Agnes.'

With what seemed to her a godlike simplicity, he lifted her bed in his arms, effortlessly, carried it across the main room and placed it opposite the fire.

'Here now, you must rest. Come.' His voice was low, gentle, certain. She was too tired to think, and obeyed him, and let him tuck her into her bed.

'Don't worry. I will tend Agnes. I have done it before. I know what to do. She will be quite safe. Rest now.'

He carried the candle away into the back part of the room, so that Julia's bed was in shadow, set it near Agnes on the mantelpiece, rearranged her covers, and then, looking round the room, went to the fire and carefully added a little coal, and when it was to his satisfaction, put out the candle, went again to Agnes' bed, and drew a chair by it and sat down.

Julia watched his movements. Everything was so simple, so easy for him. Why was he here? Why had he descended like this to save her – but he was here now, and everything would be all right. Arthur would save Agnes, she just knew it. He was always such a strong, such a good man, she could trust him, she had always known it, so safe so sure . . . She fell asleep.

Arthur sat by Agnes in the dim light of the fire. In his childhood, in a household of six children, he had had experience of scarlet fever. He remembered nights when his mother had sat up all night, remembered seeing her reassuring face as he and his brothers and sisters were settled into bed, and looked up in the dim candlelight, and were comforted by her, when there was disease in the house.

And later, when he was a growing lad in his teens, and was beginning to appreciate the strain his mother underwent, being mature for his years he had said to her, 'Mother, rest now, I'll sit up with her.' He remembered how grateful his mother had been; remembered too the long night of waiting and hoping that the fever would pass and the child be well again.

So he sat now, well understanding what was happening, that the fever would pass and Agnes be well, or the other thing, that it would be too much for the poor wasted frame, and the child be taken into God's care. Either way, it was his task now to wait, to help, and above all to serve Julia in whatever way he could devise.

She was asleep, thank God. He crossed carefully, silently, and looked down at her sleeping face lit by the distant firelight.

Poor girl, she was tired, and had lost weight. What had she been through to bring her to this? He looked round the room for a moment and then down at her face. Strange that seeing her in this shabby room, seeing her so reduced so drawn and under such strain, seeing this only made her doubly precious to him, and he thought that she had never seemed more precious – no, not even when he had seen her dancing, when she had seemed more beautiful than was possible, so light and gay in Peter Cunningham's arms, and he had seen that she was in love with that man, oh, it was so obvious, she could not hide it, and she had danced with him, lightly gliding about the room. Even then when he had looked at her loveliness and had

396

gazed on with the hopeless adoration of a man who knows he cannot possess her; even then she had not looked more precious than she did here, now, asleep in this poor bed.

He turned again to Agnes, settled her easily with his strong hands, lifting her as if she weighed nothing at all, and the child seemed to be reassured by his careful calm hands, and was a little relieved, and he sat by her adjusting the bedclothes, and dabbing her forehead with a towel.

All night Arthur sat as Julia slept, and the child passed through her crisis, and as dawn slowly came into the room, he saw that she was going to survive. Agnes fell asleep. When he saw for sure that all was well, he stood up, stretched, and took a deep breath. Drawing the thin curtain a little to one side he looked out into the beginning of the grey dawn. The houses dimly visible across the street, silent, still, the street below him empty.

He knelt at the fire, adjusted it and eased the dying coals with the poker, and as a few spurts of fire appeared carefully added a few coals to help it to mend and begin to build it for another day. He set the kettle over the fire carefully, silently; there was enough water left for him to wash his hands, and after it had warmed a little, he poured it into the bowl on the table and washed his hands and face, and felt a little refreshed. Strangely he did not feel particularly tired; hungry though. Once Julia was awake, he would go out and get them something for breakfast.

He did not want to think of what lay ahead yet. He wanted only to be here, at this moment, in this silent room, as the dawn was weakly breaking at the window, the dawn misty and dim outside, the fire here crackling strongly now, and the mother and child sleeping. Agnes' breathing was regular now, she had fallen into a deep sleep; she would be all right. He went across to Julia again. She too was still deeply asleep.

Still, better not to think yet. He must wait until they were both stronger, then they could make decisions. He went again to the window where the day was now lighter, though it was never going to get very light in this fog. He could see smoke beginning to rise from the chimneys opposite. Other families were awake, and were beginning another day. Every day a new day. He looked out, musing. Better not to think yet; better to wait. He looked round the room again. There didn't seem to be very much food. A bit of bread – yesterday's, the day before's? Some tea in a screw of paper. Milk, curdled. Yes, when they were awake he would go out and see if he could find a shop open.

Julia stirred. He went and stood over her, and as she first opened her eyes and recognised him, he said softly, 'She is safe.'

397

Her eyes closed again for a moment, then she said 'How? When?'

'During the night, the crisis passed. She is asleep now.'

Julia turned her head on the pillow. She could not think, only feel the relief.

'Where can I fill the kettle?'

'There's a pump in the yard.' She tried to raise herself, but he prevented her.

'There's no hurry. Agnes is asleep. Lie still.'

He took the kettle from its hook over the fire, and went out of the room. In the silence Julia lay peacefully. Now she could hear Agnes breathing, regular, easy. The relief was too much and tears were in her eyes. It was not possible that Arthur should have come, and Agnes should be saved. She did not deserve it. She could not stop the tears.

He came in again with the kettle and hung it over the fire.

'Agnes will sleep for a while yet. Best to leave her in peace. You stay there; I'm going out to get us something for breakfast. It's foggy this morning.'

Such a simple thing to say, but it meant normality, ordinariness, things she had not thought she would ever know again. Arthur had come, and brought normality with him. The relief. And her child safe.

He went down the stairs, and she could not stop herself from getting out of bed and going to see Agnes peacefully asleep. It was too much. God had been too good to her. She looked round the room. Arthur had made up the fire, and swept the hearth. It was all neat; everything was orderly, normal, and regular.

But she felt dreadfully weak. She returned to her bed, now in a new position away from Agnes, in the main room, facing the fire. Better to go back to bed for a little while. She lay staring into the fire, hearing Agnes' breathing and waiting patiently for Arthur. There was no hurry, he would do what was necessary, he would take care of her, she could lie quietly and wait for him. There was nothing to worry about. No curiosity yet how he had found them, what miracle had brought him here in her hour of most need.

Arthur returned carrying packages. He said little, hung his coat on the nail behind the door and began opening the shopping and arranging things on the table. He went out again to fill the kettle, and hung it over the fire.

As he straightened he looked at her, and smiled a slightly crooked, mischievous grin.

'Don't move.'

She smiled, and suddenly felt such love for him. She didn't think

398

she would ever be able to recompense him for his goodness. She snuggled back on the pillow, watching him as he methodically rearranged things on the table, clearing off old bread-crumbs, and throwing them on the fire, then unwrapping a loaf and cutting slices, and unwrapping another package of oatmeal and pouring some in a saucepan, and adding milk and water, and carefully setting it on the fire. She watched his careful, sure way, unhurried and everything so easy, stirring the saucepan.

Agnes still slept as the day dawned, another foggy dim day, and it was as if the three of them were marooned there in that room, warm with the crackling fire, and cosy. Julia lay on her side, with her arm curled round her head, as she watched this man going about his tasks. By a miracle everything was safe, everything was all right; she did not think, was just happy in his company and in that moment knew she had never been so wonderfully happy in her life. Not wanting to say anything, but only to know this moment and feel it through her, feel it in her innermost being.

He brought the saucepan from the fire, and poured the porridge into two bowls, sprinkled some sugar over them, and brought a bowl to her in bed.

She pulled herself into a sitting position and took the bowl from him.

'Better for you to stay where you are, for the time being,' he said, and of course, if he said it, it must be right. At that moment he was a wonderful kindly father to her, and would care for her.

He took some porridge himself, and was already busying himself at the fire cracking eggs into the other saucepan, and stirring them. He set the things down on the table and took up his bowl of porridge. Eating it as he walked, he crossed to where Agnes lay asleep, looking down at her in silence then returning to the fire.

'She is sleeping well.'

'Were you –' she began hesitantly '– were you awake all night?'

He didn't answer her for a moment, then said absent-mindedly, 'What? Yes. Don't worry, I'll catch a bit of sleep later.'

She finished the porridge and he took the bowl from her, and brought her a plate of scrambled eggs, and later a cup of tea. Afterwards he bent over her, arranging the bedding about her, and then stopped what he was doing, leant over her and looked into her eyes. They looked into each other's eyes.

'You've been very tired,' he said, without showing any expression. 'Stay in bed for now. Agnes will wake eventually and she'll be hungry. I'll give her something, don't worry.'

In a moment without thinking she had reached up and pulling him a little towards her, kissed him lightly on the cheek.

399

He helped her to lie down in bed again, arranging the bedding round her, and soon she was asleep.

When she woke it was afternoon, and she felt hungry again. Arthur had fed Agnes, and put to her sleep. When she questioned him, it seemed he had changed her bedclothes, washed her, and set her back in her bed; he had also washed out the napkins and her night gown, which were all now neatly ranged along the clothes horse. He had swept out the hearth again, emptied the ashcan, and brought up some more coal.

He had also been out shopping and was preparing Julia something to eat. She felt stronger now, and though still tired, knew she was past the worst.

Chapter Forty-eight

She was still lying in bed. It was five in the afternoon, and already dark outside. Arthur had closed the curtains, and they had been drinking tea. Julia had been able to brush her hair and tie it up with a ribbon, but she was still in bed in her nightgown. Arthur would not let her get dressed. Strange that for a moment as he handed her the tea, after all this time, it had only just crossed her mind that she was here alone in a room in her nightgown with a man who was not her husband. All this time, yet even now as she noticed it, it did not seem important. He had never remarked on it, or seemed to be embarrassed by it in any way, and it was just so nice, so relaxing here the three of them together, and everything, all the world outside still seemed to her indescribably remote.

'How did you find me?'

Arthur was at the table cutting a slice of bread.

'I met Rebecca Loveday in the village and she told me.'

'When?'

'Last night. I came up immediately.'

Of course. Becky.

'How was she? Poor girl, I am afraid she couldn't stand it here.'

'She felt very bad about leaving you; she begged me to bring you home.'

'Home?'

'To your father's house.'

'But –'

Arthur put down the loaf.

'Your father has changed. He wants you home very much. He wants to be reconciled. I am going to take you down when you are recovered.'

'Oh.'

She lay staring at the ceiling. Now the world was coming back, and decisions would have to be made. But to be reconciled with her father. At last.

It occurred to her Arthur must know nothing of her life here.

'Did Becky tell you what I have been doing?'

'I didn't give her time. The second I had your address I was away.'

'As you know Arthur, I have left my husband. I never intended to go back –'

She paused, uncertain how to continue.

'But now?'

'Now,' She lay, staring at the rose in the centre of the ceiling. 'When Agnes was very bad, and I did not know whether she would live or die, I thought that her illness was my fault, that it was a punishment for my sin in leaving my husband, because I had broken my marriage vows.'

Arthur listened in silence.

'Arthur, I am confused; I don't know what to do.'

'Why do you think you left him?'

'I warned him that if he ever used violence against me I would leave him.'

'And he did?'

'Yes.'

Arthur had set down the bread, and had sat on a chair by the fire. He passed a hand over his face.

'I'll kill him.'

'No, my dear.'

There was silence. Then Arthur said in a low voice, 'He released you from your vows the moment he raised his hand against you.'

Was that true? Should not she return to Peter, as she had vowed in her darkest hour, stay with him, endure whatever drunken brutality he might inflict on her, was it not right that she should endure anything rather than risk her child going through that suffering again?

'Arthur, you will never know what it was like being alone with Agnes not knowing whether she would live or die. I nearly went out of my mind.'

'You will never be alone again.' He said it quietly, not looking at her.

But she forced herself to go on.

'In that moment when I knelt by her bed, I made a vow. To return to Peter, if Agnes should be spared.'

She turned and saw him, there by the fire, sitting forward on the chair, elbows on his knees, staring down.

'You are not going back to him. I will never let you go again.'

'I must – I vowed.'

He came to her.

'I will never let that man near you again. You did not desert him; it was not your sin, as you put it. It was his drunkenness and brutality that drove you out. You are entirely innocent.'

He stood large over her.

'My dear –'

She looked up at him and as she lay there, relaxed now, feeling that she was going to survive and get better; feeling this man was feeding strength and life into her; relaxed and warm, she looked up into his face and remembered: this is the man who saved my child.

She reached for his hand, and drew him gently down to her. He knelt by the side of the bed, large and strong beside her, and she pulled him still, then released his hand, and threaded her arms round his neck.

'Oh, my darling.'

He kissed her.

Then the strain, the emotional effort that had so drained her, had brought her to this low state, was converted into an enormous desire for him, as if he were some god of old who had descended upon her when she least expected him, absolute in his power, almighty, had taken her under his protection, saved her, and above all and never to be forgotten, had saved her daughter.

She drew him down to her and they kissed gently; he was strong yet so gentle, and he ran his hand down her body and she felt a shivering thrill as his fingers ran across her breast, a yearning for him that she must take him into herself, she must, because it would be right, and her back arched up to him, he could sense it.

They drew apart for a moment looking into each other's eyes.

'Come,' she said softly.

In the dim light of the fire, and the one candle on the mantelpiece, he slipped out of his clothes, and as she watched him pull his shirt over his head, and saw his strong man's chest, his broad shoulders, she quickly pulled her nightdress off her, lay back, and let him behold her nakedness, saw his eyes as they moved down over her breasts, knew that he was pleased, that he wanted her, knew he desired her, and was glad because she desired him now, she desired him deeply within her.

He carefully pulled back the blankets and slid down beside her, and now she ran her hands round and up his back as he was over her, his long man's back, so big and strong. He was supporting himself above her, kissing her, glancing only on her lips, and then grazing across her cheeks, touching her eyes, her ears, and then

403

slipping down her neck and as his lips travelled down to her breasts, she arched her back up so that her nipples rose to his touch and as she felt his tongue on them, touching, teasing, and fondling them, there was a great rush of need for him, because she was so sure of him, so sure that he wanted her and wanted her to find satisfaction, so careful for her, and there was no hurry, because he would be careful to bring her to the very pinnacle of her desire.

In her relaxed state, her body seemed to open for him, wanting him in her so badly yet content to wait until he should have prepared her – oh God, but he was so strong. She ran her hands down his back, felt his firm buttocks, a man's body so unlike hers, not soft and curved but somehow all hard, all muscle, heavy and strong and dominating over her.

He seemed everywhere about her; sometimes his hands running through her hair, spread over the pillow, sometimes running down her back, across her thighs; and now he had one arm round her waist, and seemed to lift her as his lips caressed her breasts. Oh, it was so good, she wanted it to go on forever, touching, slipping and sliding round each other, but always slow, never hurried or rough, nothing awkward but always sure, and she trusted herself utterly in his arms.

She cried out, softly moaning, she could not help it, and he looked up for a moment, saying, 'Are you all right?' careful for her, and she said, 'Oh, yes, my darling. Oh, yes, yes,' and still he would not stop but went on, rousing her so surely until she was in a fever of desire wanting him in her so badly, and then when she wasn't expecting him, he was coming into her. Oh, it was so good, he was so big, so hard, coming in and in and in, oh God he was filling her with himself, she was powerless, helpless under him, her legs knotted tightly round his hard back, clinging on to him for dear life to save herself until at last she was utterly carried away, helpless, her head thrown back as the strong rhythm of his movements brought her through the barrier of fire, and they were floating free on a sea of pure feeling, and then afterwards lay side by side, inert, empty, thoughtless, only knowing a pure emptiness, as if they had both been made anew.

Again she woke. It was dark now, the fire low, and Arthur was asleep beside her. Agnes was crying. Julia slipped quickly out of bed, and went to her. Poor child, she was still dreadfully thin and would need careful nursing for some weeks, but immediately Julia saw that she was going to mend. She herself, though sleepy, felt new strength, sure she too was going to mend, and alert now she looked round and saw the milk on the table that Arthur had brought in that morning. She warmed a little in a saucepan over the low fire to give her child.

She took Agnes in her lap, sitting on the chair by her bed. Poor child, how light she was, but what a relief to know she was all right now, and would get better. Agnes drank her milk, and Julia settled her back in her bed. The sweating had stopped, her nightgown was dry. Julia ran a comb through her fine hair, and sat by her talking softly to her, silly things that mothers say to their children as they fall asleep, things that only little children understand, until Agnes slept again.

She turned and looked around the room. Arthur was asleep; she crossed and looked down on him. Poor man, he must have been so tired. How infinitely precious he was to her, lying there, the man who had saved her, now for a moment under her protection, defenceless in his sleep.

She stirred the fire into life, and went quickly down to the coal cellar for more coal. Then she set a kettle over the fire, and when the water was warm, slipped out of her nightgown, and naked in the firelight, washed herself all over. She combed her hair, and tied it back with a ribbon, and peered into her fragment of looking glass. Was that her? Somehow she looked different. She couldn't say how exactly. And then she thought, Am I still attractive? Am I attractive to Arthur? And then, Oh, yes, he loved me so then, just then in that bed, I know he loves me.

Arthur woke; it was nine o'clock at night. As he woke, and turned his head on the pillow, Julia was standing by him, and he looked up at her. Neither spoke, but Arthur smiled, a sly smile.

'What is it?' she said.

'Hmm? Nothing. Are you hungry?'

'Yes, I think I am very hungry,' she said.

He vaulted out of the bed, naked, and pouring out the rest of the warm water washed himself. She watched him and loved his nakedness, just loved to look at him there as he washed himself, his long man's limbs. He was lovely. Arthur seemed completely to have recovered. He dressed, and then told her he was going out for five minutes to get them something to eat.

In those few minutes he was gone, she went and tucked in Agnes tightly, and as she stood looking down at the sleeping child, thought, How wonderful it would be if Agnes were Arthur's child, and we were married, and could live together as a real married couple. Thinking these thoughts, she was still suffused with that memory of

405

him in her bed, that wonderful divine memory that would come back every so often and intrude on her thoughts.

But they were not married. Agnes was not his child. If Peter could find her he would demand Agnes from her, and there was nothing she could do. And if he could prove that she had been in Arthur Grahame's bed, she would be proclaimed an adulteress before the world, shamed and ruined.

These were the thoughts that sobered her.

Arthur came with an armful of packages, a loaf of bread, some more milk, and eggs, and some roast beef from the bake-shop. As they sat at the table and had their supper, Julia was suddenly ravenously hungry as if she hadn't eaten for days, and had never enjoyed a supper so much in her life.

Afterwards they talked.

'What are we going to do?'

'I don't know yet.' He was sombre. 'No one knows where your husband is. He's supposed to have gone to Paris. He has shut up the Old Manor House.'

So it would be safe for her to return to Stallbridge to see her father, and be reconciled with him. That was good. And Agnes could get well again.

That night they lay together in her narrow bed, in each other's arms, and as the dawn broke and they were awake, he was aroused again and they made love, silently, in an exquisite tension. He would not let go, but held her till she reached the point, constrained her tyrantlike to undergo that heavenly torment, that utter mortification, so that wrung out and all passion spent, they fell asleep again briefly in one another's arms.

Then the sound of Agnes woke her. It was another day. Arthur rose and dressed himself. He went out again to get them some breakfast, and said as he was at the door, 'I will send a telegram to your father. How soon will Agnes will well enough to travel?'

She thought perhaps in three or four days, and so it was arranged that they would travel down to Stallbridge together and she would see her father again. So long as Peter was not there it would be safe.

It would be a relief to bring Agnes down into the country, to give her a proper bed, and proper meals, and clean air to breathe.

While they were having breakfast the post came. There was a letter for her from *All The Year Round*. Mr Wills was pleased with *A Lady's Cheque Book* and the other article she had written, on the iniquity of the divorce law. He enclosed a cheque for twelve guineas.

406

She had to explain to Arthur how it was that such bounty should fall from the heavens into her lap, and laughed as she saw the astonishment on his face as he took the cheque.

'You never expected it, my dear, I'll be bound, eh? Never thought that anyone would pay me good English sterling for my thoughts?'

'And is this what you have been doing since you left your husband?'

'Of course.'

Arthur looked thoughtful, and she, seeing the shifting thoughts in his face, reached across her hand.

'You need not worry, Arthur. I am pretty sure I can support myself and my daughter with my pen. Other women do it, you know.'

407

Chapter Forty-nine

As Agnes improved and the day approached on which they would travel down to Stallbridge, Julia knew there was something she must say to Arthur, something she would give anything, pay any price not to say, but which she must say nevertheless.

She was sitting by the fire, and looked across at him.

'Arthur, hold my hand, my dear, and listen very carefully. And please, my darling, don't interrupt what I am going to say. Please.'

He took her hand.

'Arthur, my dearest, my darling,' she squeezed his hand between her own, 'we must part.'

'We will never part.'

'My dear, I pray you to listen! I love you better than my life, and will never love any one else as long as I shall live. But think.' She squeezed his hand still held tightly between her own, looking earnestly into his eyes. 'I am married. It is impossible for me to get a divorce from my husband. If he were to come back and demand his daughter, I should return to him rather than abandon her to his care.'

He listened carefully. She went on uncertainly, finding her words with difficulty.

'And think, Arthur, you are a talented man. I know you have it in you to go far –'

He was about to take hold of her, but she put him gently from her, and only held his hand.

'No, Arthur, I beg you to listen. It is not easy for me to say this – I have thought and thought about this. Do you imagine I enjoy saying it? It will tear my heart out to lose you – but only think, my dear.'

She drew a deep breath.

'Let us be practical. You are a clergyman. More than that, if I

408

may say so, you are a talented man, working now for the Bishop of London, and the Earl wants you go into Parliament – which I believe you will, my dear! I believe you have much in you to give to the world. I know that you are destined not only to make your reputation, but perhaps to become a man of real stature, and also and more importantly to make some real contribution to the general good. You are too good to waste, do you understand?'

'Julia –'

'No, let me finish.' Already tears were starting in her eyes. 'Let us think very carefully of the reality. If we were to go away together – or to stay in London – it could only be in conditions of absolute seclusion. You would be a ruined man. You could not practise your vocation, you would have no career, every avenue would be closed to you. No one with whom you could work, or who could help you in the advancement of your career would deign to know you. Your life would be empty.'

'So long as I have you –'

'Let me finish, Arthur!' The tears swam in her eyes. 'I know you love me, my dear, as dearly as I love you. But I cannot let you make this monstrous sacrifice. I am afraid, Arthur. I am afraid it would destroy our love for one another. Every day I would think that I had ruined your chances in this world. And every day I would be there to remind you of all the things you might have done – all the opportunities lost to you. A man must have his career, his work; I know this from my father. And you are capable of so much. I cannot permit myself in the selfishness of my love for you, to deprive you of all you might be.'

'This is madness!'

She crushed his hand tightly in hers.

'No. It is only the most brutal truth. When we arrive at my father's house, there must be no breath, no hint, no suspicion, however slight, of our love for one another. Do you understand? There must be nothing.'

'Julia, why live at all? Do we really want to live all our lives alone, always knowing that the other was out there somewhere, in a certain house in a certain room, knowing they were there, and unable to go them and confess our love? How can you be so cruel?'

She drew a withering sigh.

'I don't know. But I only know it is the truth, and the best thing for us both. Once we arrive in Stallbridge, Arthur, we must be as particular, as careful as it is possible to be – never a hint or a whisper, never any suggestion, my darling.'

She reached across, still holding his hand, and kissed him gently on the lips.

'Julia –'

'It will be hard at first, I know, but think, Arthur – think. There is so much for you to do with your life. Only think of your work ahead.'

He looked into her eyes. At last he said, 'And you?'

'I will be all right, my dear.' She said it with an effort at brightness, smiling. 'You saw my cheque? It was not the first. I will be able to earn my bread.'

'You will not stay with your father?'

'For the moment, yes. But I am always afraid of my husband. You cannot understand the dread I have felt ever since I left him, that at any moment he would appear and take Agnes from me. I could not endure it.'

'But you –' he found it difficult to express his thought '– you talk about my career, and you say nothing of your own. If you do not live with your father – you mean, you will come back to this room, alone with Agnes?' It seemed incredible.

Again she tried to make light of it. 'Oh, I expect I can find something better than this next time, and I'll get another girl to care for Agnes when I am out. You really must not worry. I shall survive.'

'You are extraordinary. You want to save me for my career, as you put it. Cut yourself off from me – you whom I worship above all things in the world. And then you calmly tell me you intend to take your little girl to live in a squalid room and subsist on journalism? I will not let you.'

'You must,' she said softly. 'I have told you. The world will not allow us to be together. It is a harsh and cruel fact, Arthur, and we must face it.'

He saw her solemn seriousness, and that she was never going to change her mind, and during the preparations for their journey they were in a kind of mutual misery, unable to say anything, each absorbed by the same thoughts.

As the train drew in to the station, on a cold December day, Julia saw her father standing on the platform. She got out, with Agnes on her arm, and Arthur followed behind with her bags.

She faced her father on the empty station platform, the train beside them waiting with a gentle rush of steam for Arthur to bring out all the bags. No one else got off. Julia stood, the wind catching at her cloak and she and her father faced one another in the cold wind.

410

'Hullo, Father.'

He was awkward and made half a step towards her, and then as Arthur came up with the bags, she turned and asked him to take Agnes for a moment, and freed went and clasped her father to her. She could sense his massive relief and gratitude that she had returned to him, that she had made the step to him and taken him into her embrace. He found it so difficult to express his feelings, and she had done it for him, taken him into her arms.

Then he was able to say, 'At last you have come back,' softly, so that only she heard it. He disengaged himself. 'I have the trap outside.' He saw Arthur, and went to him for a moment. 'Grahame, I shall be eternally grateful to you.'

The trap was just beyond the station gate, and Arthur threw in her bags, and his own small one. They got in, and Stone said, 'Grahame, will you take the reins?' so that he and Julia could sit and look at each other.

They stowed themselves into the little trap, she had Agnes on her lap, one arm round her, and took her father's hand with her free hand.

He examined her face carefully as Arthur clicked the horse into motion and they rolled out of the station yard.

'You're thinner. My dear, what has happened to you?'

'Don't ask, Father. I will tell you later, I will tell you everything.' She looked about her. 'But it is so good to be back. I believed I would never see Stallbridge again.'

Every inch of that drive, every field, every copse, every tree along the road, she knew them all. She squeezed her father's hand.

'And Agnes – she has been ill?'

'Scarlet fever,' Julia said, 'but she is recovered. She has lost a little weight, but I hope she will soon put it on again.'

Stone looked down at the bundle in her arms, the pale face and large eyes, and saw the resemblance to her mother. He did not know how it was but some gate in his mind had opened and he was able to feel again, and there was such a rush of love for the little girl, his grandchild. He smiled into her face, and Agnes smiled.

'Does she speak yet?'

'No. But I think she will soon – won't you, darling?'

She rearranged the shawl round Agnes.

In front of them, Arthur looked ahead, sitting easily, one hand lightly holding the reins. All the time, though she did not look at him, Julia was conscious of him there, and there was between them a sort of electrical flow of consciousness, though they never spoke to one another, or looked at one another.

411

Then they were driving through the village; they passed the Bush, and Miss Pearson's little cottage, dipped down to the ford, splashed through, passing the new school, and there were children playing outside it as they passed; then climbing again, they were passing the gates of the Old Manor House, and so on up the lane until, as the solid square tower of the church appeared through the bare branches of the beeches, Arthur brought the horse's head round, and into the gravelled drive of the rectory.

Annie was opening the door as he pulled the horse to a halt, and came flying out.

'Oh, Mrs Cunningham, you're back! I never would have believed it!'

Julia got out and the two women embraced. Behind her was Emmy Masham, who, more bashful, curtsied.

'Welcome home, ma'am.'

'Come, Julia, what would you like – a cup of coffee?' Even on this great day Stone found it difficult to do the honours, but he did his best.

'Annie, coffee in the drawing room.'

They went into the house together, and it seemed as if it had been a hundred years since she had been here, as if it been in another life. They turned into the drawing room where a fire was burning. Julia looked about her. The room had been transformed, and there were new curtains.

'Father! What have you been doing? There are new curtains in here, and everything –'

The walls had been repapered, the woodwork repainted. The room was completely renewed. She looked about her in astonishment. Then she turned, and could not help an amused smile as she looked at him.

Stone was embarrassed. 'I – er – felt it would be appropriate, seeing that you were –'

Laughing, she embraced him, so easily. It was so strange; never in all the years they had lived in that house together had they been able to embrace. Their relationship had always been so formal, so cool, and now this morning, as the logs crackled merrily in the marble fireplace, and with the feeling of freshness and renewal in this room, she took him again in her arms and they clung together for a moment.

As she freed herself, undid the ribbons of her bonnet, handed her bonnet and cloak to Annie and was peeling off her gloves, she glanced round and saw that Arthur was not with them.

'Annie, coffee!' Dr Stone called, and she went out.

412

'Come, sit down and warm yourself.' He tried to bring her to the fire. But she wanted to look about her, and walked around the room, looking again at the old family pictures, running her hand along the back of one of the old leather chairs, and then going and looking out of the curved window at the great sweeping cedar tree, so many thoughts and memories crowding into her mind, and then with a happy sigh, coming across to her father and taking his hand.

'I have come home, Father. I never thought it possible.'

Stone was awkward and muttered, 'Where is that coffee?'

Later, after Annie had brought in the coffee, Stone wanted to know how Arthur had found her, and what she had been doing, and why she was looking thinner. She gave him a version of what had happened, and he sat looking into the fire, sometimes frowning his heavy frown, his strong eyebrows working, and pursing his mouth, and clenching his jaw, at the thought of what Peter had been doing to her; and watching him as she spoke, Julia remembered all the countless times she had gone in and out of his study, seen him at his desk, the books open before him, the books scattered on the floor about him, remembered how his eyebrows had tightened and flexed as the thoughts passed in his mind.

She kept expecting Arthur to join them, but he did not.

'Julia, I have had your old room prepared for you. I have also been able to procure a cradle for your daughter. In a minute you can go up and inspect it.'

She did not mention Mr Crabtree, whom she had never met, and wondered vaguely which room he was to have.

Later she took Agnes upstairs and into her room. Everything was as it had been.

Over lunch she was introduced to Mr Crabtree, a quiet well-spoken young man of few words, and in an almost religious awe of her father, to whom he deferred at every sentence – Dr Stone says this, Dr Stone believes that. Arthur was also there, and said little, did not look at her, and though she did not look at him – or very seldom – she was conscious of him in the room, at the table, and wondered if it were going to be possible for them to keep this up. How could they inhabit the same house for a day, how pass each other on the stairs, sit at table; how could she lie in her bed that night knowing he was only a few feet from where she lay in the darkness, how do these things and keep themselves from flying into one another's arms?

How could it be possible?

During the lunch she said, 'Father, I do not want to be a hindrance

413

in any way. I beg you will continue with your work, as if we were not here.'

Although Stone protested weakly, she understood that inwardly he was relieved, and sure enough the following morning he was back at his desk, and everything was running in the old groove.

Arthur mentioned that he must get back to London, and Julia invited him to come to them for Christmas, and he accepted. Later that morning he departed for the station.

How could she have gone go on inhabiting the same house as Arthur, without betraying any sign of the love between them? How long could she have borne not to touch him, not to let any sign, however slight escape? How long before the rumour had begun to circulate in the village that the rector's married daughter was sweet on Mr Grahame?

He would be with them for Christmas, and then – she could not think further. Could not bear to think too hard about the future. At least she would see him at Christmas.

She must write to Lizzie. She was loyal to her brother, loyal to the death – it was the sort of person she was – and if she knew where Peter was would be certain to tell him, but Julia could not bear that Lizzie should learn by some rumour that she was back in Stallbridge and preferred to write directly and tell her herself.

Lizzie came to call. She was now visibly pregnant, and on a cold winter day they huddled before the drawing room fire.

'I'm glad to see you, Julia. That day in Paddington Station, I thought I would never see you again. It was the worst day of my life.'

Lizzie had had no news of Peter. After all these months, never a word, not so much as a postcard. He was supposed to be in Paris – that had been the last thing he had said to Franks. In the meantime everything was at a standstill. The will could not even be proved in his absence. It was odd and in a way most uncharacteristic, since he had spoken so often of getting his hands on the money. But it was also characteristic of his irresponsibility that his mother could not get *her* hands on the money either – on that part of it which was legitimately hers, her widow's jointure – and that as every day passed matters were arising on his estate which needed the attention of the landlord.

Rents came in, and there was no one to bank the money; but there were also demands on his money, signatures were needed on cheques, roofs needed mending, decisions had to be made about land, about crops and harvests, about the whether and when to sell, whether and when to buy, all the many things that Alicia had carried out so long and so thoroughly.

414

Letters came to Alicia, from tenants, from dealers and factors: what were her wishes about this, about that, about a hundred and one things that had to be decided, and she could have wept with frustration – except that she was not the weeping kind – that she was completely helpless to act. Not only was Peter not here to decide anything, but he had not appointed anyone to decide in his place. Everything was at a standstill.

Chapter Fifty

Julia went to the Old Manor House to see Mrs Anderson. It was strange to see the house empty, and the furniture covered. Strange to walk through the conservatory, and no Mr Cunningham in his wheelchair.

'Mrs Anderson, I want you to send over to me the very instant you have any news of my husband. Any news whatever.'

She gave the old lady half a crown.

She called at Mrs Loveday's and asked to speak to Becky, and there was a long pause, and at last Becky came to the door, looking sheepish, guilty and defiant.

Before she could say anything though, Julia took her hand and said, 'Becky, I owe you some money. When you went you forgot to take your wages.'

Becky was confused by this, as Julia had known she would be, and blushing said, 'Oh, Mrs Cunningham, do come in, I'm so sorry,'

They were standing at the door on a cold December day, and Julia went in and Becky closed the door behind her. Inside there was a snug fire burning, and two younger children playing, Becky's younger brother and sister, and her mother washing clothes.

'Becky, I felt so badly about you, being stuck in that room. I can't tell you how grateful I was to you for staying as long as you did, and honestly I don't blame you for leaving. You will let me give you your arrears of wages.'

It was also agreed that Becky should return to the rectory to work for Julia as she had done before.

But the most pressing thing on her mind was her daughter's health, and every day she watched her carefully for signs of regaining strength, of gaining weight, and getting back a bloom in her cheek, and it was an unspeakable satisfaction that Agnes grew stronger as the days passed. So long as Agnes was well and safe she could endure anything, even the loss of Arthur.

She thought about Arthur. He would be with them in a few days. Would they be able to stop themselves from flying into each other's arms and into her bed? For long stretches sometimes it was all she could think of, and what a cruel waste of every minute it was that they were not together making love. When Arthur had made love to her in her bed in London it had been the most exquisite moment of her life, and the thought of it burned still in her memory so strongly that sometimes she would have to take a grip on herself, drag her attention back to the book she was reading, or the sheet of paper on which she was writing.

Was he thinking of her too? Somewhere in a room in London, or attending an important meeting with Bishops and Earls – did he remember their love making as she did? Was it the most wonderful thing that had ever happened to him too?

Perhaps when he came down for Christmas, perhaps one afternoon when her father was shut up with Mr Crabtree: he would only have to knock at her door, let himself in and they would be in one another's arms, and would fall into her bed, and make love and it would be such utter bliss, such unspeakable happiness, naked in his arms giving herself as if she had an eternity in which to give herself . . .

She dragged her thoughts back. This was madness. But she did not know how long she could stand it. She must also make plans. She could not stay here indefinitely, though of course her father wanted her to. Already he was bringing her back into his work, consulting her about things. Mr Crabtree did all the clerical work, the copying, the abstracting, but Stone would ask her things over their meals, and she would refer him to some book, and then they would get into a discussion. But she could not stay here indefinitely; this was only an interlude before some more permanent arrangement were made.

She was already at work on articles for the magazines. She had had a taste of independence, and knew that this was ultimately where her future lay. Here, at this moment, in her father's house, she was neither one thing, nor another; no longer Dr Stone's daughter, no longer Peter Cunningham's wife. But for that short time in London, she had been Julia Cunningham, journalist, she had been received by some fairly famous people on equal terms, her opinion respected.

Christmas came, Arthur arrived. He was respectful, distant. They

417

attended Christmas Day service in church; once more she sat watching her father take the service. She talked to Lizzie and Dolly and Alicia afterwards, then she walked back to the rectory and they sat down to the Christmas goose, and drank a Christmas health to one another.

Arthur told Dr Stone of his work in London, of the Bishop, and they talked of the future. Julia thought how happy her father looked these days, how much younger he seemed, lighter in his step, and thought how close they all seemed to a happy family group. And how far apart in reality.

One morning three days after Christmas Arthur stopped her in the passage. For a moment they were alone together.

'Julia,' he said softly, 'I am returning to London tomorrow.'

She could not bring herself to speak, waiting for him to continue.

He looked at her, then

'What else can I do?'

'I have your address, so we may write,' she said softly, holding out her hand to him, and there in the dim passage, before either could think, he took he in his arms, and was kissing her wildly, smothering her with the passion of his kisses. When she was able to disengage herself she could not speak for the wild beating of her heart, the choking in her throat, already feeling the tears in her eyes.

'Arthur, I cannot – oh God, but you must go. Nothing has changed. You must go. It will kill me. But you must –'

But he had already taken her hand and was leading her, pulling her round the corner into her room. He closed the door behind them, and before either could think he brought her to her bed, all in a wild flurry, threw off his coat and sat her on the bed. Then was wrenching at her clothes, wrenching up her skirts, and then before she could help it or even think he was over her, entering her, and the most blissful blind torment she had ever known was seizing her, wanting him more than any thing in the world, but terrified that they should be discovered, in the cold morning, in that room.

It was quickly over. He pulled himself away, looking down at her, dazed, and said in a breathless whisper, 'Forgive me, I could not help myself. I love you so badly I do not think I can live away from you.' And she, lying there in the disorder of her clothes, unable to think or know what to say, could only look up at the dearness of his face and never want to let him out of her sight again. For a long minute there was this sacred silence between them, then the reality of the situation intruded again and they rose, adjusted their clothes, feeling strange, dizzy, out of all time, in a world of their own for those brief minutes.

Stone offered to drive him to the station, but Julia said, 'You are busy, Father. I will drive Mr Grahame to the station.'

In a frigid formal manner, wrapped up warm against the cold wind, they took their places in the trap. She grasped the reins and clicked the horse into motion, and for five miles they trotted through the cold wintry lanes, saw the bare branches of trees, the dull frosty grey-green of the meadows or the brown ploughed fields, past a solitary cottage, with a wisp of smoke from its chimney rising straight in the mournful grey day, and Julia felt death in her heart, that the man who was more to her than her own life was leaving her, and worse was leaving her against his will, but only because she had insisted. Because she thought it would be for the best.

At the station they had a few minutes in hand, and stood silently on the platform, unable either of them to think of anything small or insignificant enough to say, and each knowing what the other was thinking.

Then she said, 'I believe I will come back to London eventually. So long as I am able to keep out of my husband's way. It is possible he may never return, I suppose. He may just go off to the Riviera or somewhere and stay there. If I were to get a place somewhere, we might be able to see each other occasionally.' And she smiled such a bleak smile into his face, both of them conscious of other people on the platform, constrained in this public place.

The train came in, they shook hands and he kissed her lightly on the cheek, as a brother might, got on the train, and she watched as it pulled slowly out of sight, round the bend in the line.

Julia lived quietly in the rectory. Agnes grew quickly, had regained her full weight, and was a bonny plump little girl who began to speak, and had long conversations with her mother.

Julia wrote articles, little pieces, anything she could think of, sometimes amusing sketches of village life like Mrs Gaskell, sometimes serious essays on women, whether they should have the vote, or the right to their own property; at other times, she reviewed books that Mr Wills sent her – usually on domestic matters, child care, or household management; he never really trusted her on more controversial areas, and preferred her to remain 'light' and 'amusing'. Cheques arrived in the post regularly which her father duly cashed for her. She made her own living.

A letter came for her from Arthur. It was very formal, addressed her as Mrs Cunningham, and was a dry account of his work among the poor, a description of his friends, their place of work, the kind of people they cared for. He said he wished he had her journalistic skills; perhaps one day if she and her father were to come and visit, she might write an account of their work for one of the magazines. He signed himself very formally "Arthur Grahame", and there was nothing there that her father might not read with perfect ignorance of what had passed between them.

Spring began to make its most tentative overtures, the daffodils appeared in the graveyard among the old gravestones, there were catkins on the branches and sticky buds were on the chestnuts, and one morning Julia was in the graveyard, trimming the grass on her mother's grave. The gravestone had been cleaned while she had been away; she supposed her father had had it done, but was curious that he should have waited so long. It had never been cleaned before in the twenty-five years Julia had been alive.

Looking at the inscription again, and thinking of her mother, it seemed as if in all the turmoil she had been through since she had got married, she had somehow left her mother behind, had almost lost contact with her. Her childhood now was not just behind her, but behind that great mass of new experiences.

She turned away at last and was letting herself out of the gate to cross the lane to the rectory gate, when she saw Mrs Anderson coming up the lane in a hurry.

'Oh, Mrs Cunningham, wait! Wait!'

She turned, alarmed, and in a moment the old lady came up with her.

'Oh, Mrs Cunningham,' she fought for breath, 'I've just been sent this minute to fetch you. Mr Cunningham, ma'am, just arrived this morning, sent me to you –'

Julia clutched the shears in her hand tightly.

'He sent me this minute, ma'am, the very moment I said you was in Stallbridge.'

And what would he do? He would order her to return, order her to bring back his daughter. He must. Well, he should never have her. He would not dare come and take her by force. Julia's father would not allow it. He would have to go law to get her; and in that time, she Julia would take Agnes and disappear.

She drew herself up. There was no question of some foolish attempt at flight; to be overtaken on the station platform, as she had feared when she ran away before? She would face him.

'Very well, Mrs Anderson. I will come. I will come now.'

420

Leaving her shears inside the rectory gate, she set off down the lane, without waiting for the old lady who came along behind her; set off at a stiff walk, resolute. She would confront him face to face.

She went in through the gate, open now after so many months, up the gravel drive, overgrown with weeds, to the door. The bedraggled old station fly was standing at the door, and the cabby was carrying in a box.

The front door was standing open, and it was a cold morning. She walked in. There was no one about. The house was silent, the furniture shrouded in its calico covers. Everything was as it was when she had walked round before that afternoon with Mrs Anderson soon after she had returned.

It was most odd. If Peter was here, where was he? Why were there no staff? Where was Franks?

She walked into the drawing room. Everything was under covers, the curtains drawn and the room in half darkness. Without thinking she crossed to the window and was drawing back the curtains when she heard a voice.

'Hullo, Julia.' It was Peter.

She spun round. There across from her, in one of the chairs, still with its cover over it, Peter was sitting. He was in a suit with an overcoat over his shoulders, and was holding a walking stick.

'Better not let in too much light. Hurts the eyes.'

She could not see him well; she went towards him.

But even then, even in the half light, she could see that a terrible change had come over him. He looked deathly ill, white, the skin drawn back tightly over his bones, thin, frail, an invalid.

'I won't get up, if you don't mind. Not feeling too strong.'

She stared at him, conscious how rude she must seem, yet utterly unable to drag her eyes from his face.

'Peter –'

'Returned to the ancestral acres, you see. Returned to die, to be precise.'

'What do you mean?'

'Pretty obvious, I would have thought.'

He sighed.

'Worst thing is, confounded doctor won't even let me have a smoke. Could just do with a cigar. Where's Anderson? She's supposed to be brewing up a cup of coffee.'

He paused, and looked at her.

'Nice to see you Julia, I must say; you look as well as ever. Must be in the blood. The blood of the Stones.' He giggled. 'I say – that's a joke. The blood of the Stones –' Then he broke into a cough.

421

The door behind her opened. For a moment Julia thought it was Mrs Anderson with the coffee, but it was not. It was Grace Bradshaw. The two women looked at each other in silence. Then Mrs Bradshaw, without any expression, with an almost cynical twist of her head, said, 'Oh, you're here. Good. You can take over.' She turned back to the door and shouted out, 'Don't let that cab go!' Then she turned back into the room.

Peter looked between the two women.

'You know Grace don't you, Julia? Been very good to me, has Grace.'

She felt as if she were in the presence of death. There was something here outside the range of her experience. She nodded to the woman. Mrs Bradshaw said, 'The housekeeper is supposed to be making up a bed for him. There's not much you can do for him, I'm afraid. Except take care of him.'

She pulled a large man's watch from a pocket.

'I'll just be able to catch the up train if I go now. Do forgive me if I don't stay. I expect you will have a lot to say to each other.'

As she went out of the door, Julia heard her call, 'No, put that case back in. Yes, now. And then drive hell for leather. You've got fifty minutes to make the twenty to twelve train.'

The door slammed.

Julia was left alone with Peter in the shrouded room. He had not moved, sitting like a statue in the chair, with the walking stick between his legs and resting a hand on it.

'Been very good to me,' he repeated. 'But no doubt she has other – and more pressing – business to attend to.'

There was silence again.

'But,' Julia began, 'Peter, where are your servants? Where is Franks?'

'Ah, yes. Where's Franks? Never there when you want him.' He sighed. 'To tell the truth, Julia – and this is strictly between ourselves – I think Grace was just the teeniest bit in a hurry to drop me. I can tell you she was jolly relieved to see *you*.' He paused. 'So was I, as a matter of fact. I've missed you, Julia. Missed you a lot.' He paused. 'Yes. It's all very well, but these people – all fair-weather friends, Julia – not like you – you, I mean to say – I knew where I was with you – could always depend on you – until you left me, Julia. Then I went off the rails. Everything went to pieces. Didn't know where I was going, you see. So long as I had you, I mean to say, you were well, sort of an anchor – oh I know I always shouted at you, and so forth, but I suppose, I don't know, well, it was just so convenient to have you there – if you see what I mean –'

422

He looked vaguely round the room.

'I seem to dimly recall Anderson was going to make some coffee. Any chance, do you suppose? I feel frozen to the marrow, to tell the truth.'

Julia went to the fireplace and pulled at the bell-pull.

'Why did you never write? No one had any idea where you might be.'

He shook his head.

'Never was much of a hand at it, Julia. A sheet of paper now, sort of gives me the willies – put a piece of paper in front of me, the mind goes a complete blank.'

There was a silence again, and then Mrs Anderson came in.

'I've bought you a cup too Mrs Cunningham.'

'Thank you, Mrs Anderson.'

'Good old Anderson. Good thing I kept you on, now I think of it. Otherwise no cup of coffee – did you think of that, eh?'

'As you say, sir. I'll go and make up your bed now and light a fire in there. Mrs Cunningham –' She looked at Julia as she was going out, and Julia followed her to the door.

'Do you want me to send a boy for the doctor, ma'am?'

'Yes, thank you, Mrs Anderson. As soon as the bed is made up and the fire lit, we must get him upstairs.'

'Yes, ma'am.'

As she re-entered the room, Peter was stretching forward trying to reach the cups on the little table near him, and clattering them together on the tray.

'I'll do it,' she said. She rearranged the cups and saucers, and poured out the coffee.

'Good girl. My God, it's a relief to see you. Can't tell you how good it is. Thank you.' She handed him the cup, and as he took it, she heard it clattering on the saucer, as his hand shook, and was afraid he might drop it, but he managed with difficulty to get the cup to his mouth, the stick left resting between his knees, and he drank for a moment as she watched him, then clattered the cup on the saucer again. She reached forward and took it from him.

'Ah, that's better. Thanks. Anderson always did make a good cup of coffee. Credit where credit's due, I say. So –'

He looked at her. She had drawn up a chair towards him, and was sipping her own coffee.

'Julia. There you are, and here I am. In our own home. Rather nice, isn't it? Fitting. The master and mistress. Let me see, only leaves the child. Is she well? What was her name? Dash it, gone clean out of the old brain. What was her name, Julia?'

423

'Agnes,' she said softly.

'Agnes. Yes, to be sure. I wonder if she remembers her old papa, eh? Does she? Do you ever remind her of me, Julia, eh?'

'She is too young to understand these things, Peter,' Julia said softly.

'Too young.' He let out a breath. 'I could do with a smoke. Trouble is, the doctor's very strict. Frog doctors very strict, Julia. *Défense de fumer*. Blast. It's no life, I tell you. Julia, it's been miserable, downright miserable. Grace did her best for me, I give her credit for it. Mark you, she had been living as –' he giggled '– "my guest" for so many months. I suppose she owed it to me, in a manner of speaking; still, so did the others, but they all peeled off when they saw which way the wind was blowing.' He sighed again. 'Oh God, I feel rotten, can't seem to get comfortable.' And he moved in the chair. 'Where's Anderson?'

'Wait a moment.'

Julia went out and up to their old bedroom. The old four-poster bed with its venerable hangings stood where it always had, and Mrs Anderson was fussing round it, adjusting the blankets.

'I've just got to light the fire.'

'Don't worry Mrs Anderson, I'll do it myself – is that bed well aired?'

'I'll get a pan, ma'am – but don't you go getting your hands dirty.'

Julia smiled bleakly to her.

'Have no fear Mrs Anderson, I know what I'm about.'

The fire had been unlit for months. She quickly rearranged the logs, and settled some kindling beneath it, and soon had a fire alight. Mrs Anderson returned with a hot water bottle and set it in the bed.

'The boy's gone for Dr Williamson.'

Julia looked at her.

'Do you think we could get him up here between us?'

'He looked very frail, Mrs Cunningham. I fear he won't weigh much.'

The two women returned to the drawing room. Peter was still sitting waiting for them. Julia bent over him.

'Mrs Anderson and I are going to get you up to bed, Peter. Will you be able to manage it?'

'Suppose I'll have to. Got this far, after all.'

With great care, and very slowly, they raised him from the chair, and one on either side escorted him. Each taking a thin arm, half holding, half watching him, they escorted him up the stairs, into the bedroom where the fire was catching up, and sat him on the side of the bed.

424

Julia half closed the curtains. In silence the two women worked round him, one removing his boots, another his collar and tie, his shirt, helping him out of his trousers, exposing bit by bit his shrunken, withered body. Julia did not allow herself to feel. They got a nightshirt over his head, turned down the bedclothes and got him in.

He looked up into Julia's face.

'Thanks, old girl. Much better now.' And he was asleep.

Chapter Fifty-one

She went back to the rectory for lunch and told her father what had happened. She sent a telegram to Franks in London, and another to Lizzie and Alicia.

She returned to the Old Manor House to find Lizzie and Alicia there with Dr Williamson.

'He might pull through, Mrs Cunningham,' he said to her in a confidential whisper, 'it would depend.'

'On what?'

'On whether he wants to. But it seems he doesn't want to. There is no will to live, that's our difficulty. It's very strange. There is no disease that I can identify – no sign of a cancer for example. It is as if he were just wearing out from sheer indifference. As you know he has never taken the slightest care for his health.'

'Yes.'

'The best thing for him is that you are here. So long as you are with him, there is a chance he may recover. There is no doubt you are his best hope. He did nothing but talk of you while I examined him.'

'Yes, doctor.'

The doctor departed, and she and Lizzie and Alicia went up to his room again and looked down at him. He was asleep.

Then they returned to the drawing room.

'What did Peter say to you?'

'Very little. I still don't know where he has been. He talked about his friends; Mrs Bradshaw brought him down. Do you remember her? She was here in a house-party once. She delivered him into my charge, and then beat a very hasty retreat. She couldn't wait to get out.'

'What are you going to do?'

'What else can I do? I am his wife.'

'Oh, Julia,' Lizzie said, 'I can't tell you how glad I am you're here.'

That evening Franks arrived from London. Mrs Anderson had been sent in to the village and re-engaged the cook and a housemaid. Fires were lit in the drawing room and dining room, and that evening Julia and Alicia sat down to dine.

'We can take it in turns,' Alicia said.

'Thank you, Alicia, for your offer. I will make up a bed here for the time being, until I have a clearer idea of how he is. But I am not bringing Agnes here.'

'He is your husband, Julia. This is your home, and Agnes is his daughter. He is entitled to have you round him.'

'So everyone has been telling me for the last nine months.' She looked down. 'You do not need to remind me of my duty.'

Alicia reached over and touched her arm.

'Excuse me, my dear. I was forgetting.'

'Forgetting what?'

Alicia looked into her eyes. 'Forgetting Mr Grahame,' she said softly.

'Oh, yes, you know all about him, don't you?' Julia was desperate. 'Well, Alicia, since you do know all about him, I don't mind telling you, here and now, that that man means more to me than my life; that he saved my daughter when she lay at death's door, and that he has made me more happy than I knew was possible; that I have sent him away from this village, and that in all probability I shall never see him again as long as I live. And if it gives you any satisfaction, I wish you joy of it.'

She rose with a clatter from the chair, crossed and sat by the fire staring into the flames.

'I get no satisfaction from it,' Alicia said eventually. 'But we are all of us such selfish creatures. You want Mr Grahame; I want you to care for my son. There is no solution.'

Julia straightened. Without looking at Alicia, she said, 'Of course I will care for him, as long as he needs me.'

She went up to the rectory to put Agnes to bed, and then once she was safely asleep, walked back in the darkness to the Old Manor House. She did not want to think, but walked through the darkness pulling her cloak about her, feeling in a state of frozen animation, all feeling suspended. There was nothing to do but wait. It had been the very thing she had never expected, taken her utterly by surprise; yet thinking back, it seemed on the contrary, the most logical thing.

Now that it was too late, she was free to ask herself: why had she

427

not taken up Arthur's offer? Why had they not simply taken better, larger rooms together somewhere in London? She was earning money; at a pinch she could have supported them all three. Arthur – well, he would have had to give up his work with the Bishop's Fund, and his prospects of getting into Parliament – and he would have sacrificed those prospects for her, she knew – but he could have found other work. Not as a clergyman obviously, but there must be many things he could do. They could have lived together, no one would have known. She would have called herself Mrs Grahame – oh, how wonderful that sounded – she could just hear the sound of it, hear shopkeepers and tradesmen addressing her, yes, Mrs Grahame, no Mrs Grahame – it would not have been lawful wedlock, but so what? As Mrs Troughton had said, half of the couples in that neighbourhood had no documentary proof of their union, and it did not seem to bother or hinder them. Who would ever know?

And they could have had children. She could have borne Arthur's children – whereas now perhaps in the future some other woman would carry his children, bring them into the world and rear them – the thought was too painful. She and she alone had that right.

Oh, but it could never have been. What was the use of it? She was married. Peter would have found her out; she could not have hidden for ever – it would never have worked – and how could she ever have gone back to her father? No. The bubble burst.

She let herself into the darkened house, and went softly up to Peter's room. A bed had been made up for her in the room next-door – ironically the very bed in which Grace Bradshaw had once entertained Sir Cosmo Whittington, though that now seemed in a previous existence.

As she walked through the door, the fire was low and threw a warm orange glow through the room.

'Hullo, Julia.'

She went to his bedside. Only his face was visible above the sheet. In the dim light it seemed modelled like a skull, uncanny, horrible. With an effort she forced herself to remain calm. She fussed about the bed, tucking him in tightly.

'How do you feel?'

'Dog tired, frankly. Tired to death – if that's the right expression.'

'Did the doctor talk to you?'

'Doctors don't know anything, Julia, old girl. Hopeless shams every one of 'em. What did he tell you?'

'He said he was afraid you did not want to get better.'

'Ah, yes. Thought he might.' He paused. 'You know, the trouble with being stuck in bed like this is – it gives you so much beastly

428

time to think – and I hate thinking – so I just lie here, and try not to think. But still the same old thoughts will keep rolling round the brain – if it can be called that, which by the by, in my condition I doubt. Anyway, whatever is in there, the same old thoughts just keep trundling round. What's it all for, eh? What's it all for? Can't seem to see it, Julia. So long as you were there, I thought maybe I could make sense of everything, but once you went, well, I don't know –'

She wandered away and stood staring into the dying fire.

'Where did you go?'

'Hmm? Usual places, you know. Paris for a spell; of course all the chums were keen as mustard for a bit of fun, money no object now the young squire had come into his own. So we did Paris for a while, then went to Italy, careered around there. I can't remember now – Venice probably, Rome, Naples, all those sort of places, I don't remember. Then I thought we should settle in the Riviera for the winter. But all the time I was thinking what's it all for? And I'd get drunk again, but it didn't make any difference, because I'd wake up the next morning and the question would still be waiting for me.

'Grace tried to help in her way, but she's not like you, Julia. She couldn't see the problem. What's it all for? she'd say To enjoy yourself, what else? And she'd go off for a canter, or play roulette; never looked beyond the day. That's the secret of happiness, Julia, don't look too far ahead. One day at a time. That's the secret.' He paused. 'If you ask me.'

'You shouldn't talk too much, you will tire yourself.'

'What's the difference? Even if I get well, you'll go off again. Go off with the curate. You don't care whether I live or die.' He paused, waiting. 'Go on, admit it.'

She was silent, staring into the dying fire.

'You can't deny it, Julia. You love your curate. Worthy man. Upright fellow. Bit rough round the edges, lacks polish perhaps, but essentially sound. Just the man for my wife.'

'You need have no fear, I am not going away,' she said softly.

He was silent. For a long time neither spoke until she thought he must have gone to sleep, and was about to cross to him, to adjust the bedclothes, when he spoke.

'You're not going away, so long as I'm ill. So long as I'm unwell, you'll feel guilty enough to stay. But what when I'm well? Will you stay then? You don't love me.'

She couldn't look into his face. She stood by the bedside, looking away towards the fire.

429

'See? You can't look me in the face and say you love me. 'Fraid not, Peter old fellow. Your wife doesn't love you.'

'I loved you once.'

'Isn't that a line from Shakespeare? Sounds iike it. "I loved you once".' He looked away, thinking. 'Anyway, what's the difference? I married you. Mother wanted it, and she bribed me: Marry Julia, Peter, and I'll double your allowance. How could I refuse? Funny thing was, the longer we were together, the more I liked you. You're one of those people who sort of attract other people to them, as if you know what it's all about. And I began to think if I stayed with you I would find out what it's all about too. Then you left.'

'We shouldn't be talking. You'll get overtired.'

'But it's true, you see; just when I thought I could see what it was all for, you upped and left.'

'Your memory is playing you tricks, Peter. You weren't ever interested in me – the first two days of our honeymoon perhaps, until the novelty wore off. The fact is, the situation is exactly the other way about: so long as you are ill you want me here; once you get well, you'll be off with your cronies again, off to the club, off to enjoy a bit of hunting, or shooting somewhere. You just want me around you, somewhere in the background, just to know I'm there.' She paused. 'You're not actually interested in me. You have never consulted my interest or convenience in your life – never bought me a gift, never remembered my birthday, never a bunch of flowers. You couldn't even remember the name of your daughter.' She paused again. 'Forgive me for speaking frankly.'

There was a long silence in the dim room. She stared into the fire.

He drew a long sigh.

'God, I could do with a smoke.'

Eventually, she said, 'I shall be in the room next-door. I think I'll go to bed now.' She stopped at the door. 'Good night.'

As she lay in the darkness she could not get to sleep. Wouldn't it be better to kill herself? If it weren't for Agnes she almost might. Oh God. She turned in bed, the rest of her life unfolding before her. He wouldn't die; he wouldn't get well. He would just lie there, reinventing the past, feeling sorry for himself, an incubus which would suck out the life from her, bit by bit, day by day, and she would wake in the morning, every day, look out of the window and count off another day, another day of her life, gone for ever, counting off the days, oh she could not bear it.

Anything must be better than this. Why not snatch up Agnes and run away to be with Arthur? Why not? She knew very well why not.

430

She could not sleep. She would never bring Agnes here. Never let her be infected with that man's presence. Very well, she would not desert him; she would do her duty – oh God, why was everyone so ready to tell her her duty? – she would give up her own chance of happiness. But that Agnes should be involved – that this waste and misery should cast its blight over her too. She could weep.

There was no way out. She was stuck here. For ever. The only crumb of comfort was that Alicia would be here too, to share the dreary round.

Chapter Fifty-two

Several days passed like this. Julia couldn't think what to do about Arthur, but in the end sat down and wrote him a short note telling him what had happened, and what the present situation was.

Lizzie and Dolly came to visit. Lizzie and Alicia still felt uncertain of Julia; they didn't feel they had her wholehearted commitment to Peter, and at the back of their minds were still afraid she might go away again.

So after supper, in an early-summer evening, they decided to go up to the rectory to have it out with her. The two of them would get her in a corner, and extract a commitment from her. No running away.

'You stay here, Dolly. Keep Peter company for a while. We are going to have a chat with Julia. Come up to the rectory in half an hour or so.'

They took the carriage up the lane, and Dolly made his way back upstairs to Peter's room. He went in. He never knew what to say to Peter, and stood uncertainly in the room, looking down at the fire. Before she had gone, Lizzie had tucked Peter snugly in, and only his face was visible.

'Sit down, Dolly, if you want,' Peter said eventually. 'You make the place look untidy.'

Dolly wandered uncertainly about the room, and eventually sat on a chair by the fire.

'So, the womenfolk have left you to entertain me, eh? Where have they gone?'

'To see Julia,' Dolly said briefly.

'Easy to see why. They don't trust her. They want her here, by the marital bedside, doing her duty by her lord and master, mopping the fevered brow.'

'Yes,' Dolly said very quietly.

'What did you say? I can never hear what you're saying. Why don't you speak up, man?'

'I said yes,' Dolly said more loudly.

'That's the trouble, with you, Dolly, you should be more assertive. Let everybody know who you are. Let Lizzie know who you are. She walks all over you. You shouldn't stand for it. Let her know who the master is. I would.'

Dolly said nothing.

'Still, I don't suppose you ever will. She's got you where she wants you.' He paused. 'Some were born to command, and some to do as they're told.'

Peter sighed.

'I could do with a smoke. Tell you what, Dolly, now the women-folk are out of the way, just you be a good fellow and run down to the billiards room, and bring me up a cigar. And don't tell anyone.'

'Didn't the doctor tell you you weren't to smoke?'

'Dolly, don't be tiresome. Just run down like a good fellow – they're in that box by the tantalus.'

'I don't think –'

'Dolly, for heaven's sake, just do as you're told.'

For a moment Dolly looked at him, then he turned and went down into the billiard room, found the cigar box, in which there were some rather old cigars, selected one which felt firmer than the others, and carried it up. Peter was lying with the sheet up to his neck.

'Good man! Let's see – put that dish here on the side table, I can use it for an ashtray.'

Uncertainly Dolly gave him the cigar; Peter reached an emaciated arm with difficulty from under the bedclothes.

'Ah. That's better. Bit old, but no matter. There are some spills on the mantelpiece.'

Dolly lit a spill in the fire, brought it carefully across and held it under the cigar as Peter drew on it. His hand was shaking and Dolly had difficulty holding the spill under the cigar as it weaved about.

Peter inhaled the smoke, drawing on the cigar to get it well alight as Dolly went back and threw the spill on the fire.

'Ah,' he breathed. 'Dolly, you are a friend. I know I've said some mean things about you in the past, but in a man's hour of need you have turned up trumps.'

His hand shook as he trimmed the ash on the edge of the dish on the side table.

'What was it some fellow said about a cigar? A woman is only a woman, but a good cigar is a smoke? Something like that. And how right he was.'

His shaking hand knocked the dish and it fell on the floor. Dolly came quickly and set it back on the table. Some ash remained on the floor.

'Your mother will know you've been smoking,' he said after a pause.

'Yes, she will, won't she? And do you, know, Dolly, unlike you, I couldn't give a damn. Not a tuppenny damn. I suppose that's one of the differences between us.'

Dolly stood watching him as he smoked in silence for a minute. Then the cigar dropped from Peter's hand among the bedclothes.

'Damn. Pick it up, Dolly old fellow. Burn a hole in the blanket otherwise.'

Peter was so tightly tucked into the bed, that it was impossible for him to move more than his head.

The bedclothes had begun to smoulder. Dolly moved quickly to retrieve the cigar and beat the old blanket. There was a smell of burning and his hand was dirty. He held the cigar.

'I shouldn't –'

'Give it back, Dolly, there's a good fellow.'

'I shouldn't –'

'What's the matter with you? Your entire life is circumscribed with shoulds and shouldn'ts. Give it here, man, for heaven's sake.'

Dolly handed the cigar back into Peter's shaking hand. Then with an uncharacteristic shake of his shoulders he turned away towards the door.

'I'm going to find the ladies.'

'Yes, you do that, old fellow. I expect they'll be wondering where you've got to. Afraid I'll be corrupting you by now.'

'Corrupting me?' Dolly turned. 'Yes. C-c-corrupting – that's a-b-bout all you're good for, isn't it?' Dolly spoke in a low compressed voice, stuttering with the intensity of his feeling. 'You corrupt just about everything you touch, if you ask me. I mean to s-s-say, what good have you ever done? Eh? You only know how to wr-wr-wreck and r-r-ruin things, that's all you know about, spoiling, I mean, your whole life – what is it, and I mean to say – look at Julia, look at her life, just ruined and wrecked by you, I mean, the best-hearted girl in the world – after Lizzie I mean – and all you could do is to wreck and r-r-r-uin her life.'

Dolly ran out of words, and red in the face, stared at Peter. Peter was quite calm.

434

Peter sighed. 'Shut the door after you, Dolly. And tell Anderson to come in and bank the fire down in a minute.'

Dolly went out, down the stairs and out into the gravel turning space before the house. He was more upset than he had ever been. If he could have done anything to hurt Peter just then he would have – would have murdered him. It was as if Peter were some black cancer in the body politic which was his family and the network of his friends and relations. Or as if everyone he knew was linked together like a jigsaw puzzle, all fitting together to make a harmonious composition, except that there was one piece which did not fit, which pushed its way in and distorted the whole picture, forcing every other piece from its rightful place.

He looked up at the bedroom window. If only – in his black mood he wished, he wished that Peter Cunningham could be swept away – if only Peter Cunningham were dead! With a shock he confronted his own thought: he wished him dead. He always had, actually. At that he was ashamed; surely no one could be so bad that one could actually wish them dead? Confused and unhappy he stared up at the window, and then, with that curious twist of his shoulders, as if he wanted to shake Peter Cunningham out of his thoughts, turned and made his way down the drive. The twilight was gathering around him and it was a pleasant light early summer evening.

As he was passing through the gates he heard a cry from some-where behind him. At first he couldn't think what it might be. He turned, listening. Then he heard it again, a cry, and another, quickly rising to a scream. A man's voice – was it from the house? It was like a peacock's scream, strange, unearthly. In a second he knew what it was. He ran back along the drive, and as he came out before the house, he looked up, and in the darkening sky saw black smoke issuing from the window above. He knew instantly what had happened.

Dolly wrenched the door open and pounded up the stairs. As he crossed the landing he could hear the distinct crackling noise of fire over Peter's screams, and as he burst in, the room was already thick with smoke, the whole bed with its hangings alight, and Peter like some grotesque scarecrow gesticulating in the middle of it, bogged down and trapped by the confusion of bedding around him, his head still flat against the pillow, but flailing back and forth, and one free arm waving and beating about him in the midst of the bedding, roaring and crackling about him.

Dolly flew towards him, wrenching the bedding back. Peter's face was distorted with terror, blackened, his hair and eyebrows singed, his one free arm reaching out to him.

435

The swags and draperies of the old four-poster now began to collapse in a sea of flame, violent, greedy, impatient to swallow them both up. Ever louder, roaring in his ears, the flames were spreading across the floor to attack the curtains. At any moment the whole room would go up.

Like a madman Dolly fought with the burning bedding, kicking the hangings away across the floor, and almost suffocating as one heavy fold fell across his shoulders. For a second he thought he himself would be engulfed, but twisting and kicking himself free at last he began pulling Peter free from the tangled mass of the bedclothes, first by one arm so that he fell out on the floor, his nightshirt alight. Dolly could barely see, there was so much black smoke now, and the heat was almost more than he could bear. Squatting down, he took Peter beneath the arms and began to drag him across towards the door. Peter had stopped screaming, which was good.

The carpet was alight, and Dolly could scarcely breathe. He had dragged Peter as far as the door, but as he let go of one arm to pull it open, the act of opening the door sucked in a great draught of air, and the fire seemed to roar up a thousandfold stronger, a deafening roar in his ears, a whirlwind of fire and heat raging about him.

Dolly was so concentrated on his task that he forgot to be afraid. As the draught rushed in past him, sucking the flames up and engulfing the whole room in an orgy of flames and black suffocating smoke, his mind was curiously cool, and he was thinking all the time, if I can just get him beneath the arms again, and if I can just get him through the door, and if I can just get him to the stairs – so little by little he dragged Peter across the landing and down the stairs, his heels bumping on the stairs – God he was so thin, yet such a dead weight – across the hall to the door, out into the air, and so at last across the gravel on to the grass verge.

Above him, the fire was roaring out of the window, up and licking against the heavy limestone slates. Dolly straightened and took a deep breath of cool night air.

Then he knelt quickly over Peter. His face was quite black, and his hair was singed and stank of burning; his nightshirt too blackened and singed. Dolly, his nostrils filled with the stink of fire, tried to arrange him comfortably, slipped off his jacket, rolled it up and slipped it under Peter's head. He seemed unconscious, his head lolling away as Dolly placed the jacket under it, but then something made Dolly suspicious, and he leant over, setting his ear against Peter's mouth. He could hear no breathing. He sat up quickly, took one of the hands, rubbed it, blackened as it was, chafed it, then more frightened slapped Peter's cheek. What about his pulse? He felt for the pulse; he didn't know where one was supposed to look for it, fiddling about round the wrist, but unable to feel anything.

There were sounds of feet running and several people – he couldn't see how many – were running up the drive.

'Send for the fire-brigade!'

'Who's there? Is there any one inside? Where's Mrs Anderson?'

'I'm here! I'm here!'

'Thank God. Rescue Mr Cunningham – he's upstairs.'

'He's here! You'd better send for the doctor.'

Franks and Mrs Anderson and a boy were standing round him.

'Go for Dr Williamson!'

The boy dashed away.

'Fetch Mrs Cunningham and Mrs Emerson – they're at the rectory!'

Franks was away, running up the drive into the darkness.

'Mrs Anderson, if you could fetch some water. It's Mr Cunningham.'

Now Mrs Anderson saw clearly.

'Oh Lord! It's Mr Cunningham! I didn't see him for the moment. Lord, sir, was he in that?'

'Yes, Mrs Anderson, fetch some water.'

But Mrs Anderson was kneeling now over Peter, smoothing the singed hair away from his face, looking at him closely in the half light. Alarmed, she took hold of his head, turning it from side to side, then looked up with a jerk.

'He's dead, sir.'

'What? He can't be! I've just got him out!'

'He's dead, sir. Don't ask me how.'

Dolly sat back on his heels and stared unseeing at the burning house. Dead. Oh God, and he had wished him dead. Dead! And he had given him the cigar! What would Lizzie say when she knew?

'He can't be! What did he die of?'

'Don't ask me, sir! But he's dead all right.'

Dolly stared down at the body on the grass verge. What was he going to tell Lizzie? Oh Lord – and Julia?

She was waiting on the station platform. Agnes was with her. The little girl was at the toddling stage now, and every few seconds Julia had to go after her, as she would toddle off to the station master's house, or after flowers growing on the bank. Julia had left the trap in the yard outside. It was a warm afternoon in late summer, the best time of all the year, the middle of September, when all of

437

creation was poised in the last days of summer, and already the first hints of autumn were beginning to make themselves felt.

In herself she felt a lightness, as if an indescribable weight had been lifted from her.

She had never known what to make of what had happened. Peter had been all right when Dolly had left, he said, safely tucked up and about to nod off to sleep. How the fire could have started no one could fathom; a log must have fallen out of the fire and rolled on to the carpet. There could be no other explanation. At the inquest, the doctor testified that Peter had died of heart failure, brought on by distress and the heat and smoke.

Lizzie had glowed with pride as the Coroner singled Dolly out for special mention, commending him for his bravery and cool head, and ever afterwards she treated Dolly quite differently. The thought that she had very nearly lost her husband, and that he had gone into a burning house to rescue a man she knew he detested, had a deep effect on her. 'I'm not a fool, Julia,' she said privately later, 'Dolly's a heart of gold, and I am going to make it up to him.'

Afterwards Dolly had been particularly attentive to the widow; it was quite unlike him really. He had said, in a tone so solemn as to be almost farcical, that now that Peter was gone, he would like to be a help and support to her; and that she was to regard him in the light of a husband – well, in the sense of supporting and helping and all that. And she had to look seriously into his face and say that it was very kind of him, and how considerate he always was to her, and of course, if she needed assistance, she would not hesitate to appeal to him.

Alicia had been very strange; she became introverted and quiet. It was as if she could not come to terms with what had happened. Julia knew that this horrible death would affect her more than any of them and devoted herself at first to being with Alicia, listening to her as she relived that night, talking it through, and slowly learning to accept what had happened.

The house was not completely gutted. Several rooms in the upper floor of the central wing were burnt out, but the surveyors told Julia that the estate could easily cover the cost of rebuilding. She had no wish to or intention of ever living in that house.

There had been a brief mourning, and now a bare four months later Arthur was coming down, and who knew but before the end of the year Julia and he might be man and wife?

She was afraid to hope any more. Would not some fresh problem arise to frustrate them? In his reply to her letter he had not mentioned marriage. Had he taken offence at her manner in sending him off?

438

Perhaps there was some woman in London with whom he had become acquainted? These things happened. Besides he might not care to marry another man's widow. What might his family say in the matter?

These were the fears that ran through her mind; not very big fears it is true, for deep in herself there was a warmth that she could still feel from the few days they had had together in their little room in London, and from that she drew an inexhaustible draught of hope and a deep feeling of peace and happiness.

She was not in mourning. People were bound to notice, and bound to pass comment, that on a summer day she was waiting for this man dressed in a white gauzy muslin dress that flounced around her and was caught by the wind. She didn't care. She wanted to look attractive and inviting for him. She couldn't bear to let any more time go by, couldn't bear to lose any more time out of his company.

As the train came into sight, she scooped up Agnes. The train drew up, a few doors opened, and passengers were getting off. Then Arthur appeared with his little bag, smiled to her even before he had slammed the door, and came up the platform to her, with his easy big stride. He came to her, and just threw his bag down and took her in his arms, her and Agnes together, and held them both silently to himself. None of them spoke, though Agnes gurgled, giggled, and touched his face with her hand, and as he released Julia he turned to the little girl and said, 'And how's my little darling? Eh? Remember me?'

Of course Agnes did not remember him, but she took to him immediately, he was just the right sort of man to take a little girl into his big arms, and she was happy there, exploring the bigness of him, the nice way he had, and the nice sound of his voice.

He took up his bag, and with Agnes on his arm, they went out into the yard, found the trap, where the horse was stamping and shaking her head against the flies on that hot summer afternoon. The moment that Arthur had taken her in his arms Julia had known everything was all right, and was surprised with herself that she could ever have doubted him for one second.

They set themselves in the trap, she took the reins, and they clattered out of the yard and into the lane.

'And how is –'

They both spoke at once, looked at each other, and laughed. As they drew out into the country and were bowling along between the fields, Arthur took her and kissed her. But she flustered, pulled away, saying, 'Careful, I must watch the road,' and laughed.

He said, 'I expect the mare knows her way,' and took her again and kissed her, and she was more happy than she could say.

He drew back, and they looked ahead to the mare again, trotting in front of them, and he held her hand and said, 'We will never be separated again.'

Then he said, 'You know, Julia, I have never asked you to marry me?'

And she looked at him with an amused smile, and said, 'I don't believe you have.'

'You laugh, but it has been in my thoughts that in my need for you, I was unaware that you might think I had been – I don't know – taking liberties. You have a family. What is your father going to say if you tell him you are marrying the son of a farm labourer? Would it look better if I approached him and asked his permission?'

She looked at him for a moment without speaking.

'Before you came just now there on the station platform, you know, I was inventing all sorts of imaginary difficulties for us, and now I find you have been doing the same.' She smiled. 'Do you think I would allow anything on earth to stop us getting married?'

'You will have to come and meet my family. We are poor folk, Julia. My father and brothers work on a farm. I have one brother who has become a land agent, and a sister who has married a miller, but otherwise we have always been labourers. There is not much money in the family.'

'I will happily come and meet them.'

But once they were married they would be going back to London. Arthur's work for the Bishop's Fund grew ever more pressing; Julia would go with him, and occupy herself with writing and bringing up their children.

Stone was of course surprised when Julia and Arthur told him of their plans, but three months later he married them in the parish church. Julia didn't mention it to anyone but she was already pregnant. During those last weeks of summer, during walks along shady lanes in the lee of the downs, it was so very difficult for them to keep their hands off one another, and on many afternoons they had found some quiet corner of a field and lain side by side, staring up at the bigness of the sky, watching the slow movement of the clouds over them, and talking of the future, all their lives together.

You have been reading a novel published by Piatkus Books. We hope you have enjoyed it and that you would like to read more of our titles. Please ask for them in your local library or bookshop.

If you would like to be put on our mailing list to receive details of new publications, please send a large stamped addressed envelope (UK only) to:

Piatkus Books: 5 Windmill Street
London W1P 1HF

PIATKUS

The sign of a good book